# The Monstrosity or Anna Purse

### To Address Drugs and Porn, Her Story.

Josiah Hutchison

All characters, places, and allusions named herein are of fictional origin and are intended exclusively for the entertainment of the reader. (This includes those referenced in the 'Afterward.')

ISBN: 172978240X
ISBN-13: 978-1729782408

# DEDICATION

To my son.

# ACKNOWLEDGMENTS

My wife. My brother. My parents, Ron and Terry. My cousin-in-law who teaches English, Sang. And my friends, Kevin and Glen.

Thank you all for entertaining my novice notions.

~~Each~~ of you are astronauts in my eyes.

All

Sang,

Like the true teacher that you are, your feedback kindled the writing fire in my heart. Not many a man would be as honest or as patient to a relative as you were, so thank you! I consider your students and your family lucky to have you and your expertise guiding and leading them.

I'm sincerely grateful,

# Part 1 – Anna & Chad

# Part 1 - Chapter One

"I didn't know you could be addicted to this stuff," James said artlessly, tending to his locker as he geared up for the baseball scrimmage.

"Addicted to what?" Sean asked, taking the bait as he pushed his remaining designer clothes into his own space.

"Miss Doxy, what else?  Like every month."

"Oh, grow up...and get a girlfriend," another voice commented from the other side of the blue lockers, gaining a few laughs.

"When's Veronica gonna make it in an issue?" James poked at Sean.  "She's got a great figure."

"And believe me, there's no incentive for me to share her with a weirdo like you," Sean said, half-laughing at James' absurdity.

"Well, mine, mine, mine, aren't we a little selfish."

"You're sick, dude," Sean concluded like a disinterested older brother, slamming his locker closed.

"Chad!  You could hide a camera in your dorm to get the footage." James said, sitting down on the bench with his ruddy cleats.

"What for?" Chad asked, hinting at his disposition of the topic. Chad looked over the row at his jesting teammate, who stood eye to eye in height.  Though Chad had everything that could make James jealous, including the front-page action photo for the baseball program, his schoolmates had teasingly made him aware in elementary school that his nose didn't fit his face.  And though growth spurts and puberty had mostly righted the awkward proportion, he still lived with the scar of the memory. Hence, whenever someone started looking at him as intently as James was looking just then, he would self-consciously compensate by smiling as wide as his cheeks would allow.  This had become a habit because he had once overheard a pretty girl in middle school once mention to his mother that his smile was easy on the eyes.

"What for...what for? You're completely missing it! Revenge! For all those nights your roommate's kept you awake, you know," James said with conjured astonishment, drawing more chuckles.

Chad ignored the suggestion.

"Oh, you're dull...never mind," James lamented, rolling off his assault when he saw he was losing the spotlight.

"I'm not dull. I'm just waiting for somebody that's more than 2D to come my way," Chad said in delayed defense, having become comfortable in his own skin, in who he was and in what he stood for, after extensive debates back in high school with his bathroom mirror.

"Yeah right. You get your fix. You're just not ready to admit it," James argued.

"Chad, what do you say we do this twerp a favor and go warm his bench," Sean said and playfully pushed James' obnoxious head over as he passed behind him.

--- *A few minutes later, on the baseball diamond.*

The blue sky, this flawless curtain of heaven boasting the noon-day sun, forced the batter to squint his eyes under his helmet. The spectators at this game and the trickle of students from Vern Hill College watched the varsity baseball team dominate the junior varsity team.

The 'dull' pitcher, Chad Wattsworth, declined the signal from the catcher twice and with a solid movement, let the batter catch a glimpse of the ball as he transferred it to his glove. After checking the empty third base out of habit, Chad let go of the ball with impressive flare. The ball smacked the catcher's glove, delivering a final strike. Chad turned toward the dugout and saw Anna standing midway up the bleachers, scanning the field like a novice bird watcher. His instant recognition energized him, and he raised his glove in a sportsman's welcome when Anna finally seemed to be looking his way.

Settling on the third row, Anna moved along the empty bleacher and decided on a place to sit. At a loss of locating some tissue to clean the bench, she gracelessly used her hand to brush away the rain deposited dirt. Wrapped in a rose sweater, and now rubbing her silted hand, she settled in a manner to touch the seat as little as possible. Leaning forward, Anna continued scanning the field intent on finding the pitcher among the collapsing players as they grouped toward the home team's dugout. Anna, like Chad, had many conversations with her mirror growing up, and she had since determined to hate make-up or anything that would falsify her smart appearance or her temperamental skin that would turn unfairly red with any sort of sunbathing exercise. Fortunately, she had the birth blessing of having a body that made designer clothing look as it was intended, fashionable, and her full head of shoulder length and undeniably red hair, identical to her mother's, would style any way she wished, though she favored keeping it straight. Unfortunately, even in high school, boys and girls alike didn't agree with her conclusion about make-up, and her expensive wardrobe, after it was made fun of twice, self-consciously shrunk to what she liked to wear, which was the style of 'comfortable,' and comfortable to Anna Purse usually meant plaid, or jean, or frill-less solids. Her own revelation of being comfortable with her highly freckled skin came when she read her best friend's school-winning poetry entry about her, her being Anna Purse. The entry described her exquisite extra blessing of freckles and compared them to a sugar cookie having the luxury of sprinkles. Bethy Berkshire, her charismatic and poetic best friend, could have walked the runway for any high-fashion outlet from the time she was a sophomore. She too didn't agree with Anna's insistent stance on make-up, but that didn't change Anna, nor did it change Bethy from liking Anna. Anna had calm eyes which balanced the intensity and sparkle of Bethy's. Such was their friendship, and Anna had missed Bethy dearly during her first year at college while her best friend finished up her senior year of high school.

Chad's funny friend, the varsity team catcher, stepped up beside him and seemed to be simultaneously aware of Anna's arrival. He confidently claimed, "I call dibs on the third-row brunette, or is she yours, Chad? ...or maybe she's not brunette, it looks more red." The two players slowed accordingly in the bottleneck of the dugout. After realizing his claim had been ignored or unheard, he spoke again, "Chad...you there, man?"

"Me? What did you say, T.?"

Terrance, affectionately named T. by his teammates, joined the varsity as the only freshman, same as Chad had the prior year. Both players hardly had to 'try' during the tryouts to secure their spots on the roster.

"No, she's a friend, and I already asked her. A nice girl, very pleasant to be around, and smart; say...," Chad said, peering up at Anna. After falling into line for the dugout, Chad twisted around and said, "...say, you'd like her...." Then interrupting himself for sake of his turn in line, Chad skipped the final two steps into the dugout and took his place on the bench.

Terrance also sat down deep in the lineup and watched the junior players ready themselves on the field. Noting the pathetic score, Terrance then stood up and strode past the latter few of his teammates. Unlocking the dugout door that opened to the bleachers, he headed toward the spot where Anna Purse carefully sat.

As he did, a varsity baseman leaned over and whispered to his counterpart, "What's up with T.?"

Anna Purse watched and waited for Terrance to approach. "Hi, I'm Terrance. Hey, do you want to go to the fundraiser tonight?"

Without showing too much concern to the unorthodox behavior, Anna replied, "Hi, Terrance. I'm Anna. Someone else is taking me. But thank you." Noticing that Terrance was quickly attracting attention, Anna broke a little from her calm manner and suggested, "You might want to get...."

"Terrance, get your britches back to the dugout; now!" the coach clearly commanded like an irate parent. The following hash of the coach's yells and gesticulations interrupted the game. The benched varsity members, partially concealed by the dugout, struggled to contain their erupting laughs in the shadow of the heated coach.

Resilient to embarrassment and initially unaware of Anna Purse's plight, Terrance succumbed to the demands of the coach. However, while retreating from Anna, Terrance caught her blushing and responsively said, "Sorry, coach likes to yell."

Anna's lips bent upwards.

Before reinstating Terrance to the dugout and restarting the delayed action of the game, the coach poured out the rest of his fury on the freshman. He cited threats for any further disruptive, undedicated, shortsighted, or selfish behavior. He then extrapolated the threats onto the rest of the varsity teammates as each player still attempted to stoically bury their remaining amusement.

When the play of the game continued, Chad Wattsworth, a disciplined student and extremely talented second-year pitcher, stepped into the batter's box. He lifted his bat loosely over his shoulder and focused on the bicep of the junior pitcher. The ball dropped into the catcher's glove with a smack. Habitually swinging the bat down and back into position, he settled his stance once more and waited for the second pitch. The pitch hit the dirt and caused the catcher to skillfully dance to stop the ball. His roommate, Sean, meanwhile had stolen second base without much effort.

The team watched as Chad waited for another pitch.

Crack! The ball sailed over the second baseman's head, advancing Sean to third base, and with Chad's quick step he beat the ball to the first baseman's glove.

"...Mr. Neutered bringing anyone tonight?" Terrance overheard a teammate ask someone with a mocking tone.

"Chad? When have you ever seen him 'with' a girl?" another responded, causing a general snicker and glances in Chad's direction.

"He needs to get some," the first team member cruelly quipped with disdain of Chad's reputation.

Chad monitored the position of the ball in the pitcher's hand and took a lead off the base. Seeing the signal from the third base line-coach, he leapt toward second base. The right-handed batter swung, missing the ball, and the catcher launched the ball ignorantly to the second baseman. The second baseman then saw Sean blitzing for home plate, and forgetting about Chad, hastily returned the ball short of the catcher. Chad watched his line coach while rounding second base and easily made it to third before the catcher again scurried to recover the play.

A good while later Terrance jumped into a jog toward the mound after Chad's terminating throw, finishing the brutal game with a score of forty-five to one. He immediately understood the question on Chad's lips, which looked like they had just taken a bite out of a questionable sandwich. "Why not ask her then?" Terrance tried defending. "We were up by fourteen points, and the only point they scored was the first swing of the game, a mercy pitch if you asked me."

"I don't know...priorities, composure, commitment, or something like that might have been handy to remember in the moment," Chad said, joining in with the seeming unanimous movement of the fielders toward the junior team's dugout to shake hands.

"I mean it's not like I would jump up and ask a girl out during a real game. You'd agree this game was a joke."

Somehow striking a nerve, Chad stopped and turned in front of Terrance and caused an unusual look of concern on Terrance's face. With an air of disappointment Chad said, "This game might have been a joke, but you got to at least play with a little respect. Somebody still lost you know."

Unable to recover, Terrance started walking silently with a lump in his throat.

Then Chad slapped his friend on the shoulder with an apologetic smile and concluded, "Don't sweat it."

"Terrance! Blitzes! Now! Till the booth goes dark!" resounded the coach. The coach had caught Terrance starting to follow Chad toward the female crowd loitering behind the varsity dugout. Everybody around started smirking at the punitive action.

Sullen, Terrance turned to acknowledge his fate and lunged backward toward his consequence.

Chad easily made his own catch in stopping Anna before she escaped the park. "Hey, Anna, thanks for coming...and sticking around," Chad spoke with a voice hardly touched by the short jog.

"Thanks for inviting me," Anna said. "You guys were relentless out there."

"And just a scrimmage!" Chad agreed. "I guess Coach wants to see who the possible seat-fillers might be if there's an injury mid-season or something," Chad replied unable to remove his eyes from Anna's face.

"Oh, I see," Anna understood with an upward nod.

"Will I see you tonight?" Chad Wattsworth asked suggestively without finding a comfortable place to hide his hands.

Anna replied, "Sure thing."

Chad said goodbye to Anna and returned to the dugout, where he found the coach talking to his clipboard-toting assistant. After offering a few concessionary words to the coach and receiving his reluctant approval, Chad stepped back onto the field and unexpectedly fell into rhythm with Terrance as he served his punishing blitzes.

# Part 1 - Chapter Two

The two trickling teams of players crossed a sparsely populated parking lot toward the locker rooms, leaving their two teammates, Terrance and Chad, on the baseball diamond.

Bringing up the rear of the team, Coach Paddernick and his clipboard-toting assistant closed the doors of the locker room behind them and warned the players in typical coach fashion, "James, I already know about you; otherwise, mandatory meeting after you clean yourselves up!"

The assistant joined in echoing the coach's demand, "You all heard it, don't leave. The coach has some important instructions for everyone."

Showers sounded a dithering roar as the players circulated through the stalls. Lockers clapped amidst the humoring chatter of the players. Finally, with only a few members concluding their eccentric cleansing rituals, the coach entered his rhetorical dialogue:

"Gentlemen, we have the privilege tonight to interact with the elite of society, do we not? You are all required to be there, or rather to be out front of here at...," Coach Paddernick said, pausing to look down at his watch, "well, one and a half hours from now. Four-thirty on the dot is the time you need to be here. Right? Sean, give me your attention please, I'd hate for you to be the one that fouls this whole thing up."

Sean, the six-foot-two outfielder, stopped his whispering commentary. Unable to refrain from smirking out of embarrassment, he said in full volume, "Sorry, Coach P."

Coach Paddernick continued, "The outcome is critical for the funding of our program this year and for years to come. Do you want a team to play for next year? I hope so. You all own suits and ties as a requirement of filling a varsity slot. Wear them. Respect your escorts if you have invited one." The coach scanned the eyes of the players and continued, "If someone wants to talk to or interview you, all evening for that matter, you interview and talk...all evening. If a guest asks you to dance, you dance until they don't want to." Unified now by their attentiveness, the athletes began to settle into absorbing their responsibilities for the evening.

The coach continued intently, establishing his theme, "You have obligations. Yes, you have obligations, they may end at eleven-thirty tonight, but this evening really rides on you." Enthused with his own imploring, Coach Paddernick said, "In all reality boys, these are millionaires, perhaps billionaires; yes, I do believe a billionaire has been invited." Coach Paddernick looked pleased with the crowd and continued, "Network. Be respectful. Rich people hire reputable people from reputable colleges like this one. It's your gain or loss for the college and for yourself. And...," he hammered, "if anyone dares risk or compromise the event tonight with any youthful, childish, juvenile, or immature behavior...or prank, I will personally remove them from the event." Then adding a moment for effect, he exclaimed as if it brought him satisfaction, "...and possibly from the team!" Without stopping to observe whether the team felt the full weight of this consequence, he started pacing to help summarize his thoughts. "If you're not of age...don't drink; impressions are critical; in fact, we are presenting you for one purpose and one purpose only, for the same reason we call it a fundraiser." Taking a full breath like he was about to inflate a balloon, he slowed down his demands slightly, "Tell your ladies to look good, of course they're not the ones I'm worried about." He abandoned his train of thought with a twist of his head and summarized, "Suit, tie, shined shoes, hair, cologne, this is to be first class, so be first class. Dismissed!"

Terrance and Chad dodged the outpouring bodies from the locker room, having run blitzes until the lights timed out in the announcer's booth.

Chad, with a momentary clear passage, stepped ahead of Terrance through the gymnasium doors. Coach Paddernick, catching sight of Chad's athletic frame, looked up and smiled proudly saying, "Good pitching out there today, Chad. But, don't throw that shoulder out before it really matters."

"No, sir, just a time to perfect and experiment," Chad said, heading straight to his locker.

Coach Paddernick looked back down at the assistant's clipboard to resume his private discussion. The locker room door didn't stagnate for more than two seconds before Terrance made his entrance. The notorious creak attracted a glance from Coach Paddernick.

"Terrance!" Coach Paddernick spoke with a crescendo of disapproval, but his coach's heart broke his stern expression into a grin. Having intended to dish out a second helping of rebuke, Coach Paddernick instead refrained as his own youthful behavior, not yet ten years in the past, had come to mind.

# Part 1 - Chapter Three

Dark green evergreens interspersed with blossoming apple trees concealed most of Vern Hill College from satellite view. These trees stood with obvious age, guarding the scattered undergraduate dormitories and classroom buildings. Out of the concealment of these trees, starting as early as the top of the four o'clock hour, sharply dressed varsity members emerged. Most of the third- and fourth-year students arrived by vehicle, while the few sophomores and freshman circumnavigated the brick pathways proceeding from the dormitories.

As the current trend fashioned, girls wore their hair down and straight. The dresses fell below the knee with a wrinkled seam, and the rest of the material fit enough to give a smooth impression.

The guys very much looked like a baseball team with their nearly identical apparel.

Chad, not wanting to arrive first or last, timed his arrival to error on the side of early. He walked alone for sake of his roommate having departed earlier to pick up his girlfriend. As he approached the group, he observed everyone's anticipation to welcome or to be welcomed by someone. One by one, the couples matched up accordingly until everyone had arrived.

The bus arrived as scheduled with the coaches already on board. The coaches, dressed in the same looking suit, tie, and polished shoes, immediately started taking role of the members entering the bus.

Chad gladly sided up and boarded with Terrance and took a window seat mid-bus. Looking out the bus window at the array of trees, he thought back to the excitement he had felt the prior year.

"So, why the green suit?" Chad asked, unable to hold his question in any longer. Terrance had on a green suit that looked like what a card-sharping comic book character would wear.

"You noticed?" Terrance questioned, trying his best to hold back the grin that pressed forward on his face.

"Yeah, I noticed, did you wear the same thing to prom?" Chad said, reflecting Terrance's growing pride.

"No, and it's not that green. My mother agreed with the girl at the department store and said it would make me look sophisticated, so long as I wore brown slacks. It probably also helped that it was marked down ninety-percent."

Chad chuckled and redirected his gaze across the aisle to where his roommate Sean and his date sat. He raised his voice to interrupt the couple's private conversation, "Hey, Sean, you were there last year; you remember what they had for dinner?"

Sean and a few others reminisced for a few minutes before the bus departed on schedule to shuttle the players, their escorts, and the coaches to the fundraising event, taking place downtown Pittsburg.

# Part 1 - Chapter Four

Trying to emulate paparazzo hype, a photographer and his side kick took pictures of the arriving team as they offloaded from the hired bus. A royal red carpet covered the stairs and directed them underneath an expansive awning and into the many story building. The row of players, beaming at the sight of the venue, whirled their heads back and forth absorbing the classy surroundings. Exchanging excited looks, they all talked amongst their neighboring teammates and partners.

The team followed a doorman down a long hallway out of the main lobby. The passage split in two, and the doorman directed the first couple up a flight of stairs to a landing where an elevator openly awaited.

A second decorated doorman stood in charge of pressing the elevator button for each entering couple, and each pair rode the elevator separately.

A third doorman waited inside the elevator and, on all twenty-seven trips, said with a professional calm, "Hello, welcome to Vern Hill College's yearly athletic fundraiser. Your attendance is much obliged; the doors will be opening momentarily behind you. Please enjoy yourselves tonight." As soon as he would finish, the doors would open behind the couples.

Dressed in her vibrant yellow dress, made gold by the warm light, Veronica followed Sean onto the elevator and disappeared ahead of Chad and Terrance.

Terrance turned to make conversation with his friend, "She looks good, right? I thought the sun was pretty blinding, but when she stepped on the bus...wow."

"Yeah, pretty, but whatever," Chad suggested, addressing the elevator doorman with a smile.

"Good, I'm glad I'm not the only one to think so."

The elevator door chimed, interrupting Chad's chance to respond. The white glove of the doorman courteously rose to indicate that their turn had arrived to ascend.

Chad, in his distracted moment, thought of Anna Purse.

--- *A stressful moment from the week before the fundraiser.*

"You nervous?" Chad had asked Anna as he stepped up beside her outside of the lecture hall at their arranged rendezvous spot.

"Not considerably.  Why?  Should I be?" Anna had responded as she gathered the few presentation supplies that had been resting against the wall.

"It's like a twenty-minute presentation in front of the crankiest professors in the whole History department...I would have said, '...in all of history,' but you probably wouldn't think that's funny...who for all practical purposes is just quizzing you in front of everybody.  Remember how he kept interrupting the last couple?  He didn't stop.  That doesn't make you nervous?" Chad had tried to rationalize like a jittery stage actor.

"Hah!  Well, you sound nervous enough for the both of us. He likes me you know," Anna had responded while she waited for Chad to open the door to the lecture hall.

"Well, everybody likes you.  How can that be an excuse not to be nervous?" Chad had reasoned flirtatiously.

"How could you possibly know that everybody likes me?" Anna had fairly pointed out.

"Well, anybody who's spent more than ten minutes with you does.  I'm surprised that somebody hasn't asked you to the fundraiser at the end of the week," Chad had said, watching Anna's face intently.

"Oh, that's right.  That's coming up.  I'm actually going with someone already," Anna had said quickly.

"See, I told you, 'Everybody likes you.'  You should come to the scrimmage we're having before the fundraiser," Chad had recovered, still trying to diagnose Anna's expression.

"Oh, that's the day of my exam...ination," Anna had said, finally guessing Chad's intention.

"Oh, bummer.  Well, baseball's always been a great relaxer for me.  You should come over to the field after you ace your test," Chad had suggested.

"So, it's a home game?" Anna had said to recover from the expression she had made.

"Well, scrimmage...we're playing the junior varsity.  So, you'll have your choice of seating, no ticket necessary," Chad had explained.

"I'll see about it, but hey, here's the cue cards we were using the last time we practiced," Anna had said to refocus the school's star pitcher on their impending history presentation.

--- *A short second after his daydream.*

Brought to wit by the second chime of the elevator, Chad smiled at how instantaneous the memory had consciously replayed. "That took no time at all," Chad said to shew away his heightened memory of Anna Purse and to reconnect with reality.

# Part 1 - Chapter Five

The elevator door opened to reveal the vibrant color of the late noon sun as it illuminated the nearby skyscrapers. The room that Chad and Terrance had entered was elegantly decorated and organized. Servers displayed select wine bottles on pristinely folded cloths as they floated among the elegantly guests.

A master of ceremonies buzzed around informing different groups, "If you will, please join us in the west side banquet hall. We will seat you for our dinner courses. Thank you." After taking a few more steps, he repeated the same invitation.

A few pieces of tasteful furniture were positioned for guests to appreciate the coming sunset, and between two of these couches sat a hefty piece of wood on a table. Terrance dauntlessly grabbed the handle of a rendered sword associated with the hefty wood carving and looked back at his teammate for a laugh. The sculptor of the woodwork had suspended the sword and its decorated handle in midair, falling from a petrified warrior's hand. Chad could have closed his eyes and shaken his head, but instead he offered Terrance his plain unamused smile.

The master of ceremonies made it over to extend the dinner invitation to the two teammates. Terrance perked with hunger and turned to make a beeline for the door of the banquet hall, not twenty paces away. Chad, with a jerk, restrained the physically committed Terrance and immediately offered a closed-lip apology to a white vested gentleman. With subtle disdain, the man meagerly smiled and carried on with his female counterpart without further attention to the two players.

"Terrance, cool your jets, man." Chad barked as the small shot of adrenaline darkened his tense cheeks.

"Yeah, sorry, sorry," Terrance admitted hastily. "I hear food and can't help but jump at the opportunity."

"It will come whether you wait, walk, or run to it; at least show a little regard for where you are." They started toward the west side banquet hall door. "I mean, everyone knows you can catch a ball straight lined home by mere instinct, no need to prove that here," Chad said lightheartedly, trying to downplay his gruff reaction.

Terrance's mood had visibly soured, and he didn't indicate whether he had heard or not.

They both entered the grand doors of the banquet hall where the doorman handed each of the players a tall menu before sliding his finger down a partially concealed guest list. "Order what you would like from your table server; please enjoy, Mr. Chad and Mr. Terrance," the doorman welcomed. After checking off each of their names, he turned to the smiling waitress and told her two consecutive numbers in a hushed voice. To the boys he said, "Please follow Miss Courtney. She will seat you next to a Mr. Sean and a Miss Veronica."

After leading the pair to their table, Courtney arranged Chad and Terrance in such a way as to allow Chad to face the couple and Terrance to face the grand doors. Then, the assigned table waitress stepped up to the table, cheerfully dismissing Courtney back to the entrance.

After the waitress started, Terrance leaned over to Chad and whispered, "Hey, look." Looking with his eyes and throwing his head in the corresponding direction, he continued, "It's Anna. She came like she said she would, and wow!" When the waitress looked at Terrance, expecting a response. He said, "Oh yeah, I should be...." His voice attenuated as he flipped the menu back in front of his face.

"Yes, Terrance what would you like to eat, as a hunger plagued college student?" Chad asked, smiling at his private humor. He looked down at the menu then back up, trying to catch another glimpse of the other dashing girl that was with Anna. The girl had looked enough like Anna, "Maybe her sister, or cousin," Chad thought, surprised at the gender of her escort.

Chad felt the weight of multiple sets of eyes fixated on him, and snapping to attention like Terrance had, he replied, "That sounds good. I'll get the same thing they're getting."

The casual waitress chuckled and in good humor asked, "Which same would you like?"

"Ahh. Whatever Sean ordered will be fine. Thanks," Chad said to get out of the doubly awkward moment and swiftly handed back the gold bordered menu to the waitress.

"Who were you checking out?" Sean asked, causing Terrance and Veronica to laugh.

"So, Chad, I bet you're one of those types who has everything together, like you could win a staring contest. He's like this calm perfect person. Does he ever flinch?" Veronica asked, recovering the embarrassing moment and redirecting her question back to her boyfriend.

"Well, I flinched today. My first throw was hit out of the park," Chad answered, trying to mock himself. He made brief eye contact with Veronica and then resorted to toying with the corner of his cloth napkin. "I don't know. I kind of like being in control. It's a refreshing place to be...they can't swing until I pitch, and I won't pitch until I decide to."

"I don't know how you could possibly not be nervous. When I watched you last year, I could barely sit still; I would get so nervous...just watching," Veronica said, visibly shaking her shoulders as if to demonstrate her spectating behavior.

"My pitching might be nerve racking, but Sean here has the most difficult position in the game, as I'm sure he's told you."

"No, he doesn't tell me much. How's that?" Veronica replied with a hint of doubt.

"Well, any comparison would show it. Me? I warm up my arm and repeatedly throw one of five pitches sixty feet over the plate. Whereas, Sean, here, stands at rest with a cold arm and is expected to sprint, leap, and dive to catch a ball, most often hidden by the blazing sun and throw it somewhere from two-hundred to four-hundred feet across the same base...and do it fast enough for the ball to beat the runner home."

Veronica's jaw relaxed in agreement, liking Chad's comparison.

"Plus," Chad continued, "Sean is usually the one that recovers the ball and saves the game when I mess up." Chad's satisfactory answer ended Veronica's general inquiry, leaving silence and awkwardness floating across the table.

As Sean and Veronica agreeably fell into a private conversation, Terrance began his own with Chad. "Have you ever gotten drunk?"

"What?" Chad spouted, nearly ejecting the piece of ice that had fallen into his mouth. Surprised by the suddenness of the question, he responded, intent on changing the topic, "No, but I learned in a high school science class that if you drink eight gallons of water your motor skills will decline as if you were."

"I've never either," Terrance commented, unintentionally sounding distant. Terrance focused his eyes across the room and then continued, "What about girls? Would you ever get with Anna? I mean would you...," he suggested, finishing his meaning with a movement of his head.

"Get with?" Chad asked naively, shaking his head.

"Yeah," Terrance spoke as if Chad shared his sentiment, "get with like...score; well you know...the other guys talk like...like you aren't interested," Terrance said uncomfortably.

Surprised that these peculiar topics didn't attract Sean and Veronica's attention and fearing they might, Chad rose out of his seat. His movement triggered a nearby waiter to step up behind him and properly slide his seat back. "You want to get some appetizers? It looks like we just go up and take what we want," Chad said, referencing a few individuals standing around the centralized table. Before Terrance could answer, Chad started toward the table, and Terrance followed.

Nervous from the topic, Chad huddled closer to Terrance as a white-gloved waiter carried his plate and picked up the appetizers that Chad selected. "Anna is a friend; I respect her," Chad said in a hushed voice. "She," he started to add and looked over his shoulder. "I don't think girls are things to score; I mean they aren't 'things' in the first place, in the inanimate object sense."

Chad had finished selecting his appetizers and reached up to take the plate from the waiter. However, with an iron clad grip on the plate, the waiter insisted, "I will follow you, sir." Chad shook off his brief confusion triggered by the waiter and stepped back into his huddle with Terrance as if he remembered what he wanted to say.  "Girls deserve your respect, you should kn...."

Terrance interrupted by stepping offensively away from the huddle like an oppositely polarized magnet.

Raising his voice to a normal talking level, Terrance remarked, "That's the third time today you've told me I'm disrespecting someone or...," Terrance paused, letting his irritation bleed onto the collar of his great suit jacket.

A bit stunned, Chad didn't reply.

"Or...you...."  Terrance's frustration grew, and he raised and dropped his hands in objection.  "Ahh!" Terrance concluded in disgust, turning his shoulders away from Chad's path toward the table.

Afraid of attracting more unwanted attention, Chad stoically continued to his seat like he was inconspicuously fleeing a grocery aisle after knocking a glass jar of green olives onto the floor.

# Part 1 - Chapter Six

Followed by the stiff-jacketed waiter, Chad sat down, and the waiter placed the plate of hors d'oeuvres on his charger plate.

"What was that?" Sean asked, indicating Terrance as Terrance crossed to the other side of the room.

"Oh, this is a pinwheel, and that is a pile of black raspberries on cultured milk.  Or do you mean Terrance," Chad laughed.  "I don't know, he's not been himself today.  Or I guess...I guess he was being himself today."

Veronica, though obviously curious, remained silent.

After reflecting on Chad's words and seeing Chad wouldn't divulge more, Sean started to declaim his opinion of Terrance's erratic behavior on the ball field.  Before he could make a point, Courtney approached the table in front of an older white-vested gentleman and a lavishly dressed lady.  As Courtney made the introduction of Sir Byron Dorkan and his wife Kloe, Chad rose from his seat and extended his hand.  Courtney intermediated the initial conversation, addressing Byron Dorkan first, "Chad

Wattsworth is a sophomore pitcher for Vern Hill, and Sean Dowagiac is a third-year outfielder, center I do believe; correct me if I'm wrong."

Affirming his baseball position, Sean also rose to his feet and rounded the table to properly shake Sir Byron Dorkan's rough hand. "I'm glad to meet you."

"I'm delighted as well," Byron replied with a distracted smile.

Courtney interjected a final time, "Sir Byron is a local venture capitalist and investor residing here in the Pittsburg area."

Sir Byron Dorkan waited for his wife to settle next to Veronica before he sat, and Veronica smiled shyly as Kloe introduced herself, "I'm sorry, Ms. Courtney didn't mention your name, I'm Kloe Dorkan."

"I'm Veronica...Veronica Ricky," Veronica responded and immediately complemented Kloe's exquisite shoes.

Settling next to his wife, Byron's first words went to his personal waiter. Without using his name, he requested appetizers to be brought, pointing to the plate in front of Chad. Without thanking the waiter, he turned to Chad and began, "I'm fond of young athletes such as yourselves, but why you young guys so violently compete in such an unpaid venture beats me."

Allowing a nervous moment to pass, Chad realized that Sir Byron expected him to make a defense of his aspiration. He tested his voice, reasoning, "Many of us hope to play in the majors someday...where there's money. The rest just really love the sport, I guess."

"It doesn't matter what you hope for, kid," Sir Byron said with a meaningless smile. Then Byron laughed under his breath, "Money and the majors." Formulating his words more clearly, he continued, "Sure, there's money in the majors, but most all of you will be certainly disappointed when draft day comes and goes without a phone call." He finished his discouragement with a judging look at Sean. "A few may get there, I suppose," he admitted, adopting a more even keel tone. Then in a seeming change of perspective, he said, "I look forward to seeing you play this season."

Completely caught off guard and partially confused, Chad responded, "Well, thanks; do you think you'll be able to make it to a couple of games?"

"That may happen. It all depends, but if I do, I'll be watching." Having said nothing meaningful, Byron shifted his attention to Sean, "Sean Dowagiac, center fielder, what are you studying, son? And who is this fine young lady you're with?"

Sean started to answer, but Sir Byron glibly commanded, "Speak up son. I can't understand you."

Sean laughed to hide his embarrassment. "I'm studying business; I'll be applying for an internship this summer, hopefully something locally offered here in Pittsburg, but who knows; this is the lovely Veronica."

Veronica curtailed her sentence from her lively conversation with Kloe about vacationing on Molokai. "Hi," Veronica said, looking for direction from Sean and lifting her hand up with politeness.

Due to the impasse of the table, Byron also raised his hand in the same manner and authentically smiled for the first time.

Risking a moment's distraction, Chad glanced over to Anna's table on the opposite side of the room.

## Part 1 - Chapter Seven

Veronica, on a sidebar conversation with Kloe for much of the courses of dinner, finally saw fit to ask the beckoning question, "So, Sir Byron, how did you come by getting the 'sir' added to your name; were you actually knighted by the queen?"

Kloe smiled with pride, having prompted Veronica's question.

"Well, well, now," Byron said and sat back in his chair, proud to have everyone's attention. "When my first wife passed away, oh six years ago, maybe seven now...." He paused, massaging his jaw in thought. "When she had passed, I moved back to England to get away from it all. You know, all our memories, our house, her family, and such here in America. It was harder than you think," he said and paused again. "So, I left. I quit my job investing...I would never recommend that to anyone, by the way, not to have a job in my situation. There's too much time for self-pity and the wallowing...despite the fact, there's so much opportun...."

"Byron," Kloe injected kindly, "tell my Veronica about the queen, not about your self-pity, please."

"I'll tell your friend about the queen, but these two young gentlemen are soon-to-be contributing members of society, Veronica too, if she aspires work outside the home. I'll get there, sweetheart," Byron promised softly and continued, "There's endless opportunities out there for all of you, yourself included, Veronica."

Veronica sent her eyes safely to the tablecloth as she forced the corners of her mouth to crease out of politeness.

"In England, while I did little to improve my situation, I ran across an advisor of the Queen; we would eat lunch together regularly at a quaint little downtown cafe. The food was great, and it was there he told me what I'm about to tell you. He said, 'Byron, I'm sure you've heard it said, good things come to those who wait, and though, that may be true with religious people, I don't think it applies in business. Good things come to those who work hard. Good things come to those that have investors. Good things come to those in the right place at the right time. And good things come to those that have connections...to people."

Kloe turned to Veronica with bored eyes and apologetically explained, "He'll eventually get to the queen."

Hearing his wife's apology, Byron responded, "Yes, dear, the queen is coming, but this is how I got to the queen." Stopping for a moment, he respooled his thoughts. "My friend offered to introduce me to the queen, and upon introduction, the queen, quite intrigued with my love tragedy, had me sit in her tea room and tell it to her from the start as if I was her afternoon entertainment. She kept inquiring as to the details, 'Mr. Dorkan, give me the details,' she would say. So, I entreated her to all the details, so much so that dinner was eventually called for. And she kindly extended me an invitation to dine with her and her immediate family that evening. My friend, bored to tears, finally won his leave, but I stayed on. The whole ordeal afforded me by the queen, come to find out, was in fact an extemporaneous interview for an eligible widow of her cousin. This of course was all unbeknownst to me; I thought she was merely infatuated with the fact I was a heart-broken widower. Anyway, at the end of my story, at the end of dinner, she asked me politely one last question. She asked...."

Kloe physically perked up, agitated with excitement, as she tapped Veronica's hand.

"'Would you humor me in making acquaintance with my recently widowed niece's daughter this weekend at the Windsor Castle?' Shocked, I said, 'I wha...wha...would be delighted to.'"

Veronica inhaled some of Kloe's instinctively feminine excitement.

"The castle was amazing, my first time, but the queen's niece's daughter was more amazing." With that he stopped, speechlessly admitting the cheesiness of the line. "I was knighted after the wedding. It was a grand event that others could do actual justice in describing, but all I remember is Kathryn Elodie Ogilvy. I call her Kloe, if you haven't discovered that fact already."

Kloe, physically attractive for her age, had the charming wisdom of a mother and the reputable stature of a trustworthy friend, one who could not only read people's emotions but could see right through to the heart of people, and she could do this without using one unnatural question and without gossiping her instinctive discoveries thereafter. She had already determined that Veronica saw Sean, her boyfriend, as a temporary cuddle-buddy. Chad, she easily decoded from how he listened to her husband that he was single and was distrusting of his hardworking father. Then it was obvious to Kloe after watching Sean's repeated glances at Veronica that he had two supportive parents at home.

The students each listened, expecting more from the pompous storyteller.

"Much rides upon a good name. Your good name, Sean, will get you more than your resume...." Sir Byron continued practically applying his tale until the master of ceremonies lifted his voice over the chatter, "We hope you enjoyed your dinner courses, stay if you please, but I would like to invite you all out to our dance floor on the east side of the building." Bowing slightly as if honoring the crowd for their attention, he said, "Thank you all," and left the banquet hall through the grand doors.

Looking back at his audience and seeing he had lost their attention completely, Sir Byron turned to Kloe and asked, "Kloe, my dear, would you care to waltz?" His question fell among the commotion of the personal waiter removing her half-eaten plate. After the waiter stepped aside, Kloe relaxed her face and focused on her husband.

Veronica looked on like a camera operator waiting for a director to call action, admiring Kloe's composure.

Inferring that she had not heard his first proposition, he repeated himself, this time attempting to mimic the accent of the announcer, "Would you care to waltz with me, darling...on the east side of the building?" The poor impersonation of the master of ceremonies made Kloe's smile erupt with pleasure.

# Part 1 - Chapter Eight

Addiction lies in its consequences, and it lies in wait.

--- *Seven years earlier in a humble apartment.*

"Come on, sleepy head," Sandy had greeted, throwing a clean pair of socks at Romney from inside the small master closet.

Romney John Daniels had sat up with a fright and exclaimed, "Are we late? Are we late? What time is it?"

Sandra Daniels had laughed and had spoken her muffled answer into the densely-populated closet. She had come out to find Romney upright and handsome on the edge of the bed in a sleep coma, so she had repeated, "It's eight-thirty. You said you wanted to be sure to be up at eight to be 'Ready-ready.' ...You remember?" Her own attractive eyes couldn't pull away from the magnetic qualities of her husband's dark hair and jawline.

"That feels like thirty minutes ago," Romney replied, letting his blond-haired wife's admiration fuel his strong legs into motion.

"Well, it'd be fairer to say three-and-a-half hours, but I know that feeling," Sandy had said as smartly as she looked, laying Romney's conservatively priced suit on the crumpled bed cover. "What do you want for breakfast?"

"Fifty-million dollars," Romney had said, thinking forward to the imminent business pitch he and his business partner were scheduled to give in an hour and a half. He tilted his head out of the snug master bathroom to indulge in a two second look at his wife's perfect profile.

"I still can't wrap my mind around that figure, but you're the college graduate," Sandy had replied as she walked out of the conservative bedroom, glad to have caught her husband's eye. "I meant more like what do you want to shove down your throat for breakfast?"

"Something simple. My stomach's already starting to float like a butterfly sanctuary," Romney had responded, as he worked himself up onto his sleep deprived feet and hobbled toward the adjoining bathroom.

Sandy had walked out of the room and then around the sofa to pick up a dark blue corner cushion. After tossing it onto Romney's partner's head, she had playfully greeted, "Good morning, Jack."

Jack had reacted almost identically to her husband, except Jack had accidentally rolled to the side and had collapsed on the floor. "Good morning. Are we late?"

"No, but you need breakfast, if you're going to convince this 'Sir Byron Dorkan' to fund your little skyscraper business," Sandy had said still in the brightest of moods, turning her playful nose and shoulders to her kitchen.

"Oh," Jack had groaned and had relaxed his round head and stocky shoulders back onto the thick brown carpet with a thump.

"How about something simple?" Sandy had suggested as she started opening and closing things.

"That would be perfect. ...You making lunch too, after this meeting flops?"

"Oh, shut up. You're going to make this billionaire a billion more dollars," Sandy had encouraged before sliding the pantry door open and closed again.

"We should send you over to give the pitch," Jack had said, after seeing Sandy come back into view.

"Okay, and what would I do? Dance for him...or them?"

"At least you'd be believable," Jack had reasoned, finding some motivation sprouting in his upper body muscles to raise himself up enough to watch Sandy's light figure float productively over

the counters. Jack had watched Romney race out of the
apartment bedroom half-dressed from his high-speed shower to
give his attractive wife an enthusiastic embrace and partially wet
kiss.

"This is going to be an awesome!" Romney had exclaimed as
he bounded back into the bedroom to put on his plain business
suit and green patterned tie.

"An awesome what?" Jack had asked, putting words to Sandy's
curious expression.

"Breakfast!" Romney had shouted from the other room.

--- *Seven years of hard work later.*

After the spectacular launch of Jack and Romney's real estate
development company, conveniently called Hense and Daniels,
Romney had been thrown an ugly curve ball on the home front.

All the demands of operating Hense and Daniels along with
the responsibilities of raising a two-year-old daughter left
Romney with very little time to sit and think. On this specific
day, the day of the well-advertised Vern Hill fundraiser, after the
mail carrier delivered a most disturbing letter written by a lawyer
on behalf of his wife, he couldn't prevent his thoughts from
disrupting his focus at work. The proposition of the letter set
him off-kilter, and he eventually told his executive assistant that
he needed to take the rest of the day off to gather himself. After
a call to a business friend, someone who would keep his marital
business private, he ventured over to his friend's office, looking
for a therapeutic conversation. He soon found himself alone in
a conference room, waiting on a spare moment his business
friend, a lawyer by education, promised to make for him. The
free minutes of silence set his mind to wandering.

"Addiction spreads, arguably so, like a disease; a disease that
spreads to every area of a man's existence." Romney Daniels
remembered the drone of the addict at the help group he had
attended in the colder part of the year on behalf of his wife.
"Hence, the game of containment, the prognosis, grows
convoluted. The longer the struggle, the longer trails of tears,"
the anonymous participant had spoken so personally as he read
from a wrinkled sheet of notebook paper.

Jeff Dunnire opened the door to the conference room at
Scales Architecture Company and saw Romney sitting in the first

of seven available chairs. Romney still gazed out the tall windows, waiting for some voice of reason.

Jeff, who had slowly opened the conference room door, grinned at the surprise on Romney's face when the discordant sound of the door hit the metal frame and startled him. Despite the initial wordless conversation, Jeff detected the context of his friend's visit and subdued his amusement. Taking the liberty to pick up the unfolded letter lying out in front of Romney, Jeff sat down in a chair and started scanning its contents. Understanding the entirety of Romney's predicament after glossing over the legalese, he vigorously stood up and said, "I'll do it, but I need a favor from you first. I'll give you a minute to consider it." Jeff intentionally paused, hoping to ignite his friend's interest. Jeff, a casually dressed optimist with a purpose in life to help any neighbor in need, had a lovely wife and a son, who was about to enter kindergarten.

"You'll do what?" Romney laughed, looking for clarification.

"Represent you, or help you settle, or whatever. I still have my license to practice law. Somebody else is just going to run you over with fees and bad advice. Nothing is more important...in my mind anyway," Jeff said but caught Romney starting to lose his smile. "Anyway, I have a majority of our board members sitting in the next room over, convinced my bootstrapping business method is the single factor behind our recent lack of growth." He paused, hoping to further entice Romney by his inference, "They're suggesting we completely flip our ratios around. ...Definitely not a 'what would Romney do' solution. I need somebody to talk some business sense into their big noggins. Would you...?"

"Yes! That's something productive I could do," Romney said with a youthful burst of confidence. His face awakened as he recalled the recent dinner-long conversation he had had with Jeff and his wife on the topic.

Jeff Dunnire gladly led Romney into the next conference room to reinforce his level-headed approach to business.

After contritely answering the few objections posed by a loud board member in response to the testimonial that Romney had offered, Jeff escorted his friend out of the conference room and

walked like his foot was attached to the conference room door
by way of a bungy cord.

As if picking up mid-thought with an upward pointing finger,
Jeff bade Romney a rushed farewell by saying, "There's much to
talk about; I'll call you tonight."

## Part 1 - Chapter Nine

The business distraction and the sunlight briefly refreshed
Romney Daniels. As he proceeded to the curbside, he refocused
his eyes down the street to look for a gap in traffic. It was
difficult to conceive the reasoning, but Sandy Daniels, his wife
of seven years, had gone through the trouble of hiring a lawyer
to file for a divorce. After arriving at his sporty sedan across the
street, he slumped down into the driver's seat. A man coming
out of the café several feet away from his passenger door caught
his attention. The man walked with a brown leather portfolio, a
showy watch, and purpose. "Those portfolios are certainly the
thing these days," Romney commented to himself after noting a
clear 'F.P.O.' monogram on the cover. Nevertheless, as the rush
of cool air conditioning started pumping out onto his face his
mind took off wandering again.

"Honey, I'm home," Romney had shouted in classic fashion at
the end of a work day more than a year ago. He had only heard
a little scuffling in the kitchen. After hanging up his light jacket
and slipping off his work shoes, he had started perusing the mail
and rounded the hallway corner into the dinette area. Sandy was
moving about, having apparently just thrown something away.
Lowering the insignificant mail pile for a moment, he
approached Sandy for a tired kiss. "Hi," Romney said, noticing
her breathing rate was heightened. "You been cleaning?"
Romney had asked, assuming from her hovering position
between him and the trash can.

"I'll take that for you," Sandy had said convincingly, offering
to dispose of the advertisements.

"Why, thank you," Romney had said, surrendering the few
pieces of junk. He began retreating, which had seemed to put

Sandy at ease. They had chit-chatted about their bedroom upstairs at their mansion on Washington Street as Romney gladly changed out of his work clothes. April, Romney's daughter was two doors down at the babysitter's house. Nothing alarming had happened until he had recalled an advert in the junk mail pile that Sandy had thrown away, a rather insignificant ten-percent discount for some local merchandise store, and Sandy couldn't stop him before he had started digging through the trash. With Sandy conspicuously frantic at his back, Romney had pulled a needle out from the trash can and had ignorantly said, "I'm sure glad that I didn't jab myself on this."

Sandy hadn't replied, and her cold expression had gone unnoticed.

"This looks pretty serious. Is it from the pharmacy? ...Cause the label isn't very clear," Romney had commented after a moment's thought. Then Romney had reached back into the trash can with curiosity and continued, "I'm going to give this number a try. They really shouldn't...."

"No!" Sandy had nervously interrupted.

It was that moment that Romney had seen a similarly labeled vial trapped between a banana peel and a piece of mail and jumped to the conclusion. "Are these drugs? Are these drugs, Sandy?" Romney had questioned and repeated needlessly, having seen his answer plainly written on her face.

"It's nothing. It's nothing you need to worry about," Sandy had unconvincingly said.

"Sandy, we have cash blowing around here like leaves in the fall, you could do anything under the sun. Tell me this wasn't drugs," Romney had vented, watching the painful effect his words were having in Sandy's eyes.

"I'm sorry," Sandy had said through forming tears. "Please don't let...."

"Enough of it," Romney said, snapping his head to the side to clear his mind.

Romney Daniels continued toward Washington Street where he hoped to find his wife at home. He repeatedly tried to reign in his disjointed thoughts over the course of the drive, especially as his car approached the gate to his rather sizeable house.

"Here," he said, testing his voice. Three knocks stirred some movement within the house. A rather lovely set of eyes appeared between the curtains, followed immediately by shrieks of joy. Romney heard his daughter reporting, "Daddy, daddy. Mommy, it's daddy."

Romney Daniels' heart filled with the same feeling, and he stepped inside with a glad enough smile on his face. After squeezing his daughter in an airborne hug, Romney set April down and greeted her with welled-up emotion, "Hello, Pearl."

## Part 1 - Chapter Ten

Professionally framed photographs lined the front hallway of Romney's mansion. Romney's favorite picture still stood in a hand selected silver frame on the entrance table. "You truly are stunning in white," Romney said of the wedding photo as his daughter ran off to retrieve something of importance from another room. Romney heard his animated child scuffling back around the corner on the hardwood floor in a two-year-old's hobbling run. He knelt to receive her colorful handiwork, and said, "April dear...."

"Do you like it, daddy?" April interrupted with hope of her dad praising her. Yet, without giving Romney a chance to respond to her advanced vocabulary, April Daniels started bouncing around the foyer with an unpredictable spurt of energy.

"I do, April. Is mom home?" Romney asked, already knowing the answer.

"She's in the kit-chin," April said as she took her artwork back from her dad.

Romney rose to his feet and toured a few reluctant steps down the hallway. "Yet, maybe this will change," Romney said to himself.

"What will change, daddy?"

Romney had gotten used to his two-year-old speaking like a four-year-old and didn't consider her present comprehension anything short of normal. "April, why don't you go play in your toy room for a bit," Romney said, offering to assist her over the small playroom gate.

"Okay," April agreed with a glum voice.

"Well?" he asked, pulling out the folded envelope from his jacket pocket after he rounded the corner to the kitchen. He noticed an open needle lying on the counter and barely hung onto his temper. Biting his tongue, he tore his focus from the depleted package and furrowed his eyebrows trying to home in on what mattered in that moment.

Leaning on the kitchen counter like she was bartender waiting for an order, Sandy finally said, "Hey, hunk, what are you doing here?" and sarcastically raised her eyebrows.

Romney held up the letter and proceeded again to engage his wife.

"Oh boy," Sandy said indifferently, keeping her attention to herself and checking the bubbling pot of noodles on the stove.

"I...ae." The words formed incoherently behind Romney's tongue from Sandy's interruption. "I still love you, Sandy, and before you shut me out forever, I want to...," Romney said, interrupting himself for sake of an inconvenient idea.

"You want to, you want to...he says it's all going to happen one way or another," Sandy passively argued, acting like she was waving her own letter through the air.

Romney replied in his best British spy voice, "Accompany me to the fundraising dinner for the Vern Hill varsity baseball team tonight; you and me. I'll arrange a babysitter, and we'll have a grand ol' time."

Romney John Daniels waited.

Romney saw how Sandy's chest rose and how her face subtly shifted and twitched. Sandy inhaled twice to respond, but from Romney's vantage point, his proposition slowly overcame her unspoken objections.

"Okay, but...."

"Ah," Romney held onto his perception of victory.

"Okay," Sandy Daniels repeated lethargically, finishing the conversation as if she saw her agreement as doing her husband a favor. Then with another careless motion, Sandy left the kitchen for the upstairs bedroom.

Romney noticed a slight detour in his wife's track for the stairs.  Picking up a small cell phone that rested lifelessly on the sidewall table, she glanced back at him.  Romney caught a glimpse of what he thought was a smile on Sandy's face, and he returned a skeptical smile as his shoulders exhaled, finally releasing the tension that had been mounting throughout the day.

A muffled voice from the upstairs hallway reached Romney's ears around the same time he was searching through his phone contacts for the number of Alexandra Richards, their babysitter.

## Part 1 - Chapter Eleven

Alexandra Richards had been a wonderful help to the Daniels family for two long years, and, while speaking to Alex Richards' mother, Romney heard the little joyful voice consenting in the background of the telephone.

After finishing the short arrangement, Romney stepped into the toy room over the child-gate, holding his jacket.  Romney called to April, who was still contently playing in the center of the toy room, "Let's get your shoes on, Pearl."

After receiving no response, he swung his spring jacket over his shoulders and shimmied the twisted right sleeve onto his arm from behind his back.  "Hey, April, come.  Let's get your shoes on, and we'll walk over to Alex's house."

"Look, dad!" April Daniels said, holding up a knickknack that she had threaded with a strand of her doll's thick yarn hair.

"I see; hey, come, let's get your shoes on," Romney said forgivingly as he exited the playroom into the hallway to grab April's pink jacket.

After a short impasse, mostly due to April's continued interest and desire to retain hold of the knickknack, Romney reiterated, "Do you want to go play with Alex?"

Finally understanding, April took the knickknack and threw it toward the shelf of other toys.

--- *Moments later while walking along their residential street.*

"Yes, I see, honey, it went over there. Thanks for kicking the rock out of the road," Romney spoke, looking up at the Richards' home five minutes later. Unable to maintain his chosen walking speed for sake of his daughter's demand for attention, he said, "Alex is your best friend, right? And she is a good friend, isn't she?"

"Yes?" April questioned, intending to state a fact.

Answering the front door, Mrs. Richards apologized, "I'm sorry, Rom, we are in the middle of...well, could we pick her up in about an hour? I thought that's what you meant on the phone."

"Yes, absolutely. No problem at all, April wanted to play, and, tell you what, I'll just bring her back in an hour. Sorry for the misunderstanding," Romney apologized.

"And Romney, I know Alex enjoys babysitting April...she really does, honest to God, but umm. And please don't take this the wrong way, we love having April over, but recently it's been...been more of a burden for me with work, and with Dave traveling more. And we can definitely watch her tonight. We want to help, but...."

The wordy excuse ended with Romney maintaining a polite smile to hide his inward disappointment, and after sincerely apologizing, Romney picked up April and returned home. After following April into the foyer, he quickly lifted April over the gate back into her toy room where she recommenced her toy threading.

## Part 1 - Chapter Twelve

Romney buttoned up a crisp shirt and checked the length of his stiff cuffs by reaching his arms out toward the mirror. He continued dressing, but he frowned after knotting a green patterned tie and feeling the snugness of the collar on his neck. After reforming the tie into a better knot, he ran his hand over his collection of watches, pausing to note the time on one of them, and he remembered how he had come to have so many.

--- *Five years prior and on his birthday.*

He had arrived home, like usual, a week before his company planned to break ground on their first project. Fiddling with his keys, Romney had paused to erase the day's-worth of tension from his face. But before he could grasp the door handle, the door had swung open, and Sandy had said, "Here hold this," while handing Romney an oblong present. Sandy had disappeared and had returned with a Hawaiian shirt. "Here give me that," Sandy had instructed, asking for Romney's briefcase with buried excitement.

"Sandy, I'm tired. Nobody would leave me alone to make any progress today; it was all, 'Happy Birthday, Rom! So, what are your plans tonight?' ...over and over. I hardly had time...."

"Oh, poor you. You're such a great boss that your employees care," Sandy had countered, easily penetrating Romney's unfounded grumpiness. "Hold on," Sandy had continued, dashing away into the first-floor apartment. She had returned a moment later with a granola bar and had insisted that Romney change into his festive shirt on their small porch. Within a few minutes, Romney was opening his oblong shaped present from the passenger seat of their economy car while chewing the snack Sandy had retrieved for him. Sandy had driven through the streets with some hidden agenda, hiding every clue with a grin as to the purpose of the long-jewelry-box-looking gift. When Sandy had pulled back in front of Romney's office without relinquishing any meaningful piece of information, Romney had almost gotten upset. Sandy though had continued in her positive spirit, "Awe, come on, Rom; live a little!"

The assertion had preoccupied Romney until Sandy had navigated him back up the elevator to the headquarters of Hense and Daniels. When the doors had opened, Romney couldn't repress his smile. He had instantly reddened with embarrassment as nearly every employee, some with their families, yelled in unison, "Happy Birthday, Rom!" Each employee had stood there waiting in a half circle, holding a small box below a flimsy banner made of office paper that read, "It's about TIME we celebrated you. HAPPY BIRTHDAY!" Romney had gone around the room, thanking everyone, and he individually opened nine small gift boxes, which had all turned out to be watches per Sandy's instructions. Romney couldn't stop smiling on the drive home as he held onto his oblong shaped watch organizer. Then once back at their apartment, Romney discovered the romance that Sandy had planned.

The entire memory pleasantly flashed by him in a few seconds. Then, Romney lifted his suit jacket over his shoulders, feeling the silk slide up his sleeves, and selecting his most recent addition to his watch collection, one from Jack Hense, he watched the second-hand tick a few times before the doorbell chimed. Not expecting anyone, Romney Daniels set the watch down and galloped down the stairs to the front door. Ten steps behind, Sandy Daniels made her way to the top of the staircase and paused long enough to see the face and jacket of the guest through the half-circle window above the door.

Romney freely opened the thick front door.

"Hi," Romney Daniels greeted, not knowing the uninvited guest who looked like a trespasser who might whimsically decide to graffiti the mailbox on his way off the property.

"Yeah, I'm here for the lady of the house," the boy asked with fallacious eloquence.

"I'm Romney Daniels, who may I ask is calling on the lady of the house?"

The boy contorted his face without answering as he chewed on something.

"I'm Romney Daniels, owner of this house, husband to 'the lady,' who are you?" Romney prompted again.

"You said that, dog" the boy said with annoyance, "I'm Spence, and I'm here to meet this lady...if she's not here...well then it doesn't matter to you then."

"'Pence' as in a penny or 'Spence' as in Spencer?" Romney asked.

"Spence. Do you answer questions or just ask them? Is this lady here or not?" Spencer asked with displeasure.

"Not...and not because of her not being here," Romney replied. "Something is fishy."

"Forget it, man," Spencer blared without remorse. "You tell her, 'She owes me double.'" Spencer backed away and turned toward the mail gate across the grass.

Romney smiled at his small accomplishment until he felt the sting of his wife's repudiating swat on the back of his head as she flew by him and called out to Spencer, "Wait!"

Romney couldn't overhear the interchange from the center of the yard, but he watched, feeling helpless as Sandy bought what Spencer was selling.

"I'm going to get ready for your little evening thing," Sandy informed as she came back in the front door.

"Are you going to be high?" Romney accused unfairly.

"Maybe."

"Sandy!  No!" Romney objected sternly.

"No, or what, you're gonna divorce me?" Sandy stabbed and kept retreating inside and to her bedroom up the stairs.

Romney eventually pressed back through the front door and stepped in to find April playfully bombing the kitchen floor with cereal from a discovered cereal box.

After escorting April once again to the babysitter's house, he waited on the doorstep for a minute and listened to the babysitter's mother, a cheerful woman aptly named Felicity, as she called for her daughter to answer the door.  Alex, a flourishing eleven-year-old, obediently found the door, opened it, took a glance at Romney's attire, and whistled with approval. Romney nearly blushed, but he successfully held off the crimson from his cheeks, knowing the whistle's meaning was obliviously and innocently mistaken by the eleven-year-old.  Then Romney Daniels returned to his mansion after Alex disappeared inside with his daughter.

After ascending the stairs, he entered the master bedroom and looked at Sandy.

"I'm not ready yet.  I'll meet you down in the car," Sandy said glibly, entertained by a television talk show host as she pulled her socks over her unusually bony ankles.

# Part 1 - Chapter Thirteen

The moment after Romney sat down in the driver's seat he unlocked and belted up his personal carry weapon as he usually did.

After a good ten minutes of waiting and a few episodes of annoyance, Romney realized with astonishment he hadn't put his watch on his wrist. With no promising indications of Sandy from his vantage point, Romney got out of the car and walked into the house through the garage door.

As Romney banged through the garage screen, Sandy emerged from the front door in her semi-fashionable attire. She walked confidently toward the front of the purring vehicle, and when she finally noticed that Romney wasn't inside, she paused as her conscience reminded her of how much she was dreading the rest of the evening. She mimicked how her husband would have chided her, saying, "Just climb in, dear," and willingly agreed to the opportune cop-out. So, she sunk down into the idling car, closed the door, and put it into motion out of the driveway and down the street.

Romney shook his head after he stepped out of the door to find that Sandy had completely disappeared with the car. He looked down the road, and perhaps heard the roar of the engine at the stop sign around the bend.

"Okay, I'll meet you there then," Romney rhetorically stated, knowing that Sandy had as much intention of meeting him at the fundraiser as he did of arriving to it dressed in a pink tuxedo.

After calling a limousine service to escort him to the event, he took a seat in his pricey suit on the steps of the porch to wait.

For a while he replayed Sandy's actions that evening. Finding it of no use to exert anymore of his energy, he let his thoughts drift to appreciating the consoling weather.

A short while later, a limousine driver, named Santiago, beeped the horn twice to alert his unobservant customer.

Santiago started awkwardly laughing at Romney's short retelling of what had happened, and Romney didn't fault him for it either.

"I can imagine the nine-one-one operator's reaction," Santiago reacted, admitting his harmless intention.

Romney injected his own spin on Santiago's infectious attitude. "'Ummm, so, sir, what your telling me is...your wife has your car?' They'd think I was crazy."

Santiago motioned with his hand to hide his amusement, and after seeing the mood of his passenger change, he said, "Man, I sure am sorry for you, sir. Where can I take you tonight?"

"Thank you," Romney said, responding to Santiago's motion. "To Vern Hill College, for the fundraising event. Do you know of its whereabouts?"

"Yes, sir, right away! Will you be needing a ride home, sir?" Santiago said with a recomposed voice, looking back to see whether his laughing had offended his passenger.

"I think I may; will your services be available if it turns out that way?"

"What time'r you thinking, sir?"

"Oh, let me see," Romney said with a pause. He mulled over the impossibilities for a minute. "Ten or eleven?" Romney asked with uncertainty in his voice.

"I'll call it in," replied Santiago. And with the matter somewhat settled, the limousine pulled away from the curb.


## Part 1 - Chapter Fourteen


The thrill of trouble pulsed through Sandy's fingers. As if someone would soon be in pursuit, she used the powerful engine to accelerate toward her outlet.

Too impatient to wait, she held her dispenser in her hand. The car would drive well enough, so she let go and took the vile. If the car's steering had not been aligned, she would have left the road. Then time slowed down as Sandy succumbed to the almost pure chemical that flowed into her blood.

The engine idled as she coasted the car to a stop. In contrast with the surroundings, Sandy parked the car, and stepping out of it, she looked as forlorn as the windows lining the street. Instinctively, she lifted her glossy purse over her shoulder. The car may have locked itself, and it concerned her little. She took a full moment to breathe the sweaty air but could not rouse the sense of smell to detect the putrid fragrance of it. She walked to the entrance of an alley. "Dead end," she thought, following the far brick wall up to its high ledge with her eyes. "Hello," she called. No one answered. She stepped inside and smiled. "Alone at last," she told herself, walking carelessly halfway deep into the alley.

Lifting the lid of a heavily utilized garbage bin, she looked inside to determine the value of its contents. The door to the corresponding shop next to the bin looked well used. Layers of aged liquid stained the steps, revealing the daily trail of disposed trash. The door swung open, startling Sandy. The unlucky trash man appeared with his daily luggage. Hesitating at the sight of Sandy, the man looked her over judgingly. Sandy backed away, repulsed at the look of gruffness that grew on the man's face. Once the trash man completed his mission, Sandy continued playfully all the way to the back of the alley. "Artistic; in fact, this could be art if people would just be willing to come look," Sandy convinced herself. Then she turned around and walked back to the opening of the alley. She stood, looking right and left. Then again...right and left. "Hmm, I guess he's not coming after all."

A city bus stopped across the street, dropping off day workers that were headed home. A sense of guilt slowly welled up in her chest, "I did this, I brought myself here." The guilt quickly shifted to shivering...then hot shivering as the sun struck her forehead. She retreated to the shelter of the alley. A curl of wind rounded the corner of the alley, created by a passing truck.

She forgot why she was sobbing and returned to the garbage bin. Lifting the lid again curiously, she tried to determine what the man had discarded. Poking the trash, she suddenly had the desire to untie it. "People discard good stuff all the time. What a shame. They don't know what they're missing. That man shouldn't be called the trash man. What's this? What's this? Well it's a loss now. These people! If they would just stop throwing these good things away." She lowered the lid to her side. "Ick," Sandy said to herself, looking down at her shoes. "Where is he? I knew I couldn't count on him. Romney where are you, you and your fancy car, your fancy job with your suits, and your fancy child. You spoil her, and you can't even see it."

Sandy started toward the exit.

"Phbb. He doesn't understand," She said from her scattered thoughts. "That's a pity. It's a good thing that I can make all of his problems disappear," Sandy sang. Then she dug through her purse to find her phone, and once she found it, she instinctively dialed the number. "This is Beverly. Uh-huh."

## Part 1 - Chapter Fifteen

Romney Daniels knew the city well and passed by numerous memories as the limousine patiently started and stopped on its way toward the fundraiser.

"Santiago, are we thinking of the same fundraiser?" Romney asked, unsettling the driver with his question.

"You're wanting the Vern College fundraiser, sir, no?" Santiago indecisively answered, glancing back and forth between the road and the rearview mirror to discern the deliberation of his passenger.

"That's the one, but are you planning on rounding the block or something; it's right back there. Isn't it?" Romney asked, enveloping his question with uncertainty.

"No, I don't believe so, but if it makes you feel better, sir, I'll call to my dispatcher, and he'll check for me," Santiago offered, assimilating Romney's tone.

"If you would do that, I would be grateful; I'm almost certain that the fundraiser was right back there last year," Romney resigned, sinking back into the cushioned seat as he listened to Santiago talk over his radio.

"My dispatcher doesn't know, sir; I was going to drop you off where my coworker said he was going to drop another person earlier...before I took your call," Santiago said and looked back at Romney Daniels for instructions. After noting his passenger had overlooked his subtlety, he asked, "Do you still want me to go there, sir? Or do you want me to swing back around for you?"

"Keep going, keep going, I'll double your tip if you're right," Romney bet with a cursory smile and turned to look back out the tinted glass toward the shops lining the street.

The city continued to pass by the window slowly.

"It looks like you'll be doubling your tip, sir," Santiago said, bending under his window shade to confirm the street signage.

Romney also leaned forward, interested in locating the telltale signs of the fundraiser. "Yep, that must be it. Forgive me for my doubt, Santiago," Romney said and handed the proud chauffeur his promised courtesy.

Romney climbed out of the vehicle and onto a red carpet. Then after straightening and buttoning his jacket, he proceeded into the venue. Romney didn't recognize any of the few guests arriving before or after him, though a familiar looking stranger introduced himself as 'Michael Gallant' and extended his hand to Romney.

"Romney Daniels. A pleasure," Romney replied.

The stranger turned to observe the luxury of the foyer. Looking up with the stranger, Romney thought of all the wasted space that was spent in the name of lavishness. Then he turned back to Michael Gallant, but instead of speaking, he sighed at the discovery of his gun still strapped to his side. Eventually, one of the three elevators opened, and an attendant promptly invited the two guests on board. A courteous manager of the waiters placed his hand on Romney Daniels' left arm as he exited the elevator and said, "Kind sir, what a pleasure to have you here tonight. Are you here together?"

"All-one. Thank you," Romney slurred, placing his fist over his mouth. "Sorry. I'm alone," Romney apologized as he handed over his invitation.

The perceptive manager somehow seemed aware of Romney's situation, and instead of calling the first available waitress, he called the second waiter in line. "Fievel, would you tend to...Mr. Daniels tonight," he beckoned, reading the name off the invitation.

"Thank you, sir," Romney replied and visually made acquaintance with his waiter. Then after stepping into the visually stunning lounge and taking a relaxing breath, Romney called Fievel to his side and started walking down the stretch of windows. "Fievel is it?" Romney asked casually to clarify he'd heard the name correctly.

"Yes, Mr. Daniels," Fievel responded attentively.

Turning his head mid-stride, Romney asked, "Where would a guy go around here if he was hungry?"

"Right this way, Mr. Daniels," Fievel prompted, directing Romney with an open-faced hand. "They should be seating now."

"Good."

Fievel professionally waited with Romney as the doorman in charge of arranging the guests introduced Courtney.

Courtney smiled as welcomingly as a bouquet of fragrant jasmine when it was her turn to speak and invited pleasantly, "If you would, please follow me."

## Part 1 - Chapter Sixteen

Courtney's hair swung around as she turned back to Romney, who trailed a few steps behind her. "Will this table suit you? You'll be the trailblazer tonight, if that's all right."

"Of course, of course, this will be fine. Thank you, Courtney," Romney said, seeing Fievel walk up behind him.

Trying to show his good humor, Fievel sensibly asked, "May I bring some appetizers for the famished Mr. Daniels?"

Still unbuttoning his suit jacket, Romney addressed Fievel's hesitation with a courteous smile and nod. Romney sat and started spinning his treasured ring around his finger after a few moments of surveying the room. After another short minute, Romney looked up to find Fievel placing a plate full of appetizers in front of him. Expressing his gratitude, he squeezed a flaky bun. But catching sight of Fievel again, he paused for the waiter's arm to stretch in front of him and lay down another plate of good-looking food. Romney turned around to again thank his disappearing waiter before looking the plate over. Then he burst with laughter as Fievel laid a third plate to the right of his other two plates. "You take my words seriously!"

"There's more, sir, there's more," Fievel answered jestingly, understanding Romney's meaning.

"I know, I know, but the meal, God gave me a stomach to fill, not my eyes. Thank you," Romney hugged the knot forming in his stomach. "Thank you for making me laugh, but please take it all away, mind this bun."

Fievel gladly obliged, leaving only the pastry for Romney to finish enjoying.

Utilizing the appropriate utensil, Romney spread butter on his swirled bun, but noticing Courtney's approach, he replaced his knife and appetizer on his white plate. Courtney arrived closely followed by two attractively dressed guests. Sharing her familiar smile, she began her introduction. "Mr. Daniels, may I introduce Julianne Purse and her daughter Anna. Miss Purse is a gold supporter of Vern Hill's athletics department and her daughter currently attends college there."

"It's nice to make your introduction, Julianne and Anna. I like the name similarity."

"Plthis is...," Courtney and Romney spoke over each other. Both stopped and fought each other for second place with their eyes. Flushing a little, Courtney picked up, "This is Mr. Romney Daniels, Chief Operating Officer at the local property development firm, Hense and Daniels, here in Pittsburg."

"Thank you, Courtney," Romney said, dismissing Courtney back to her duties. Romney motioned for Fievel to assist the daughter, and the two waiters stepped in and out skillfully to allow the two ladies to take their seats.

"The appetizers will impress you both; Fievel, might I bother you to return with those plates you had so pleasantly brought earlier?"

"Oh please, I'm famished; aren't you, Anna?" Julianne asked.

Anna amiably showed her agreement.

Fievel and the other waiter coordinated the plates they brought and displayed them in front of Julianne and Anna.

"So, Mr. Daniels, C.O.O. of company partly named after yourself," Julianne started.

"Call me Romney, please. May I call you Julianne?" Romney politely interrupted.

"Oh, sure," Julianne responded.

"Unfortunately, yes. Hense is my business partner's last name, and it only made sense to balance the name with the other co-founder. Time was so little in that phase of the company. I promise I'm not that egocentric."

"Well, if I didn't have a daughter that shared most of my name, as you observed, I might have made such an accusation. Where are you from, Romney?" Julianne asked.

"Chapel Hills now, and what about you both? I take it, Anna, you are residing on campus at Vern Hill," Romney inquired.

"No, it's not...not so," Anna said too quickly.

"Anna's living at home with me across the river on Riverview Avenue. The drive is barely anything, and I get bored with myself when she's not there to keep me company."

"Or out of trouble," Anna added.

"Hah," Romney laughed.

"She's my little protector."

"By that she means I take out the trash and do the dishes," Anna added.

"Oh, Anna dear, don't put yourself down. You do more than that," Julianne said sarcastically.

"Riverview Ave. That's the street that has the grand view overlooking the city," Romney stated with inquiry, interrupting the playful banter.

"I'd say so," Julianne confirmed. "I've lived there for ages and couldn't part with the place after my parents died," Julianne said, surveying the appetizers.

"Oh, I'm sorry to hear. I must say, if it's not rude, you two certainly don't look like mother and daughter." Romney offered.

"Well, I'll be," Anna said, acting offended.

"No, no...not in any way saying...."

"I'm completely kidding. We get that all the time. We might as well be sisters," Anna clarified apologetically.

"My parents passed tragically when I was younger," Julianne said, redirecting the dialogue to what she was thinking. After pausing, she concluded, "My grandmother raised me, but she's since passed as well."

# Part 1 - Chapter Seventeen

Anna released a giggle, looking down at the purple fruit she had picked at with her fork from the small dish of ambrosia centered on her plate.  Her half-smile, however slight, caught Romney's periphery.  "I'm not a big on the town kind of guy," Romney explained.

"Still, we need to get you into the city after the sun goes down. Obviously, you're unaware that it's improper for the C.E.O. of a company to be so uncultured." Julianne continued.

"C.O.O.."

"Titles...it's a piano bar.  I dual, or entertain if you will, with this classical pianist on occasion.  Goodness, I'd take a night off to culture myself, if I weren't heading up the entertainment," Julianne said with full steam.

"She takes most nights off," Anna added with a smirk.

"You're not helping my case, Anna dear," Julianne bantered, waiting for Romney to react to her insistent pecking.

"Anna, what made you choose, Vern Hill?" Romney redirected.

Alerted by her name and excited to speak, Anna replied, "history."

"History, you say?  And what portion of history affected your decision most?" Romney asked in echo to prevent Julianne from inserting a remark.

The question made Anna unconsciously wince her eyes, and after catching Julianne's attention from her pause, she apologetically asked, "I'm sorry.  What?"

Finding her puzzled look adorable, Romney set to apologizing, "No, no, I'm sorry.  How about I choose one question at a time, instead of combining three and punishing you to sort them all out."  He smiled, appreciating her gentle resolve, and asked, "What intrigues you most about history?"

"About history," Anna replied, looking away as she formulated her response, but her eyes came into focus on an approaching waitress.

"Hi, Mr. Daniels, Miss Purse, and Miss Purse," the waitress greeted, locking her knees and hugging a writing pad.  "Have you enjoyed our appetizers?" she asked almost rhetorically. Seeing the beginning of an affirmative nod from Romney Daniels, she added, "Hand prepared by our Chef Marco in the kitchen tonight...."

Romney interrupted and asked, "I'm sorry, but what's your name, miss?"

"Abigail," she said happily, hiding behind her writing pad.

"Abigail, a lovely name," Romney said. "Is Marco, actually Chef Marco's last name, or is his last name actually Cannavacciuolo? Because I had heard wind that Chef Cannavacciuolo from Butler's Station was running the show tonight. For all practical purposes, he makes my lunch every day. He's right across the street from our corporate office."

Abigail held her grin while Romney explained, then she sheepishly admitted, "That sounds right, maybe? But I don't know; he wouldn't tell me." Seeing her guests all smile at her mannerism, she expounded in her defense, "I asked him how to pronounce his name yesterday when I got here, but he just told me, 'I've hired a butcher already; you don't pronounce my name correctly, so you...just call me Chef Marco to all the guests.'" She said, imitating the syntax and tongue of Chef Marco.

Romney enjoyed the accuracy of Abigail's impression and replied, "That's the one, Chef Cannavacciuolo...a stubbornly fantastic personality!"

Abigail made haste to explain their options and take their orders. After gaining confidence from the pleasing demeanors of her guests, she queried Romney, "Cannavacciuolo, you said. Right?"

"Right! You nailed it...and the first time even!" Romney praised.

"I'll go give Chef Marco some heat about his name and your orders right away," Abigail promised, still gripping the writing pad.

"Well, that was interesting," Julianne condescendingly commented to the table.

"Yeah," Romney replied instinctively before detecting her sarcasm. Turning back to Anna, he saw her lips eager to speak.

Triggered by Romney's attention, Anna said, "I'm intrigued by how time, unforgivingly, buries history...regarding my intrigue with history that is. History lets you gawk for as long as you want at it and catches you up in the wonder of what actually happened," Anna continued happily. "But still," she said, "I find it fascinating to look back on real dilemmas, what people did, to see how things turned out...and all interchangeably."

"Good answer," Romney encouraged without looking away. "So, a true passion for history in general, which period or segment in history excites you most?"

"I love the early painters of the renaissance; so maybe the fourteen to fifteen-hundreds. I guess it helps that more of their history is preserved," Anna said.

Immediately sensing Anna's delight and commencing from her pause, Romney recalled an article he had recently skimmed. Leaning back and crossing his arms, he asked Anna as if examining her, "So, who do you think actually painted the Mona Lisa first, was it Da Vinci or Gioconda?"

"Leonardo Da Vinci painted Mona Lisa," Julianne interjected at the preposterous question.

"I don't know," Romney confidently bluffed, "Was it Da Vinci that first painted it or did Gioconda paint it ten years earlier?"

Anna blushed.

"Gioconda, La Lisa Gioconda, is the name of the painting, in Italian; she couldn't have painted herself," Julianne said, taking her casual focus back across the room. "Well, I guess she could have, but she didn't."

"Actually," Anna said, "it might be best, currently described as La Joconde, in French, because...."

"Ladies, ladies – and gentleman – you look beautiful tonight." The whole table turned to find Terrance wheedling next to Anna with a confident smile.

"Oh. Hi, it's Terrance, right? Good to see you," Anna said, unsure of the correct name. "May I introduce you to Romney Daniels and my mother, Julianne."

Terrance abruptly paused his pertly self-assertiveness, as if the introduction had jarred his memory, and then dramatically sat down next to Anna. Picking up her hand, he whispered loudly enough for the others to hear, "Anna."

Anna could see his teasing eyes.

"...if you were a flower, you'd be a rose...." Terrance paused again with a concerned look on his face as if waiting for his stage partner to speak her line.

Anna couldn't help uncomfortably grin and look away to keep from laughing. She yielded, "Why, Terrance? Why would I be a rose?"

"Because you always blush red every time I come near you."

Julianne let out a cynical laugh and replied, "Oh...that's a good one; Terrance, my boy, if you were a flower, you'd be a rose's stem, because you look sharp and you're wearing green!"

Terrance succumbed and unintentionally repeated, "That's a good one. Anna said you were Julianne?"

"Still am, Terrance," Julianne replied and smirked at Anna with amusement.

"Anna, I hope you don't mind me joining you, but...," Terrance said, pausing to allow the waiter to place his appetizers in front of him, "...my table was beginning to be a bit of a bore."

"Oh, sorry to hear that," Anna sarcastically sympathized, causing Terrance to snort his own laugh.

"See, it's paid off with better company already," Terrance said, grabbing a pinwheel swirled bun and taking a bite. "Mmm, good stuff."

Seeing the newcomer from her perch on the side of the room, Abigail stepped up beside Terrance and began, "Hi, my name is Abigail."

"Hi, Abigail," Terrance interrupted, smiling with his indulgent lips.

"Ha...hi," Abigail smiled courteously in reply. "Have you had time to look over our selections off our menu tonight?"

"Oh, no need; I already ordered," Terrance said, turning to face Anna again. Then in slow motion, he turned back to Abigail with a ghostly look on his face. Abandoning his act with his own laughter, he realized the recent waiter had leaned over and begun whispering an explanation to Abigail's other ear.

Anna stated, "And, Romney, just what is spanakopita."

"Ooh, you should have ordered it. Chef Marco may run an Italian restaurant, but he's definitely a master of Greek food."

"It's not on the menu at Butler's," Julianne accused.

"Oh no. That'd be unforgivable. Friday's," Romney said, hiding further information in his cheeks. "Next time you go, go on a Friday, and check the carry out counter. If you beat me to lunch, you might get some."

"What did you order, Terrance?" Anna asked politely to include her acquaintance.

"Well, whatever animal a mig-non comes from," Terrance said, concealing any hint of joking. "Did you look at it?"

"The filet mignon? I did," Anna said.

"Surf and turf, baby!" Terrance said with tainted sincerity.

Dinner arrived and was consumed amidst their general chatter. Then voicing the general sentiment at the end of the meal, Anna said, "What a delightful meal; don't you agree, Rom?" Anna blushed a second time and swallowed the lump that had instantly formed in her throat at her informality. "Do you go by Rom?"

The silhouette of the master of ceremonies timely heralded the announcement of dancing and the next phase of seating for the six-thirty dinner courses. His polite bow, framed by the grand doors of the banquet hall, triggered the commotion of the guests.

"Splendid indeed, Anna," Romney returned after the announcement. "And yes."

"Who might this be?" Julianne asked inquisitively, noticing a six-foot tall athlete approaching.

Anna shifted her focus to Julianne but pivoted around at the suggestion of her mother's eyes. "Oh! It's a classmate." Anna said.

"Hey, Anna...Terrance," Chad replied, smiling diffidently. Circling his eyes past Terrance to Romney and Julianne, Chad put his left hand in his pocket and stepped toward Romney to make his introduction. "Hi, I'm Chad Wattsworth."

"Hi, Chad, I'm Romney Daniels. I seem to recall a picture of you on the front page of this season's baseball program. You pitch for Vern Hill, no doubt?" Romney asserted, firmly greeting Chad's stronger hand.

Moving his neck to view Julianne's face and shoulders, Chad agreed, "Yes, sir."

Julianne naturally read the admiration in Chad's gaze and reached her slender hand in front of Romney. "Chad, it's nice to meet you; I'm Julianne Purse." Keeping her eyes open for Chad to appreciate, she placed her fingers in Chad's hand.

Without shaking her hand, he gently squeezed her fingers and stuttered his response, "...Julianne, is it?"

"Hey, that's what I said," Terrance interrupted. "It must be a thing."

"Chad, would you walk with me? This here is a stately man," indicating Romney, "but, he's effectively taken," Julianne said.

Terrance turned again to Anna and asked, "Well, if that's a thing too, Anna, do you boogie?"

Anna stared at her mother in disbelief for the first hanging moment, and the terrible moments that followed she couldn't peel her eyes off the couple, hoping to still catch Chad smile in her direction, or look at her, or at least acknowledge her presence in some manner. As her eyes strafed around the table, she noticed Romney's silent observation and hastily answered Terrance, "If boogie means, I'm done eating and ready to dance, then, yes, let's boogie."

Romney saw Anna's strained smile as she glanced at him once more.

## Part 1 - Chapter Eighteen

Chef Marco faintly heard the hum of music from his work space. Looking up at an empty order clip, he smiled to express his satisfaction at reaching the middle marking sound of his contracted engagement. He dipped his knife in an infusion of lemon, vinegar, and water. Then, wiping it clean with a damp muslin rag, he tapped his cutlery to a mounted magnet.

"Jimmy!" he commissioned to his sous chef, raising his voice to carry his articulation across the kitchen, "è ora di cominciare tutti una volta di più." Waving his hand in a lassos motion, he stepped in the direction of the double swinging doors to watch the changeover of guests. After passing through the swinging partitions into the banquet hall, Chef Marco immediately set eyes on the familiar face of Romney Daniels. "Ahh! Ha-ha...," he proclaimed in Romney's direction. Eagerly stepping over, he grabbed Romney by the arm. "I should have recognized your name on the guest list, my friend. How are you, Mr. Daniels?"

"Chef Cannavacciuolo!" Romney said, delighted to see his aliased acquaintance. After affectionately standing and letting the famous chef pump his hand, Romney candidly said, "When did you change your last name to Marco?"

"Oh? Oh...," Chef Marco laughed while he made the connection. "Oh, no sweet Abigail couldn't get it right, so I teased her a little; that is all," Chef Cannavacciuolo answered with his familial air. Looking at Romney's wrist with his right hand yet engaged in his greeting, Chef Cannavacciuolo observantly asked, "What? You are not with your favorite time-keeper? How will you tell the time, sir?"

"Not tonight. My wife wasn't able to make it," Romney said, revealing his disappointment with a subtle depression of his shoulders.

"Oh, that is too bad; you need to bring her by the Station more often now," Chef Cannavacciuolo replied naturally and leaned in closer to Romney, "...or has my food been to her bad?" After holding his serious expression, his lips broke into a teeth-filled smile, and the sight of the bus boy cleaning the nearby table reminded him of his cooking his duties.

"Addio," Romney bid to his acquaintance and intentionally dropped his napkin on his plate. Unobtrusively stretching, he stepped behind a few guests as they walked toward the exit of the banquet hall. After a few minutes of walking alone, Romney found a space in front of the large west windows to relax. The cushions were comfortable, but the sun was too intense for Romney, so he glanced around to find Fievel.

Rushing to Romney Daniels' glances, Fievel petitioned, "May I bring you something, Mr. Daniels?"

"Nothing in particular, no; but I was wondering do you have any shades for these windows, so I might sit here on one of these couches and watch the sunset?" Romney asked.

Fievel showed his apology, "No, sir, I don't know of any." He paused, trying to ascertain a deeper question that lingered on Romney face. "But I will tell you from being here last night that seeing the sunset was amazing. You won't want to miss it! Give yourself maybe twenty more minutes, and the sun won't be so

blinding then." Seeing that his response satisfied Romney,
Fievel turned to reclaim his discrete position next to a wall
ornament.

"Thank you, Fievel," Romney said to his retreating waiter.
Holding up his hand to decline a passing beverage concierge, he
decidedly rose to his feet and continued to follow the crowd
moving toward the dance floor.

## Part 1 - Chapter Nineteen

Dressed in his green suit jacket and brown slacks, complete
with a beautiful hand in his and a mask of confidence on his
face, Terrance led Anna to the dance floor. Terrance pardoned
himself between two older couples that stood chit-chatting
around the floor without letting go of Anna's soft grip. Anna
followed, smiling as she heard her heels tap the waxed surface.
The conductor displayed a pleased smile on his swiveled head,
intending to welcome his first daring guests to begin their
dancing. Returning his face to his four instrumentalists, he
visibly inhaled while lifting both of his nimble hands to signal a
reprise to the top of the medium tempo waltz.

"How about some hip-hop?" Terrance audibly requested,
turning to Anna with a cocksure grin.

The perplexed conductor, swaying slowly with the tempo,
asked, "H-ip pop?"

Without inhibition, Terrance blurted out, "Yeah, you
know...hip-hop." Terrance moved his shoulders and rolled his
body artfully.

Anna put her fist up to her mouth to hide her amusement and
glanced at the confused conductor who still careened around
without losing his tempo.

The obliging conductor broke the nervous moment, "Oh you
mean...heap-hop, wit a big down beat like-dis." The conductor
pointed at his bass and repeated his interpretation of Terrance's
request. "Hold 'E,' for heap-hop." He silenced the musicians
with a swipe of his hands and quickly tapped his desired beat on
the black metal stand. The violinist smiled as if he was freed

from a stuffy room. The bassist, with all starkness, pulled her bow heavily across her low string in time with the tempo. The other two instrumentalists exchanged looks and repositioned themselves. The conductor's hand lifted and brought forth the impromptu rhythmic song. Turning back around to smile at the young dancers, he said proudly, "Now you can dance heap-hop."

Brilliant in his own way, Terrance clapped and fell into fluidly popping and moving his limbs. When he twisted an imaginary hat around his head, the crowd started gawking while the chatter stopped. A voice of amazement rippled through the onlookers when Terrance fell into a simple break dance and athletically jumped back upright to his loosely coordinated feet. Flipping his jacket down, Terrance danced it off and hung it around Anna's shoulders as enticement for her to join him in his dance. Anna's color slowly changed as she started sliding the jacket off after Terrance had spun away from her nonverbal refusal.

"Come on; you gotta know some moves too," Terrance miffed to Anna as he continued coordinating his four limbs with unpredictable style.

"Noha...," Anna managed to respond and hesitated back further toward the onlooking crowd.

Romney Daniels had made his way to the sideline of the dance floor and watched for a short minute.

The conductor spoke up reactively from his careening stance, "You dance good heap-hop, sir."

Romney stepped forward, intending to welcome Anna off the floor to save her from the humiliating attention of the crowd, but the moment he had reached her spot on the checkerboard, he saw Coach Paddernick rush into the area with a staunch look of censure. With two more quick steps, Romney caught Anna's periphery while Terrance caught stage fright from seeing the resolute expression of his coach.

"Both of you come with me," Coach Paddernick pronounced barely loud enough for those on the dance floor to decipher, leaving the rest of his threat to be implied by the crowd and his listeners.

Realizing he might be an accomplice, the paling conductor frigidly turned his back to shun the dance floor tribunal. The

failing hip-hop beat had brought to the foreground the
murmuring sounds of the audience.

Easily guessing the implication of the coach's hushed
invitation, Romney raised his voice to interrupt Anna's
obedience. "Anna, would you care to dance?"

It seemed for a moment that the silence around the room fell
completely as the quartet had ceased to play and the gossip of
the crowd had suspended. Coach Paddernick joined Terrance's
frozen pose, anxiously pausing to allow Anna to answer. Barely
glancing back an apologetic look to Terrance, who stood
enervated in submission, she said, "Yes, thank you."

## Part 1 - Chapter Twenty

While moving with her escort toward the grand doors of the
banquet hall and looking more than ever like Anna's sister,
Julianne began, "So, you pitch."

"Yes, I pitch...or try to at least," Chad replied, offering a shy
glance at the floor before refocusing on her inquiring expression.

Julianne reached her right arm over and took hold of Chad's
forearm, leaning into Chad and giving an inference of
admiration. Then she let her silence work its magic.

"You came with Anna?" Chad said on cue and looked down
again, accepting the slight added weight of Julianne's off-kilter
walk. "She said that she was going with someone else already
when I invited...when I talked to her last."

"Anna turned you down? What a shame," Julianne remarked.

"Well, she didn't exactly turn me down, I never pressed to find
out how she came by her own invitation," Chad defended in a
kind manner.

Julianne's face fell into a satisfied grin and said, "Anna's a gem,
I couldn't ask for a better companion." Then Julianne squinted
her eyes and lifted her hand up to shield the sunlight.

Chad Wattsworth, seeing Julianne's discomfort, in one
spontaneous maneuver stepped up to block the nuisance with
his athletic frame. Julianne smiled in appreciation as Chad
continued walking backwards out of the banquet hall and into

the outer lounge. Julianne dropped her hand from her face and held it out in suspense for Chad. Positioning her head in Chad's shadow, she looked at his silhouette with difficulty for his reaction. After glancing behind to judge the pace of the crowd, Chad turned back to find Julianne's hand waiting for his. Fixated on Julianne's hand, he studied her fingers for a moment. Then Julianne latched onto him abruptly to stop his rearward stagger and to keep him from colliding into a waitress. Caught off guard and nearly missing his step, Julianne helped him maintain his balance.

Chad said, "Why, thank you. That would have been embarrassing," as he watched the waitress move away with two half glasses of wine.

"Chad," Julianne said, drawing Chad's lively attention, "how old are you?"

Chad smiled and replied, "Twenty...not old enough to drink, if that's what you're asking."

"Would you mind if I...?"

"Not at all; no, please don't let me stop you," Chad said appealingly.

Identifying the air of silence after Chad's accommodating response, she said, "I don't need to have anything tonight."

Chad offered his arm again to Julianne. Side by side they slowly migrated around the perimeter of the lounge toward a cove of couches.

"So, I take it you've had some bad experience with alcohol?" Julianne said, verbalizing her suspicion.

"Yeah," Chad replied. "How'd you guess?"

"I'm sorry; I shouldn't pry," Julianne said, looking away from Chad at another handsome individual.

"No, no. It's nothing to hide. My dad...," Chad said and paused to mull over his story.

"A man of pauses," Julianne smirked.

"Ha, no my dad...," Chad started again, recalling the memory vividly.

Julianne laughed, pushing Chad's strong arm.

"I mean...my dad was belligerent a little growing up, because he drank every night," Chad said, finally completing his thought.

"I'm sor...."

"I would stay...," Chad spoke over Julianne.

"Go on," Julianne prodded.

"No, you first."

Julianne waited stubbornly, then seeing Chad's insistence, encouraged, "I was only going to say, I'm sorry to hear that. And you were saying, 'You would stay....'"

"Yeah, I would stay after practice to avoid him...after everyone left, I would pitch a bucket of balls countless times before walking home," Chad conceded.

"That's probably why you're so good," Julianne said, gently grabbing and shaking Chad's shoulder.

"Yeah, I wouldn't say that. I'd rather have had a dad to pitch to...," Chad spoke lucidly. "I don't know, I think he would have been a good dad if he didn't drink the way he did. He could have loved my mom...but that's all past now. He's a lot better," Chad said, looking at Julianne's face, noting the welcoming lines of her lips.

"That sticks with you though; you're stronger because of it. Don't you think?" Julianne said, enjoying the transparency of the conversation.

"Well, yeah. It's formed certain behaviors of mine, but what about you, mystery girl?" Chad posed, trying to loosen his nerves.

With her eyes, Julianne took the challenge and said, "I don't know. Ask me something, and I'll tell you...no secrets." Sinking into a seat, she stiffened her arms into her lap.

"Like where do you live? Are you in school? What do you like to do?" Chad asked in rapid succession, feeling as if some resistance had disappeared while he took a seat beside her.

Freeing one of her hands from her lap and rolling her shoulder up a bit, she speechlessly opened her mouth to answer, but stopped short of speaking. With the muscles in her face tensing up, she glanced at Chad's eyes.

"Who's pausing now, Ms. Julianne?" Chad resounded, evoking a short laugh.

Removing her gaze to the fringe of her shimmering dress, she started, "I live with Anna across the river, and I've long graduated...." Lulling to display her youthful face, she looked to see if her comment had registered on Chad's forehead. "And," she sincerely shrugged, "I like playing the piano."

When Julianne checked Chad's face and caught him staring, her smile widened.

Catching Julianne's look, Chad darted his eyes to his own lap and started tapping his leg with his fingers.

"What's the matter?" Julianne said, with grinning concern. "You're acting like a boy that's never sat next to a girl before."

Taking a breath and turning back to face Julianne, he said, "Maybe I haven't."

"Oh, yeah right," Julianne said confidently, while inwardly diagnosing Chad's strange sprout of anxiety.

"But I like it," Chad let out, seeing a distancing thought appear on Julianne's face.

"Well, that's encouraging," Julianne laughed sarcastically. Humored with Chad's disposition, she slowed down her movements and reached over to slide Chad's hand onto her opposite shoulder. "I like it too. Where do you live, and what do you like to do...outside of baseball and pitching alone after practice?" Julianne said while smoothing her free hand over the ruffles that had formed on her lap.

"Well, on campus," Chad answered, hesitating in response. "And," Chad continued, leaving his trapped arm put, "I'd like to hear you play the piano."

"That's fair, but that's called flirting," Julianne accused. "Do you really want to hear me play?"

"Do I lie?" Chad asked, trying to cover his embarrassment.

"Well, they don't have a piano stashed away around here anywhere to pound out my tunes on, and the piano shop has long been closed, so you'll have to either follow me home or come to Piano Taps, where I play once every other week," Julianne flirted back.

"Like this week?" Chad asked.

"No, you'd have to wait an extra week."

"An extra week! Unacceptable, that's too long," Chad said jokingly, liking Julianne's push from her shoulder.

"Well, the night is still young; shall we take advantage of it?" Julianne asked boldly, suggestively leaning forward to prove her intention.

"Okay."

"Okay?" Julianne asked in surprise.

"Do I lie?"

"I don't know, do you...I don't know, do you?" Julianne teased at Chad's quick reuse of the sharp phrase. "Nobody's going to miss you around here for the hour we're gone. But I must warn you, I'm pretty good," Julianne coaxed.

"Well, shouldn't I be the judge of that?" Chad asked, looking around. "Should we let Anna know? I don't know where...."

"Oh, Anna's grown up with her own agenda these days, I don't worry about her much," Julianne downplayed.

"You want to go now?" Chad replied innocently, expressing the pinch of caution that had suddenly overshadowed the growing minute of confidence.

"I mean there's no rush, but the clock will strike midnight and eventually I'll turn back into a sleeping pumpkin."

Chad stalled for a few contemplative seconds.

"Come on," Julianne said to counter Chad's deliberation. "Let's go have some fun," she encouraged and took Chad's hand from his lap. Chad allowed Julianne's forward spinning motion to motivate him off the couch toward his anomalous pursuit. Then Julianne beckoned her personal waiter and informed him that they would be leaving.

The waiter a bit perplexed fidgeted about and ineffectively mumbled, "I'll call your car right up."

Julianne looked at Chad who looked back at her, having similarly heard, "Ickle or bar it up."

Their mutual glance caused the waiter to rephrase, "I'll go call your car right away."

Before the waiter could turn to go, Julianne asked, "Oh, Julian! Have you seen my daughter, or actually could you just tell her I'm leaving?"

"Right away, ma'am," Julian replied with purpose, twirling himself off to complete his assignments.

## Part 1 - Chapter Twenty-One

The waiter hustled to the manager who had finally finished his greeting duties. Flagging the manager's attention, he shared the two important pieces of information.

A void filled the air as the quartet from around the corner waned. "Is everything okay?" the surprised manager asked, voicing his concern.

"I believe so. Both were in the best of spirits," Julian said between breaths.

Lowering his volume and speaking as if touting privileged information, he whispered, "A little love struck it appeared."

"The Purses?" the manager responded poignantly.

"I don't know his name, a ball player, tall, strong looking. Of course, that's no help. I'm headed to inform the younger Ms. Purse now," the waiter said capriciously, almost dismissing his manager.

"Inform her of what? I'm confused; just..., go, go, just...."

Hanging onto his concern, the manager dismissed Julian with a wave of his hand. He finished his thought alone, muttering under his breath, "Well...if anyone ever needs a reason to avoid overachieving." Stepping over to a stylish box, the manager lifted the lid and fingered through a mass of gold colored envelopes. Stopping on one to read the label, he rotated his head to better decipher the name. "Julianne Purse," the manager read from his canted position, appreciating the calligraphy with its swooping type. Removing the envelope from its hiding place, he tucked it under his arm and proceeded to locate the deemed love-struck couple. "By the exit no doubt," the manager guessed.

Julian walked and weaved quickly through the gathered crowd, searching for the young Ms. Purse. As he bolted around the dance floor, a waltzing musical piece began to fill the empty space. He continued till he rounded the corner and faced the blazing brightness. Stepping by the wooden statue, he surveyed the arrangement of couches set ready to observe the sunset. The waiter bypassed a few guests that had gathered around the nearby cocktail bar master and headed for the banquet hall where the second course was in full swing.

He decelerated toward the doorman, greeted him with a smile, and rushed his question. "Have you seen the younger Ms. Purse?"

Upon hearing the person of interest, the attentive doorman suggested, "Look for a ball player wearing a green suit-jacket."

"The green suit guy, yes, okay," the hustling waiter said, leaving in the same fashion as he had arrived. After asking a different coworker, "Have you seen the 'green-suit guy,'" he headed directly for the service elevator and stepped up beside his manager.

Stalled by the closed doors of the elevator, the welcoming manager with his hands folded together turned briefly to his subordinate and asked, "I hope you've had more luck than I've had trying to catch this elevator empty."

The hustling waiter turned, having had a chance to let his heartbeat catch up with his pace and answered, "She's with the green-suit guy."

"Yes, the green-suit guy. I see," the manager replied calmly.

Julian noted the white curls jutting out from behind the manager's ear as he faced the elevator doors.

"This green-suit guy...he's downstairs?" the manager peacefully inquired.

"Alec said he might be. I don't know."

The manager turned to look at Julian for a moment. Then after considering his words, he said, "Tell you what, why don't you swing around again. I'll go downstairs and say farewell to the elder Ms. Purse, and if by chance I see the younger version with the green suit guy, I'll be sure to inform her that her elder is leaving. Agreed?"

"Yes, sir," Julian answered without much thought.

The manager peacefully stepped onto the elevator and turned around, but before the doors closed, he instructed, "If you don't find her shortly, go ahead and grab a wine bottle."

"Yes, sir," the ambitious waiter submitted again.

After the doors dismissed the waiter, he exclaimed, "The car, ahh." Putting his feet back to work, he scurried to the house phone in the waiter's hallway and told the operator, "Valet, I need the valet desk."

"One moment please," the unhurried female voice on the other end said. "Valet?" a female voice seemingly questioned.

"Yes, I need to be connected to valet," Julian said, without having lost a bit of his excitement.

"This is valet," the valet voice replied in the same unhurried tone of the operator.

"This is valet, really?" Julian inquired with surprise.

Without a shift in animation, the valet voice responded, "Really here till I go home. How can I help you?"

Julian clarified, "You sounded exactly like the operator, that's funny. I couldn't tell the difference between your voice and hers, but yes...who?" Julian lifted his fingers to his temples and stretched his brain. "Yes! The Purse's car please."

"Someone left a purse in their car?" the valet voice asked to clarify. "Do you have the tag number or last name?"

"It's Purse. No, I don't have the last name...I mean the tag number."

"I'm sorry each guest was given a valet ticket with a tag number; you'll need to check back with the guest. Get back to me, and I'll send one of my valets out to search for it," the valet voice said without apology.

"You said you could look up the name; Purse is the name, Ms. Purse, I need you to pull up Ms. Purse's car, please," Julian said, letting a hint of desperation rise in his plea.

"Is this Julian, by chance?" the valet voice asked.

"Yes, I believe her first name is Julianne," the hustling waiter responded.

"No, I mean are you Julian?" the valet restated.

"Yes, I am, is this the valet desk?" Julian let go if his temples and looked up at the fluorescent hall lights that tracked along the top of the blank wall.

"Mr. Hoffman just stopped by the desk and called up Ms. Purse's car, saying that you would probably be calling shortly, so we've got it covered, thanks...and what's that?" the valet voice said, speaking to someone away from the phone. Letting her voice fluctuate with an air of humor, the valet voice repeated,

"Oh, Mr. Hoffman says, no green-suit guy in sight.  Thanks, Julian."

## Part 1 - Chapter Twenty-Two

The two novice dancers faced each other, feeling the heightened weight of their limbs from the pressure of their audience.

"Do you know the waltz?" Romney initiated.

"Mostly," Anna replied, containing the concoction of nerves and reprieve that pulled at her stomach.

"Good.  A waltz, good sir, if you will!" Romney announced to the conductor, forgetting the crowd.  "Don't worry, you're in the slightly over-confident hands of a novice dancer now."

Her smile held in her laugh while she lifted her delicate hands up to accept his posture, placing her pale forearm on his square shoulder.  Anna could see Romney counting in his head, and she smiled even more.  After a nervous two seconds, she felt the stiffness in his jacket breathe and push her back into the waltz.  The dance felt like one long inhale and exhale, and as the quartet ended their musical piece, Romney almost took Anna through one extra step.  Stepping back, he visually thanked his younger partner with a courteous smile.

"Another?" Anna asked, raising her arms for the second concerto movement.

"Gladly," Romney said more at ease, drawing her in again.  Noticing that the floor had somehow filled with dancing couples, Romney started counting the dancing rhythm again with small nods of his head.

"So, Terrance?"

"Yeah," Anna said, blushing.  Looking down, she saw a metal device clipped inside of Romney's blazer but continued, "I hope you don't judge me for that."

"Oh, for sure, I do," Romney spoke sarcastically, hoping to evoke a smile.

Anna laughed politely and felt Romney releasing his guiding hand to lead her into a slow spin.

"You did well...dealing with his unpredictable-ness," Romney complimented, retaking her waistline on the downbeat of the song. The violinist strummed vigorously, skillfully playing a continuous melody over the accompaniment. Seeing that the suggested topic cast a shadow on her prior gleam, Romney let it go. Romney redirected Anna in a half-step move that she didn't recognize, but clinging close to his center of balance, she trusted her feet to rock in unison with his. Having changed directions, she saw the prior crowded corner and reason for his skillful step.

"What novice you are," Anna accused, scolding Romney's misrepresentation with her thought.

Knowingly at his skill's edge, Romney fumbled and readily surrendered the rhythmic movement of his feet. "Oh, you caught me," Romney said facetiously and let go of Anna's waist with an embarrassed version of Anna's jittery laugh. "Anna, this is fun, but I have to admit that this looks awfully suspicious, being married and dancing with...."

"Ms. Purse," Julian greeted, landing his target on his second circuit around the lounge. Waiting for the couple to part and face him, he continued, "Please excuse me for interrupting your dance, but the elder Ms. Purse instructed me to inform you, Ms. Purse, that she is leaving."

"Was she being accompanied by someone else?" Anna asked as if she had staged her question. She searched patiently for the answer behind Julian's proud smile which immediately began to dissipate.

"Yes, I do believe she was escorted by another, ball p...."

"Thank you," Anna said, cutting off Julian's response. She indicated Julian's dismissal with a faint smile and turned back to Romney, raising her arms to dance as she did.

Romney compassionately moved back into his prior dancing position, but after noticing her flushed cheeks, he suggested, "Walk with me to watch the sunset, will you?"

"Sure," Anna modestly acknowledged, releasing his responsive hand. Anna felt reprieved and said, "Thank you." Then she started following Romney off the dance floor. After rounding the southeast corner of the lounge, the more agreeable light of the sun hit her face as she finally stepped into rhythm with

Romney. With an air of accusation, she asked, "Why do you have a gun strapped to your belt?"

Their private conversation in earshot of a few other guests, Romney openly laughed as his thoughts flooded again with his reality. "That's a long story, but in short: my wife ran off with my car tonight in a...well, a misunderstanding. Really, she doesn't like me carrying the whole defensive weapon thing. My daughter is with the babysitter – soon to be put to bed – at my house where I've promised my wife that I would never keep it, and my lock box is in my car...which I'm hoping is still with my wife. Hence, the safest place for my gun, that you've keenly noted, is unfortunately and uncomfortably on my hip."

Attentively listening, Anna replied, "Okay, so what's the long version?"

Romney lifted his chin and laughed again. Arriving at the wooden statue, Romney and Anna stood behind the occupied couches. Turning to find Fievel, Romney caught sight of his waiter and a second waitress in tandem carrying two chairs in his direction. Fievel arranged the patterned chairs side by side in full view of the horizon. "As promised," Romney said acknowledging his waiter's timeliness.

The waitress that accompanied Fievel bowed to Anna quietly. Romney Daniels helped Anna Purse sit in her cushioned chair, and after settling beside her, he sighed, welcoming the peacefulness offered by the day's conclusion. Letting his free hand fall to the outside of the chairs, he stored his other hand protectively in his lap. After a minute of realizing the beauty found in the passing light, he asked, "When was the last time you stopped to enjoy a sunset?"

"The sun rises on my window and wakes me up every morning. It's been a while."

"Yeah." Romney looked around and saw the warm light illuminating every visible corner of the lounge. "Breathtaking," he exclaimed.

Anna realized Romney had turned toward her, and though the light concealed her blush, her cheeks suggested how she had interpreted Romney's statement. Trying to recover, she said, "So, tell me about your daughter."

Romney smiled as if Anna had opened the window to a stuffy room and began, "April. I love her. She turned two years old last fall, so I guess that would make her two and a half. Blond, beautiful, big eyes, and her hair is long enough for pigtails now."

Anna interjected, "Do you have a picture of her?"

Ashamed, Romney balled his fist then stretched his fingers while saying, "No, I don't, but I should. I carry a picture of my wife in my wallet though."

Intrigued by the notion, Anna asked, "May I see her?"

"Sure," Romney said and removed his wallet. Removing the treasured photograph of Sandy with a slide of his thumb, he handed it to Anna and apologized, "I'm sorry if I seemed to be venting about her, she's an amazing woman covered by a debilitating addiction...not all her fault"

"What's she addicted to?" Anna asked curiously, because Romney had offered. "And it didn't sound like you were venting about her."

"A downward spiral of drugs, to what depth I don't really understand," Romney said, laughing uncomfortably at his accidental confession.

"Oh," Anna consoled. "What do you do with that?"

"Unpleasant things," Romney answered. "Try taking food away from a starving person or putting a bandage on an anxious child. It hasn't gone well," Romney explained. He briefly smiled, then straightened his face. Looking out to the sunset again, Romney observed how the sun looked like a sinking mountain from its colors interacting with the clouds.

"I'm sorry," Anna expressed gently, looking away to give Romney privacy. "If I can help in any way, I'd like to," Anna offered, after a moment of silence.

"Ahh, don't trouble yourself. Unless you babysit by chance, but I'm sure you're busy, being a college student and all. You've helped already."

"I'd love to, and Julianne doesn't work; well she works kind of...but doesn't have to. In fact, I think she needs something productive to do."

"No, I wouldn't want to burden your mother."

"No really, it would help her stay out of trouble. I mean she wouldn't endanger your daughter ever, but she's a good person, even if I...," Anna said, speaking freely from her heart, but she paused to recover her statement. "And she loves kids! Though, you'd never know until you saw her around them. Please! I know you would never ask for our number, but I insist." Anna said, excited to be of use. Then she stood up and turned around and waved over Fievel. "I'd like a pen and paper please," she ordered.

"You're too kind, Anna. Thank you," Romney conceded sincerely. "Can I offer you a ride home? Or is that too forward?" Romney asked, surprising himself with his own words.

"Was I that obvious?" Anna said, shying away her eyes and using the bit of remaining sunset as an excuse to look away.

"No, not at all, I'm sorry. I shouldn't have offered."

"No, no, I'm glad for your company. It would sure beat sitting around alone to toil and boil over Julianne and Chad. Imagining...anyway. I'll only share a cab ride if," she started but stopped when she noticed Romney's fist nervously balling and relaxing again. "But that's a bad idea, you're right, it would be better for a single attractive girl to call a cab and ride home alone across town to her house, without a purse, or ID," Anna said, smirking with sarcasm.

"Anna Purse has no purse," Romney observed then offered, "I have a driver, Santiago, he drives me all the time, or more so these days anyway. He'll take you home. I'll call the cab as the unattractive married man to go pick up my daughter."

"I couldn't do that, Mr. Daniels, I trust you to properly escort me, and if you won't, I'll be the one calling the taxi. And if you prove to be stubborn, then I guess we'll both be saying our goodbyes from the taxi line," Anna said, showing her resolve.

"Okay, that's unreasonably reasonable. You don't mind leaving this throbbing party early, do you?" Romney asked, thinking of his appointment with his sleeping daughter and the extra time he needed to stow his gun, both on top of taking Anna home.

"Not at all," Anna spoke unrestrainedly, but the thought of encountering Chad Wattsworth with her mother rollicking at her destination immediately clouded her thoughts like a fizzing can of soda.

# Part 1 - Chapter Twenty-Three

"Hang here for a bit, I have to make a scene," Romney said, slapping both of his knees before standing up.

"What?" Anna humbly alarmed.

"I need to give some goodbyes to some good folk," Romney clarified. "Don't worry; it doesn't involve hip-hop or breakdancing."

Anna Purse chuckled and reshaped her hair over her ear and said, "Okay, just don't forget about me."

Romney Daniels surveyed the sparse crowd of moving guests, obviously looking for someone. Turning around, Romney noticed Anna's inquisitive gaze. He shrugged his shoulders in her direction, letting his arms swing outward and back again to answer her.

Anna let her shoulders rise as high as Romney's had, chuckling to herself.

In view of Romney Daniels' backside, Fievel watched the playful exchange between the two. However, a nudge from his female cohort immediately wiped the amused grin off his face.

"They didn't come together, did they?" the curious waitress asked.

Fievel shook his head and stepped away in trail of Romney.

Romney seemed to be retracing his steps to the dance floor, and as he did, he scanned the scattering of guests. Romney finally succeeded in his swerving search. "Romney," the bellowing voice came. "Romney Daniels, it's good to see you!" Sir Byron Dorkan said stepping back from his private interview with his crumply white vest. Kloe Dorkan's face lifted with practiced excitement, silently saying her own welcome in the shadow of her husband's commanding pomp.

"Byron, how goes it?" Romney said, extending his hand in greeting.

"It goes well; have you met Michael here, Michael Gallant?" Sir Byron Dorkan asked.

"Yes, once; Romney Daniels, it's good to meet you again. This is your first time at the fundraiser; is it not?" Romney asked, cordially shaking Michael Gallant's hand again.

"Yes, and what a great venue...."

"Roger, Roger!" Sir Byron Dorkan bellowed again. "How's that daughter of yours?" Sir Byron Dorkan asked, grabbing Roger Berkshire's hand after Romney's. Shaking Roger's large shoulder, he smiled as Roger returned the same genial grasp.

"Bethy's doing fine. She's finally enrolled in college now for the fall, here at Vern Hill," Roger Berkshire informed.

"Ahh, if I could get my boy interested in college; Roger, you know Chief Operator Romney Daniels, and this is Michael...."

"How's your little girl, Romney," Kloe Dorkan asked discreetly, selectively stepping into the circle beside Romney.

Revamping his objective, Romney elevated his answer for the crowd of friends. "Oh, she's wearing pigtails now at home with the babysitter, which reminds me," Romney said, holding up and then hiding his empty wrist. "I actually need to run out early to put her to bed."

"A shame you couldn't stay; who's your date tonight?" Kloe Dorkan spoke with equally intensity.

The defining question garnered the attention of the congenial group. "Anna Purse, a new friend," Romney enunciated.

"Anna Purse! No, couldn't be," Roger Berkshire chimed in at the inconceivable connection. "Anna's a good girl, you know Bethy and Anna grew up together. My daughter's already talking about having Anna room with her at Vern Hill in the fall," Roger said.

Romney Daniels waited for a pause, and as soon as he lost the limelight, he caught Fievel's attention with an obvious beckoning motion. With his pocket book in plain sight he removed a fifty-dollar bill with a pinching swipe of his thumb and forefinger. Placing the bill in Fievel's hand, he authentically spoke a word of gratitude to his waiter. As he stepped away to return to the picturesque view, Kloe followed him. She quickly caught up with him in a few lively steps.

Kloe wrapped her arm through Romney's as he slowly maneuvered.

"How's your wife?" Kloe said with concern, after obtaining enough space for privacy.

Romney paused to collect his thoughts.

After seeing his facial expression change, Kloe continued, "I haven't seen her in a long time and think of her often; would you tell her I'd like to see her, or talk to her, or whatever she wants." Having silently discerned the information she sought, she lightly detached from Romney to reverse her course.

"I will. You know I will; thank you, Kloe. She'll come around," Romney said before Kloe completely broke away.

Smiling to the room, Romney returned to surveying the guests.

The welcoming manager stood out from the rest, and approached Romney, asking, "Will you be leaving so soon, Mr. Daniels?"

"Yes, and such a pleasant dinner and dance tonight; thank you," Romney said, bowing slightly.

"Would you kindly go with our favor?" the manager asked, extending a golden envelope that had elaborate cursive penned on the face.

Openly receiving the golden envelope, Romney agreed, "I look forward to supporting the Vern Hill College's baseball team this season. I hear they're poised to do well in the conference play." Walking away from the manager, he used the golden envelope as a flag to beckon Fievel once more.

"Could you place a call to Pitts Limousine Service, and request Santiago to pick me up in ten minutes or so?"

"Right away, sir," Fievel said, spinning directly toward the waiter's hallway.

Romney walked back over to Anna, who had rotated around to the side of the chair to watch the flow of guests. "Are you ready?" Anna asked with a relaxing smile.

"Yes; could you carry something for me by chance?" Romney asked.

"Sure," Anna answered.

Romney offered her his left hand, and Anna took it with polite appreciation as she rose from her chair. Then as soon as Anna had her own balance, Romney extended the golden envelope in a delivery type fashion.

"What is it?" Anna asked with interest.

"It's for safe keeping...for now. I'll let you open it in the car if you want," Romney promised, and dropping his own hands to his side, he walked slowly toward the centralized elevator. Anna followed, proudly handling the curious envelope as Romney indistinctly removed his pocket book and took out a business card and another single fifty-dollar bill. Folding them together, he put them in his pocket.

Fievel met Romney and Anna at the centralized elevator and illuminated the elevator button with a proud smile. "Fievel, you serve well," Romney said, reaching into his pocket. "I would be honored to refer you, if you ever need such a reference for a job," Romney said, sincerely extending his hand with the second fifty-dollar tip.

Nearly objecting, Fievel closed his speechless jaw and stepped backward as the elevator doors split open. "Thank you, sir," Fievel finally mustered.

Anna saw Fievel's smile crack open from between the closing doors. As the elevator began descending, the elevator attendant looked at length at Anna Purse. Then looking away and up at the overhead panel, he shook his head as if trying to ward off sleep. Unable to contain his stoic composure any further, he said to Anna, "You look like a twin, if I might say." Romney looked up and saw the operator looking at Anna.

"You probably just saw my mother," Anna said, re-curling the bang of hair that had fallen over her cheek as she glanced down at the floor in response to the comparison.

"Must be so; my apologies, miss. It's been a long night; it's good to know my mind isn't playing tricks on me. Goodnight now," the elevator rider said with reflective abashment as Romney directed Anna ahead of him through the open doors.

Walking as new friends would, Romney and Anna crossed the exalted lobby. "I noticed the ceiling coming in. Look at it," Anna said, lifting her eyes again to appreciate the illuminated decorations. "I love how the latticework brings down the loftiness of the room, making you feel more at home," she observed.

"It's its own form of artwork, and it's expensive...and labor-some," Romney commented.

"It's worth the extra penny, I'd say."

Romney smiled and huffed, anticipating the reaction of his reply, "And especially if it's not your penny that's extra."

"Well, of course," Anna said, punching Romney's suited arm. "But you must admit it's pretty to gaze at."

"Projects go belly-up quickly, when the managers go too big, too far, and too fast...treating decor, as you say, as a personal vendetta while losing form, function, and the ability to finish the whole in the process," Romney said with an air of contempt. Pausing to hear himself speak, he chided himself saying, "Sorry, that's my job coming out of me. I'm the guy responsible for destroying the dreams and visions of my architects."

Having refocused her appreciative eyes back on the ceiling for a moment, Anna peaceably responded, "Somebody has to bring the dreamers back to reality, I guess." Anna proceeded ahead of Romney again, toward the valet guarded doors. A valet dressed in a collared white shirt and a reflective vest greeted them and pulled the door open to the sidewalk. The sound of rollers smacking a crack in the pavement reached Anna's ears as she cleared the edge of the open door. A strike on Anna's shoulder spun her ninety degrees off balance. "Ho!"

Romney, though an arm's reach away, along with the valet, who stood even closer, both panicked and reached in vain to stop Anna from falling. The valet holding the door saw an empty board on wheels reeling across the red-carpet underneath both sets of velvet ropes. A second and larger valet, that had just finished relocating a car in the garage, haphazardly caught the board rider with his chest. Fortunately, the valet's breadth and weight allowed him to absorb all the boy's inertia.

Frightfully, the board rider clung to the larger valet. The grimace of the intimidating man sparked a hasty string of apologies from the boy. "I'm sorry, I'm sorry, I'm so sorry," Jonathan Wickfell said. After fearfully patting the broad valet on the chest and dusting the valet's shoulders to straighten his collared sleeve, the boy turned back to observe the damage.

Anna had already returned to her feet with the help of Romney and the door valet. Rubbing her shoulder and smoothing her brilliant orange dress, she glanced up and hearing someone ask, 'Are you okay?' she replied with a startled voice, "Yes, yes, I'm okay; that came out of nowhere!"

Another valet scurried to the commotion, carrying the long
board. "Is everyone okay?" he asked in a timbre that reflected
his hustle.

"Yes, I'm okay, I'm fine," Anna said again.

"Good, good," Jonathan Wickfell answered, not having
recovered from his own shock. "I'm good, are you good?" he
asked the large valet. "Hey, thanks for getting my board; I'm so
sorry, I know you're all dressed up and everything, and...,"
Jonathan said apologetically. Looking down, he saw his
backpack that had landed at his feet. "They say distracted
driving is dangerous, well let me tell you!" Everyone looked at
Jonathan Wickfell, giving him the judgment that he deserved.
Seeing his precarious position, Jonathan turned and focused on
Anna. Seeing that she appeared to be the only casualty, he asked
again hesitantly, "Miss, did I hurt you?"

"Yes, I'm fine; I mean, no, you didn't."

After seeing her frazzled face and analyzing her response for a
second, Jonathan replied, "Good. I'm sorry, but if it helps any,
you look great in orange; doesn't she look great?"

"Man, you'd look good in orange, which is what you're going
to be wearing if you don't skedaddle before I call the police," the
broad valet said, taking up Anna's defense.

"No, no there's no need for that," Anna interjected.

"I know, I'm just playing with the kid," the large valet said with
a smile to convince Anna but immediately looked back at the
intruder with vexation.

"Yes, right, that's good, that'd be good. I'll be going now,"
Jonathan said, dropping his board to let it roll across the carpet.
Ducking under the velvet ropes, he kicked his board another few
feet and bent under the second crimson rope. Looking back half
in fright and half in relief, he pushed off and skated away,
bending quickly around the far corner of the block.

Santiago pulled up to the curbside and stood up out of the
short limousine. Moving around the back of the car, Santiago
said, "It's good to see you again tonight, sir." Then reading the
silent excitement on everyone's face, he asked, "Was the party
good? I mean the fundraiser?"

# Part 1 - Chapter Twenty-Four


Santiago shut Romney Daniels' door in chauffer style. Then without hesitating, Santiago stepped forward and into the driver's seat of the car. Stringing his seatbelt easily across his chest, he asked, "Where to, my friends?"

Anna helplessly directed her thoughts to her looming destination. "I don't have anywhere to be," she proclaimed.

"Well, I'm taking you home...sometime tonight, right Santiago? Back me up here."

"I press the gas pedal, sir; you tell me when and where," Santiago said, dodging the spotlight. "Though if it helps you out, I could start the meter," Santiago smiled into rear view mirror half-seriously.

Anna laughed and then jumped in surprise when someone tapped the side window. Flagging a golden envelope at eye level, the valet spoke something through the closed window. Recognizing the envelope, Anna automatically looked down at her empty hands. Romney observed the same and asked Santiago to roll down Anna's window. The opening window caused the valet to stop his waving for a second and repeat, "Ma'am, I believe you dropped this."

"Thank you," Anna replied, taking the returned envelope and watching the valet step back onto the curb. "Wouldn't want to forget this," Anna said, turning to Romney.

"Oh no! We would have been at a loss for sure."

"What is it?" Anna asked again, puzzled by Romney's tone.

"I'll tell you, if you tell Santiago where to drop you off."

Anna paused, thinking of what more she could add to sweeten the deal. After coming up with nothing, she said to Santiago, "I live on Riverview Avenue, on the other side of the river."

"Yeah, yeah! I know where that is. Right away, ma'am."

"This is Anna Purse by the way, Santiago, a new acquaintance of mine," Romney added, realizing he had neglected to introduce her.

"I wasn't going to ask, but it's nice to meet you...Miss Purse, right?"

"Yes, please call me, Anna."

"Anna? Certainly, whatever you'd like, Miss Purse."

Cheered by Santiago's humor, Anna started picking at the envelope and turned her attention to Romney. "So?" she said, lifting her eyebrows expectantly to remind Romney of his end of the bargain.

"So, you're holding Vern Hill's yearly request for financial support for their 'athletic programs,' or their 'baseball program' might be more accurate," Romney replied.

The anticipation in Anna's eyes deflated like a punctured bicycle tire. "Well, if that's the case, here, you open it."

"Or so I think, one can never be sure," Romney said, holding a serious face long enough to be convincing.

Anna held onto the envelope at Romney's retraction, but at the threat of looking flirtatious, Anna let go of her end. Romney immediately tore open the golden envelope to find exactly what he had predicted. "It's what happens every year. Unfortunately, the dinner before the letter is your only recompense." Romney conceded his foreknowledge as he scanned over the predictable letter.

"So, you did know!" Anna objected, acting betrayed.

"Well, you never know, but I wouldn't have waged against it."

"So how much are you going to give Vern Hill; I go there, you know. So, you'd be supporting my college," Anna said, sinking her hands deeper into her lap.

"Your college, yes, but do you play baseball?" Romney said cunningly.

"I'm an undedicated fan," Anna answered, understanding Romney's bait.

"I hadn't thought of that; in that case...," Romney said. "In that case," he repeated, "how much would you give?" Romney watched Anna think for a moment, making time by dancing her eyes across the stitching of the black leather seats. "Or how much would you have me give?" Romney rephrased, clarifying his meaning.

"What do I have to work with? Or can I give you a percentage?"

"Twenty-five."

"Thousand?!" Anna said with disbelief, but then, considering his position in comparison to her mother's, she thought it relatively proportionate.

"Well, if you said a hundred percent, that'd be the thick of it," Romney defended before seeing the corners of her mouth.

"Zero."

"Percent or dollars?" Romney said, holding a serious face for a moment.

"Dol...," Anna started, interrupting herself as she detected Romney's antic.

"Why zero?" Romney asked to rescue the topic from embarrassment, resisting the urge to tuck his hands under his arms.

"Your wife and your daughter, Sandy and April, right? You've set your priorities straight already; support for Vern Hill would be...," Anna said, trying to think of the word that best described her point, "...misdirected. Don't you think?" Romney didn't interrupt, and still analyzing his face, Anna followed his gaze to her knees where the crinkled fringe of her dress had scrunched. Smoothing her hand over her knees with a new vibe of discomfort, she looked back at Romney who hadn't moved. After realizing his eyes, though directed at her knees, were not actually focused on them, she asked, "Is everything okay?"

Snapping out of his reflective daze, Romney said, "Sorry, I was tabulating. You're right."

Feeling like she needed to turn the tide, she asked her prodding question, "So, why do you carry a gun if it offends your wife so much?"

"Well, there's the classic arguments, that you can't win a gunfight with a knife, and the right to bear arms to prevent tyranny and such, but for me...," Romney started. Unable to think of a statement of reasonable length, he relaxed and explained, "Well, I believe life is precious, and if the possibility exists of someone threatening the life of my wife or my daughter, I want to be able to protect them. Just owning a gun won't do it. So, hence, I carry it tirelessly." Hoping to show his candor, he asked, "Why? Do guns make you nervous?"

"A little. I would worry about accidentally shooting myself or someone else if I ever carried one."

"I won't try to convince you that guns are safe, but that's the risk; the risk that I hope routine precaution will avoid in my case," Romney said, backing off his hobby horse.

"So, if you don't have your car and you've vowed to not store this gun in your house, where are you going to keep it?" Anna asked, recalling his assertion from their earlier conversation.

"I have a gun safe at my apartment, so I'll drop it off there before I go to pick April up," Romney answered without much thought.

"How far is your apartment from your home?" Anna asked, unintentionally softening her pronunciation of home.

"Oh, it's right here in town, actually right on this side of the river," Romney said, stopping short of elaborating.

"Right here?" Anna asked with annoyance.

"Well yeah, right around the corner, down a little, left, then right, not far. Santiago knows," Romney explained, disturbed a bit by Anna's disturbance.

Without acknowledging Romney's explanation, Anna leaned forward and commanded Santiago, "Turn here and take Romney to his apartment; he shouldn't have to go out of his way just to take me home."

As Santiago committed to the turn, Romney interjected a moment too late, "No, what? Oh well. It's no faster this way. It's on the way back, but okay, never mind."

Anna looked at him in disbelief, believing more in his hospitality than his honesty in that moment. She peered at Romney like he was a con-artist and asked, "Really?"

"Really, I have to come back through the city to get home to get my daughter to bed," Romney assured without a modicum of falsehood. "But this works just the same," he continued, relaxing his shoulders. Thinking a moment more, he looked back and tacitly exchanged a grin with Anna, who looked childish.

"Daughter," Anna agreed, having forgotten the fact. "Chapel Hills, I got it. My apologies."

After debating a few moments longer, Romney decided to ask with general curiosity, "How do you know I live in Chapel Hills?"

"You told my mother at dinner. Didn't you?" Anna testified.

"Ah, now I look silly.  And you live at home with your mother on Riverview Ave," Romney admitted.  Embarrassed, he confessed, "I don't know how I forgot that."

Both Anna and Romney sat silently, each battling their own pride until Santiago pulled to a stop a few seconds later in the well-lit turnaround of Romney's condominium apartment building.

"You can wait here while I run upstairs, or feel free to come sit in the lobby," Romney offered.

"I'll come in," Anna said, but pulling the car door handle, she found it locked.

"Sorry, Miss Purse, I'll get that fussy door," Santiago apologized, rushing to push the unlock button again.

Anna sat patiently, and a moment later both left side doors flew open.  Both Santiago and Romney started climbing out in unison until Santiago saw Romney proceeding ahead of him.

"Thank you, Romney," Anna said, accepting his hand as she stepped out of the car.

"Welcome; I'll be just a minute.  It won't take long to stow.  Oh, here allow me," Romney stepped out in front again to open the door, but before he touched the handle, the door automatically began to open.  Retreating a step, Romney glanced back at Anna, who stood smirking at his instinctive reaction.  Romney conceded his bewilderment with a smile of his own as Anna walked through the automated doorway still wearing her smug look.

"So, how much do you charge for babysitting?" Romney asked, following Anna through the door.

"Charge?  Oh, I don't need money."

"Oh, a privileged girl, I see.  Jenny, this is Miss Anna Purse," Romney said, splitting his attention to the front desk attendant.

"Welcome back, Mr. Daniels, and it's nice to meet you, Miss Purse," Jenny greeted, rising to her feet from the stool situated behind the clean counter.

Romney pressed the ascending arrow, making the elevator's doors spring open.  Stepping into place for launch, Romney instinctively tapped his floor number three.

"I'm not spoiled," Anna reengaged coltishly, having followed Romney inside to defend herself.

"What? Did I say you're spoiled? Not my intent, I think working for money, as a principle, is important...developmentally."

"Well, yeah!" Anna said, finding herself closed into the elevator from her obstinate pursuit.

The elevator quickly rose and stopped. "I mean, it develops a sincere appreciation for things that in turn you're able to go and buy, all the while preventing gluttony," Romney spontaneously continued as the elevator sprung open to reveal an elegant table, vase, and fern.

Anna agreed but found Romney's matter of fact speech grounds for teasing. "So, Romney, do you have a shorter name that people call you, like Rom?" Anna restated her hanging question from dinner.

"If you prefer," Romney consented, pulling a toothless key out of his pocket.

"Insincere, unappreciative, and glutton. Are those the terms that you think of when someone offers you a free service as a friend?" Anna fisted her hip and fixated on Rom's creased forehead.

"Wow, I need you to edit my words, before I go making a buffoon of myself again in public. I said that, didn't I? I promise it sounded much better in my head," Romney said, waving his key at room number fourteen, which caused the deadbolt to snap. Pushing the door open, he stepped inside and stopped.

"Romney, I was just giving you a hard time," Anna apologized, reaching out to touch Romney's arm imploringly.

"I know, and please call me Rom; but please wait here, Miss Purse. Besides I should be the one apologizing," Romney said, unapologetically shutting the door. Anna stood satisfied in the short hallway for a moment alone. The door no sooner closed, then Romney opened it again. "I said I should, but I didn't, I'm sorry for inferring you were unappreciative, insincere, and gluttonous." The door closed again, and Anna bit her lip as she glanced down the short hallway.

# Part 1 - Chapter Twenty-Five

"Do you know when this bridge was built? "No, no, it's a neat story, I promise," Anna said to an inquisitive look on Romney's face.

"Tell me, please," Romney Daniels replied after erasing his expression. "I'm not a history buff, as you well know," Romney said, enjoying Anna's spirit.

"In 1954, George Brown, a general contractor, was commissioned by the transport authority of greater Pittsburg to renovate the existing bridge: widen, fix, reinforce, and so on. But new cracks were discovered halfway through the project, and George Brown went to the transport authority to renegotiate his contract. He argued that the sunk investment and further costs would bankrupt his business. After the transport authority refused to redirect more money to pay for the deeper fixes, George Brown, in the spring of 1956 rolled up shop and walked off the job, leaving the project at an impasse," Anna spoke with vigor, enjoying Romney's laugh. "Excuse the pun," Anna said, shyly stealing a glance at Romney's unspoken compliment. "Anyway, the transport authority, having mistakenly called Brown's bluff, initially asked for him to reconsider, but George Brown would only reconsider for twice the payout of the original contract. After a year of failed negotiations, the engineer that had drawn up the initial reconstructive plans, who was aware of the unaccounted damage, proposed a solution to the transport authority right before they opened up a second bid to fix the bridge."

"What was that?" Romney asked attentively.

"He proposed deconstructing the entire bridge and starting over with a more economical design. When quizzed about the increased cost of the new build, he drew attention to the part of his proposal that he himself would front the cost, but only with the transport authority's consent to set up toll booths and tolls for a minimum of three years and up to ten if a preset profit margin wasn't met."

"Interesting," Romney encouraged, personally admiring her impressive recollection and fluid speech.

"Yeah, what the transport authority planners didn't foresee was how lucrative three years of tolls would turn out to be. He made millions more than George Brown would have, even with the renegotiated contract."

"Anna, you're an impressive storyteller!" Romney honestly confessed. "I hope you have the opportunity to tell my April a story or two."

"Daniel Mills."

"Who?"

"Daniel Mills, was the name of the envisioning engineer. Your last name was Daniels, which made me think of the story," Anna said with disclosure. In an instant, her demeanor changed, and losing the fire in her voice, she observed, "Oh look, home." Filling her lungs, Anna turned to Romney and said, "Thank you for rescuing my night."

"Hey Anna, I have your number here, but I'd like to introduce April to you before I just drop her off."

"Of course," Anna agreed, with an optimistic smile.

"What day are you available next week? I know you have classes," Romney asked in a businesslike tone.

"Wednesday?"

"Okay, I'll call and set something up for Wednesday; maybe lunchtime?"

"Sure."

"Hey, Anna," Romney readdressed to change the subject.

"Yes?" Anna said, pausing her exit from the short limousine.

"If I can be of service to you in any way, here's my business card. Call me, okay?" Romney said, having already drawn out his pocketbook. He comfortably picked through the plastic cards stacked behind Sandy's picture. Sliding out a tarnished card, he handed it across the car to Anna, who had one leg straddled out on the edge of the driveway.

Anna closed the limo's door and walked up the shared driveway. She half tried the door handle of the car parked in front of the garage. The interior light turned on, and Anna's shoulders dropped in judgment. She pulled the handle a second time to open the door and stretched into the driver's seat. After what appeared to be a few stubborn attempts, the garage door jolted to life, and Anna climbed back out of the seat, quickly locking the car in a mechanical manner. Without looking back or waving goodbye, she entered the garage and closed it behind her with her reclaimed purse on her shoulder.

"Santiago, home please," Romney ordered, choosing to slide to the opposite side of the car.

"Right away, sir, but before I forget, I want to tell you about something that I saw suspicious, that I thought you'd be interested to know."

"Suspicious? Anna's just a friend I met tonight, that needed a ride home."

"No, no, when you went up to the apartment, there was a car that pulled up and stopped, facing me on the other side of the street, like this," Santiago said, positioning his hands. "I didn't think anything of it a-first, other than all his windows were dark. But, before you got inside, he rolls down his window and stuck out a camera or something. It was kind of creepy; then he drove off," Santiago said, picking up speed as he talked.

"Yeah, that is kind of creepy."

"I looked for him to come back, and when you came out again, another car that looked like him drove by too fast to see," Santiago finished, waiting to see if this testimony worried Romney. "Are you a famous person or something?"

"No, not in the paparazzi sense," Romney answered.

"Then, does that not just freak you out kind of, sir?" Santiago asked, spouting his itching question.

Romney's phone rang with its two alternating tones. The caller identification flashed an unfamiliar number on the small screen. Romney answered and lifted the phone to his ear, "Hello, Romney Daniels."

"I need your help now, let me drive you home."

"Sandy?" Romney tried to decipher the whispering voice.

"No, this is Anna."

"Anna, are you okay?" Romney nearly shouted with confused concern, lunging for the door handle and crashing out of the back seat onto the pavement with the cellular phone clamped to his ear. After up-righting himself from his clumsy maneuver, he immediately surveyed the half lighted house. After seeing the porch light illuminate, he heard the click of a door in the phone. Daring to speak again, he asked, "Anna, are you okay?" Seeing

Anna's figure appear in the spotlight of the porch lamp, Romney, still uneasy, started toward her. Hearing a whimpering in the phone, he asked more sympathetically a third time, "Anna, are you okay?"

"Just overwhelmed."

"Understandable," Romney said, releasing the tension in his shoulders. He could see Anna standing, though distressed, safely alone from his new vantage point.

"Let me drive you home," Anna requested again through the cell phone. Hesitating to explain further, she peered into the night toward Romney's indistinguishable figure.

She heard the opening of a car door, and looking down at her phone, she saw that she had somehow missed the fact that it had disconnected. Hearing a second throw of the limousine door, she looked up to bid its departure. Then, in a moment of delight, she jumped like a girl finding surprise concert tickets taped to her door and took seven galloping strides to throw her arms around Romney.

Romney allowed her embrace empathetically and waited for her release. "There and back again, promise?"

"Yes, yes, of course..."

"Promise?" Romney restated and emphasized with his insistent gaze.

"Promise," Anna replied, feeling a ping of childishness tingle her neck as she rustled through her purse to locate her car keys.

## Part 1 - Chapter Twenty-Six

"Stop shivering," Julianne said sarcastically.

"I can't help it; I'm sorry, I shouldn't be here," Chad finally explained with a pounding heart after hearing the back door open and close the second time.

"Relax. Relax, stop shaking," Julianne laughed as she reached out to console Chad.

"I can't; I'm sorry, I shouldn't...," Chad recited, nearly tripping over himself as he scrambled away from the bed. "...be here."

"Don't be ridiculous. You can be where you want to be," Julianne said, curling up in resistance as she searched for a basis for Chad's incoherent reactions.

"It's not you, it's me," Chad said, worrying about Julianne's new tone.

"I can tell," Julianne chuckled, dismissing the guilty expression happening all over Chad's face.

"I'll pay for whatever you want; I'm sorry."

"Pay for what. Chad, you've got to settle down."

"I'm leaving."

"Okay," Julianne agreed, seeing Chad already fleeing the room. She raised her voice apologetically, "I'll drive you."

Muffled from the hallway, Julianne understood only part, but enough of his desperate reply, "Campus's...taxi." Confused, Julianne sat frozen in her thoughts, intentionally avoiding the convicting corridor that Chad had opened with his peculiar remorse. Julianne finally smiled and laughed at what she found absurd. A false cool light construed the room. Tired of her thoughts, Julianne jumped up to slap off the disgusting lamp. Then she split the draped curtains and swung open the patio doors. Washing herself with the mild wind, she immersed herself in the city's bustle across the river. The pollution of light made the stratum of clouds glow. Some white blossoms had fallen onto her outdoor couch. Sweeping most of them off with her hand, she reclined on the remaining few. Once settled, she felt a heat grow in her chest, and unable to resist further, she returned and continued her gaze at the skyline and sounds of the city.

## Part 1 - Chapter Twenty-Seven

Chad felt frazzled and could only bring himself to recite a few self-accusing pejorative phrases. Once he had breached the confines of the house on Riverview Ave, he slumped down with his jacket on the concrete porch step next to the garage without noticing that the red sedan was missing. The cement step in front of the porch made him restless, and he paced in a flustered circle, moving his hands uncontrollably from gripping his head, to crossing his chest, to a nervous slack by his side, and around again. Finally, he cushioned his head against the narrow stack of brick on the side of the garage, scuffing his foot repeatedly on the pavement as he did. He mulled through the possibilities of getting home to his dormitory but could only conjure the thought of his dormitory classmates and of Sean waiting with prodding questions. Looking down the street he saw the glow of a gas station. Resolute on not re-entering the house to call the campus taxi, he started out down the sidewalk toward it. The downhill slope and pull of Kearigan Street gave him the few minutes he needed to settle down. The floodlights from the station's overhead canopy expelled the darkness but equally highlighted the oil stains littering the pumping and parking area. As he approached, he saw no cars in the corner lot and no attendant in the store. He entered through the sticker painted glass door, ringing the unavoidable door chime as he did. He rang the desk bell once, hoping to call the attendant out to make change from his twenty-dollar bill. He rang it again after an impatient minute. "Apparently, the bell doesn't call anybody," Chad remarked snidely.

Seeing donuts on display and thinking them appetizing, he planned to buy one as an excuse to make change. Opening the display case, he chose the most appetizing looking pastry. Returning to the desk to pay, he instinctively took a bite. Looking with disappointment at his selection, he rang the bell again with full anticipation of the attendant appearing. Looking back at the rest of the donuts on display, he transposed his look of disgust on the rest and decided that all of them must have been a day or two old. Turning around, he took another dry bite of his donut pastry. The second bite tasted thicker than the first.

Scanning the store, he located the pay phone outside. Leaning over the counter to appease himself, he still did not see anyone. Then he set his partially consumed donut down and walked out of the store to see how much the pay phone would cost. The sticker covered glass door chimed again as he exited, and taking a breath, he held the air and puffed his cheeks before he picked up the phone as if to make a call. Automatically discounting the operator's voice as the pre-recorded instructions, he hung up and

two coins fell into the change tray.  Looking around
flabbergasted, he laughed and half-expected to share his
amusement with the missing attendant.  He ran his eyes down
the metallic chart to see if the ejected coins would pay for a call.

"Ha," Chad exhaled.  Picking up the receiver, he dialed the
campus's eleven-digit palindromic number from memory.

"Pittsburg Way City Taxi," the busy dispatcher greeted.

"Yeah, I'm a Vern Hill college student."

"At Hops?  I have another Hops to Vern," the dispatcher
presumptively shouted to another dispatcher.

"No, I'm on Riverview street or avenue or something across
the river," Chad corrected.

"Never mind," the dispatcher indirectly apologized to the
coworker, "Riverview Avenue, do you have an address?"

"No, um..." Chad confessed, swinging his head around to see
if he could see the street sign.  Sure enough, he saw the street
sign and replied, "Kearigan Street, the house is on the corner of
Kearigan Street and Riverview Ave."

"Okay," Chad heard the dispatcher say on the other end of the
phone, followed by the tapping of keys from a keyboard.  Chad
waited.

"Okay?" Chad questioned after a few seconds.  Looking up,
Chad still saw no movement inside of the convenience store.

"I have a driver on that side of town, say give him ten
minutes.  The corner of Riverview and Kearigan, right?"

"Right, ten minutes," Chad answered, and as he did the
dispatcher took his cue to hang up the phone.  Chad did the
same and re-entered the store to pay for his dried pastry.
"Hello," he called and waited for a reply.  No one answered.
Five minutes or so passed with no change.  "Ahh," Chad
exasperated, watching the small wall clock with growing anxiety.
After he couldn't stand waiting any longer, he grabbed the rest
of the donut, shoved it into his mouth, and bolted out the door.

He arrived back at Julianne's house with an uncomfortable and
guilty cramp in his gut.  Returning to the concrete step, he
identified every car that drove past, childishly expecting each to
be a police car coming to arrest him for shoplifting.  He
rehearsed his defense, considering his improbable fear.  Then
twenty more minutes or so passed with no sign of a taxi.  Finally,

a familiar red sedan pulled into the driveway. The car stopped, and the driver, concealed by the brightness of the headlights, left the car running for long seconds. Then out stepped Julianne, from what he could tell, and Chad shook his head, trying to make sense of the scene.

"Chad?" the voice questioned. Anna saw Chad scrunch his face in confusion.

"It's Anna," Anna prompted, knowing she had probably blinded him with the headlights. "Do you need a ride home?"

"That's kind of you to offer, but the campus taxi should be arriving any minute," Chad responded, having had plenty of time to secure his earlier emotional breach.

Resisting her spiteful spirit that threatened to interrupt, Anna calmly moved to the edge of the porch step and slowly sat down five feet away from where Chad uncomfortably stood. Chad acknowledged Anna's wordless token and smiled nervously. Anna said nothing for a while, keeping her hands folded over her waistline and vision straight ahead. Shivering in her sleeveless dress, Anna repeated, "Are you sure?"

A taxi cab answered her question.

Chad's feet lingered for a heartbeat. "I'm really sorry, Anna," he said, hesitating to elaborate. Then springing into a jog for the waiting taxicab, he turned back only in time to see the porch door swing closed. Ducking into the cab, he spontaneously thanked the driver for coming.

--- *A minute earlier inside of the Purse's Victorian house.*

Completely disconnected with her surroundings, Julianne eventually heard the arrival and cessation of a car. The gentle wind fell silent for a moment. Then, after recognizing the voice of her daughter addressing someone, she hastened inside to script a convincing charade of her night.

Anna entered the house a few minutes later with disgust on her face. "Mom! Or should I say, cougar!" Anna accused, finding her mother tranquilly reclined on the loveseat.

"Is that what you think of me, Anna dear?"

"It's not too hard to contrive, when that's what you...Chad's a good guy, he has a reputation around campus for being a good guy. Why do you have to go toying with minors?"

"He's not a minor, Anna dear. But boys in their handsome suits are certainly more fun when their speech isn't slurred and when they aren't tripping over their pickup lines," Julianne said, undisturbed by Anna's charge.

"He's my friend, and I introduced...and you started hitting on him almost immediately."

"It's hard to ignore lust on an attractive boy's face," Julianne defended.

"What! What are you talking about?"

"You're upset, Anna dear. I didn't taint your little boyfriend, but I did do you the favor of rustling him up before he started toying around with you."

"He's the only respectable guy I know on campus, Mom!"

"That's even more a reason to be skeptical, Anna dear. He obviously doesn't know what he wants or how to go about getting it. Oh look. Now you have me talking with gibber-jabberish logic," Julianne argued, pausing to laugh at her vagueness. "This Chad might have the impression of having chastity, or a good reputation as you say, but if he's going to take my bait at a glance, what do you think he's going to do to you when you throw your bait out there for him to nibble on? I'm proud of you for turning him down by the way when he asked you to this fundraiser fling."

"And you think that makes sense. That taking him home would accomplish something? You're not going to mother me out of the fact that you just wanted to hook up like you were fifteen again."

"Oh good. I'm glad you brought that up. You can rest assured that we didn't do anything you wouldn't approve of. Literally, he barely took his jacket off, much less his pants."

"Who's supposed to be the eighteen-year-old here? Nothing about this is normal! Why can't you just stick to your one-and-done men from the bar? Like that's a good enough example for me anyway," Anna said, throwing her frustration around over the prospect of her mother's behavior being intentional instead of selfish.

"Not all of them are one-and-goners, Anna dear. In fact, Frank and I are dating tomorrow night."

"Do I know Frank?"

"Very funny, it's not a different Frank, but I'm getting hungry. Do you...."

"You just ate! And...and why did you leave me?" Anna said, remembering her other frustration.

"Oh, Romney was going to give you a ride home."

"How did you figure that? You up and ran off with Chad, leaving me...you never talked with Romney," Anna accused.

"It was written on his face, just like Chad's fascination."

"And I suppose serial killers are just as obvious."

"They're usually pale and awkward."

"Well great! If you ever lose your thumbs, you'll have a job waiting for you down at the police station, profiling suspects."

"You're too funny; so, are you going to drive, or do I have to drive myself to go get food?" Julianne asked merrily.

"Oh, goodness gracious, Mom!"

*--- At the same moment on the opposite side of the Montague river.*

The taxi driver sped away with the tired engine whining as it tried to stay on schedule. The driver seemed to converse with himself, encouraged only by a few breaths of agreement and the same courteous smile from Chad. Chad watched the vertical steel columns of the Mills Bridge flicker by in rhythm, making the east bridge and the reflections in the water appear like an old silent film with its visible frame rate. After diving into the city from the short down slope at the end of the mostly flat bridge, the taxi lurched to a stop in traffic. Minutes came and went, creeping by more quickly than the car in its driving efforts did. The lack of progress gave Chad a few moments to gawk at pedestrians with their peculiarities. Happy for a diversion, he neglected to hear the beginning of the driver's question. "What? Sorry, I missed that," Chad said with apology.

"What dorm? You want me to drop you off...or where at?" the driver responded again.

"Swanson Hall?" Chad asked, looking for the driver's understanding.

"Yeah, okay," the driver affirmed after a lengthy second and indifferently continued his self-bantering discourse. Pulling up to the appropriate hall, the driver dismissed his customer by cranking his torso around in his chair and collecting Chad's smallest tip for his service. Astonished at his receiving anything at all, he sent Chad off, insistently saying, "Thank you, sir. God bless you!"

Chad looked up at the old knotted trees that created a canopy over Swanson Hall's front entrance. The trees matched the aged look of the brick. Then pulling open the transparent door of the dormitory, he turned off the main hallway to the staircase. He pounded each step as tomorrow's events began presenting themselves. The familiar announcements posted on the bulletin board by the entrance reminded him of one, which reminded him of another, and a girl descending the stairs in formal attire bearing a wincing smile reminded him of yet another. The appointed mandatory team meeting earlier that day became clear in his memory, having missed it for cause of Terrance, for cause of Anna, for...Julianne. Chad hung his head and groaned as if tired of repeating the same exercise.

He reached the top floor and pushed through the precautionary fire door. His door was the first on the left side of a long hall. After digging out and inserting his key, he rotated the handle and pushed to find the door stopped by the interior chain.

"Sean?" Chad said equally as a question and implicit command.

Chad heard two voices talking in an excited hush. One laughed and the other giggled in echo. Rapid footsteps came toward the latched door. "One second," Sean petitioned.

"What's going on, man? I'm tired," Chad moaned.

The latch chain rattled, "Hey, Chad, I need a minute."

"What for?"

"A little privacy that's all, you don't mind. Do you?" Sean said in a fluster as he opened the door to his shoulder.

"Who's...."

"Veronica; and I don't want to embarrass her. Well, you've told me yourself, 'You don't really want to,'...well, you know," Sean dropped his voice as he talked and looked back into the room.

"Yeah, yeah, alright, I don't want to know."

"Give me ten minutes."

"Take as long you need, I'll be sleeping in the game room," Chad said, turning back to the stairs.

"Oh man, you make me feel bad," Sean remonstrated to his sullen teammate.

"Oh, don't worry yourself," Chad said, showing his fatigue. He breathed in to expound but stopped short of divulging any details into his night.

"You okay, man? We missed you on the bus," Sean asserted, sensing his roommate's trouble.

Chad continued walking away with no response and noted the door latching behind him as he re-entered the stairwell. Fatigued by the drain of the night, his thoughts fell to the strange smile of the girl he had passed while ascending the cascade of stairs. Chad tried to recall her face, but gave up to mere conjectures, unable to determine whether the girl was smiling or whether the girl had been holding back tears. He leaned more toward the latter, which would account for the short heaving gasp he had heard echo from the bottom of the stairwell. He briefly empathized with her speculated tragedy as he entered the first-floor game room. Stomaching the distress, he dropped his weight onto the middle of an abused sofa and collapsed into a coma of remorseful sleep.

## Part 1 - Chapter Twenty-Eight

Romney Daniels woke up early on the fat couch in the front room of his mansion on Washington Street. Stretching his arms, he looked around at the familiar space of the living room. The room felt surreal compared to the vividness of his dream, where Sandy had just informed him a fraction of a second prior by carelessly saying, "Look who came home," and, "Oh, by the way, I crashed the car again." Certain of his dreaming, he checked around for Sandy.

Checking around generally seemed like a good idea, so he continued his search on foot, heading up the stairs to the bathroom. He nearly stepped on Sandy's purse strewn on the hallway floor. Tautly curious about the state of the car, he carefully opened the bag. Upon discovery, he removed the keys and noticed her paraphernalia. The open needle worried him for

April's sake, so he stepped with pep into the bathroom to get his usual supplies. After giving a provoking look at his reflection, he opened a child-proofed drawer and removed a plastic glove. Donning the glove, he set out for his Friday pre-morning's work.

--- *Two hours later, Romney found his assistant attentively waiting.*

"Hey, Mr. Daniels," Saundra Lent said, rising to her feet with a pile of papers to follow her boss into his conservative office.

"Hello, Saundra. How's the day looking," Romney Daniels asked.

Saundra gave Romney a friendly welcome as she poised at his desk ready to explain the standard bombardment of early office calls and paperwork. "Mr. Hense wants you before you leave for lunch."

"Good, I have lunch blocked for a personal meeting."

"The foreman called and is questioning the permits in regard to the reassessment."

"Okay."

"These are in need of your permissive signature, and I'll be leaving an hour early for an appointment."

"Very good, thank you."

"Oh, and I almost forgot," Saundra said with an eager smile, removing a rawhide brown portfolio from under her notepad.

"Oh, wow. You got right on that request."

"Did you ever doubt?"

"No, thank you."

"Of course; you paid for it," Saundra said, retreating to her ringing phone.

Romney took a second to touch the thick soft leather cover, boasting its rough unfinished edges. Romney took a few more moments to transfer and arrange his deep blue ink pen, half-depleted notepad, few business cards, and reference papers into the portfolio. After his surprise and pleasant diversion, he delved into his mid-morning work, all in preparation for the weekend. Halfway through his cumbersome reading of the updates, he made a call to the foreman to reassure him of the validity of the city permits.

"I talked with the inspector myself. No, no, yes, Hue Jackson understood and takes a more lenient interpretation of the 1985 building codes. We intentionally left the bridge wall standing to

grandfather the project. Well, what do you need? Okay, I'll
have it to you shortly; are you in portable 'A' at Lundberg?
Right, anything else? Very well, I'll have that right along."
Romney hung up the phone, and called through his open door
to Saundra, "Saundra could you pull up the divorce order, I
mean the court order from last week for the Lundberg site and
send the Judge's ruling for the tree removal. I think the
summary will be fine, fax it to portable 'A.'"

"Right away," Saundra replied.

"The foreman has protestors dismantling the fence insisting
the ruling was in their favor," Romney needlessly rationalized.

Time rocketed as usual.

"Sandy, what time did Jack tell you?" Romney said, hitting his
forehead for using his wife's name. When he received no reply,
he looked up from his calculations and shook his head,
frustrated that his mouth had betrayed his distracted thoughts of
his wife. "Saundra, do you recall what time Jack wanted to
meet?" Romney said, inching up the caliber of his voice.

"'Eleven-ish,' is what he said. You know how he is," Saundra
finally replied, when her typing fingers had found a spot to pause
for a moment.

"Thanks," Romney said, noting the hour had arrived.
Grabbing his new portfolio, he strode out of his office and
glanced in the mirror before he exited. "Hey, Mitchell just e-
mailed me about time off could you respond to him saying,
'Whatever he needs,' and asking if he's found a temporary point
person while he's out?"

"Sure thing."

"Hey, Theresa" Romney greeted in passing.

"Mitchell Reed, I just got to your...," Romney said, extending
his hand.

"I don't know how you expect me to work with my hands tied
behind my back. It's the fourth time the funding for my
project's budget has finally been approved a week after my
contractors need their money to start."

"What do you need, Mitchell?" Romney defused, closing his
eyes calmly as he retracted his hand from the employee who
always dressed in a white collared shirt and cotton tie.

"What do I need? I just told you," Mitchell said with heat, having a sizable nose that could flare like the top flap of a steam engine's smoke stack.

"I'm sorry, what do you need from me, Mitchell?" Romney repeated sincerely.

"You need to get off your high and mighty horse and stream line the budget payouts, no more of this tier one to tier two and two-to-one pony show."

"That's not how this company succeeds, Mitchell. The accountability among team members is the purpose of the cross-project budget approval. I don't think I need to explain it to you, but tell you what...," Romney said and continued wincing, "...come up with a proposal that would adequately replace our tier accountability program and present it to me or Jack, and we'll see if we can't go about incorporating your suggestions for streamlining the budget approval process. We sink-or-swim around here based on cash flow, but for now the resistance of our tier reviewing achieves the balance we need."

"With that said, here's my next 'second-tier' proposal to my 'first-tier' commander," Mitchell Reed said with sarcastic submission.

"Thank you, Mitchell. I'll look this over by the end of the day and call the meeting to approve it pronto," Romney graciously said, slipping the few pages into his rawhide portfolio. Tall windows illuminated the entire office, giving the open-beamed ceiling a warm archaic glow, and he continued his walk across the spacious room to Jack Hense's office.

"Romney!" Jack cheerfully greeted before Romney had a chance to announce himself. "We need to accelerate the off-loading of Fenndale," Jack commanded.

"By how much?"

"A year and three months."

"A ye...okay...we would be digging into our profit-estimates."

"By thirteen to nineteen flour buckets, I know; Theresa ran the comparison for me already. I've been tipped on three new properties. It's going to stretch us, but it's double on the acquisitions and at three years the number of possible tenants will put us in eleven-digits territory."

"Three freshwater properties that I don't know about? What tips are you getting?"

"Not here, Philly and Morestown."

"That's personnel expansion, new market entry, and do you think we can pull enough profit out of Fenndale to get us on our feet? It's only at seventy percent occupancy now, and if Theresa is right...."

"Can you?"

"Ah, I...well, such a quick offer will only attract profiteers. We'd have to be lucky."

"Ah. Well, see what interest you can muster, and pull together the master minds to postulate a launch campaign. I'm going to sit down with Byron to see if he's interested in staying on board for another round. Pending his interest, we may let Fenndale run full term," Jack said, partially distracted by a new message arriving in his inbox.

"How about this," Romney responded to maintain the momentum, "send me the files confidentially, and we'll put a team of seven together to run scenarios and prioritize the properties based on our current capacities and strengths. From there we could present it again confidentially to a larger team to decide which property suits us best and then go forward publicly from there...after offers are accepted in writing."

"Yes! Shoot me your two names, and I'll shoot you my two or three, depending Byron's acceptance," Jack agreed with his typical furor and passion for prospective ideas.

"Good. I'm out to lunch now and swinging by Lundberg afterward; do you have anything to send that way?" Romney asked to dismiss himself.

"No. But enjoy. I hear they're protesting the trees," Jack Hense related, letting his cheeks rise and showcase his opinion.

"Yeah, I'll talk to them," Romney said, double-tapping the door as he departed.

# Part 1 - Chapter Twenty-Nine

Romney parked on the side of the street, two stores away from Crumbles Cafe, directly across the street from Scales Architectural Company. Looking to his passenger seat, he picked up his new brown portfolio, thinking to write down a few ideas for the expansion as he waited for Jeff Dunnire to join him. However, the presence of Mitchell's budget, and more so the topic he came to discuss with Jeff, caused him to set down the portfolio and leave his car empty handed.

He paid one of the parking meters that were rhythmically placed on the street and made his way to the front of the cafe. He glanced through the window as he neared the entrance. Lively couples chatted face-to-face over tables inside, and the comforting sound of the tiny bell jingled as he opened the door. The ropes that made a short horseshoe shape in front of the payment counter overflowed with people, giving Romney plenty of time to peruse the menu with the other customers ahead of him. After standing at the end of the line for a few minutes patiently waiting, a few more customers trickled in behind him. He scanned the room, looking to see if Jeff Dunnire had slipped in unnoticed. Jeff looked every bit of a family man, embracing his thinning hair along with his wife-selected apparel that ranged from starkly professional to awkwardly comfortable. Romney didn't see Jeff but settled on watching an oblivious couple chatting lively a few feet away. The boy, wearing an out of season gray beanie, watched his animated table mate while she in turn talked and shrugged. Occasionally the boy would divert his gaze downward while flipping his straw around his empty water cup still filled with melting ice.

Nearly to the register, Romney flipped out his phone and dialed Jeff's number from memory. "Hey, Jeff; are you good for the turkey-brie sandwich today?" Romney asked and heard his answer behind him echo through the phone.

"I'll grab a table," Jeff said, moving toward one of the remaining vacancies. He watched Romney order and pay for the lunch, taking an order token in exchange for his payment. Jeff rose to greet his friend and noticed him exhale his tension as they sat down together. "Okay so...," Jeff instigated, trying to determine an efficient entry point for the litany of information that he needed to convey.

"So is right. Thank you for your time. You tell me how much it's worth, and I'll pay you for...."

"Don't be ridiculous, this is about you and Sandy. I've looked over the letter, but before we get to that, first off, I need to know your disposition, your story. But even before that, how are you? How's your little girl?" Jeff asked. Jeff's reaching motion down to his brief case encouraged Romney to take a moment of preparation. Jeff laid a legal pad of paper and a stylish pen on the table, and then he leaned back, relaxing his hands out of sight.

"I love Sandy, so, though the letter was somewhat of a shock, I kind of expected it," Romney said and paused, realizing he spoke his thoughts instead of answering Jeff.

"Okay, tell me about it. What do you think? Or was there a point in time where her love for you started to fade?" Jeff said spontaneously, repositioning his hands atop of his knee as he propped up his leg to visibly accommodate Romney's jump to the pressing topic.

"I probably got carried away at work. No, April was born. April was born in August, and by November I began to admit to myself that her behavior had swung, and then I caught her."

"Oh, thank you. That looks great," Jeff Dunnire said, complementing the server as she arrived with the food. "Continue, please, her behavior had swung."

"Well, she didn't let her mother come for New Years as she has for...for as long as I can remember. And when I asked her about her reasoning, all she said was that she didn't want her there. She started going out more, which was fine with me because I wanted her to get away from the continual responsibilities that come with an infant. The only problem was that she would lie about where she was going. I didn't really care, well I should say I didn't care until that day I found her package in the trash, and...."

"I'm sorry; sorry to ask, what package?" Jeff interrupted.

"Her needles, she was doing drugs. That's what she called them a few times anyway. Sorry, it seemed like a hip term in the moment. They're syringes and vials mostly."

"What type of drugs?"

"I assume heroin, and probably prescription drugs; the amount of money she was going through, it had to be more than one. I think in January alone I watched twenty-eight thousand dollars disappear, and I say 'disappear' meaning spent on un-producible things."

"Wow, I never would have guessed," Jeff reacted, picking up his sandwich.

"Please, please eat, I'm losing my appetite," Romney said with redress.

"Oh no, I have much to tell you about the entangled divorce system, procedures, paperwork, and such. You'll have plenty of time to regain your appetite," Jeff said, dismissing Romney's politeness. "Twenty-eight thousand a month, that's unsustainable; what happened then?"

"Hhh, I bought a needle disposal trap," Romney quipped, half-expecting Jeff to laugh. "She didn't care, well, that I bought it, or about the proper disposal of her needles, even for April's sake. I couldn't convince her she had a problem. She would just laugh at my 'interventions,' as she'd call them," Romney said, feeling a pinch of emotion. "Afterwards, without fail, she would ask for more money, or try to cash my checks, or try to open lines of cash credit, or make an excuse for whatever. It had to be cash," Romney said, finding his rhythm, but paused in observation of something behind Jeff.

Jeff attentively turned a little to look.

"Say, if you saw someone you know stealing a cookie, how would you go about stopping them?" Romney asked.

Jeff froze as Romney abruptly rose to his feet and rounded the table toward the exit of the order line. Following Romney with his eyes, neck, and shoulders, Jeff watched Romney say to an apparent acquaintance, "Spencer, right? I'd like to buy your lunch today." The guy named Spencer didn't object and stood rather stupefied along with the female cashier, who slowly accepted his payment. "Put two cookies and two bottled juices, on the, the, the, whatever you call it...bill, thanks," Romney said, snapping his fingers as he thought. He laughed with embarrassment at his own illiteracy.

He smiled at Spencer and then took the receipt back to his table, picking up a juice and a cookie before he did. Romney heard a voice from the middle of the line say, "I guess you're the lucky guy today."

Jeff echoed, "So who's the lucky guy?"

"Sandy's dealer...one of them anyway. He stopped by the house yesterday afternoon."

"Stop, stop, you just bought her drug dealer's lunch?"

"Call it, suspected loss prevention. So anyway, I closed off her access to our checking accounts and opened plastic lines of credit, credit cards, for her and myself, so she could buy literally anything she wanted," Romney said, heightened from the intervening exchange. "She agreed to attend a recovery class, and I think it helped initially. That was exciting, but she didn't stick with it." Romney paused again, contemplating his cold sandwich. "Oh! She crashed her car, and I'm convinced she was high when she did it. That's what really set me off. April was in the car, and she just fell asleep, Sandy did, in the middle of the day! I took her license away and cut it into pieces in front of her. I was mad," Romney said, dipping his eyes to the table for having admitted to his rage. "I eventually apologized, and at that point from having attended the recovery class, and at the personal recommendations from the leader, I started laying down some boundaries, specifically regarding April's safety, and acknowledging the addiction. I told her the rules and the natural consequences, which she repeatedly disregarded. This is getting to sound like a sob-story; I'm sorry."

"What were some of the rules," Jeff said, quickly swallowing a bite, "and consequences, if you don't mind me asking?"

"I wouldn't stop her from buying or using drugs, but April could not be with her when she did. She said, 'Of course.' Our neighbor a few doors down said that they would be available to babysit anytime and any day, that is until yesterday. She had a limo service that would take her and pick her up. She only had to pay the cleaners out of her accounts, or else she had to do the work herself. Let's see...what else? I asked, not demanded, that she attend the recovery class with me that met once each week. I think that's all."

"That all sounds generously fair."

"Well, immediately when the money wasn't there to pay the workers, she said she was leaving, and she took my car. She left for a while; I want to say a week. No more than the usual expenditures appeared on her cards. Then she had a debit card in her name. Oh, my head is starting to spin."

"Well, why don't I talk for a bit about the pro...."

"Oh, but there's more," Romney said, and having already unwrapped the cookie, he restively broke off a piece and put it in his mouth. Not sure of why he felt proud, he continued, "I finally got in contact with her, this is around this past December, after countless headaches, and convinced her to come home. I remember her saying, 'It's so kind of you to start caring about my well-being.' And I still don't know if she was being serious, sarcastic, or just spaced out at the time, but that was a punch in the gut. So, needles to say, I mean needless, sorry, at her request I've been living between two places. I'm usually staying in the city apartment weekdays and caring for the mansion on weekends. April's whereabouts...."

"Aye, and she wants to divorce you for...," Jeff remarked, opening a manila folder he had placed on the table, "indignities and desertion. Well, good news for you, it's only been since December, I think you said, that you've moved out, even though your continued presence on weekends would easily negate that alleged fault. Go ahead and eat; at least you ordered a cold sandwich from the get-go." The restaurant had started emptying of the lunch crowd, and the employees behind the counter began to neglect their posts for diversionary dialogue. An audible joke and witty remark caused a bout of laughter among them. "This is troublesome for you, from what I gather," Jeff said, genuinely struggling for the right words. "Cheryl has suspected something for a while, and even if you had brought it up before now...gosh, I don't know what we, Cheryl and I, or what I could have done."

Romney didn't feel troubled as he had successfully off loaded his private burden and consequently rediscovered his appetite, but he nodded, thankful that Jeff understood his plight.

"This could all disappear with a few pen strokes, or let me rephrase, we can do this one of two ways: one, concede that divorce will eventually happen and proceed with a settlement, or two, fight...fight for this love of yours," Jeff said with a subtle smile, suggesting the difficulty hidden within the phrase. "Which, in your case, means hoping Sandy will change her ways and mind. Sandy's lawyer will inevitably fall back on the argument that your marriage is irreversibly broken, because the only thing I detect as a possible indignity was you destroying her government issued driving license."

"Not my proudest moment, I'll admit."

"Yet, going to court is only going to effectively draw out the date of divorce, and mostly becomes an officiated argument on how to divide the assets. Though your first words were...."

"I love her," Romney recalled and meant what he had said.

"And court proceedings may give her more time to recognize and recover from her addiction," Jeff said, nodding to convince Romney of the meager hope of the tactic. "So, besides all that, I've assembled the paperwork here to dispute the current accusations, include as much evidence as you feasibly can, and return it to me as soon as you can. Regardless of whether you want to settle or not."

"I don't want to settle, in fact I won't."

"Well I'm not going to take your answer till...."

"Not while there is still a glimmer of hope."

"There is, but I haven't heard your answer yet."

"Okay, but I'm not one to disregard...," Romney said, stopping to continue his reasoning intuitively.

"And Romney," Jeff said, leaning on the table and setting down his pen, "you love her, I know, and I'm not a counselor, I'm council, but if you are in for the fight to win in the way I perceive you want to, you're going to have to forgive, and forgive, and forgive again. You can't run away or bury the difficulties anymore. No sooner than next Friday will I accept your answer. See if you can send me this information on Monday. Well, let's say Tuesday to give you a workday to get to the banks and government offices."

Romney stood up, dusted off his gray suit pants out of habit, and glanced at his hands retrospectively to see if he had just smeared crumbs onto his clothes. "Thank you," Romney said again, extending his clean hand.

"All for a friend," Jeff replied, following Romney's lead out of the cafe.

# Part 2 – Anna & Spencer

# Part 2 - Chapter One

Anna Purse felt refreshed after her long weekend of recovery. The commencement of the first of her two summer semesters was less than an hour away, and the vibrance of the campus thankfully distracted her memory away from the disagreeable event of the fundraiser that had finished off the spring semester. The sun that periodically forced her to squint in the occasional light that flickered through the tree coverings touched and warmed her freckles and emblazoned her hair to every shade of fiery red. The sun made freckles elsewhere too, on the manicured lawns and on the vainglorious spring flowerbeds, and the heart of Vern Hill's campus beat with a similar array of radiance. A hollering student attempted to reunite with a classmate that was fifty yards away and drew the attention of a couple of other scattered students. The campus tour also paused as the guide stopped to watch the random heralding. Repositioning her shoulder bag, Anna exited the covering of trees and detected a whirling of wheels behind her. Concerned from her previous collision with the board rider at the fundraiser, she tried to locate the source of the sound. The wheels began clicking rigidly and retarding. The dichotomy of sunlight made seeing into the harbor of trees difficult, but Anna kept to her walking. The smoothed concrete sidewalk bordering the trees had a gentle downward slope under Anna's feet, and after a few more steps, the towering athletic complex came into view.

The board rider, closing the gap quickly, watched Anna step off the concrete onto a wood chipped bed. Smiling with a friendly wave as he rolled toward the athletics facility, he made eye contact with Anna and noted her familiar smile. Gravity pulled him away toward his destination.

Anna had smiled at her childish apprehension, and she too had noticed the vaguely familiar face. Sticking her hand into her pocket, she removed a dainty wrist watch. Seeing that she had enough time, she set out anew down the gentle decline and past the group of lecture halls to see if she could find and meet the board rider. She easily tracked the skateboarder to the point where he had disappeared around the corner of the athletic complex. Rounding the corner of the complex, Anna heard the crack of a bat followed by shouts and hollers from the baseball diamond. In too short of time to decipher the verbal raucous, a baseball cracked down onto a car windshield. The single smash was startling, and the players and coaches who had been shouting adamantly turned away from the fly ball that had somehow been hit foul to such a height and distance that it cleared the protective netting over the backstop. The practice resumed, and from her distance, Anna spotted Chad Wattsworth, dressed in baseball practice attire, standing erect with convincing athletic prowess on the pitching mound. Anna watched Chad pause with his right hand tucked behind his back and admired how he drew his arm around like the catapult it was and let go of the ball. After following the ball to the catcher's mitt, Anna located the fly ball that had settled next to the damaged car and decided to do the good deed of returning the ball to the dugout. After watching indulgently for a few minutes, she tossed the ball next to the dugout for someone later to find and returned to her curious pursuit of the mysterious board rider. Making her way through the welcoming glass doors of the athletic center, she walked around the indoor running track, peering through the transparent walls of the weight rooms and through those of the indoor basketball court. After passing the friendly looking receptionist again, she asked, "Did you see the skateboarder that just came in? I'm looking for him." The receptionist admitted she hadn't. So, Anna looked at her watch again and decided it was time to officially start toward her first class of the summer semester, instead of wandering the campus aimlessly.

## Part 2 - Chapter Two

Jonathan Wickfell looked as smart as his name looked wicked, and though his smarts highly benefited his schooling they also limited his athletic abilities. Still when he looked in the mirror to measure his height with a yardstick, he would always scowl when the measure would never quite read six feet. Yet, smarts and height don't define the shape of your face, and Jonathan Wickfell had a decent face, one that might or might not win a notable-mention ribbon in beauty contest. Jonathan threw his towel over his slender shoulders and pushed through the exit door of the locker room. His gym shorts had a classic reflective stripe down the seam and swooshed as he walked to the weight-room where many of the natural athletes on campus worked as fitness trainers. "Hey, Sean!" Jonathan said, signaling his Monday instructor. The six-foot varsity outfielder smiled, recognizing his fellow classmate.

"Back again, eh?"

"You know it. I'll stop coming after I can dunk that basketball," Jonathan said, joking at his honest ambition.

"Oh, you'll be happy then. I'll take you shopping for some springboard shoes and fix you right up," Sean said with jest, picking up a five-pound medicine ball and handing it to Jonathan. "Rotate and hold."

Jonathan looked at the pink medicine ball with dislike and stretched in accordance with Sean's commands.

"Okay, all the way down to touch the floor...all the way. You still have three inches to go," Sean coached, demonstrating how far he wanted his classmate to reach.

"Ahhh."

"No, don't bend your legs, we're stretching your haunches, keep them straight."

"Ahhh, I can't...how can I not do that. I mean, you're what? Like four inches taller than me! Ahhh."

"You're red in the face man, flexibility isn't related to height. Come on, I'll review the racks first and then I'll give you some aerobic exercises to do in sets by yourself."

"How was that fundraiser last Friday night? Or was it Thursday," Jonathan asked, seizing his only chance at firsthand information.

"It was cool, you know, suits, ties, rich people calling out your name and singing your praises. But it was a chore after the first thirty introductions."

Jonathan laid down at Sean's bidding on the weight equipment and having remembered the motion, demonstrated the exercise for his student instructor. Focused under a bar of weights, Jonathan asked, "What was your favorite pert?"

"What?" Sean asked, hearing the question but not understanding his last word.

"I mean what was your favorite part of the evening?" Jonathan clarified after relaxing his muscles and replenishing his lungs with oxygen.

Sean Dowagiac grinned sublimely. "Veronica, of course."

"Of course," Jonathan repeated. After sitting up and taking the clean towel that Sean extended to him, he said, "It would be nice to have someone like Veronica."

"Like being the key word, and don't get any ideas," Sean said lively.

"I mean...," Jonathan said, trying to justify his statement, but he abandoned his attempt as he pressed his arms together, saying, "It would be nice."

"It's easy," Sean replied, seeing his response had stirred some inward emotion of his classmate. "Here, sit up, and remember the goal of this one is to rotate the shoulder. Remember to extend, then pull it in. Good. I mean it's easy, you just find a girl you like and ask her out or something. She likes you or she doesn't."

"Yeah," Jonathan said, finishing the practice rotations in a depressing slouch. "Do you know Erica?"

"Sophomore, works over at Crumbles Cafe, in some liturgical major?"

"Yeah."

"Sure, doesn't everybody? Cute girl."

Jonathan followed Sean Dowagiac over to a lengthy wall mirror and appraised his peer's athletic frame. "Is she seeing anyone?"

"Seeing anyone? How should I know? Ask her. Push-ups, sit-ups, leg-ups, stretch, don't forget a little water between your sets," Sean instructed, pointing out one of five lists on the wall next to the mirror. "You're going for heart rate, rhythm, and endurance."

"Well, I was thinking you might know, because she's friends with Veronica and all."

"Well yeah, that sure would be convenient for you if I knew, now wouldn't it," Sean said insincerely, while turning to dismiss himself for the next waiting student.

"Would you ask her...for me?"

"Ask her? For you? Dude, what kind of relationship are you hoping for?" Sean said, unable to restrain his astonishment.

"I mean it would be nice to know if she was going out with someone before I made a fool of myself in asking her," Jonathan quickly defended.

"You mean you want me to ask Veronica or to ask Erica?" Sean asked, trying to clarify his uncertainty.

"Well, I meant Veronica to see if she knew, but if you're up for asking Erica directly, well, that would be just as good," Jonathan suggested as sarcastically as he could.

"No! Just as good? If you're too scared to converse with a girl long enough to figure out if she's interested, you're after...you might as well as...well, what's the point?"

"I think I like her," Jon replied unsure of what to say.

"I think I...," Sean repeated, wanting to remove himself from his precarious position without committing to something and more so without insulting his classmate. He physically dropped the tone of intensity in his voice and said, "Go ask her; that's the least you can do for yourself. You can spend your time better than wrenching your heart all around over the what-ifs; or maybe that's what you're after. I don't know," Sean advised, motioning with an open hand, indicating the counterpoint to his own directive. "Somebody that just sits wishing on the sideline, isn't in love with the game, they're in love with the idea of the game," Sean said, and hearing his own advice, he smiled with satisfaction as he dismissed himself to the next student waiting for his attention.

"Yeah...thanks; push-ups, sit-ups, leg-ups, and don't forget a little water...and stretching!" Jon repeated, looking at his apple colored expression in the mirror.

## Part 2 - Chapter Three

Anna Purse followed a classmate into the square intimate classroom. No more than thirty students could have squeezed into the class, and most were still yet to arrive. Anna sat next to the classmate to look friendly and set down her class books. Before she had completely settled, the tall girl with naturally tan skin leaned toward her and secretly disclosed, "When Professor Kovan starts talking I heard that he locks the doors to the classroom."

"I know, I heard that too," Anna Purse responded with a similar plea to satisfy the silence. "Do you believe it?"

Two more students arrived through the door at the back of the classroom. The friendly girl paused and looked around before answering Anna's rumor defying question. "I don't know how much I do, but I also hear you can't fail this class."

"Right," Anna agreed, enjoying the features that made her classmate's face pleasantly dance with life.

"Right."

Without a word, Professor Kovan entered the room ten minutes to the top of the hour. The few chatty students readily identified his presiding decorum and hushed their conversations. The arriving students also followed suit as if instinctively adopting the code of silence. On the hour, exactly, he started his teaching. The professor had already made it through his introduction and course expectations when the door to the back of the classroom swung open and a final student entered. With wet combed hair, the student carried a duffle bag and a long board. The professor stopped speaking and looked up at the interruption.

Anna noticed the long board but couldn't identify any of the markings on the board from her vantage point. "Darker hair and different apparel," she judged, convincing herself for the moment that it wasn't the same board rider she had pursued to the gym.

"You must be Jonathan Wickfell."

"Yes, sir," Jonathan attentively replied.

"We saved you a seat up front; come sit down," Professor Kovan said indifferently.

"Yes, sir," Jonathan replied and began walking toward the remaining open seat. The sound of nylon rubbing his duffle bag swooshed with his steps.

"Don't enter my classroom late again, Mr. Wickfell. I'd rather you not come at all than disturb the other students who planned...and succeeded in arriving on time; understand?"

"Yes, sir."

"I am not Ludwig Wittgenstein, and this is not an elementary school," Professor Kovan said, emphasizing the gravity of his abstruse point with a moment's pause.

"'If people never did silly things, nothing intelligent would ever get done,' would they?" Jonathan said, having misinterpreted the humorlessness of the professor's remark.

Having interrupted the professor again, Anna caught a sliver of a smile on the professor's face as he turned back around to face his opposition.

"Kudos, Mr. Wickfell, you read the first chapter, but, 'Whereof one cannot speak, thereof one must be silent.'"

"Yes...."

"Uh...," Professor Kovan interrupted, raising his conducting hand as quickly as he spoke.

A few students chuckled; everyone else patiently observed. Then Professor Kovan turned his back to the classroom and continued, "There are only two exams and therefore only two chances to pass this class. Be on time or don't come at all, but whatever you do...do not come through that door late. This is a math logic class, a class of math and logic, which is merely a form of language whereby we can more effectively transmit abstract ideas. And it's important, and in fact, it's the very thing that sets us apart as humans within the animal kingdom. So, follow along."

Jonathan Wickfell had caught sight of Erica, the Erica, on his way to the front of the classroom, and after losing the spotlight, he divisively took the opportunity to look over at her as he opened his duffle bag to remove his class materials. Anna, who blockaded most of Erica, her friendly classmate, from Jonathan

Wickfell's view, caught sight of his curious eyes and diverted her gaze back to the orating professor.

Ten minutes passed, and catching herself daydreaming, Anna snapped back to watching the white board that was beginning to fill up with cryptology. A few minutes later, having the same symptoms of sleeping while wide awake, she innocently lost muscle control of the pencil she held. The mere sound of the pencil falling may not have disturbed anyone, but her clumsy reaction seemed to cause Professor Kovan to stop and turn. Barely making her voice audible enough to effectively apologize, she began, "I'm sorry...."

"Professor, wouldn't 'x' be over 'b' and not the other way around?"

The professor visually identified his accuser and then sought out his alleged mistake.

"The late Mr. Wickfell is correct, please forgive my scribble," Professor Kovan confessed and continued with the corrected formula till the hour and a half long class ended.

As Anna rose to her feet along with the rest of the dismissed class, the friendly acquaintance said, "I'm Erica by the way; do you have time to grab lunch?"

"Erica? Hi, I'm Anna, I'd love to. What were you thinking?"

"Well, I don't have that long. I have to be to work by twelve, but the cafeteria is right around the corner," Erica suggested.

"Sure, I have till one. Where do you work?" Anna inquired, happy to have made a friend.

Following the flow of students down the side aisle and out the classroom door, Erica clasped her two books and notepad tightly to her chest. Anna walked equally beside her, searching her brain for an interesting topic. This struggle was complicated by the fact that Erica had ignored or didn't hear her prior question, so Anna decided to abstain.

"So, are you dating anybody?" Erica tritely rummaged with a smile.

"As in a boy? Oh, no. You?"

"Who'd want to date me? Hah," Erica laughed reflectively.

Anna couldn't tell if Erica truly meant her question, so she indifferently said, "I feel that way sometimes. But when I see the guys that my mom brings home, I tend to think most guys aren't interested in anything but...well, not interested in the same things, or you know...want what I'm looking for in a relationship."

"True that!" Erica responded, clarifying her questionable sentiment with another laugh.

"I don't mean everybody. I know someday some guy out there will be responsible enough, I mean...well, that's what I'm hoping for, you know...a good guy."

"Yeah, do good guys exist still?" Erica rhetorically remarked and saw Anna smile sheepishly. "What!" Erica defended, detecting some interior monologue happening inside of Anna. After letting the anticipation build with no apparent reply, Erica chided again, "What! I was kidding...kind of; I know some good...."

"No...," Anna interrupted, seeing that Erica had misread her silence.

Erica hushed and pushed open the exterior glass door, letting Anna pass before her. A chatting couple took Erica's action as a courtesy and proceeded behind Anna. "Tell me."

"It looks like it's going to rain," Anna said with embarrassment and looked up at the sky.

"That's not it."

"It's nothing."

"But nothing's making you blush," Erica said, shifting to a teasing tone.

"Well, you said, or asked, if there are still good guys out there."

"Yeah?" Erica replied.

"And I think I met one yesterday, but...."

Erica looked up at the sky, to avoid the possibility of disclosing any jealousy. "There's always buts."

"Yeah," Anna replied concisely in agreement without any apparent intent of elaborating.

"Yeah? You're like pulling teeth! But what?" Erica asked, accepting Anna's courtesy of holding the cafeteria door.

"But he's older," Anna said, tipping her head side to side as if to say, "...not just a little either."

"Maybe that's the way to go about it; go find an older responsible guy, like you say."

"And kind of married?" Anna added, squinting her eyes as if trying to see someone on the far side of the bustling cafeteria.

"Kind of, how can someone be kind of married?" Erica petitioned with a laugh.

"Well he is, but she...yeah. Don't look at me like that; you're the one who started prying."

"That's ridiculous! I could see you thinking about it for like a whole minute before I asked," Erica said, liking Anna more every minute.

"Yeah, 'thinking' about him, wait what do you mean by that?" Anna asked but immediately vetoed her question by saying, "I don't want to know. Food, I'm hungry."

Erica laughed again which made Anna expose more of her blushing smile. "You know it then. There are still good guys out there." Then as Anna placed her order to the cook, Erica added, "They're just all married."

Anna sat down at a table and waited for Erica to maneuver to the opposite seat. As Erica positioned her plate, Anna leaned forward, anxious to make a comment.

"Erica!" the pitch of voice almost shrieked, inferring the excitement of the coincidence.

"Veronica!" Erica matched Veronica's animation while rising to her feet.

"So, you have class now too?!"

"Sure do. Veronica, this is Anna; Anna, Veronica."

"Oh, you're cute as a button," Veronica said in Anna's direction, and turning back to Erica, she asked, "Do you have cover?"

Erica nodded and reached into her purse as Veronica fashioned her excuse.

Anna followed the story, something about the fundraiser, a boyfriend, a classmate, Sean, a morning alarm, and clothes not fitting. All the while listening, Anna self-consciously replayed over to herself her various interpretations of Veronica's first impression. Lunch quickly passed under Veronica's gab, and as soon as Chatty Cathy's drawstring ran out, she jumped up and went on her way, saying, "Call me. It sure was nice catching up with you and your friend here over lunch."

A pleasant silence fell in the wake of Veronica's departing.

Sensing the shared relief, Erica turned to Anna and apologized by raising her eyebrows and letting out deep breath. "Hey, I'm going to head out for work, thanks for sitting here and keeping me company."

"Yeah sure," Anna said amiably. Anna followed Erica's lead as she stood and gathered her disposable dishes. Using an extra napkin, Erica dabbed her water and proceeded to wipe down the table.

"Thank you for that. Hey, you never told me if you were dating anybody," Anna said, resorting to reusing Erica's opening line.

"Oh? No. Did, but that's over." The lunchroom staff, readying for another wave of students, went about their cleaning, clearing, and restocking duties.

"You work on campus?" Anna inquired.

"No, over at Crumbles Cafe."

"Well, aren't you going to drive?" Anna asked, expecting a logical excuse as to why Erica had turned away from the parking lot. Taking a quick step back to avoid a bicyclist, she restated her question with a quaint motion of her hand toward the parking lot.

Erica immediately connected the dots and confidently said, "No, Crumbles is this way. It's just a ten-minute walk."

"Walk? Phooey, ten minutes, it's on my way to my next class."

Erica smiled at Anna's hospitable resolve and indicated her answer by happily taking three steps and linking her arm through Anna's.

"Tell me about him," Anna dared asking, "if you're okay talking about it, that is."

Erica contorted her lips to the side, understanding the topic clearly. She thought about the engaging question and resolved, "Ask me again sometime. Okay?"

"Yeah, sure." Anna replied.

"But you are the first person to ask; and I mean that," Erica confessed, "...I mean that you need to ask me again sometime."

"Time is good, though I'm not sure how I could relate. I've never dated, or wanted to...even, cause of my mom."

"Lucky," Erica said with a smile. Then with a complete polar change of emotion to lighten the mood, she said hoarsely, "You're so lucky."

"Why? I see gorgeous girls like you and Veronica with boyfriends and all, and you seem happy."

"Have you...no." Erica gave up on asking her question.

"Have I what?"

"No need," Erica replied, shaking her head. "Woah, is this your car?"

"Yes, kind of, and no. It's my mom's, but she doesn't drive much, so it's mine for the afternoon."

Erica walked around to the passenger side of the clean car. Anna started the engine with the key and fastened her seatbelt. Erica followed suit. "You're good at changing the subject too, you know," Anna accused light-heartedly, testing the depth of their new friendship.

"And look at that, you called it like an hour ago, rain, sure thing," Erica leaned forward toward the dash to get a glimpse of the dark gray cloud overhead. "And look, it's moving across the parking lot."

"And you were going to walk," Anna chided.

"Yes walk, there's nothing wrong with walking. Besides, that's before I knew you had a sporty ride."

"What time do you finish?"

"What?"

"Like what time are you done with work?" Anna asked, knowing her intent of offering to drive her new friend home. "I assume you live on campus?"

"Yes and no; I mean no and yes. You're not going to pick me up, and yes, in the Hampton dorms. Room 23B."

Anna smiled in response to her friend's feistiness.

"I've seen that smile once today already. You're too kind, Anna."

The pattering noise of the rain turned into thundering slaps on the car hood, making detailed conversation nearly impossible. Anna pulled up to Crumbles Cafe after the short drive and still felt sorry for Erica, knowing the short ten feet to the café door poised to sufficiently drench her friend. "And don't pick me up," Erica reprimanded.

"Well, I can't until you tell me what time you finish. Tell me what time you finish; I'm coming for a night class regardless," Anna spoke as loudly as she could after Erica had cracked open the door to leave.

"Six, but I'm walking home...regardless," Erica said, slamming the door and retreating to the covering of the café awning.

Turning to send off her friend, Anna could see joy behind the waterfall of dropping rainwater. She beamed, enjoying her own prospect of kindness. Then a bolt of lightning split the sky, followed by a roar of thunder. Timidly, Anna pulled away from the curb and reversed her course around the next block, re-passing Crumbles Cafe after she did. Thinking she saw Erica through a window lofting her hair up over the neck tie of her apron, she privately bid her friend farewell again and headed back toward campus.

With the windshield wipers splashing the amassing rainwater, she saw a person on the side of the road ahead of her. The narrow shoulders forced her to slow down as she approached the man. The young-looking man had his light jacket folded up over his head in a vain attempt to stay dry, or at least to keep the general flood of water from obstructing his vision. Anna's heart began pounding with sympathy and pulsed further from the defying notion colliding with her mother's firm prohibition of picking up strangers. The college-age-looking boy had a longboard wedged under his far shoulder and a sopping wet duffle bag on his left. Anna almost resisted, but after noting the color of the boy's nylon pants, she cracked her passenger window and yelled as loudly as she could, "What's your name?"

The boy, squinting at the car, heard the indistinguishable voice and instinctively responded at the top of his lungs, "What?"

Anna had stopped the car, and the boy, having continued two more steps, returned and ducked toward the cracked window.

"What's your name?" Anna emphatically questioned again for sake of the ambient noise and her pounding heart.

"Jon," the familiar stranger shouted.

"What's your full name, Jon?" Anna asked in fear, insistent on convincing her remaining doubt before committing to the irreversible consequences.

"What's your full...," Jon began, objecting amidst the shifting beat of water pellets, but he stopped when he recognized the face behind the crack in the window. "Jonathan Wickfell! You're in Professor Kovan's ten o'clock math logic class...," Jonathan said like a light switch had flicked on, and he saw his classmate reach over to pull open the door handle.

"Quickly!"

## Part 2 - Chapter Four

The windshield wipers waded through the water for a while until they started squeaking on the windshield. Responsively, Anna Purse parked her wipers as she continued driving to campus.

"Hey, thanks for the lift. I'm sorry about soaking your nice leather seat here," Jonathan apologized.

Satisfied with the result of her risky behavior, Anna drove on in silence for a moment. Then after assessing the conscientiousness of her passenger, she facetiously commanded, "Don't let it happen again, Mr. Wickfell."

Jonathan turned to Anna with alarm, not knowing how to respond to the sudden reprimand. Noticing his rescuer's capering smile, he laughed dryly to relieve some of his tension.

Anna's smile grew wider. "Are you heading back to campus?" Anna asked, forgetting to renege her antic.

"Yeah...Swanson Hall, do you know it?"

"Am I a student at Vern Hill?"

Jonathan, again unsure of how to read his driver's manner, turned quietly to watch the cars ahead cut their wake through the pools of water that had formed on the road. Jonathan laughed as Anna slowed the car enough to turn onto the weaving campus road. "Either you're witty, or I'm dull," Jonathan confessed after his sudden laugh. "I guess both aren't necessarily mutually exclusive," he surmised, but he immediately blushed at his comment.

"I don't usually have such a sharp tongue like that. Sorry. You should feel my hand still shaking from trying to decide whether or not to pick you up."

"Well you're shaking, and I'm shaking. At least you won't be catching a cold from your shaking," Jonathan said, shivering at the thought of cold. He leaned away to open the door with his drenched duffle bag and long board snug to his chest but stopped and said, "You know you look familiar."

"Yeah, I know. It took me the greater part of the morning to figure it out, but you ran into me at the fundraiser last Thursday night," Anna said, looking at Jonathan's face.

"No! That was you! I am so sorry, that's so embarrassing. Let me know how I can make it up to you. If you want a study buddy or something, let me know," Jonathan offered, firing spontaneously.

"I'll be fine, I'm sure, but thank you," Anna replied.

While walking heavily on his heels a few steps backwards, the thought struck him as the car zoomed around the circular course to the exit. "Her name!" he scolded, kicking his foot at his sinking realization. With a dissatisfied grin, he redirected himself to the dorm, and trusting gravity, he threw himself instinctively onto his long board. Hopping off a moment later, he greeted, "Hey, Chad," as he passed the campus star.

"Hey, man," Chad automatically responded and lifted his weathered backpack over his shoulder. Looking back momentarily to see if he should have recognized the student, he admitted that he didn't know for certain and walked into the waving trees that still were dripping from the downpour. As he rounded the corner, he detected a red car accelerating through an intersection parallel to his path. Seeing the frame of a girl and remembering Julianne's similarly colored and shaped vehicle, he started replaying that prior Thursday night's events and cringed as he remembered declining Anna's offer to drive him back to campus.

--- *At the same moment in the spotted sporty car.*

Anna Purse looked at the center console of her speeding car and noted the time while beads of water moved in synchronous waves over the roof. A minute later, she found herself periodically looking out over the Montague waterway through the vertical beams of the Mills Bridge. Then she heard her cellular phone ring as her car barreled out of the bridge's steel framework. She quickly decided to brake and turned abruptly onto a small service road at the entrance of the Duquesne Tunnel. She parked her car and stretched to the rear seat with an unorthodox twisting of her body. Returning upright, her blood having rushed to her head, she pushed the hair out of her face and stared at her lifeless cellphone. Then "Rom," scrolled slowly across the display, and the phone buzzed in her palm. Returning the call before listening to the message, she pressed the phone to her ear.

"Anna Purse!" Romney answered.

"Hi, is this Romney?" Anna asked to be sure.

"At your service...well, hoping for your service actually. I promised to call and set up an interview."

"Wednes...."

"I pick April up around 5:30, and we could get together for an introduction," Romney began speaking his thoughts, assuming Anna's reply.

"I have class tonight, how about Wednesday morning before lunchtime," Anna said positively.

"Ooh, I'm leaving for Morestown early; wait! Didn't we already say Wednesday when we parted, oh, the night before la...I mean Thursday night? That's right, I'm sorry; the Morestown trip just popped onto the schedule late this morning. How about Tuesday sometime around or in between your classes? Say noontime?"

"Eleven might work, but it can't be for too long."

"Fair deal. I'd also like to introduce April and Sandy to your house, not necessarily on Tuesday, and, remind me, I have a key to give you for our place. So, if you ever need to drop off April, you can."

"Okay."

"I hope to convince Sandy to come to our little meet and greet."

"Okay."

"Where would be a good place to make the introduction?" Romney asked, trying to nail down all the details.

"Umm...," Anna stalled, racking her brain for a convenient location.

"I don't want to intrude on campus, but if you're going to be there, it would work."

"I could come early," Anna agreed.

"What time is your class?"

"Twelve."

"So, eleven then?"

"Sure," Anna said, smiling at the self-realized solution.

"Great, call me at this number if things change."

"Okay," Anna said with her eyes closed.

"Okay, I'm looking forward to it. I know April is going to love you. We'll talk soon," Romney concluded, hanging up the phone after hearing Anna's shy closing reply.

Opening her eyes, she found herself staring up an incline toward a service road that switched back to some sort of elevated guard house or service shed. Having hastily parked perpendicular to the bustling road, Anna found herself listening to the roar of the cars entering and exiting the tunnel entrance. Waiting for her window of opportunity, she timely flew backward fifteen feet into a small break in traffic and tested the integrity of the car's floor board with her excited foot on the gas pedal. Fortunately, the small area of dry pavement at the tunnel entrance gave plenty of traction to send the powerful car into and out from the depth of Mount Lincoln.

Seven minutes later, counting from the time Romney had ended the phone call, she pulled into her snuggly square driveway. Hoping the garage door opener would miraculously work, she maneuvered as closely as she dared to the door while repeatedly pressing the transmitter. After digging her thumb repeatedly into the plastic, she gave up. Releasing the brake, the car shifted backward, and she opened the car door. The damp bottom of her purse touched her forearm as she slid it onto her shoulder. Recalling the reason for its dampness, she privately laughed at how much wetter Jonathan was. Once inside, she trained her eyes on the small notepad of scribbles that she had jotted from her summer class. When she looked up to address the patter of feet on the almost white carpet, she saw her mother's face paling in comparison.

"I'm pregnant."

"Don't be ridiculous, mom, you're not pregnant...just hormonal."

"I've been pregnant before; I know what it's like to feel pregnant, and I feel pregnant."

Anna didn't bite at her mother's insistence. Instead she proceeded up the staircase toward her room. Halfway up the incline, she asked skeptically without slowing her progress, "From Thursday night, with Chad?"

"No, I thought I told you. Didn't I? He ran off," Julianne responded, glad to remind her daughter of her clean hands.

"Why don't I call your new confidant, Chad, and he can console you," Anna said, stopping for a moment on the stairs.

"I know I felt something kicking, or swimming around in there; maybe it's just food poisoning," Julianne defended with a reflective muttering before Anna's bedroom door clicked closed. Then suddenly the feeling came over her again, and she rushed to the service of the toilet.

Hearing the faint but conclusive sounds of her struggling mother, Anna felt partially vindicated as her eyes began to well up with tears from the reminder of the fundraiser. She blinked away a few of them and tried looking at her window bordered with her pretty curtains for comfort. After a few minutes of staring at her white curtains, she fell asleep on the plush white comforter covering her bed.

## Part 2 - Chapter Five

"Anna dear," Julianne said after knocking lightly on her bedroom door like a dripping downspout. Listening for movement and cracking open the door out of curiosity, she peeked her head inside and repeated, "Anna dear, it's four-thirty. Were you going to take a cab back to school?"

"What? I thought you were sick," Anna lethargically replied, having become conscious at the intrusive sound.

"Oh, that. What a relief, but I'm starving; so, were you driving or calling someone to come pick you up?"

"I'm coming," Anna said, rolling to her side on top of her covers. Remembering her agenda and her six-thirty class, she rolled out of the bed. "I'm coming," she reiterated with annoyance to herself.

Picking up her books and keys to the car, she stomped groggily downstairs, out through the front door, and waited for her mom in the car. Her mom calmly walked up to the car through the floating exhaust a few minutes later.

"Anna dear, you didn't have to park so close; the neighbors have plenty of room to get by if they need to," Julianne commented in her usual composed and unhurried manner.

"Yeah, I know, but the garage door opener isn't working again, and I thought proximity...well, never mind, but are you sure you're up for working tonight?"

"Oh yeah, but I want a hoagie beforehand!"

"A hoagie, as in a sandwich?"

"What else? The whole thing, no sharing to save money, or the earth, or starving people or whatever you say."

"Or nineteen hundred calories at one sitting; I wanted to pick up a friend from Crumbles Cafe at six...ish."

"Oh, a new friend?"

"Mom, 'a new friend?' Yes, a new friend. What am I supposed to do with that? I'm completely capable of making friends."

"And what's his name?"

"Well, I did want to talk to you about something different, – Erica, is her name – that is, do you remember Romney Daniels from the fundraiser?

"Of course, he seemed to be hiding something," Julianne pondered audibly while opening her purse and flipping through a few items in search for an eye mirror.

"Hiding? So, he's a generous caring individual one day, and he's got secrets the next."

"Like he just got served with a divorce letter," Julianne continued.

"Anyway, he has a daughter that I offered to babysit for."

"Oh really! Is she cute?" Julianne responded.

"She's two-and-a-half with hair long enough for pigtails. I'd call that cute." Anna saw in a glance Julianne's interested smile flatten. "What?" Anna asked, sensing her mother's quenched enthusiasm.

"Eyes on the road, Anna dear, you know that makes me nervous; is she cute?"

"I haven't seen a picture of her, but...."

"She's two-and-a-half with pigtails. Is she well behaved?"

"How am I supposed to know; I haven't met her, but I'm going to tomorrow."

"Tomorrow?"

"Yes, before my class at twelve...at eleven. Well, meeting at eleven before my twelve-o-clock class; I was hoping you would come with me, so I could help him. Or, so we could help him out by babysitting." Her mother sat stoically in thought, and Anna disobediently glanced over to read her mom's silence. "It would help me earn some money."

"I don't like two-year-olds...money? You've never had to work for money; why would you work?"

"That's a good question. Why do you work, mom?"

"Ah! Smart girl," Julianne muttered. "Because it gives me an audience and the satisfaction of their applause," she spontaneously defended.

"And me the satisfaction of helping a friend."

"Oh, you're friends now? You have two new ones, Erica and Romney, a boy after all."

"And actually, if you're counting, a two-year-old, named April, makes three, who I'm meeting tomorrow, and I would like you to meet her as well."

"I don't want you meddling around with married men," Julianne said, adopting her motherly tone.

"Mom, babysitting...not daddy...," Anna said, abandoning any further implicating counterpoint.

Julianne flip-flopped and said, "I'll babysit in a pinch...or so that you can attend class, like you say."

"So, you're not coming to meet him and April with me?"

"No, you're a big girl."

Julianne looked up and saw the distinct Piano Taps sign, and out of habit she prepared to disembark by unbuckling her seatbelt. Anna noted the sound with irritation and hesitated over pointing out her mother's roadway hypocrisy. Unable to resist, she criticized, "And you think taking my eyes off the road is dangerous."

"I love you, Anna dear, show's over at eight-thirty; sometime around nine, unless you hear from me, okay?"

"See you then, mom, and thank you!" Anna added before Julianne let go of the closing door.

"For what, Anna dear?"

"I love you too," Anna rephrased to avoid recounting her mother's permission to babysit.

"I love you too, Anna dear."

Anna took off, noting the time, and it dawned on her like the change off a traffic light that she had forgotten her mom's hoagie sandwich. She swung around the block again to see if her mother had emerged to lay claim to her requested dinner, but, after a few seconds of waiting and placing one unanswered phone call, Anna declared, "She doesn't need nineteen hundred calories...even if she was pregnant." Glancing up at a stop light, she tapped her fingers on the steering wheel. "She's not pregnant," Anna said again to her dashboard. "Oh, now I'm hungry."

As she was approaching Crumble's Cafe a spot on the street opened for her to easily park. Swinging the car into reverse, she paralleled into the spacious spot. She got out with excitement and peered into the long front window to find Erica. A boy, college age, stood inside the door and courteously pushed out the door for Anna to enter.

"Busy beyond belief, huh?" the college-aged male commented to Anna.

"Yeah, I'd say so," Anna replied, unconsciously gripping her purse.

"Anna!" the voice came from Anna's left. "I told you not to come, but you did!" Erica said ecstatically, approaching to give Anna a quick hug on her track back to serve another order. "Busy; let me know if you can't find a spot, kay?"

"Kay," Anna said infected by Erica's pleasure.

Anna turned back to observe the growing length of the line and the courteous young man, who was handsome enough to take any excuse to look at, if even for a moment. His attractively messy hair was a bit brighter than Jonathan's, on the blond side of the spectrum, and the only thing she noticed in her moment of gawking was that he looked a wee bit tired under his eyes. Anna perhaps looked for a moment too long, because the tired eyes caught her own and made her heart suddenly pump fresh oxygen to her face.

"So, Anna, I'm Spencer. I'm sorry, I overheard your name. Are you meeting anyone?" Spencer asked, forcing his hands further into his black leather jacket.

"Hi, Spencer, I might be." Anna had chosen a loose-fitting white shirt to wear, and matched with form fitting blue jeans, she had once again succeeded in modeling a classic look without any effort.

"I just see there's not much room to sit, and if you're not meeting anyone, well, all these tables are set for two it seems."

Anna followed his train of thought but felt uneasy about the inferring offer, so she silently reached across her chest and grabbed her purse with her second hand. Spencer laughed and made his polite apology by turning his eyes to the wall to grant her the privacy he had spoiled. Anna's phone rang. Expecting her mother, she immediately answered it. "Hey, mom, sorry."

"Hey, Anna, you're going to be so excited!" The voice on the phone bubbled with glee.

"Bethy, sorry, excite me!"

"I'm going to be attending Vern Hill in the fall...or starting in the fall at least. I had initially planned to attend and was accepted at Grayson as you know, but the program filled up, which was a little disappointing. Anyway, do you still need a roommate this fall? Because you know we have to room together if I'm coming to Vern Hill."

"Wow, Vern Hill, no joke, like we planned yesteryear, right?"

"You don't sound as excited as I thought."

"No, no, I can't wait to show you around; you're going to love it; I'm just living at home with my mom that's all, so I can't promise that we'll be rooming together," Anna said, slowing down her final words and bracing for the certain disappointment.

"Oh, don't worry about it; we're going to be hanging out too much anyway."

"Yeah, but I don't know. With you enrolling and everything, I might have to reconsider my arrangements," Anna said, feeling her heart drawn to the possibility of independence. "Oh, I can't wait to introduce you to people and the campus. I mean you're already familiar with the area, but it's changed a little since you left."

"My mom and I have visited my dad in the city a few times over the past two years. But this will be new, I can't wait!"

Finally internalizing the implications of the news, a smile crept onto Anna's cheeks. "What program did you choose, oh, hold on. I'd like a turkey hoagie cold, and a non-caffeinated tea...like chamomile or something," Anna ordered, still holding the phone to her ear.

"Seven forty-three."

"Oh, oh, give her my discount, she's a friend," Erica instructed in passing.

The cashier punched another two squares and said, "Two ninety-four."

Anna smiled at Erica as she walked away, having already grabbed another plate of food to deliver. Anna paid with a more than adequate bill, and the cashier handed her the plenty of change. Instead of fussing with reorganizing the change in her wallet, she deposited the loose bills into the clear pitcher marked "YOUR TWO CENTS - Tips for the team - THANK YOU!!!"

"Sorry, Bethy? I had to order here at Crumb's."

"No way! Hey, is Scooter still working there?"

"I don't know let me ask. Hey, miss, do you know if Scooter is working here still?"

"Oh, yeah. Hey, Scooter!" the cashier barked through the serving window to the kitchen.

The familiar wrinkled face popped up with its normal merriment and generally recognizing Anna, he said, "Hija how are jou! Good to see jou!"

"Bethy says, 'Hi!'" Anna called out over the babble.

"He does! Oh, I remember those days," Anna heard Bethy say into her ear.

"Oh, say, 'Hi,' to Bethy for me, ja?"

"Okay! He says, 'Hi.'"

"That's great. Well, I got to go, I'm going to call you all the time now. I mean more than I do already!"

"You better, Bethy," Anna said happily. She hung up her phone with one hand and received a table token in the other. Then she turned to the cafe seating area, looking for an open table. Scooter, dressed in his cooking apron, walked out to hand deliver Anna's plate, saying with his wrinkled smile, "And 'tis is special for jou for being a friend to Bethy." Anna took the plate, smiling her thanks, and looked back to survey the seating-scape again. A mop-headed boy rose out of his chair a few paces away, and Anna uncomfortably recognized the Spencer guy from the doorway.

"Please, please, sit here. I'm done," Spencer implored with his mouth full. He supported his words by taking his plate and brushing his crumbs from the spot with one swipe of his free hand.

"No, no, sit down. I...."

"No, no, it's not anything, please take it. See, I'm leaving," he said, stepping back away from the table.

"Well, thanks," Anna said graciously, and after sitting down, she watched Spencer walk from one side of the cafe to the other with the same purpose of finding an open seat.

On his return pass, Anna called the name she mostly remembered, "Spencer, sit down already. You're too kind."

"Thanks," Spencer said, pulling the chair out across from Anna. "I don't know; I thought a spot would open up faster," Spencer confessed and took another bite of his sandwich. "Hey, I don't mean to make you feel awkward again, but I just enrolled at Vern Hill for the fall, and I haven't...well, I've only been on the campus tour. What do I need to know, like hang out spots or bad professors and such?"

"You're going to like it. I mean, it's school – no way around that – but the professors are great, and the student government always has some campus wide event going on it seems. Every club under the sun that you can imagine, like a carnival of options! Will you be living on campus?" Anna said, beginning to trust Spencer.

"I haven't decided yet, but it's an option. Do you recommend it?"

"Oh yeah, for the first year especially. You'll get plugged in so much faster and make more friends that way."

"What clubs are you involved with?" Spencer asked, having trouble diverting his gaze from Anna's moving jaw line.

"Oh, nothing right now, but you'll see me at a home baseball matchup occasionally," Anna replied, before stretching her mouth around her sandwich.

"Oh, you mentioned 'clubs under the sun,' so I thought you might participate in a few," Spencer said rationally. After a moment of silence while Anna chewed, he asked, "If you could be in a club on campus, which one would you be in?"

After what seemed like a few more minutes of talking, Erica stepped up to the table, having already removed her green apron and said with a cheery smile, "You ready?"

"Yeah! Hey, this is Spencer, Spencer...," Anna said and hesitated. "It was nice talking with you."

"Ahh, the lucky customer from the other day, I remember your face; it's nice to meet you, Spencer," Erica greeted, already having made the connection.

"Yeah, that's me; I've never had someone pay for my food like that. Lucky, huh?"

"Hey, thanks for waiting, Scooter had me stay a few minutes over to help with the cleanup."

Anna had not noticed the number of empty tables. Looking at her watch and recognizing the real time, she emphasized, "We've got to go."

"Hey, it was a pleasure; can I call you sometime?" Spencer said, sensing his last moment of opportunity.

"Yeah, sure," Anna said, already moving in the direction of the exit.

"Tell me your number; I promise not to sell it, tell it, or yell it to anyone," Spencer prompted.

Anna closed her eyes as if she needed to stop everything in order to remember her personal information and recited it, cramming the ten digits into half-a-breath.

"I'll see you later then," Spencer said, smiling underneath his mop of hair.

"Yeah, and if not, on campus this fall, right?"

"Absolutely, but it better be long before that," Spencer objected, saluting his farewell to the girls as each looked in his direction one last time.

Anna hurried to her car across the street with Erica following close behind with her periodic double steps to keep up. "I'm sorry to rush you, but I have to be to class in fifteen minutes."

"Well, you don't have to fuss about me."

"Oh no, I lost track of time in my conversing," Anna corrected.

"More like flirting," Erica teased.

"Oh no, really?"

"You gave him your number after giggling with him for like an hour and a half. That's flirting if it was ever to have a definition," Erica said.

"He's going to be our classmate this fall; I thought I was being cordial," Anna excused.

"And cutesy in response to his, what would you say, handsomely and gentleman-like behavior."

"Do you think so?" Anna selfishly inquired while accelerating toward her school. Predicting her arrival time in her head, she estimated four minutes for walking to class and one to sit down before she would technically be pulling a 'Jonathan Wickfell.'

"You didn't do anything less than normal. He's cute, and that's why he's always flirting with girls after he comes in. He knows it, so, 'be careful,' is all I'm saying."

"Has he ever flirted with you," Anna asked with curiosity, admitting her guilty position.

"He tried, but the café was slammed at the time," Erica excused. "And I had a boyfriend."

"Same one as earlier?"

"Maybe," Erica said, pausing like a guilty suspect. "So, tell me what's your major? Spencer got an interview before I did, so I need to figure you out before I lose my chance," Erica said, veering off the uncomfortable topic.

"History," Anna replied, turning into the grand parking lot a minute earlier than expected.

"Oh, you're one of those girls," Erica said with heavy sarcasm.

"What? I love it!" Anna defended, attune to Erica's comical banter. "What about you?" Anna asked with serious interest.

"Linguistic Anthropology."

"Really?"

"What? You don't see me as a linguistic anthropologist?" Erica equally returned.

"No...yes. But I'm going to be more careful about what I say to you from now on, now that I know you'll be analyzing all my words. That's my attempt to be funny by the way," Anna said, mimicking Erica's less than serious tone.

"Joking, huh? I figured as much, which is why I think you're going to make an excellent first case study," Erica replied, making Anna's gut release a laugh.

## Part 2 - Chapter Six

"Please, please...."

"You're begging me now, you're begging?" The walls were little insulated, and anyone above, below, or to the rear of the apartment would have easily heard the defined sobbing. With a bicep that drew fear, the brandished metal piece sounded a single crack as the raging man carelessly hammered the delicate surface. "You're a worthless runaway, and I should make your sister work, seeing that you're incapable...."

"No! I'll go, I'll work, I will, I will, I promise. Please...."

"See you don't have to beg me girl; you're beautiful. I'm looking out for you all the time, but you can't be giving your product out for free without collecting, and you can't be skirting your end of the deal. I put a roof over your head." Reaching over the polished counter that he had carelessly chipped, he grabbed a box of golden crackers and supported his claim, "I provide food for your family. Here."

"You do, you do, thank you."

"Don't treat me like this; two days you haven't brought in a dime," the manipulator said, assessing the girl's attempt to smile gratefully amid uncontrollable sobs.

"Could I have, could...," the thin jaw bone spoke, but either for sake of aching too much to finish or the associated anticipation of reprisal, she shied away from her request.

"Could you have what, sweetheart?" Trist Palanco asked with a softer almost mocking voice.

"A little," she quivered.

The six-foot bear rose to his hind legs and aimed his rage, understanding the little meaning of her request. He thoughtlessly let his anger pull the trigger of his gun, and a new hole further tortured the innocent couch. The frail girl leaped toward the perceived safety of the door, but the breadth of the human animal acted to restrain her, if only to make another imprint of horror in her memory. His thumb print would later show on the corner of her jaw. He dared, "Do you want to ask me again?" The girl shivered, and if her body hadn't taken over in fright she would have collapsed. "Next time I see you I'll be collecting something."

"Mm...."

"What?" he snarled, using his capacities to shake the entire life he squeezed.

"Ye...us." When Trist let go, she had already resigned herself to the approaching darkness, but her body again unconsciously snapped into resistance, clinging to some unknown shred of light. The enslaved then angel flew out of the apartment dressed in fear.

Triston Palanco took a deep breath, relaxing the muscles in his face as he carelessly watched his laborer politely close the front door. Picking up the box of orange crackers that the girl had deserted, he grabbed a handful and began walking to answer the new knock.

"Hey, Spence!" Trist heralded with his altered mood and extended a burly arm to invite a brotherly embrace.

"You got to ease up, man, or she's gonna run again. And one of these times she's going to get lucky and figure out how to get the police involved."

"Jessica Patsy? Naah, she's too scared to cheat."

"I'm just saying for your sake. I've got nothing to do with her. Hey, you get a shipment yet?" Spencer flipped right to his intent. "I'm down to two packages. You've nearly run me dry."

"Of course, but I need to pay Wiffet tomorrow for it, so I need some money."

"Money, where's the money I gave you for it already?"

"It's gone, man.  You know how money is," Trist excused as he sat down to test his tortured couch with his full weight.

"Man, you owe me, and now you want more; where's the payout?" Spencer said with growing frustration.

"Owe you what?  You roll in it.  You got to let go of it sometime or later," Trist sassed to his middle benefactor. "Besides, the way I look at it, you're in debt to me to get your fix, so ease up, and we'll call it even."

"Whatever," Spencer walked to the locked closet to restock his pockets from the dwindling stash.

As Trist surveyed his accomplice reaching through and removing a concealed key from the disfigured drywall, he added, "You know Wiffet will come looking to you when I don't pay him tomorrow."

"Thanks, you need me, so nice to know," Spencer replied, as he pocketed enough product for the night.  Counting in his head, he put three packages back.

"Wiffet sent me new stuff, good stuff."

"How would I know, I don't get my fix anymore,"

"You did, and you keep coming back.  And even though you think you're all puritan, I see you skimming."

"Samples.  You sample the product, you hook 'em; once you hook 'em, you clean 'em; and once you clean 'em out, you disappear.  You know I don't cheat you."

"I know, I know.  Did your dad drop any change in the neighborhood of ten genies around?"

"Ten grand?  Don't bring up my dad.  You know I wouldn't talk to him even if he called," Spencer said with an expression of buried stress.  He prevented his forehead from greasing the wall with his arm while he digested Trist's new money trouble.

"What are we going to do then, Spence?" Trist asked, his grizzly eyes peering at the apparent aggravation of the free-bird.

After a sigh of tension, Spencer relented, "I know a girl, who orders three times that much in a month and is desperately hooked, you can get it from her.  She goes by Beverly sometimes over in Chapel Hills, she's almost spent anyway, and her man's catching on." Spencer looked away anxiously as if he had somehow just made a guilty confession.

"Thanks, you sure?  Sandy's been playing almost two years."

Spencer looked up at Trist, questioning him with snappy eyes for knowing Beverly's true name.

"I'll check into it," Trist assured as he watched Spencer queerly leave his apartment in seeming response to his pushiness and his knowledge of Beverly's private details.

Spencer rhythmically galloped down the decline of stairs, hitting the ground with his preset direction. The sirens he heard in the distance didn't faze him. Reaching into his first accessible pocket, he positioned his fingers to the sides of his cellular phone. Removing the phone, he stopped to pick up the package that had fallen to the ground and thumbed the plastic encased contraband back into the bottom of his pocket. Having maxed out his address book with numbers and pseudonyms, he slowed his gait as his thumb hovered over his phone's keypad. Struggling to recall the number of his little sister's house phone, he put pressure on his sinuses to piece together the memory.

A machine answered. He waited for his cue. "Hey, baby sis, it's me. I know I've been gone for a while and that dad hasn't been too happy with me. I don't know what you think of all that, but I got word from Kathryn that you're moving off to college now, well, here in Pittsburg anyway. Anyway, I met a girl here recently that I kind of get along with...okay, I kind of like her. But she's going to show me around the campus, and maybe I'll get to introduce you when you arrive. Kathryn didn't know or tell me when you were starting. But I want to help you move in and get started and stuff. I know dad probably told you why I left and what I'm 'doing,' but I'm clean now. And I want you to make your own opinion of me. Will you do that for ol' Spence here? Okay, I'm rambling, don't tell dad I called, he'll try to put me under house arrest or something. Love you sis'. Okay, bye."

"Great, just the convincing sounds I need in the background," Spencer scolded himself as he turned to gawk at the two patrol cars that had blared through the intersection during the final words of his message. To cheer himself up he turned to his reconnaissance interest of the moment. Also, from memory, he dialed Anna's phone number, and encountering a messaging system, he left his rosy and sanguine, "Hoping to see you," and "...get together for, I don't know, I guess we could call it a date" message, together with other extemporaneous sentiments.

# Part 2 - Chapter Seven

Anna laughed at the nervousness of the boyish voice on the phone message as she backed through the exit door of her lecture hall building. The transparent door gave way a little more than she expected, and she would have stumbled if her elbow had not found the glass when it did. Nevertheless, the discomfort of her funny bone only made the exasperating message more entertaining and magnified the excitement that charged and pounded within her. As the message ended with his clarifying phrase, "I guess we could call it a date," she looked up, unintentionally smiling at an oncoming couple. Veronica recognized her and sprightly greeted, "Hey, girl!"

Anna replied, "Hi, Veronica," in her passing. After taking a brief pause to appreciate the tall athletic type ushering Veronica, she continued toward the emptying parking lot. Still holding the phone to her ear, she listened as the subsequent un-played message began. "Hey, Anna, this is Romney," Anna heard the familiar voice and listened to its impressing closing. "Okay, call me back, bye now." Even though she needed to start driving to stay on time, she replayed her two voicemails. "Oh hi, Anna? This is, well, Spencer, from this evening. I'm sorry; I couldn't wait to call," she listened to the boyish quiver in his voice. Then Romney immediately followed with his businesslike glib, "Okay, call me back, bye now."

"Nothing like how he sounds in person," Anna analyzed as she finally started the car. Feeling girlish and giddy, she rolled down her windows, and she turned on the crisp stereo. "I'll always love you," the song resumed mid-line from where it had lastly been silenced. Too happy to sing and too happy to think, Anna inhaled the humidity that lingered from the earlier rain. Passing the cafe, she smiled to the sound of complimentary guitars waving from her speakers. The music played through the green light as if in tune to traffic and slowed at the command of the yellow signal. As Anna pulled up to Piano Taps, she saw Julianne was tending to a pathetically dressed girl. Julianne sat

closely with a consoling arm over the back of the pretty-blond
figure.  Anna noted the contrast of Julianne's refined apparel, her
handbag, her jewelry, her makeup, and manicure.  Nothing was
spectacularly gaudy by any means, but the fragile blond had
nothing in comparison; nothing but a short skirt, a loose t-shirt,
damaged tall-heeled shoes, and her head in her hands.  Anna's
empathetic heart shamed away any pride left over from her
judgmental conscience, and she stepped out of the car toward
the pair.

The girl looked up startled, then looked at the perfectly
polished car, and then returned her horror filled eyes to Julianne,
ready to flee.  She tried to get away from Julianne's increasingly
adamant introduction of her daughter.  Julianne perceived some
connection between the style or color of the car and her instinct
to run.  "Please come stay at my house, Jessica."

"No!"

"Is it the car you don't trust?"

"I can't...I can't...I just can't.  Besides, Trist would hunt me
down and kill...and kill you too," Jessica Patsy said emotionally,
having already moved five paces away to maintain her getaway
options.

Julianne started to authentically weep, "Who could possibly do
something so horrid!"  She couldn't finish her thought out loud,
but rashly shuffled through her bag, looking for some mediating
token.  Jessica had again begun to make her escape when she
heard the contents of Julianne's handbag spill out onto the side
walk.  "Jessica, don't go without this," Julianne frantically
implored and grabbed all the cash out of her pink wallet.
Throwing the cash into her shoulder bag, she scurried to toss in
her mirror, her lip stick, and a spare pair of socks.  Hastening her
few steps to the stalled girl, she placed it on her shoulder while
having another desperate idea.  "And these," Julianne added,
sliding her shoes off with ease and hanging them by the heels
over the side of the leather bag.  "Sell it all, use it, do whatever.
It's yours.  Just please don't let whoever's doing this to you
continue to do this to you!"

Jessica considered her advice for a long moment.  Her feet,
though stationary, battled.  Julianne stood as still as stone,
committed to stay until Jessica made her ultimate move.  A few

cars swooshed by the puddle of rainwater that had collected on the far side of the street. A man also offered his inquiring gaze as he circumvented the standoff by stepping into the road, and he glanced at Anna also to make sure that he himself wasn't an intended target.

Meanwhile, Jessica's barricade had begun to crumble. Anna could tell that she slowly gave in by how she nervously elevated and teetered her shoulders. Jessica finally whimpered and offered a shame filled smile. "I don't have a place to stay."

Julianne hushed her momentary grin, afraid of reiterating her initial offer with too much haste. She waited instead for Jessica to further expound the humbling remark. Stoically, Anna watched, and for the first time in a long time she was completely unashamed of her mother.

Jessica fancied the small hope for a moment, the hope brought about by her new status of owning a used leather purse and having pretty shoes to wear. Then finally, she consented with a bitten lip and nods of her head.

Julianne caught the broken girl in her arms, and as she did Anna moved to collect the few remaining items left on the ground from Julianne's life-saving gesture.

# Part 2 - Chapter Eight

Romney Daniels looked at the trustworthy watch he had classically wound earlier in the morning as he entered his office building. Only a few flights of stairs remained ahead to challenge the final stretch of his morning commute. His wife in a seemingly upturned mood had dropped him off and promised to return after a morning brunch with a friend.

"Hey, Jack," Romney said, passing the elevator with a welcoming gesture.

"Come on, Rom," Jack Hense invited.

"The stairs are calling me, Jack, I'll race you up."

"I'll win," Jack bragged blandly.

"Oh yeah?" Romney laughed.

The elevator doors cut short the challenge and set Romney on his course up the six short flights in the rectangular stairwell. Invigorated as he reached the top of his climb, he pushed through the security door after waving his badge. Jack Hense stood with his stocky shoulders leaned against the wall, waiting with his eyes attached to a business document. "I told ya," he said, without looking at his joint founder.

"Oh, grow up," Romney Daniels jestingly countered his friend's boyish bragging.

"Hey, Mitchell," Romney said to the approaching personality.

"Here you are, Mr. Daniels, typed up as requested; all my ideas for restructuring the project approval process, and I've even thought through and suggested the implementation stages. I think everybody feels like me about the tediousness of the tier one and tier two teams interfering with each other. Who really wants or needs a disconnected, different, and out-of-touch project team hampering and stalling their project anyway. It only results in retaliatory...well, there's no need to draw out a long explanation here since it's all written down there. I know I'm ready for a change."

Jack Daniels looked with curiosity at the loose sheets of paper covered by a sheen of black letters that Mitchell offered to Romney.

"Thanks, this looks like you've spent a long weekend on it," Romney responded as he glanced over the top sheet of the well-handled stack of paper.

"Well, if it makes my life easier, and helps the company succeed, why not work through the night, eh?"

"Hold on. Jack, I'll be over at say nine to discuss the two's," Romney called as Jack took the opportunity to politely remove himself from the impromptu meeting.

"A new project?" Mitchell inquired at the familiar terminology.

"Yes, big. In fact, this would be ideally timed if we could get...well, walk with me Mitchell. I'd like to hear you orate your propositions, so I can get a framework, or more so, so I can interpret your ideas," Romney said, picking his words from multiple thoughts parading through his mind.

"It's all quite simple and explained in the outline. I don't see why I would have to explain it again when I've already gone through all the trouble of writing it out for you," Mitchell Reed complained as he followed his leader in his white collared shirt and cotton tie.

"Well, if you're going to be pitching this to our leadership team, I want to see how it sounds out loud," Romney quickly rationalized.

"Me pitch? What do they pay you for?"

"I figure it's your ideas here, so you should get the credit. And if you're passionate about seeing this change, you'll be willing to stick your neck out and risk your name to see it realized."

"Ri...."

"And if you're willing to put your name alongside your effort, which is obvious from the amount of time and verbiage you've produced, it will be easier for me to climb onboard and push for its implementation," Romney continued, turning his back on his executive assistant to face Mitchell once inside his outer office.

"Sir," Saundra interrupted.

"One second, Sandy," Romney answered and paused to recompose his thought. "And Sandy, Saundra...Mitchell, I'd like you to sit down with Saundra sometime today. She is a master at formatting and grammar." Romney could see Mitchell's jaw stiffen. "You're going to need copies and we will probably only have maybe five minutes to make your case and present your ideas to the leadership team."

"I've taken my own time and my whole weekend, unpaid mind you."

"I know. I see the product, but you also need to understand that fresh ideas are often opposed and often seen as radical. If it's not clear, straightforward, and repeatable, it's going to be overlooked or at best misunderstood."

"You haven't even read it; how do you know my proposal doesn't pass all of your criteria?" Mitchell said, growing with characteristic heat.

"I will, but I need you to know that even if this is a perfect exhibit of genius, our leadership team will more than likely gut it." Romney said and paused, realizing that 'gut' didn't communicate his point. As Mitchell inhaled to resist, Romney continued, "The team will more than likely take your best ideas; no, they will most likely use your single page, concise, to the point proposal as a starting point; so you need to recognize the possibility that the final outcome may be considerably different, even counterproductively so, after it leaves your hands and everyone else tries to write their ideas in and throughout it."

Romney could see Mitchell's irregular breathing pattern.

"You haven't even read it."

"You're right, that would be a good place to start," Romney said confidently, ready to surrender his offensive. The acceleration of the lopsided conversation resulted in his feeling guilty for his honest attempt to bring light to the realities surrounding the stack of paper. Romney turned around as Mitchell stood red in the face, unable to articulate himself.

Saundra, who stood reticently observing, took his posture as a cue to begin, "Sir, a Mr...."

"Oh, Mitchell," Romney beckoned, after shifting part of his attention to his assistant.

Mitchell stopped his despondent retreat and replied, "Yes, Mr. Daniels?"

"Do you have the document file associated with this, I'd like to commission Saundra here to put together an example summary, for you to approve of course, after I have a chance to look this over?"

"Right away, Mr. Daniels."

"Hey, Mitchell," Romney called again, having swiveled around, but Mitchell had already disappeared out the office door.

"Why do you tolerate his relentless insubordination?" Saundra suggestively questioned.

Romney looked up from his intense focus on the document and construed his face to beg her pardon for not having paid attention. After a moment, his brain caught up to his ears and he comprehended the criticism. His assistant interpreted his perplexed brows as a scolding and immediately apologized, "I'm sorry, it's not my place; it's breeding ill will, and I don't want that on my conscience."

"No, it's a fair question, with an easy set of answers. One, he's a genius, and two, he's loyal to his job description. And as far as I can tell from this, this took more than one weekend's time. What is this, like sixty thousand words?"

Saundra laughed, despite not knowing if Romney meant his guesstimate for comedy or proof. "Oh, sir, I almost forgot, a Michael Gallant is waiting in your office to speak with you about your financials."

"A who?"

"He said you'd understand."

"I didn't invite anyone in to discuss my financials," Romney intentionally claimed out loud, noting the half-opened door to his office.

"Oh, my apologies, sir; I let him in; I'll usher him right out."

"No, thank you, I'll do the honors. But I am a bit disappointed, we have a direct policy in place to prevent uninvited strangers from gaining entrance."

"I'm sorry, really, I am. He sounded as if he knew you on the phone, and he really was most polite when he called up to be let in."

"Hold on," Romney lifted a finger, disbelieving the distinct sound he heard from behind the door of his office.

Saundra heard the sound the second time. "Oh, this couldn't be more embarrassing," she exclaimed, raising her hand to shield her right eye.

The sound he had heard was of someone snoring, and when he checked his office, the visitor, a middle-aged man in an extremely light gray suit, appeared to have fallen asleep in one of Romney's two plush chairs. Romney couldn't restrain his humored smile. "Don't sweat it, Saundra. It'll all work out. What am I saying, I trust your judgment more than my own most of the time, especially when it comes to character assessment," Romney said, changing his delivery responsively to incorporate his own apologetic overtones. "Well, while we have the time, my Sandy will be here with April around nine-thirty, and we'll be out of the office around ten to meet a new babysitter," Romney said and immediately perceived the impact that talking about his family had on mending Saundra's expression. "But before that, right before, I'm meeting with Jack to discuss our two's."

"Okay, but I do have a question," Saundra reluctantly asked.

"Shoot it to me...wait! Yup, Michael's still asleep; go ahead."

"Do you really expect me to edit Mitchell's...I don't know what you would call it?" Saundra mustered.

"What else do you have to do when you get off work?"

"Oh, shut your trap already," Saundra retorted, seeing Romney's true answer in the false height of his cheeks.

"No, I'll read through it and highlight what I'd like edited and formatted. Hopefully no more than one to two pages...hopefully," Romney said, meanwhile deciding that the nap timer needed to ring. "Besides, all these pages can't be completely covered in verbiage; I'm sure he has diagrams and charts filing up most of this." Romney gave up on perusing the top page as he entered his office and quickly started flipping through the half-ream of paper but stopped short of his desk. "Nope. It's all verbiage," he corrected to Saundra out loud. "Oh, well maybe one 'org' chart," Romney backpedaled, while raising his eyes to assess the intruder, who had instinctively awakened with the approaching interoffice conversation.

"Hello, sir,"

"Hello, Mr. Gallant. I would say you have thirty seconds before I call security, but seeing that we have no personnel with such titles, you have thirty seconds to tell me why you deceived my secretary into letting you up," Romney instructed with confusing civility.

"I'm Michael Gallant with F.P.O., Financial Principle Organization. We met twice at the Vern Hill fundraiser. I'm sorry to come uninvited," Michael spoke rapidly, looking committing to his cause.

"You do look familiar," Romney said, unintentionally lowering his guard.

"I wanted just a minute of your time to offer you direct access to a private investment fund that my team at F.P.O. is starting. High yields, one hundred thousand minimum buy-in, some...."

"Do you have any literature?"

"No, not on me, but I'll be sure to fax or send them to your office right away," Michael apologized, and removed an enrollment sheet of paper from a monogramed portfolio and prepared to hand it to Romney.

"Any references?"

"Not that I'm allowed to disclose."

"What's the fund's strategy?"

"Confidential, I'm sure you understand; I was talking with Sir Byron Dorkan, and he seemed to hold you in high regards."

"Is Byron buying in?"

"I'm not authorized to disclose the fund's contributors, but I do plan on meeting with him later today."

"Ah, I see," Romney replied, and after a brief pause continued, "Well, let me walk you out."

"May I check back with you to see if you're interested or have any further questions?"

"I'm sorry to say, but you weren't able to answer the ones that I've asked already. I think I'll stick with my professional team of brokers."

"Oh, we're not brokers...investors, investors that group investors and provide the capital for promising startups, like Timco Net; Timco's turning a second year three million profit...unheard of, right?"

"Right, Michael walk with me please," Romney directed, retracing his steps in anticipation of Michael's compliance. "Do you have a business card where I can contact you and your supervisor?"

"Certainly," Michael Gallant strode closely behind, happy to comply with Romney's request.

Romney took the card and slid it under the thumb that grasped the half-ream of paper. On the way to the elevator, Mitchell Reed stepped out of his cubical with a small memory drive in hand. Restraining overt frustration but flaring his nostrils, he pushed it into Romney's path. Romney received the requested token and said, "Great! I'll probably get around to finish looking this over by the end of the week."

"Take your time," Mitchell carelessly approved as Romney continued walking.

"Is that the author?" Michael curiously questioned, as he continued following Romney.

"Of this? Yes."

"Wow, you've got your hands full."

"You say so, but it's how all good things start."

"Well, thank you for your time, and I hope to hear back from you within the week. Oh, by the way, we hope to close the tier one – the highest earning echelon – at the end of the month. So, don't deliberate over it too long. Ciao!" Michael said, saluting goodbye with two fingers like a con artist that was completely comfortable with his game.

Romney slowly took the remaining few paces beyond the elevator to his new destination, while scanning the business card for clues to the stranger's reputation. Finding only a typical run of the mill business card, he looked up to find Jack conversing with his cheery secretary.

"Romney, let's get this show started, what da-ya say?" Jack welcomed and motioned Romney through the mahogany door frame.

"That's why I'm here," Romney replied, gladly stepping toward the privacy of the second room.

"Is this the new form of exercise?" Jack asked as Romney closed the door behind him.

"The stairs? No just the whim of an optimistic morning. Sandy dropped me off today, and I...."

"No, I mean the strengthening of your hand muscles by carrying around a ream of loose-leaf paper," Jack said, smirking as he took a seat opposite his office couch.

Romney followed suit, sinking into the couch and apprehensively construed, "Oh, Mitchell, oh my. Well, you saw him hand this to me; he's wanting to restructure the company to expedite cash flow for the separate projects."

"Restructure? That's a bit out of his domain don't you think?"

"I encouraged it, and we're going to be restructuring if this move makes it past the brainstorm. I'll let you know if he has any applicable ideas in here sometime this weekend. We're leaving tomorrow, right?"

"Right, who'd you come up with for the seven; Sir Byron, the billionaire with pride to spare, is 'all in' by the way."

"You're going to laugh at mine, so you go first," Romney suggested, wiping his face with his hand as he intuitively reviewed the two names he had weighed with their associated reasons.

"Rick and Theresa, how about you?"

"Well, Rick was my first as well, then Mitchell Reed," Romney said with sincerity to avoid the possible slant of humor.

"I think Mitchell would offset the team, counterproductively so."

"Well, that's my reason for including him.  He's brilliant and outspoken.  He's seen three of our projects start to finish, and he'll certainly oppose weak 'sound good' ideas."

"No, I see your point, but Mitchell is so 'to the point' that others will shelve all their ideas just to avoid his tractor beam.  Nothing against him of course, other than perhaps his misuse of company paper," Jack reasoned, letting a smile reappear on his face.

"So, one veto, Theresa and Rick...Abdul?  He might not have the computing power, but he'll pull the team's ideas together, and I'd have to check, but I think he might be from Morestown."

"I think you're right, anyone else, because I know li'l boy George has been itching at the reigns," Jack said, paying close attention to Romney's reaction.

"Li'l...yeah, we could let him tally the stairs."

"Awe, come on.  We have to include somebody who has the endurance to run and get seven cups of coffee.  Besides, you're the one climbing the steps these days."

"You know, all poking aside, I would like to see him develop his abilities, and he's going to get swept up by someone else if we don't let him off the bench.  Li'l boy...George, okay seven it is, why don't you send out the private invitations, and we'll meet after lunch for all the details so that people aren't cranky," Romney said agreeably, standing up with the morning's agenda and phone calls already returning to mind.

"Let me know how that late-night reading goes," Jack instructed as Romney cracked the mahogany office door open.

Romney pointed the manuscript at Jack with a raised eyebrow and dryly retaliated, "You're funny, really funny.  See how I'm laughing?"

# Part 2 - Chapter Nine

After making multiple calls to both Lundberg and Fenndale properties, Romney checked his watch. "Saundra, Sandy should be arriving any minute now, in fact she should be here already. I'm in crunch mode to get through this phase one sell. Theresa will be calling with the answer to hosting Fenndale's public release. The literature and marketing assignments still need to be sent out as you know," Romney updated, while running his finger down the scratch off list he had significantly shortened.

"I'm working on that right now," Saundra assured.

"Before you break for lunch would you schedule the limousine, must seat six, preferably eight," Romney requested and heard Saundra pause to scribble the new instruction down with her pencil.

"Nine-forty, come on, Sandy," Romney said, rooting for his wife. "In five minutes, I'll start the process," Romney privately determined, still wanting to give his wife the benefit of the doubt. Romney frantically rolled out a floor plan for the high-end market contracted to fill the second floor of Lundberg Place. Excited and nervous at the same time, Romney referenced the three-page contract for Wellshop Foods in attempt to visualize how invasive to the street the marketplace was proposed to be. The phone rang in Saundra's office. In the moment of distraction, Romney bumped Mitchell's unbundled papers into the waste basket off the side of his desk. "Oh bugger," Romney vexed, interrupting his task to collect the fallen papers. "Almost nine-fifty," Romney muttered, as he finished squaring off the collected stack. "Saundra, anything?" Romney knowingly petitioned, stepping over to the outer office window to scour the street for a sign of Sandy and April.

"No, sir, you'd be the first to know, but I know you have to go meet the babysitter."

"Well, not just meet the babysitter...introduce April to the babysitter. Her name's Anna Purse by the way. Here, I should give you her number and address for future reference," Romney explained, picking up his phone to find the information. After orating Anna's personal information to Saundra, he toggled to the phone number for his wife. After three unsuccessful calls, he surrendered to reality. "Sandy's not coming," Romney audibly concluded while searching the phone for an alternate number to call.

"I'm sorry to hear that, is there anything I can do?" Saundra concurrently offered, having paused at the sound of his disappointment.

"No, it's my problem; but I don't understand, she has April, or had April, maybe she's playing with me again," Romney said, addressing his empathetic audience.

"I could call the hospital," Saundra brainstormed.

"We'll let me call the Richards' first," Romney replied, slightly waving the ringing phone at Saundra, "...to see if she dropped April off...hi, Felicity. Yes, this is Romney; hey really quick, did Sandy drop off April last minute like? She did!" Romney said, relaxing his shoulders. Having a new plan, he moved to grab his suit jacket from the wall hanger. "Well, that answers my other string of questions. Oh, me too, though if this is anything like it has been, I'm sure she's just mindlessly out-and-about doing her thing," Romney dispassionately assured and lifted his hand to Saundra's attentive eyes as he slid on his silk lined garment.

"I'll lock it, don't worry," Saundra said, halting Romney's flippant return toward his office door.

"Thank you," Romney mouthed. "But I'll be by to pick April up. I'm coming from work, so fifteen minutes or shortly thereafter. What's that? Oh, okay...oh don't worry at all, we're actually meeting a new babysitter," Romney disclosed, shutting himself into the elevator along with the mounting pressure of the new time constraint. "Yeah, you all need a break, I understand. Oh, no, no, I know she loves April, but...," Romney exclaimed as he hastened through the small lobby. "I agree, and I think this will be good for everybody, but Fel...," Romney said, trying to interrupt while hailing a taxicab. "Felicity, Sandy kind of left me in a bind, so I need to let...yes, thanks...I'll see you in twenty to thirty minutes; bye now." Romney let out a sign as his thumb continued working the buttons of the phone. "Hey, Anna," Romney greeted, skillfully concealing his fluster. "Hold on a sec," Romney said, leaning forward to tell the taxi driver his first destination. "Hey, Anna, thanks for waiting. I'll be to Vern

Hill, oh, what would it take, an hour if I'm lucky," Romney confessed, revealing his predicament.

"No problem, I'll be waiting on the benches near the grassy area next to the baseball theatre parking lot. I can't wait to meet your little girl," Anna said as she had rehearsed. "Oh? We'll let me ask," Anna replied and hugged the phone to her shoulder. "Hey Mom, you want to babysit this afternoon, right? She says, 'Yes,'" Anna hastily relayed the answer. "What? No, she's just downstairs trying to cook. Okay, looking forward to it, oh and don't be weirded out by what I'm wearing...well, you might be. Okay-bye," Anna said, hanging up the phone with a pulsing glee. "I told him," Anna confessed to Jessica.

"Ms. Patsy, would you care to eat fish for lunch?" Julianne called out from the hallway as she approached Anna's bedroom. "And what in this square house are you wearing, Anna?"

"I told you she'd object with a 'square house' comment," Anna said with a playful tone to her new friend.

"Think...I think it's perfect," Jessica timidly said, turning red at Julianne's reaction.

"...ly suited for a masquerade. Are you going to wear that to campus?"

"Well, April's almost three years old, and I think she'll love it. Say what you'd like, but I'm not going to stand out. It was either a princess, or a peasant...or a knight, I guess. It's Renaissance day, remember?"

"I remember that I've never participated in such humiliating activities."

Confused by Anna and her mother's aggressive dialogue, Jessica suggested, "I think she looks right out of a fairytale."

"Thank you, Jessica," Anna said, jabbing at her mother's overly disapproving gaze.

"I don't know how this is going to work, but Romney might need a babysitter after our meet and greet."

"Today?"

"Yeah, right after our meet and greet. You're available, right?"

"Today?" Julianne repeated.

"Yeah, right..."

"Yeah, yeah, right after your meet and greet."

"So, you'll need to drop me off and pick me up, I think. I've already put the car seat in the car for you," Anna said, smiling at her full-length reflection in the closet mirror.

"Should I get dressed as your hand maid then?" Julianne quipped sarcastically.

"No, that would be a little over the top wouldn't you say, Jessica?" Anna replied, disclosing a smile to the frail girl sitting on her plush bed.

Julianne walked to the door, saying, "I'm not getting out of the car with you dressed like that, 'Renaissance' or any other day for that matter." Making it to the stairs, she asked, "When did you have time to put the child seat in the car?"

"Early this morning," Anna unashamedly shouted back.

"But he didn't ask you to babysit till just a few moments ago. And not even you, me!" Julianne pointed out, appearing back at the white trimmed opening.

"You said, 'Yes.'"

"I said no such thing," Julianne corrected with a dissenting air.

"Oops."

"Oops yeah," Julianne echoed, but her consternation turned into a smile.

Anna perceived the shared excitement from her mother's candid grin.

"I'll be off then, well...hmm."

"What no fish then?" Julianne protested.

"You're dropping me off, right?"

"Right. Jessica though, I'm sure she's hungry."

"She should come too," Anna arbitrarily said without hesitation.

"I don't want to interfere."

"Oh, you wouldn't be interfering, Jessica. We'll eat on campus while Anna here attends her fairytale themed meet and greet," Julianne explained. "My treat...or more so we'll use Anna's meal voucher things; don't worry." Her guest shyly smiled her thanks, tucking away her apprehension. "It's like you planned all this," Julianne said, directing her charge to the tulle clad princess that proudly paraded through the bedroom door.

"I'd call the car seat thing more anticipation than planning. I wouldn't want to leave little April behind if I could help it,"

Anna begrudgingly hinted after marching passed her mother's post in the hallway.

Julianne looked for sympathy from Jessica Patsy, who had attentively stood up from her seat on the bed like a deer watching traffic on a highway. "She's still a teenager, you know that, right? This 'adultness' of hers is new."

"She'll figure it out," Jessica replied, unsure of what to say.

"Oh, I hope so, she already thinks she has."


## Part 2 - Chapter Ten


Spencer rotated the key of his car, killing the engine. With his contained intrigue, he confidently crossed the Vern Hill campus under the spread of trees. Smiling a few times in passing, he kept a watchful eye on the students. Some students walked in pairs and some alone. A few sat at the outdoor cafeteria tables, eating. After a few minutes of his meandering, he timed his pace to a certain student on a converging track. He trailed behind the student that he guessed to be returning to his dormitory. Casually, he fit in and took advantage of the unsuspecting student. The student smiled as he swiped his key through the reader and hoisted the door open in courtesy to Spencer, allowing the actor to trespass ahead. Spencer turned sideways tipping his ball cap in thanks to the student, while fully cognizant of the security camera he shunned with his backside. "You done for the day?"

"Nah, only for a bit," the naive student answered.

"Too bad they don't let us carry swords around campus, huh?" Spencer said cynically, staggering backwards.

"Ha, I'm sure they'd think sectarian clashes would ensue if they ever did."

"Complete and utter chaos, no doubt," Spencer said indifferently, having achieved his objective. He continued down the corridor branching off from the student. Halfway down the hall he tapped, waited, transacted, and left as confidently as he had come with his back to the camera. As he rounded the corner to the left of Swanson Hall, the roadway rushed with commuting cars.

"Hey, what are you doing here?" a voice challenged him in passing.

"Oh, hi...Erica, right?"

"You guess that from my name tag, for all you know my real name could be Jill; you're not attending classes here yet, are you?" Erica suspected.

"No, but I will be in the fall. I just wanted to tour around the campus today to find my bearings."

"Well, the tours are conducted from the registrar's office across the lawn in the building closest to the parking lot; other than that, you need an escort and a visitor's badge to walk around," Erica instructed.

"Would you escort me to the office? I didn't know."

Nervous in her composure, she looked toward her destination then back to the awkward confrontation and agreed, "Okay, but I don't have much time." The actor kept up with Erica, keeping his hands sheepishly concealed in his pockets.

"So, what are you here studying?" Spencer questioned after a half-minute of her hurried pace.

"Linguistic Anthro...language," Erica answered, trying to maintain simultaneous haste and blitheness. "What about you...in the fall?" Erica compulsorily returned.

"I was thinking History," Spencer said as he stepped up to open the registrar's door obediently.

"Well, you're here, you can sign up for a tour now," Erica said.

Flustered from his rejected courtesy, Spencer piped, "Okay; hey, how do you know Anna?" His attractive escort warped her tall neck around and she looked at him as if caught in deceit. "You two seemed close at the cafe," Spencer rationalized.

"Class; have a good tour." Erica contritely answered to avoid further disclosure.

"Thanks, Jill," Spencer said, using her defensiveness to subconsciously entertain himself. Spencer entered the office and joined a short line. After reservedly scanning the room and the people in line, he glanced over his shoulder to ensure his escort had vanished. Then feigning a misplaced item, he smiled arrogantly and escaped the trap. After twenty steps of his

freedom, with a solid blip of his heart, Spencer stopped with
surprise, seeing what looked like Anna less than thirty yards
away. Spencer took three steps toward the sky-blue dressed girl,
but he froze up as he reviewed her posture. He coolly rolled off
his excitement by making friendly eye contact with a nearby
biker and moved around to a shady bench. He sat down and
pulled out his phone as an excuse to loiter, hoping to see why
Anna stood waiting. He enamored himself over the silliness of
her bell-shaped costume with its conservative rectitude, and how
the sleeves covered her two bent elbows. Smartly, he divided his
attention among other scattered students to avoid drawing any
suspicion. This act lasted for ten minutes before the charade got
old. "Goodness kill me already, how long has she been waiting?"
Spencer coarsely asked himself like a grumbling union worker.
Trying to reestablish his fancy of surprising Anna, he looked
around and found two birds chirping and striking at each other
in contest over some discarded food. Spencer heard a crescendo
approaching from behind him, and at the hum's peak, a golf cart
whined at full speed around the corner. The grounds keeper at
the wheel whirled by, and Spencer watched him until he heard
the brakes warble to a stop in front of the cafeteria. Then
surprised and confused, Spencer tried to clear his eyes, and he
flashed back to locate the first Anna, thinking he had somehow
originally mistaken her identity. Careening back to the two girls
he saw sidestepping the golf cart, his mind latched on to solving
the conundrum. "Twins?"

Anna saw an approaching taxicab, but having built up so much
anticipation, she had to think twice to bring Romney Daniels'
image to mind.

As the taxi pulled up snuggly to the curbside the door opened,
and two little feet energetically hit the sidewalk. "But daddy, it's
a princess, a real princess."

"And a real street, my little lady."

"Is she going to disappear, daddy?"

"No, April, not if she's real; okay, go ask her if she'll play with
you," Romney said, smiling at Anna. Turning around, he
addressed a few words to the cab driver who seemed to
understand the last-minute instruction, and the driver pulled

away from the designated drop off area. Romney found April already hugging Anna.

Not more than an edge of a second later did April let go and proclaimed her action to her father's enjoyment. "I hugged her, daddy! Did you see me hug her?" April emphasized like a talking play doll.

"Yes, I did. What's her name, Pearl?" Romney suggestively asked his dear daughter.

"I don't know what her name is," April honestly confessed, losing a sparkle of pride in her acknowledgement.

"She says so many words; I'm so impressed," Anna insisted.

"They say she's advanced for her age," Romney replied.

"Daddy?"

"Oh, and Julianne, it's good to see you again, and thank you for lending me your daughter's services," Romney greeted Julianne as she approached.

"And who is this?" Julianne petitioned, overcome with giddy-gaga. She stooped down to April's eye level and tried introducing herself.

"Daddy?"

"This is my daughter," Romney said, answering the obvious. "April, do you want to say hi to Ms. Julianne?" Romney encouraged to his suddenly shy child.

"I like your pigtails, April; they're even prettier than I imagined," Julianne asserted patiently from her squatting position. After April further buried her face into the pocket formed in Romney's dress pants, she revealed a sliver of her bright blue eye, so Julianne instinctively initiated the long bygone game by hiding her face in her hands.

"So, is this afternoon going to work out?" Romney asked generally in Anna's direction.

Julianne joyfully accepted the indirect request, "It sure is, the car seat's already to go. I'd keep this adorable one forever."

"Daddy?" April pleaded, cranking her head up to beg for attention.

"What, Pearl? Do you want to play with Ms. Julianne today?" Romney asked, sinking to the popular level to lend his ear.

"No."

"You don't?"

"What's her name?" April questioned childishly.

"Ms. Julianne, and she wants to play with you this afternoon while I finish work."

"Noo...the princess."

"What's the princess's name?"

"Yes," April said, affirming her aim by vacating her hiding spot. "That one."

"Why don't you ask her," Romney encouraged a second time.

"No, she's pretty."

"She's pretty? That's all the more reason to ask her."

"April," Anna beckoned conservatively, bending down to speak.

"See, she knows your name," Romney reasoned.

"This is my mother, if you play with her for a little while, then I'll come and play with you; deal?"

"Dear, she's two-years-old," Julianne objected.

"And a smart one too; so, what do you say, April?" Anna said in defense. "Deal?"

"Deeal," April giggled at the sound of the word, merrily tossing her arms out from her torso.

"My name's Anna, and I'm going to babysit you once in a while, 'kay, Pearl?

"That's what my daddy calls me," April observed.

Anna glanced up at Romney for approval, but at that moment Jessica brought Anna's purse in range so Anna could hear her muffled phone ringing. "Hello?" Anna answered, finding the phone in time.

"Gotcha!"

"Who is this?"

"Look up."

Anna obeyed, looking into the freckled trees.

"Spencer, who else? Are we on for Friday?" Spencer said, relieving the suspense.

"Spencer! Sure, I don't see you; are you here?" Anna asked, still trying to uncover the specter from the shadows.

"Great, oh man, that's great, we'll talk later then. I see you're kind of busy; I don't want to intrude."

"No, no if you'll wait a minute, you can walk me to class," Anna offered, noting a strange look on Jessica's face.

"I'd be honored; I'll wait here."

"Wherever here is, okay-bye," Anna said, laughing at her inability to see her admirer. Anna hung up her phone to find the closing of the conversation as Romney waved at the taxicab that had realigned itself with the drop off point.

"This will work great. Thanks for the help! Work is cramming in like the usual, and oh, I was going to ask, – I feel bad – are you available tomorrow morning?" Romney surveyed, having returned to converse with Anna.

"Sure, what time?"

"Well, I lost Sandy again."

"Lost her?"

"Oh, your guess is as good as mine; if she shows up, I'll call you. You know how to get to Washington Street, right?"

"Oh yeah, blindfolded," Anna claimed, seeing Romney smile at the joke. "Well, that might be a little far-fetched."

"Oh no, I'm sure there's a built-in compass rose to that dress somewhere."

Anna blushed, saying with a false air of nativity, "That's why I wear a battery pack on my ankle." Anna lifted the bell of her dress enough to reveal a shimmering shoe, as Romney waited for her punch line. "You see the wiring is sewn into the fringe, and...I don't know what I'm saying," Anna admitted, laughing to ease her surging embarrassment.

"No, I'm right with you; run a current through a coil and make a magnet. Hey, is that your friend?"

"Oh, Spencer; he didn't want to intrude," Anna said, finding the friend Romney had detected at the tree line. "There he is."

"Hey, I'll let you go; I so...appreciate tomorrow. Don't keep your friend waiting; take care." Romney said, pulling himself toward Julianne who was already escorting April to the child-seat-clad car.

Anna followed for a few steps and watched Romney oversee the loading of his daughter as Jessica made motioning suggestions to Julianne from the front passenger seat.

"You know April's going to make you wear that dress, right?" Romney shouted on returning to his chauffeured ride, pausing long enough to see Anna's understanding reaction.

After two swings of her shoulders, she spun about on one foot, and meandered toward the cafeteria. Oblivious to her surroundings, Spencer playfully draped his arm over her shoulder. Lifting her shoulders to convey her discomfort, Anna entertained his electric questions about the sky-blue dress, the themed event, the buzzing campus, and the puzzling double-take.

## Part 2 - Chapter Eleven

"Hello...Julianne!" Romney said, warmly greeting the unfamiliar voice. "I'm finishing now...no, you don't have to feed her. I'll be out the door here...," Romney said and listened to Julianne's assertion over his office phone line. "I meant I'll come to your place to pick up April. What? Anna? Well tell her...oh, I know she won't change her mind. Yeah, it would help me out for sure. I'd save a few bucks and precious minutes driving, but won't that be inconvenient for you guys?" Romney asked, leaning back at his desk and visually acknowledging Saundra's presence in the doorway. "Anna? Okay. What time?" Romney asked. "Do you know where Butler's Station is? Right across the street. Yes...well, let me know how I can repay you. I know I'll be calling again. I'm glad she behaved. Sure, bye-now," Romney said, instinctively moving his office phone back to the receiver.

"I know you're about to head out. Here's the limousine reservation – assuming the trip tomorrow hasn't been rescheduled after the meeting – Michael Gallant called and offered a wordy apology, I printed the expired proposal you had me format and edit last year, and did Sandy ever call or show up?" Saundra asked after orating the string of last-minute details of the day.

"No, and I'll be hot on your trail. Oh, you're the expert here, what would you suggest for binding or keeping all of Mitchell's papers together?"

"A parcel envelope."

"It won't get mailed?"

"No, just a blank one," Saundra assured, walking out of the office and returning with an orange blank office envelope. "See, no postage, and we will write on the front: 'Mitchell Reed's Restructuring Proposal,'" Saundra said, obeying her own suggestions.

"That's great. Thanks," Romney said graciously, manipulating the large document into the confining package. Before he succeeded, his private phone rang.

"Hello, Romney Daniels," Romney said after answering the phone. "There shouldn't be insufficient funds," Romney defended with concern. "How much is she trying to withdraw at once? I didn't know there were limits," Romney admitted, grabbing a pen and paper in anticipation of taking notes. Interrupting his finger's intent, he conveyed, "Sandy is authorized on the account, is she there now? Is she in danger? I mean you seem to be hinting at there being something strange going on. Like I said, I don't – from my understanding of how it all works – need to authorize the transaction," Romney objected, squeezing his eyebrow muscles. "I understand; go ahead and do it. Unless you think she's in danger or under the control or influence of somebody else, in that case...well, why don't you call her into an office or privately ask her. Sure, the manager...tell you what, I will authorize the transaction for her. Just do the full ten thousand and hand her a twenty-dollar bill and tell her it's from me. Well, then do it as a second transaction, you can run it on her card, yes. Well, then tell her that her husband would like her to withdraw an extra twenty dollars, and whether she does or not, she'll get the message," Romney said, creatively navigating the repetitive hurdles. His tidy secretary peeked her head into the office one last time to say farewell and departed. "Okay, thank you for the call," Romney said, waving to acknowledge Saundra's departure. He clicked through a list of e-mails, read and replied to a bold highlighted one in the list and routinely rounded up the work scattered on his desk. Passing through the pipelined walkway toward the exiting elevator he exchanged a few words with Theresa about the next day's departure.

Theresa enthused, "George is coming!"

"I know. He's got to be excited," Romney magnified as he rounded the corner into Mitchell Reed's unmanageable cubical.

"Hey," Romney said, holding up the packaged document to gain Mitchell's attention. "I didn't have time to look into this at all today, but I'll try to get to it before the week's end."

Mitchell, obviously distracted by another task, didn't answer or change his blank expression.

"I'll see you late Thursday or Friday, and we will talk it over; don't work too late."

Mitchell replied some unintelligible words while refocusing on his work, letting Romney progress toward the awaiting lobby and curbside. Once curbside, Romney looked at his decorative watch and determined that he had a few minutes to wait. He waved off the taxicab that approached to claim the regular trip. Smelling the scent of the Italian restaurant across the street, he rashly decided that food might be a meaningful thanks to the Purses for their superfluous kindness. The pause between the two traffic lights also pushed him to spontaneously commit to the luring destination. With a firm grip on his portfolio and orange package, he hustled across the four-lane drag and entered the carry out door of Butler's Station where the friendly counter manager greeted him and assisted him. As usual, the spanakopita was sold out for the day, so Romney settled on April's favorite snack of chick-peas instead.

Wrapping the warm brown carry out bag over onto itself twice, he reversed his course and laughed at the passing of the familiar red sedan. A second taxicab pulled up to his curbside at the improvised signal of his raised food bag. Again, waving off the second vendor with an indiscernible apology, Romney crossed the street again to wait for his ride home to circle around the block.

"Hey, were you waiting long?" Anna asked Romney from her lowered passenger window.

"Not at all," Romney replied, trying to discern with his expression which door he should enter. "I saw you all swing by. I'm sorry; I had gone to Butler's to pick up these Peppery Chickpeas. They always throw in fresh bread. Any takers?" Romney advertised. After a few curious looks, Romney asked, "Mind if I break into them myself?"

"Please do," Anna invited responsively, cracking the bond of silence. "That's right; you know the chef you said at the fundraiser."

"He's a character, you'll know if you meet him."

"I could tell from your brief exchange before Terrance tugged me to the dance floor." The mentioning of Terrance momentarily sent each of the passengers to their own private recollections of that night.

"Daddy, can I have some?" April asked, humming the last syllable weakly as if her tepidness was the key to unlocking the food bag.

"Sure, Pearl, how many would you like?"

"Two," April said after thinking through her answer. Her two little fingers proudly proved her excitement.

"How about five at a time?" Romney countered.

Not understanding how five could be more than two, April hesitantly agreed.

Anna queried Romney for assurance of her driving direction as he opened the appetizing bag. "You can cross here and go the state road, or you can work your way through the city," Romney optioned, subconsciously holding a pointing finger up to his preference of the bridge crossing. The freckled arms of the driver followed Romney's suggested lead.

Then halfway across the bridge to the state road, Anna asked, "May I try some chick peas?"

"Of course, you certainly qualify."

"They must not be too peppery." Julianne concluded.

"Oh, they're peppery," Anna critiqued.

"Here, try some," Romney said, lifting the bag over his shoulder without turning around to address Julianne.

"No thanks. I'm surprised that April likes them if they're so spicy; Anna never did. In fact, you should watch Anna carefully to make sure she doesn't go into anaphylactic shock," Julianne said, shifting to her characteristic contest.

"Mom!" Anna objected, and leaning toward Romney, assured, "I'm not allergic, I mean I might not care for garbanzo beans, nor any non-green bean in general, but I'm not allergic."

"Good to know."

"I mean these are great, thank you," Anna apologized, her cheeks swelling to the color of her straightened hair as she turned the wheel onto the state road.

"Bread?" Romney offered. "It's kind of rudimentary; do you like bread?"

"If it's soft," Anna honestly testified.

"French bread from an Italian joint that serves Greek food. It's soft inside," Romney optimistically proposed.

Anna shared an encouraging laugh and said, "Sure break me off a piece."

"Oh, it comes in slices, so long as you don't mind me handling it."

"No, that's fine."

"Here, I'll even rip off the crust; you do like non-green bread, don't you?"

Laughing erupted from the back seat, capturing the duo's attention. Julianne excused her outburst by saying, "I think April would like another five spicy garbanzo beans."

April added with a little uncertainty, "Peas."

"So polite, aren't you, dear," Julianne said, selecting five more chickpeas from the opened bag. Her daughter directed the car with her directional memory, rounding the final curve onto Washington Street.

Romney hopped out into the street after Anna partially turned the car into the driveway. "Here's for babysitting, driving, gas, and the hassle," Romney established as he handed a single bill to Anna. Sensing resistance, he continued, "Split it with your Mom, if it's too much."

Anna smiled and after subtle movements of her lips, said, "Not bad for a first paycheck."

"You can get back here tomorrow before seven? The car's available and all?" Romney asked with a referencing glance at Julianne who had finished relocating to the front seat.

"Looking forward to it!"

Romney held April in her ruffled dress and sent the babysitting team away before entering the security code for the mail gate. Once inside, feeling the presence of home and her toys, April flew to and hurdled the child gate. Then, obeying the voice of her father, she took her shoes off and matched them together. Romney reclined on the front room couch for a few moments of reprieve, but he recalled his strange phone call at the office and instead searched the garage for a clue of Sandy's whereabouts. With no traces of Sandy having returned home, he returned to his portfolio and cracked open the portfolio with the breakdown of the properties to be assessed over the next two days. Deciding that details wouldn't change his impressions or instincts, he canted his interest to Mitchell's package. Interrupted by the sound of the gate trigger over the security system and April's energized reaction, he set all the material aside in one motion to get up and welcome his wife.

Inconveniently, April stood in the swing of the closed door, and after quickly ushering April out of the way, Romney caught the door before it slammed into the doorstop. Regardless, April began fussing from Romney's restraint, and the distraction drew Romney's tone and facial language into management mode. "Sandy," Romney called imploringly, stopping his wife next to the island counter. "I got a call today; April, go to your room." The two-and-a-half-year-old's fit exploded further, and without parleying further, Romney hoisted April up to his chest and transported her to the toy room and closed the child proofed door. Returning to the stairs he looked up amid the crying screams, hoping to locate Sandy. A clank and a few steps that reverberated from the kitchen changed Romney's course. Talking to Sandy's back, he approached and started anew, "I got a phone call today...Sandy!"

Sandy saw Romney's horrific reaction. "Leave me alone!"

"No, I won't; what happened."

"I said leave me alone!"

"Sandy, I got a phone..., no, you need to go to the hospital. That's not an accident, and even if it was, it needs to be looked at!"

Sandy ignored Romney, and without a word or inch of hesitation, she strode in five determined steps toward the hallway. Romney caught Sandy's thin arm in passing. Scared for an instant, he helplessly watched Sandy react as he had many times taught her, pulling him forward off balance with the rotation of her body toward the granite counter. She unconsciously grabbed the hardest object, the only object worth grabbing, and yelled as he barely caught his equilibrium with his following foot. Nothing was in focus except his black sock losing traction, and Sandy's swinging object...whack. Then Romney's head caught the countertop as he fell to the floor.

# Part 2 - Chapter Twelve

Anna, having already isolated the house key in her lap, flipped over Romney's business card to review the mail gate security code. She surveyed the grass patterns in what looked like a patted down shortcut across the long-bladed turf. Choosing the long road, she walked on the driveway up to the entrance. Two half-moon brick steps rounded the front door. Detecting a faint crying, she knocked lightly. The crying continued, and after a toiling minute, she decided to knock more forcefully. Deducing that no one should be sleeping, she touched the illuminated doorbell and started listening for something other than the faint crying. As seconds marched by like an invading army, Anna could barely restrain her yearning to minister to the child. She rang the doorbell firmly, hearing its ding-dong chime inside of the house, and April continued her unsuccessful call for attention. Rattling the key that she had attached to a simple chain, she tried thinking of her options. April's distress continued but gradually shifted to a more tolerable pattern with pauses. The change encouraged Anna to ring once more, and she listened even more intently for any movement or footsteps in the house. After asking the slight breeze, "Hello, is anyone home?" she took a deep breath and decided in a moment to act. Inserting the key to open the beautiful door, she heard the bolt click open as she nervously twisted her hand. "Romney? Mrs. Daniels? ...April?" she announced with her light steps, hoping for an immediate explanation. "April? This is Anna," Anna spoke toward the sniffling sound behind the closed front room door. Tapping rhythmically to signal her intent of opening the door, Anna's arm, that held the handle, burned with adrenaline. The pathetic face glistened under the covering of tears and crushed Anna's heart as she softly shrunk to the floor. The precious girl wiped her short sniffle with the long back stretch of her arm.

"Where's your dad, April?" Anna asked softly.

"He didn't close my window."

"He didn't? Would you like me to close it now?" Anna offered, but April started crying uncontrollably anew with deep heaves. She helplessly hugged up to April, wrapping her arms as best she could around the child and smelling the odor from April's backside as she did. The blond child didn't resist, and Anna tried to ignore her senses. "Would you help me look for your dad?" Anna asked. While the proposition shot a full dose of fear up her spine, the question seemed calming to April. Stepping over the gate ahead of April, she hoisted up her little friend who welcomed the help with two raised arms. Anna pattered behind April who ran instinctively toward the last place she had seen her parents together.

"Oh goodness no. April!" Anna quailed on sight, unable to restrain the child.

"Daddy...wake up, daddy," April suggested with a turn of optimistic innocence.

In a whirlwind of uncertainty, Anna tried to remove April from having playfully saddled Romney's motionless repose. She nervously gave up, combing her hair with all ten fingers as she lost control of her breathing. "April honey, Pearl, you need to get off," Anna said, quaking as her eyes swelled.

"I want to sit on my daddy, it's how I wake him up when the sun comes up," April confided, incapable of seeing the oddity of her dad sleeping in the kitchen.

"Okay dear, but why don't I change your diaper before your daddy wakes up," Anna tried suggesting.

"My daddy will do it, don't worry princess." The princess in Anna tried to smile at April's cheeriness but could only see her own hand visibly shaking. "Daddy, wake up. Do I need to tickle you?"

Anna quickly bent down and placed her hand peacefully on Romney's back, wondering if he was breathing. Dark black blood matted the hair on part of his crown. "Romney," Anna investigated nervously five inches away from his ear, gently pushing his shoulder. Her emotion started dripping on the floor next to Romney's head.

"Why are you crying, princess?"

"I'm not...I am, Pearl, because I don't know what to do," Anna confessed. More tears rolled off her flush cheek. She apologetically wiped a drop off Romney's shirt with the cuff of her loose cotton jacket.

"Why don't you call somebody. That's what mommy does when she feel's sad," April said, seeming to become sensitive to Anna's disposition. Taking it upon her own shoulders to remedy the situation, April climbed off Romney's back, and began pulling off his socks. "It's time to wake up, daddy!" April commanded and struggled.

Anna retracted her hand and replaced it as a strange sensation alerted her palm. Bending down even farther she held as still as she could, trying to convince herself that, Romney's lower back had risen and fallen at least one time. Realizing April continued to tug at Romney's bare toes, Anna gathered enough sense from the pause to hurry back toward the play room. Seeing the phone on the far kitchen wall she veered in subconscious obedience to April's recommendation. "Hi, hello," her voice quivered. "Um, I need help. I, I, I don't know. It's the mansion on...68 Washington Street; I, I don't know if the address is right. The house of Romney Daniels. He's not moving. Anna Purse; I babysit his daughter. Sh, she's here, yes. Okay." Anna took a deep breath at the instruction of the dispatcher, and after she finished releasing all the air in her lungs, she heard distant sirens start to blare. The siren signaled hope in her heart, and her foresight reignited. "I'll open the gate...don't be rash, okay; I'll be right back."

"I hear a fire truck, daddy, I'm going to go look, okay? I'll be right back too," April assured, bolting obliviously to the couch in the front room.

Frantically on mission, Anna opened the empty garage and hastily scanned the walls of the opening garage in hopes of finding some keypad or button to control the gate. With a long draw the sirens began to amplify. One glance back and the words appeared as if by providence: "Security Gate Inc." She pressed the same gate code. Nothing changed. Then she found more words printed on a label below the keypad as she felt her forehead get hot: "Press pound." She pressed pound. Nothing changed. The siren began to wind up again then shut off half way up its deafening scale. She punched the code and pound key in a desperate last attempt and turned around in time to see three fire fighters emerge in partial gear as well as the driveway gate swinging open. Her frightened face spoke for her, and in the absence of her words, two of the volunteers separated and quickly entered the house. The third fighter remained and started talking to Anna. Then, remembering April, Anna left the courteous volunteer mid-sentence and reentered the house. The two volunteers labored on Romney, who had been flipped over to face the ceiling. With one volunteer barking indistinguishable commands, the other volunteer responded by running out of the garage door. Anna thought she saw Romney's eyes open while rounding the far side of the kitchen island to join her little friend on the living room couch. They peered together with fascination at the rotating lights and saw three more emergency vehicles arrive. Anna noted a gurney skillfully fly out of an ambulance at the hands of two workers while a police officer impeded a neighbor that had approached to question the raucous. When Anna's sense of smell returned to her, she asked, "April, where does your dad usually change your diaper?" and felt suddenly lethargic.

"Up there's, are you going to change my diaper?" April responded, overemphasizing the tail of the question.

"Show me where, and I will."

"Okay," April consented, climbing off the couch one leg at a time and running to grab the railing of the staircase.

Making a mess of the mess, Anna finally finished the diaper change by helping April wash her hands. She observed April's lighthearted smacking of the water as it flowed around the sink bowl. "Okay that's enough, let's go down and see if your dad's awake." Anna remembered the two questions, the name of the hospital and the last word. The rest of the event felt like a faint dream. "Yes, I will look after her; okay, let me find a pen. He's alive?"

"Yes, but quite disoriented from being unconscious."

"How did you guys get here so fast?" Anna asked to ask something. Without hearing or understanding the reply, she finished filling out the short form with her contact information and quickly tried to re-read the form as she handed it back. Then the final volunteer left through the garage, and the firetruck coasted away.

April fell asleep for a nap a minute or two before a lady named Felicity arrived with a few curious questions. Then shortly after Felicity left, Anna gave way to her own fatigue on the front living room couch.

## Part 2 - Chapter Thirteen

"Hey Anna!"

"Romney?"

"Yes, is April with you?"

"Yes, yes, hey, you scared me!" Anna excitedly scolded.

"Yes, sorry...I'm naturally fit for that job; hey, is Sandy there?"

"No...no she never was; are you okay?"

"Never better. Hey, I have a big favor to ask. The doctor here won't release me, and I need the information from a folder and portfolio I left on my sofa in the living room, I guess last night...it is Wednesday today, right? ...and my cell phone," Romney energetically petitioned Anna, hinting at the gravity of the request in his voice.

"Sure."

"Hey, what room am I in? She's going to bring them to me – one sec' Anna – yeah, okay," Romney said from his end of the bedside hospital phone. "Three-fourteen, that's the third floor, room fourteen at UMC Hope downtown."

"Okay."

"Oh, that would be great. I'll take you out for lunch to make it up to you. Wherever you want to go."

"Okay."

"And take your time, because at this rate I'll be here all night and all day tomorrow; you're not looking for a job, are you? 'Cause I'd hire you in a heartbeat."

"Oh, I just landed one that I like, but thanks for the offer," Anna responded, unable to avoid absorbing Romney's spirit.

"Oh," Romney laughed. "Now where is it?"

"What's that?" Anna asked.

"I forgot where I put it...my cell phone charger; if you could...."

"Oh, right."

"No clue," Romney admitted, after a contemplative pause.

"That's okay. I'll snoop around the house for it, if that's fine with you."

"Certainly. But be careful. If you find any needles or strange pouches; there's a sharp objects disposal bin on the wall in the hallway bathroom. You can't miss it. Call me back if you can't find it," Romney said in rapid tempo before hanging up the phone.

"Okay," Anna agreed and rolled off the couch. She saw the two mentioned business items on the arm rest of the opposite sofa, and carefully gathered the items after a five-o-clock yawn. Waking up a little more, she stepped over to place the requested papers on the foyer table. Attracted to the lonely silver framed photograph that occupied it, she picked it up and appreciated the tarnished grooves and polished ridges with her thumb. Then hearing April's stirring, she appreciated two other family pictures as she ascended to the second floor. After greeting the two-year-old, she conversed about their planned trip to the hospital as she wandered about in search of the phone charger.

"Poke."

"What are you doing?" Anna said with her eyes still set on the mission.

"Poking you," April said, giggling as she followed Anna.

"Why are you poking me? – Hi, Mr. Daniels, you must like to keep track of time with all these watches of yours...the bathroom? No, I haven't looked there yet. Sure, give me a second. – Oww, April that hurt," Anna said, grabbing April's hand to prevent another jab. "No, she's just poking me for fun with a hair pin," Anna explained, traveling to the upstairs hallway bathroom. "Friday? I think I'm kind of dating someone this Friday. How about the weekend?" Anna shyly asserted, finding the spaghetti string charger loosely wrapped in the corner of the bathroom vanity. "Of course, family first. You know, you were right; here it is. – April what's wrong?" The child's teary eyes and frozen expression of guilt grabbed Anna's attention. "I don't know. I'll ask – April, are you okay?" Anna asked, setting the charger down on the hallway carpet. After opening her arms, April's cry began to boil into sobs on Anna's shoulder. "I don't know, but I think she was sensitive to my reaction or she thought that she hurt me with the hairpin," Anna reasoned to Romney. "Yeah, it'll probably be thirty minutes to an hour before we get there," Anna said, speaking the first guesstimate that came to her mind. "No, I don't have anything to do for the rest of the day," Anna laughed at Romney's overly concerned rhetoric.

Hanging up the phone and reclaiming the charger, Anna rose to her feet with April clinging to her neck. Anna felt the warmth of April's breath through the shoulder of her loose jacket. Carefully stepping to not bounce the child, she saw a pair of individuals walking outside the hedge and on down the street. She stopped for a moment while swaying the hiccupping child. "Look, look, April, there's a deer."

April responsively twisted around in Anna's arms to see. "The people?" April questioned.

"No, a deer by the trees. See how it's lifting its head, looking for predators, and it's watching the people walk by; do you see it?"

"Does it see the people?"

"Oh, and there's a fawn; it's really little right behind it! You probably don't see the baby deer, do you," Anna said, carefully starting down the stairs one step at a time.

"I want to see the baby deer," April eagerly said, releasing Anna's neck to pursue her interest.

"April not here; wait till we're at the bottom of the stairs, please."

"But I want to see the baby deer too!"

"April, please hold on," Anna pleaded, knowing that she didn't have the firmest hold of April's slipping dress.

April insisted, and Anna managed to set April steadily onto her feet halfway down the steps. Then the focused two-year-old began carefully stepping down the stairs as fast as her method would allow. Jumping off the bottom step and landing on both feet, she headed straight to the couch and clambered up to the window. "I don't see it, princess. The baby deer's gone!"

"Well, not from this angle, the hedge is in the way; but, why don't we get your shoes on, and I'll walk you across the street where we can look together."

"Otay," April said, belly-riding off the couch onto the floor and running with equal intensity to the kitchen to retrieve her little slip on shoes.

Anna followed to accomplish the same feat, gathering her personal gear and the requested items for Romney. As the bolt locked behind the girls, the younger, in her passionate hurry, ran and stopped suddenly to ensure her princess friend had not abandoned her. Hustling a few more yards across the grass, she repeated her pause to check Anna's progress. With one last dash, April shook the iron gate and peered through the rails only to view the impediment of Anna's red car. "Can I see the baby deer now?" April asked anxiously as her overseer unsecured the mail gate.

"We'll see; if it's still there you'll be able to see it," Anna assured, looking both ways before leading her trusting companion into the street. "It might be gone though. No, look it's in the trees. Do you see its head, well not the baby deer, but the momma dear?"

"Is the baby deer there too?"

"I don't see it."

"You don't see it anywhere?"

"No, I'm sorry, April, do you mind if I call you Pearl like your dad does?"

"Can I pet it?" April asked, setting out into the knee-high grass assuming the answer to be yes.

"This one's not to pet, April; can I call you Pearl?" Anna blindly petitioned, loading the bundled papers and personal belongings into the front passenger seat. "Why don't you come and climb into your car seat, and we'll go see your dad. I'll even let you carry his phone charger."

"No, I just want to pet the deer; otay?" came the distancing voice.

"April, there's thistles and bramble weeds all through there; I can see them. Come out, please."

"It's otay. I have shoes," April confidently asserted, pointing down and awkwardly as she lifted up one of her feet to display the evidence. The simple action caused her to lose her balance, and she clumsily sat down on a thicket of weeds. Her babysitter hastened her pursuit through the unevenly cut swaths of grass to prevent any deeper progress. "I don't see the baby deer," April further acknowledged from Anna's arms. "Did they go look for pre-dators now?"

"No, they don't go looking for predators; they look out for predators, so if they see one coming, they can run away!" Anna said with childlike animation as she turned toward the car.

"Like I run away from my daddy," April giggled at her contrived parallel.

"No, not exactly. The predator wants to eat the deer...how do I explain?"

"The predator wants to eat the deer for dinner?" April completed Anna's outrageous statement. "No, that's naughty," she rhetorically concluded, wrinkling her nose with disbelief.

"Well, it's not naughty, it's just that...it's just...that the predator doesn't want the same thing the mother deer wants. And the momma deer knows that if she doesn't look out for predators, that the predators will probably hurt her baby," Anna explained, feeling satisfied with her deconstructive, but age appropriate, answer.

## Part 2 - Chapter Fourteen

Anna clung to her book and her notepad as she walked along the brick pathway. The thoughts of dating by and far overshadowed the lecture, the chatter, and even the hunger all brought on by her late morning class. She flowed through the busy lunch line, having pinned the thin textbook and class notes under her arm. She scanned the students around her, wondering if Spencer would appear again to surprise her. Without knowing Spencer's agenda, she halved her usual sandwich order and forewent the complimentary sides. Settling into a busy spot, she ate at a pace designed to pass the time while devoting as much of her attention as possible to scouting. After a change of students, specifically one that vacated the space to her side, her eager attention slowly shifted to a novice artist and his energetic sketching one seat away from her. Oblivious to the world, the artist drew his imagination onto the paper. Slowly small faces formed on the white pad. Enjoying her undetected perch, she forgot about her plans for the day and instead began guessing at the next movements of the artist's pencil. He periodically grabbed a rubber eraser, and taking gentle care, he touched it to the page at a quarter of the rate he did the pencil. Anna couldn't tell the point where one image finished and the next one started, but she watched the collage grow in a clockwise direction around the page. With the second book-matched page filled with graphite to the short satisfaction of the artist, he paused to smile for a moment and looked briefly around the lunch room. He hesitated though when he saw his female audience. The artist tried to refocus, but his pencil looked as if it had nowhere to go on the page. Another nervous smile in Anna's direction pricked Anna to blush. "I'm sorry if I interrupted you," Anna said, shifting her eyes between his knuckles and the frames of his glasses.

"Don't be, if I wanted my ideas to be secret, I didn't pick a very good place or time to put them down on paper," the artist crackled, trying to find his voice.

"What's the project?"

"The project? Oh nothing," the artist downplayed, tapping his utensil rapidly on the solid table.

"Whatever! You either have a beautiful brain that's vying to be seen, or you have some purpose for drawing that emphatically."

"Nah, it's all silly stuff," the artist denounced and closed the small drawing pad to hide his embarrassment.

Feeling sorry for her intrusion, Anna looked back to her last few bites of sandwich. After a moment, she pulled in another breath to speak and turned to find the artist shyly retreating with his notepad and creative tool in hand. "Hey!" Anna called out in a detaining attempt.

"Hey Anna, you didn't eat already, did you? Because I'm taking you out; you know that, right?"

"Spencer!" Anna said impulsively. She wanted to jump up and hug her date but felt a sudden burst of reluctance.

Sitting down sideways in the chair next to her and partially blocking her into her fixed seat, Spencer placed his elbow on the table to support his chin. "So, you ready for an evening of excitement?"

Noticing that Spencer had dabbed a touch of effort into his appearance, which subtly improved his look and smell, Anna replied, "An evening? It hasn't struck noon yet."

"An evening. You're not busy, are you? I'm mean, Friday night is a given, but you got to seize the day too, right?" His rosy date showed confidence and rotated her exposed knees toward him. Spencer stood up and brushed up against her arm to relieve her of her tray.

"Oh, thank you," Anna said modestly, rising to her feet after releasing the tray.

"Why you're welcome, my lady," Spencer sublimed, overdoing an old-fashioned bow. "...Or is Renaissance day over?" he asked, looking up with his head.

"My chivalrous lad, catch me if you can, for your charm has brought me to faint," Anna teased and collapsed playfully back into her seat, letting her head faint onto her forearm.

"Medic!" Spencer yelled, causing Anna to upright herself with alarm. "Come on. Let's get out of here," he shifted, accepting the immediate punishment of Anna's scowling eyes and flaring cheeks.

---

"Rom, you're a hard one to track down," Jeff Dunnire exclaimed, meeting Romney as he exited the reconnaissance team's return shuttle.

"I have all the info in a folder upstairs, what's the lens for?"

"Hold still. Did you downgrade your travel budget recently?" Jeff asked after taking a flash-less photo.

"No, I was supposed to go to Philly and Morestown on a survey, when this happened," Romney said, motioning a halo over his head.

"Yeah, this...tell me about 'this' please, because I learned from my wife, who heard from Janice, who heard from Theresa, that 'this'...wasn't an accident," Jeff spoke with a teasing air of frustration.

"Ah, I deserved it."

"No, you didn't, if I might say so, not at least from what I heard. And domestic violence is a very serious issue, especially when it comes to custody of children. And the scales unfortunately aren't tipped in your favor."

"I mean, I remember grabbing her, and she responded how I taught her, jerk, smash, run," Romney interrupted while he led Jeff through the vaulted lobby of Romney's office building.

"Well, maybe the rumor mill's done its workings. What my wife relayed to me is that you tried to take your wife to the hospital, and she knocked you unconscious," Jeff said, touching the ascending arrow centered on the tile wall.

"That's what I told Theresa."

"Is that what happened?" Jeff inquired with an expression of concern. "You can trust me, Rom. You kind of need to anyway."

"Yeah, honest to goodness."

"You didn't by chance get an earlier picture, did you? Because it's all black up there, but so is your hair, and – other than looking like you have a baby tumor – it doesn't look that bad," Jeff admitted but sensed he had struck too close to a nerve. "Is Sandy okay? How bad was she, or do you even remember?"

"I've never seen anything like it. Vividly, she had a multicolored bruise along her eye cavity. She had her hair concealing most of her face, which was strange, so I can only assume she didn't want me to question," Romney described, nodding his hello to Saundra in passing. "She had just taken ten thousand dollars out of the bank. I know because the bank had called for my approval, citing some in-house requirement for cash withdrawals above five thousand on authorized users."

Jeff took the liberty to shut the door. "I don't want to alarm you, but don't be surprised if you're arrested and hauled off to jail like a criminal."

"Arrested?"

"You grabbed her, didn't you say?"

"With the intention of helping her get help."

"No, no, I'm not accusing you of wrong doing. Her lawyer, if he's crummy like he seems, will take pictures of her injuries and juxtapose it with that testimony, letting a judge infer the rest...to push the divorce case along to his advantage," Jeff quickly explained, leaning forward almost to the point of standing up from his recently seated posture. "You see? Now it's bogus, yes, and it would only stick if the judge was sleeping. But anyway, if you do, get arrested that is, call me! And I mean it, don't worry about April, I'll make all her arrangements. Okay?"

"Well, thank you."

"Whatever time of night," Jeff clarified. "Have you seen her since?"

"Sandy? No," Romney said poignantly.

When Romney electively paused to look out his generously sized window, Jeff moved on, inviting, "So, let's look these documents over."

"Sure," Romney said, moving to gather a file from the built-in shelving on the back wall. "And I didn't get a picture, that I know of, but there's Anna Purse, the babysitter that found me and who called the paramedics. There's the paramedics and the doctor that admitted me...and there's the soon to be string of medical bills, I'm sure, for proof."

Jeff briefly looked up from his initial scan of the folder's contents. Lifting his left cheek into a half-smile, he positively declared, "Don't worry a bit, the law is designed for good people, and you're a good person, Rom, just temporarily immersed in a not so good situation. Have you reconsidered your position?"

"Position? Not a chance, but I'm prepared for the outcome whichever side of the fence the end finds me on," Romney answered, gleaning the context from his glance at the open questionnaire in the folder. "I appreciated your summary page and questionnaire by the way. It was helpful in being able to visualize the processes and reasons and all."

"Hah...you're welcome; I'm sorry, I don't mean to laugh – I know ambiguity is the biggest cause of apprehension, so I'm glad that little summary helped. – I was looking at your listed priorities in the event of a settlement...irony, that's all," Jeff explained, knowing the sincerity and rationality of his friend.

"She's my number one priority, but like I said, 'whichever outcome...,' which is why I continued listing my objectives," Romney reasoned, pinching a silk bookmark that stuck out the bottom of a book on his shelf as he leaned back in his office-chair.

"Well, you listed April seven times after as the remaining objective. Usually both parties are pointing fingers. But you're highly generous, and with your permission," Jeff said, clearing his throat, "I'd like to add a few protective measures, like limited alimony, a trust account for April, seeing that your finances are well off. More than likely the lawyer is contracted to receive the greater share of your estate's settlement, so if we can divert a significant portion to other sheltered places, more money will eventually land where it's supposed to go."

"Okay. But keep my objective in front. My hope is for Sandy, and it will continue to be until the matter is final," Romney said, stopping short of a full objection.

"Tr...."

"Any wording or aggressive posture that's embittering in nature, I don't want; in fact, you can put it this way in your correspondence: 'I don't want to settle; I want Sandy,' no. Nix the negative, 'I want Sandy.'"

"With Sandy you'd get everything."

"Right, weird angle, but right," Romney rallied with a bright countenance.

"Hey! Before I forget, Cheryl and I want to have you over Monday night for dinner. Why the weird day of the week, I don't know, but let me know sometime before Monday night. I won't cook pork, I promise!" Jeff said, jabbing his finger in Romney's direction.

"All right, I'll give Sandy a call and see if we can fit it onto the schedule."

Jeff paused. Then putting off his intuitive dialogue, he smiled and said, "Well, I can't wait to see the both of you, and April's definitely welcome! Though you both might want to enjoy the time unencumbered...'s up to you." Tucking the folder under his left arm, he rose and grabbed the hand of his friend. "I'll let you get back to catching up on work."

"Actually, Anna brought my phone and all of the documents to the hospital that Wednesday, and I telecommuted basically through the entire first part of the survey," Romney explained, escorting his suited friend to the door. "Now Jack told me that he thinks I used the ol' bump-on-the-head excuse to get out of the five plus hours of driving!" Romney said, chatting as his multi-skilled friend stowed the few papers in his briefcase and lifted his briefcase to his shoulder. Then raising his hand to Jeff in farewell, he said, "I'll see you Monday night."

"Monday night, don't forget," Jeff echoed, removing the preoccupation from his face before he disappeared out of Romney's well-lit office.

Saundra sliding a clip over a few sheets of paper followed Romney back into his inner office. After listing a few non-essential items of business, she turned to leave Romney to his work, but stopped short and relayed, "Mitchell stopped by."

"Yeah, I've only made it through a quarter of his material; I thought I'd have time."

"Yeah, he stopped by a little frustrated about all the funding not coming through for the 'tier one approved' expansion proposal."

"The expansion proposal? You're kidding, right? I put that through immediately," Romney said in surprise, giving Saundra all of his attention.

"Uh, well he showed me where you had signed off supposedly, and I took the liberty to use your authorization to disperse the funds this morning," Saundra explained with frozen knees, recognizing the possibility of a grave error.

"That's no big deal. I'm sure he just creatively coined a different label for the grounds restoration project," Romney said, turning his attention away to the face of his desk. Before Saundra took his dismissing cue, he audibly debated, "Though that was last week. Maybe that's what all his big fuss is about; the foreman did mention the contractors haven't broken much ground...well not exactly 'breaking ground,' but kind of in the sense that that's what they're doing...excavation. Sorry, you can

go; I'm just babbling," Romney acknowledged and wrote a
reminder to check accounts on his growing agenda.

## Part 2 - Chapter Fifteen

April Daniels sat on the floor of Anna's room imagining that
the doll dressed in pink had a real appetite. Tinkering in the
stitched squares of the white bed comforter, she pretended to
prepare her pink friend a meal by grasping the air and passing it
to the curly haired doll. The doll smiled politely and keeled
backward, to which April chided, "It's not time to sleep yet. You
need to eat your dinner." Complying with April's compulsory
hand, the doll up-righted herself and again smiled politely.
"What else would you like to eat, baby?" April parentally asked.
"I want to eat...," April said in a pitchy voice, pausing at the
presence of screaming. The disagreeing voices echoing from
another part of the house pushed April away from her playtime
spread and trapped her between her imagination and reality. She
shivered at the unfamiliar voices, unable to understand the
pleading or the period of distant thumping. Her instincts
influenced her expression and strange emotions. "Why are you
yelling?" she innocently asked toward the open door. She
listened with shudders and finally discerned a clear set of familiar
words. "I'm leaving! Get out of my way." Then the string of
discontentment continued in its prior foreign language. With
quick breaths and a pounding heart, she rushed to her feet,
frantically grabbing her dinner guest with her polite consent.
"Don't leave me, I'm coming too!" she worriedly informed, and
repeated her plea two more times with her hand pushing the wall
and her left foot pounding each step of the staircase as she
descended. "Stop!" April heard her freckled babysitter stress
amongst other imploring. "Let...me go...," April heard her other
friendly babysitter detest amidst her restraint. "Please!" April
watched her freckled babysitter throw more vain words at
impressive speed and watched the other friendly babysitter
collapse in resistance to the floor. Convulsing in tantrum type
movements, April watched to see how her flailing idol would be

punished after such disobedient behavior. After more tense moments the friendly girl found a more peaceable rhythm in chanting, "I deserve it, I deserve it." She cried, "Help me, Julianne." Grabbing and flattening her face with her hands, she added, "I need help, you'll help me, right?"

"Jessica, I want to help you."

"Let me go get what I need."

"No, Jessica! You're the one that told me you'd be going through this. You're the one that said that if I want to 'help you' to 'prevent' you from going. You can do this! It's just withdrawal," Julianne coached and held a nervous hand out unsure of whether another episode would ensue.

"No, I need my d...."

Julianne heard the ring of the doorbell, and at the same instant, Jessica saw April's two frozen blue eyes. Julianne separated for the front door, having forgotten about her babysitting duties from the raging atmosphere of the past few minutes. Jessica unconsciously scratched her at her face as her addicted brain fought with her frail body, and seeing her window to pursue her pressing urge, she started for the garage side door around the kitchen corner.

"Don't go without me," April providentially spoke, which stopped Jessica long enough to allow Julianne to step back around the brown leather couch and into her path. Romney began his observation of the interchanging argument and decided to try the door handle when Jessica roughly resisted Julianne's handhold. The door opened, and the muffled bellows of Jessica's wrath became clear.

"You don't understand. I need my fix!" Jessica argued without realizing Julianne was no longer blockading the exit due to a painful strike she had placed on Julianne's jaw.

Julianne's side had subsequently collided with a heavy bar stool, and though back on her feet, she still retreated from Jessica's space, having come to terms with her belittled influence. Julianne could see Jessica struggling, rationalizing, shaking, and sobbing, but she couldn't hear or understand her speech any longer. Through her own tears, Julianne saw April crying.

"Julianne, would you tend to April and maybe show her how to play the piano?" Romney asked and calmly took Julianne's position. He assessed Jessica as she irately and emotionally battled her demons in the hallway leading to the garage. "Jessica, who gave you that bruise on your chin?" Romney asked, anticipating his calmly worded inquiry would be drowned out by Jessica's internal distress. He heard a chord triad on the piano from across the room, and as if a medium had been found that bridged Jessica's sound mind to her muscle control, she closed her lips and trained her glassy eyes on Romney's face. "My wife," Romney said, momentarily resisting where his conscience commanded him to go. "My wife had a bruise under her eye earlier this week, and instead of trusting me to help her, she pushed me away and hasn't returned home since. I don't know where she is or if she's safe right now," Romney admitted, bowing his head. "She does drugs," Romney said, looking back up to see how Jessica would relate. Having recalled Jessica's name and the short explanation of her relationship to Julianne, Romney felt blind in the matter. "But I love her, and I want her to come home," he testified. After losing what felt like a divinely inspired flow of words, he looked back into Jessica's eyes. With an honest posture, he leaned forward slightly in Jessica's direction. He wanted to compliment her in some way but immediately stopped himself. Dismissing his ambition, he instead smiled at the struggling girl who stood looking both physically and emotionally cornered in the tiled hallway.

When Jessica saw Romney smile, she fully expected Romney to take advantage of her like so many other men had.

"Have you heard the story of Jesus?" Romney asserted. He heard April try a few of the piano keys amidst Julianne's peaceful composition, and he saw Jessica shake her head to confirm she had not. "If I may humor you with my poor rendition of it, of the story," he said, leaning back and sliding off the bar stool to a reclined position on the floor. "The bible records a certain account of Jesus, of some religious teachers...and of a woman that's said to have been caught in the act of having sex with somebody else other than her husband, which in the olden days was a crime punishable by death," Romney said, observing the level of interest in his audience. "Unlike the religious teachers,

Jesus would have dinner with poor people and cheats and foreigners and play with little children...like April. The religious teachers for some reason hated Jesus for doing these things," he continued, pausing after setting up his short narrative. "So, the teachers, the religious teachers, tried to trick Jesus into defying the law of the land with trick questions, hoping to in some way prove him a lawbreaker," he explained, naturally animating his hands.

"Why would the religious teachers hate Jesus for having dinner with people?" Jessica asked, loosening the protection of her crossed arms.

"The teachers were jealous, and probably lots of people stopped obeying their religious rules and started listening to Jesus's way instead of the teachers'," Romney answered and scratched his cheek in search of a point. "Well, Jesus one day entered the market place and talked with a few people that were excited to greet him and shake his hand. Then a few children teasingly grabbed and hung onto Jesus's legs. One of Jesus's friends tried to rebuke the children and pry them off Jesus." His arms continued demonstrating the action of the story. "Jesus said, 'No, don't send them away, for my father's house belongs to such as these children.' His close friend was taken aback, and Jesus continued to play and laugh with the children. After a small crowd had formed around them, a group of religious teachers pushed through the shield of people, barking instructions for the kids to return to their parents," he narrated, scowling his face to show Jessica what he meant. Seeing her captivation, he continued, "The teachers were followed by two strong men who dragged a poorly dressed woman through the dusty road. The woman had obviously been putting up a fight, because her clothes had been torn and hair had been grabbed more than once. The two brutish men had obviously dropped the woman many times on their march. That's when the leader of the religious teachers, who was in charge, pointed to the ground in front of Jesus, and the two brutes followed the leader's order to dump the woman at Jesus's feet. The crowd was silent, and everyone saw that the woman was hurt and scared. The parents pushed their children away from the scene, and the religious leader peered into Jesus's face. The woman obviously feared for her life, thinking that Jesus was in fact a judge and that the surrounding mob of people were going to kill her. Then the religious leader yelled loudly enough for the whole crowd of people to hear, 'We have caught this woman in the very act of having sex with a man who is not her husband. Our law says to punish her by throwing these stones at her. What do you say, Jesus?'"

Antithetically, Julianne played a soothing melody in the background.

"Let him who is perfect cast the first stone," Romney continued, releasing the tension. "Jesus yelled out his response as loudly as the leader had yelled, and then he bent down to the ground," he explained and mimicked his explanation by leaning forward into a squatting position and pointing two fingers to the floor. "He started drawing in the sand next to the woman who lay awaiting her punishment. Lots of people guess at what he drew, but I can't help but think that he squatted down next to her," Romney spoke and motioned for Jessica to sink down to his level. "...to position himself in the line of fire...to protect her in case somebody threw a stone at the girl," Romney reached out his arms to indicate a circle of protection. "...in order to give the religious teachers time to honestly reflect on his one simple requirement," Romney added with conviction.

Jessica shivered but this time not in a fearful manner. "Did anybody-throw-or...were they perfect enough to?" Jessica eagerly stuttered with her tired voice.

"Well, the older ones quickly realized that they weren't perfect, and each one of them dropped their stones. Then the younger ones after seeing their elders give up, initially picked up the dropped stones with hatred in their eyes," Romney said, but seeing a rumble of worry shake Jessica's shoulders, he reached out and laid his hand on her as a sign of comfort. He continued, "Slowly, the younger ones realized that they too weren't perfect as Jesus had demanded. So, it turned out that all the woman's accusers had left her alone with Jesus."

Jessica felt relief as Romney removed his hand from the corner of her shoulder.

"Jesus asked the woman the obvious question, 'Where are all your accusers?' And the woman replied, after looking around,

'There is no one, sir. No one is left.' Then Jesus replied with his now famous words, 'Then neither do I condemn you. Go and do no more wrong," Romney said, finishing for but a moment. "Now the story ends there, but I can't help but think that Jesus, being who he was, helped the woman to her feet, learned her name, and escorted her home to her husband, where she no doubt would have had to confess her wrongdoing," he elaborated, offering Jessica his support in her rising to her feet. "She was still bruised all over and embarrassed, but she was saved from the greater punishment; I think you'd agree," Romney concluded, leading Jessica into the living room to find April dancing her doll on the baby grand piano and Julianne finishing her melodramatic performance.

## Part 2 - Chapter Sixteen

"Hey, baby sis' or mom it's me...I guess...Jess...Jessica, I go by Jessica now," Jessica recorded on the voicemail and forgot what she had called about. A long pause happened. "I can picture my fifteen-year-old sister's face," Jessica whispered from behind her wet eyes to the social worker hovering next to her shoulder for support.

"Good. Go on, darling."

She took a deep breath and remembered her purpose in calling. "Hey baby sis', I know I haven't been by to see you in a long time, but things are looking better. I'm going to a place, a place some nice people are helping me get into," Jessica spoke, searching for sanctioned words with difficulty. "You probably won't see me for a while...not anything new, I know. Don't hate me 'kay? ...Umm...," Jessica recorded candidly, trying to peel open a lid of truth. Her lip trembled, and she courageously admitted, "You were right, you were right a little...." She wanted to explain, but the fear from her experience swelled up her vocal cords. "...Trist...hurt...," Jessica heaved, stopping short of her intended disclosure. "...but...," Jessica hiccupped and tried again. "I hope to...find you...after. Win...I'm better, baby sis', I'll be thinking...this time...umm." Jessica Patsy stalled out. At twenty-years-old, she visibly shuddered, being ratcheted between her shaky nerves and the censure that the case worker had repeatedly emphasized before the call. Before crumbling completely, she forced the words, "Bye baby sis'."

Jessica apologetically handed the phone back to the tall police officer. The smiling social worker, twice her age tried to explain the purpose of the document she had set in front of her as they sat down together. All Jessica heard was the second to last word, "...protection...," and she thought of how Romney had extended his arms. After the social worker rose to her feet and clicked her inch-tall heels a few times toward the door, she lulled, and recognizing her client's dismay, she spoke her name while offering her an accompanying hand. "This gentleman is going to fingerprint you for the record; come with me." Jessica followed slowly, and the social worker tenderly encouraged her with a half-hug motion, escorting her down to the end of the hall.

"Will he find my baby sis'?"

"I don't know, dear, but you need to be safe too; you said your mom is with your sister," the social worker gently alluded.

"I don't know," Jessica humbly admitted, trying to interpret the stoic motion of the officer.

"Well, you can always hope, dear. And...," the social worker said, inhaling to expound, but hesitated. "You can always hope when you don't know," she reiterated with an appeasing smile. "Would you like me to accompany you all the way to the shelter?"

"Mmhmm," Jessica answered, again with split attention, catching a view of her friends through a window lined hallway.

Julianne saw the final look on Jessica's face and waved frantically hoping to show her last inch of support. "Where do you think they're taking her?" she confided to Romney.

"I don't know, but you said you needed a ride to work. How do you plan on getting home?" Romney asked, preoccupied with entertaining April.

"No, you're the one who suggested that you drop me off, and the taxi fares aren't outrageous like they used to be," Julianne responded, still distracted by the opposing empty hallway.

"Well, should we be going?"

"Where to?" Julianne asked with confusion, splitting her attention away from the lobby window.

"Work, right?"

"Oh, not tonight. My boss knows I'm hit or miss; hey, is it true about...hold on," Julianne walked up to the front counter of the police station. "Miss, do you know where they are taking Jessica...to which shelter, a women's shelter, right?"

"I'm sorry, ma'am, we can't disclose that information for her safety," the lady stringently answered from behind her mid-tone desk.

"Right, okay," Julianne said and smiled appreciatively as she swallowed the coarse answer.

Having gathered April's few belongings, Romney had April holstered in his arm ready to leave. "True 'bout what?" Romney reminded Julianne of her question.

"Oh, they wouldn't tell me which shelter Jessica is being sent to; I kind of would like to visit her, to check in on her...to see if she needs anything."

"I know she'll be in the best of places," Romney asserted as he pushed through the door that had entertained April with her reflection for a minute. After considering the shortness of his tone as he crossed the parking lot, he sympathetically added, "I hope she'll recover quickly." Julianne's phone rattled inside of her purse, and Romney looked over and saw her lifting her cellphone to her ear as she rounded the spacious passenger van Romney had recently acquired.

"Hi, Anna?"

"...Rembrandt is nothing like Renoir...yeah portraits...well, the color for one...Oh, hi, mom. Spencer and I are going to swing by his friend's house before we head home," Anna lively informed. "I'm sorry to ask, but it would save me a minute if you could pick up the car from school. Maybe you could ask Romney when he comes by to pick up April," Anna suggested.

"Sure, what time...Anna? What time? Anna? Okay, that was short and to the point. Romney would you be so kind as to...."

"Drop you off at your car? Not at all, I mean certainly. Is Anna okay?" Romney asked, having overheard a few of Anna's last words escape from the telephone as he brought the van to life with the key.

"She seemed cheery enough," Julianne reacted and fell into a silent mood. Her chauffer accommodatingly drove on without interrupting her intuitive dialogue. Before she released her seatbelt after arriving at her red sedan, she coldly stated, "I don't like this Spencer."

Romney remained silent, unsure of how to tactfully empathize.

"She didn't sound at all like herself."

"Has she dated before?" Romney interrupted.

"Not like this," Julianne replied, letting worry creep into her voice.

"Call her back. She'll appreciate the concern, and you'll communicate that you care in the process," Romney counseled. "You know, I don't know why I stooped into that luxury sport car all these years. This van drives so much more comfortably with your feet flat on the floor," Romney reasoned, intending to change the subject. However, seeing Julianne still in her daze, he offered, "I'll be available all night if you need me, okay?"

Still not able to loosen the look of worry infecting her freckled face, Julianne let out a smile as she got out of Romney's van.

--- *Ten minutes after Anna's phone had dropped the call.*

"Hey mom!" Anna said from the passenger's seat of Spencer's car as she watched her date ascend the flight of stairs up to the second floor of a weathered apartment building.

"Anna?" Julianne answered, struggling to manage both the small silver phone and the steering wheel of their red sedan.

"Sorry, my phone service here is spotty, and Spencer finally lent me his."

"Anna dear, I'm driving; give me chance to pull over," Julianne said, and temporarily laid her phone on the leather seat.

Anna patiently waited, looking out the car's front window at the blue gray apartment complex. "Hey, mom, Spencer is bringing me home now, I should be home in thirty minutes or so," Anna declared, after giving her mother what felt like more than enough time to park the car somewhere. Her eyes rolled back and then came into focus on the dark colored dashboard, and she leaned forward to inspect the silted surface. She scratched with curiosity, trying to remove the dust that seemed to have evenly settled on the textured plastic. "Good luck cleaning that off your dashboard," Anna judgmentally thought aloud. "Hey, mom," Anna queried again.

"Anna darling, are you okay?"

"Yeah, did you catch that? Spencer's bringing me home now; we should be there in, say thirty to forty minutes, if he ever finishes with his friend," Anna said, having grown tired and a bit short tempered after spending the two meals and the movie together with her tireless escort.

"Okay good, I'm in the car driving home...obviously; Romney dropped me off at your college. Will I see you soon then?"

"That's what I said, mom, like in forty minutes."

"I take it you had fun?" Julianne pressed.

"Sure, I'm just tired and ready to get home to bed," Anna explained and relaxed her neck muscles as she released a breath into Spencer's cell phone. After finishing the call and placing the phone in the cup holder at her side, she continued to listen to the sound of her breathing. She smiled kindly at a mother who was rushing her small daughter quickly by the front of Spencer's car. Unbeknownst to Anna, Spencer had parked in his usual spot in front of Triston Palanco's apartment. The mother seemed overly cautious, as if taking a shortcut through a fenced piece of property. Looking around for some explanation as to the mother's stark worry and finding none, she double-checked the locks on Spencer's car. Then considering that she hadn't seen anyone else in all her minutes waiting, she relaxed again. Breathing deeply to further pass the time, she felt beads of perspiration begin to form on her forehead. Considering her options for less than a split moment, she impulsively grabbed her purse from the carpeted floorboard and exited the black car. She spent a few moments debating whether to leave her purse inside the polished coupe, but the surrounding tired and dented vehicles made her decision clear. Taking after the example of the overly cautious mother, she stepped briskly toward the stairs of Spencer's friend's apartment. Detecting two voices from the open window above her, she climbed half of the staircase like a girl returning from a shopping spree, but she slowed when she thought she heard someone inside the apartment say, "Just let her go. They're only worth so much anyway."

"Who? Let her go? I loved that girl like a baby sister, and she ran out on me!"

"She was spent, come on admit it."

"What? She hadn't even begun to repay all the stuff I gave her, she still owes me and bigtime...," the frustrated voice erupted.

Anna strained her ear, trying to ascertain the context of the conversation. Confident that Spencer had entered the apartment in question, she couldn't identify his voice, but her nerves began to rattle after one of the voices chuckled.

"You're laughing? She left and is going to do something stupid...."

Anna heard a strong fist hammer something in the apartment as she tried to get closer to eavesdrop.

"Cool, cool it, m..., and keep it...."

As a passenger train blared from somewhere across the south flowing river, Anna realized that she cast a tall shadow on the wall next to the door.

"I'm not going to let her run me into the ground after I've stuck my neck out for her all these years. She needs a beating, and when we find her...."

"No, now come...," the tamer character tried to reason.

Anna's nerves caused her legs to shiver in place.

"...better tell me if you find her," the temper flared.

"Well yeah; she might deserve it, but I'm not beating...you lost me there."

"I'm gonna find her!"

"Right on, right on," the second character strangely harmonized without concern.

"And if I don't, I'm gonna break-in her sister," the enraged character promised.

Anna finally took a painfully quiet step back down the stairs listening to the angry voice drowned in the second short farewell horn of the passenger train.

"I'd wait a while, man, on the sister; she's too young," the level-headed responder said more faintly to Anna's ears as she crept down the steps.

"Too young the better! At least I'd get some minor entertainment for all the money I've shelled out on Jess..."

"Jess," Anna recognized and doubled her hushed pace to the bottom of the steps. Acting on the presumed connection, she hastily crossed the cracked blacktop to the sidewalk that paralleled the incoming road. Turning right, she hustled further toward a stop light and crosswalk. Anxiously, she pressed the crosswalk button five times, then proceeded immediately through a gap in traffic. Crossing the street again, she walked intently away from the apartment complex. She didn't slow down until she scurried passed a well branded gym in front of some devalued plats. Deciding in a moment, she rounded the aged brick corner and clanged the gym's entrance bell as she proceeded through the side door.

"Can we help you?" a healthy-looking boy with a cap of pure blond hair asked.

Smiling briefly after filling her lungs to respond, Anna said, "I'm waiting for someone to come pick me up; can I hang here for a bit?" After the boy nodded with a bit of confusion, Anna took a seat in the corner of the lobby and continued checking the front window every few seconds.

"Anna?" the familiar voice asked through the front glass then pressed through the welcoming door.

"Spencer! You sure came...quick." Anna reacted matter-of-factly as the door to the gym slammed closed.

"You gave me a fright, girl. I thought some bad man would pick you up."

"Why would you think that?" Anna responded.

"Well, it's not the best part of town. I'm so sorry for making you sit so long. Tr...my friend...lost someone recently, and...well, he's not taking it very well. I saw you walking away from the...from his window. Do you need something?"

"Like a towel and water from sitting in that hot car for thirty minutes," Anna excused playfully, looking back at the blond smiling boy who pointed responsively to the water machine at the far end of the lobby.

"Do you want to go grab some ice cream? Ice cream will cool you right off," Spencer suggested, digging around for a reciprocal response with his eyes. "Besides, I know the best place in town, and it's not cheap either," Spencer said, waiting for Anna to proceed ahead of him through the door he pushed and held open.

Calming herself with private assurances, Anna let her voice crack, "No, I think we need to save some allurement for a later date, don't you think?"

"Right on, right on, girl; let me take you home then. You had a good time today, didn't you?" Spencer asked, subtly prying to figure out the real basis for Anna's queer maneuver.

"Dinner was great," Anna affirmed, her heart having skipped a beat. "I haven't spent that much on dinner...ever, I think," Anna lied, playing to Spencer's ego.

"I'm sorry about your phone; were you able to get your mom on mine?"

"Oh yeah, and thanks by way. She's expecting me home in twenty minutes now," Anna said, placing extra weight on her reference to her failsafe measure.

"Are we twenty minutes away?" Spencer playfully asked, opening and closing the car door for Anna.

After dodging the expectation of answering through the open window, Anna watched Spencer circumnavigate the front of the car with his confident gait. Brainstorming her exit plan in the pause, she waited quietly while Spencer reclined and turned the engine over with the key. Then beginning her charade, she said, "I think I know where we are. Is Pitt Stadium right over there?"

"I'm pretty sure, yeah," Spencer agreed, stealing a long look at Anna's top as he waited for a green signal at the crossroad.

"If you cross a bridge to downtown, you'll hit Pitt Ave," Anna said while catching a view of Spencer's appreciation. "The light's green," Anna intentionally interrupted, then continued, "You'll follow Pitt toward the Mills bridge, but before you get there, you'll turn onto Pitt Washington Way; a right and then a left and then you're there."

"Got it! Am I going for time or for accuracy?" Spencer joked, trying to ease up the perceptible tenseness of his date.

"Safe...."

"...or safety?" Spencer arrogated, commandeering Anna's reply. "Safety? You got it," Spencer finished, seeing Anna smile thinly.

Feeling good about his mild accomplishment, he flaunted his mediocre driving skills from stop light to stop light. "Pitt Washington Way you go; I walk this street a lot when I'm bored," Spencer commented.

"What do you do when you're not bored, like for work?" Anna interviewed, trying to keep relations as normal as possible to hide her shortness of breath.

"My dad's rich, I haven't had to work a real day in my life," Spencer boasted, but realizing how the proposition made him sound, he recovered, "I mean I'm not a dead beat, I'm enrolling in college in the fall, and maybe one day I'll be as successful on my own. I don't know."

"That's a noble aspiration. What are you planning on studying? It's right there," Anna asked while pointing her finger at the high-rise condominium apartments.

"I was thinking History," Spencer sheepishly disclosed.

"Because I'm into history?" Anna accused, holding the door-handle of the overpowered vehicle with her fingers.

"Well maybe...partially...yes; that's not weird, is it? I mean I'm not into the painters as much as you are, but the struggles between civilizations, the dictators, the wars, the Reichs, the cultural clashes; I can watch it...."

"Oh, you don't have to walk me in," Anna stressed, holding up a protesting hand to Spencer as she departed the car for the entrance.

"What kind of barbaric guy would I be if I didn't escort a fine lady like you to the door?" Spencer retaliated, catching up to Anna who obligingly continued in her failing ploy.

Anna walked in through the door and up to the receptionist without waiting for Spencer to close himself inside the lobby. "Hi, Jenny, three-fourteen...Rom?" Anna requested with glassy eyes, as Spencer tried to continue to make his chivalrous case from five feet behind her.

"I mean, what do you think; do you think I could benefit society as a History major? Is everything okay...you forget your key or something?"

"Yeah, my mom's not home yet," Anna nervously rationalized, glancing away at the smartly dressed receptionist.

"Well, I'll keep you company until she gets here," Spencer ignorantly offered.

"Hello, Mr. Daniels, two guests arrived, and asked for you. One's your escort from last weekend, I believe, and a gentleman is with her. Should I have them wait for you in the lobby or send them up?" Jenny respectfully asked loudly enough for both mid-evening guests to understand.

"I'm okay waiting by myself, you can go. I had a good time, thank you, Spencer" Anna said as convincingly as she could.

"Jenny, is it?" Spencer said boldly, leaning into the counter. "Could you let me walk this fine young woman up to her apartment...three...fourteen?" he said, swiveling back to Anna to clarify the address.

"I'm sorry, Mr. Spencer, but that's against our policy that I'm sure Miss Purse knows well about," Jenny stated without a hint of falsehood. "Mr. Romn...Rom, will be right down to greet the two of you," Jenny continued, smiling as she extended her arm over the clean counter to indicate the seating area.

The bell of the elevator grabbed the attention of the guests before Jenny had finished her invitation. Romney Daniels walked out of the steel framed opening with a smile on his face. It took only an instant for him to recognize Spencer and the helpless look on Anna's face. While forcing a continued smile, his eyes changed. "Anna, so glad to see you," he addressed pleasantly, and with a side hug, he shoved a familiar toothless key into Anna's open hand. "Spencer! It's good to meet you again. How are you?"

"I'm here with Anna; I'm going to stay with Anna."

"No, I'm afraid not," Romney disinclined, stepping provokingly forward to allow Anna passage to the elevator.

"You'd better get out of my way; it's my duty to protect that girl," Spencer aggressively said, pushing into Romney to pursue Anna. "Get out of my way, fool," Spencer threatened again with a push when Romney didn't budge.

"Gentlemen, I'm calling the police; this is unacceptable behavior on this private property, and you, sir, are now trespassing!"

"Right, call the cops on the guy trying to defend his girlfriend...private property my mmhmm...you and I both know this isn't your 'private property,'" Spencer retorted with inference.

"Would you like Anna to see or hear you right now, Spencer? Please leave Anna alone," Romney coarsely instructed after realizing he had a voice again.

"That's her decision, old man; you think you're her dad or somethin'?" Spencer condescendingly argued. "Why-you worrying about her, don't you have a little girl you think you're protecting? Yeah?" Spencer bluffed. Spencer scared himself at how easily the villainous threat flowed from his mouth. The vocabulary repulsively reminded him of one of Trist's tirades. Pridefully, he pushed Romney once more toward the elevator and stormed off to his midnight-toned vehicle.

## Part 2 - Chapter Seventeen

"Did you actually call?" Romney asked the rustled receptionist after making certain Spencer had departed.

"No. Did you invite him here? Because he's a firecracker," Jenny replied.

"No. But thank you for helping me out of that...," Romney said, swiping his hand around at the empty lobby to indicate what he meant. "You're the hero, Jenny, thank you," he emphasized again as he dismissed himself. His chest still quivered as he leaned his back into the side wall of the elevator. Then Anna's concerned face appeared as the elevator doors opened to the third floor.

Relieved to see Romney alone, Anna scolded herself, taking a guilty glance at the floor.

"It's good to see you, Anna," Romney said ready for an explanation.

"I'm really sorry for bothering you. I didn't want...I don't know, I didn't know how to get out," Anna apologized.

"Are you okay?" Romney asked.

"Yes."

"I have to ask, 'Did he hurt you?'"

"Yes, no, I mean no," Anna said flippantly, looking up at Romney's attentive eyes to confirm her true answer.

"Did he assault you in anyway?" Romney pushed.

"No, no, nothing like that. I overheard him talking with his friend, and they were talking about horrible things. Then they mentioned Jess, and I spooked," Anna sporadically explained like a driver who had survived a freak car crash. "I heard him yell in the lobby; what did he say?" Anna asked, shrinking her shoulders with curiosity.

"Oh, he vividly explained how he would make a horrible boyfriend for you," Romney said, gradually submersing his answer in a smile.

"Oh, now you want to be funny, Mr. I want to wear a stinky old t-shirt around the house when I'm at home," Anna bantered, but her emotions rapidly welled up in her eyes and chest.

Romney wrapped his arms responsively around Anna when she finally released her tears. As Anna pulled away, she offered a composed smile, then laughed, having become conscious of her pitiful state.

Romney self-consciously looked down at his shirt and jested, "Well, well, now...you can't call something stinky unless you've smelled it, and you just did...besides there's...."

"Awful," Anna remarked, repressing her laughter while attempting to conceal the tip of her freckled nose behind her fingers.

"Awful! But there's a reason. Hey, you'll be okay here for a minute?" Romney asked.

"Sure," Anna easily answered.

"I'll go get April from her room and then get you home. The moment I mentioned your name, and that you might be downstairs, she nearly went berserk," Romney lively explained while stepping towards his apartment door. The bell of the elevator stopped Romney's momentum and made both Anna and him shoot their attention to the steel doors.

"Good evening, Romney," the middle-aged gentleman saluted after a passing look at Anna.

"Henri, good to see you," Romney courteously acknowledged, returning a step toward Anna. "Let me grab April, and we'll get you home; Henri and his wife go to my church," Romney explained in response to the questioning look that had fleeted across Anna's face.

"Oh, what church do you go to?" Anna curiously asked, following Romney over to his apartment door.

"A nondenominational-denomination one, north of town," Romney said, trying to fit his hand inconspicuously into one of his front pockets. After producing nothing, he patted his other pockets.

Anna watched his peculiar behavior critically for a few seconds before realizing what he was doing. "Oh, sorry, I still have that," Anna admitted after momentarily debating whether to tease him.

"Oh good," Romney relieved, accepting the toothless key from Anna's hand.

"I'll wait out here," Anna declared, moving back towards the spine of the building.

"Thanks, I'll be just a minute. April, I know, is so excited to see you. She hasn't stopped talking about 'Anna' and her baby deer adventure all week," Romney commented as he heard his door latch click open. "April! Woah, woah; how'd you get out of your room?" Romney chided in surprise.

"Anna!" April sang in a beeline of excitement to greet her friend.

"Are you good with her?" Romney asked, seeing the shared joy on Anna's lips.

"Oh yeah," Anna confidently replied.

"I'll be right out then," Romney reiterated before letting the door bounce on its security latch. He hurried to grab a diaper bag, a toy, and a nighttime treat for April. Then he changed into a collared shirt and belted his denim pants. Scanning the room for any other necessary items for the late night round, he flicked off the last light switch and secured the door in the presence of April and Anna playing in the hallway. Anna hushed April in response to a crescendo of giggles.

"Don't tickle me," April playfully pleaded, clenching her arm close to her side before inviting another tickle by lifting her elbow again high in the air.

"Hey Pearl, are you ready to take Anna home?" Romney inserted to the laughing interaction.

Anna couldn't resist tickling April again.

"I want to go too," April illogically objected while giggling.

"Okay, then hold Anna's hand," Romney said, silently communicating his parental ploy in his eye contact with Anna.

"Oh, your shoes," Romney stated, blitzing back to the door of his apartment.

*--- Minutes later as Romney unlocked his van in the parking garage.*

"What happened to the…your sporty thing? It fit you so well," Anna observed as she rounded the opposite side of the plain black van. April hugged her dad's neck as he carried her to the sliding door.

"I seem to sense an air of sarcasm coming from somewhere nearby. Do you hear it too, Pearl?" Romney replied, finding Anna framed in the light tint of the front passenger window.

"Do you think I'm childish, Rom?" Anna freely asked, sliding into the front passenger seat.

As Anna's eyes flickered and sought Romney's reply, April let her dad finish buckling her into her day-old car seat. "Sit by me, Anna!" April hopefully requested.

"Not this time, Pearl. Here, I brought you a treat...and a toy!" Romney sternly said, trying to placate his daughter.

"But I want Anna to sit next to me," April whined.

Romney displayed his unwillingness to give into the request by closing the driver side door, and Anna turned around to smile an apology at April. In a fit, April randomly flung her toy into the front seat nearly grazing Anna's forehead.

"April!" Romney reactively shouted with consternation. Then seeing Anna's surprised face, Romney lowered his voice amidst April's continued rant, saying, "I'm sorry, Anna; leave the toy there. She didn't hit you, did she?"

"No, but I can sit back there with her," Anna offered.

"Do you hear that, April, she would have sat back there with you," Romney scolded as he backed the car up into the full garage. "Normally, I'd welcome you to do as you wish but not in light of that," Romney explained in an unconcerned voice.

"That's his number!" Anna announced, holding up her vibrating phone. "What do I do?" Anna asked, looking flatly at Romney.

Distracted by the inputting of the code to exit the parking garage, Romney didn't answer at first. "I'm sorry, was that

Spencer that called you?" Romney asked as he checked the cross street for traffic and let the quiet van slide down the ramp and into the street.

"Hold on. He just left a message," Anna informed after a disconnected few seconds, fidgeting with the phone in one hand and displaying her anxiety with other. "Yeah, I think he's leaving a message," Anna reiterated.

"Hey," Romney said, trying to gain Anna's attention away from the phone held to her ear. "Hey."

"What!" Anna said with worry.

"Hey," Romney repeated resolutely, "Spencer is just a boy, just like me, and it would appear that he likes you. I walked all over his pride tonight." Romney searched his thoughts for reasonable words. "Give him a chance to be human, blame me, if you need to, but you don't have to do anything...anything you don't want to," Romney said. "But before you do 'do anything,'" Romney interrupted himself, checking the cross-street before he continued, "...it would be good for you to know that Spencer has sold drugs to Sandy." He finished his advice by shaking his head, ashamed at how long it took him to confess to Anna his knowledge of Spencer's identity.

"You owe me lunch," Anna suggested, returning from her noisy thoughts without hearing anything Romney had said after he had spoken Spencer's name.

"You got it; when and where?" Romney mechanically responded, trying to figure Anna's angle.

"My class ends at eleven on Monday; the brickyard, around the corner, behind the gym...Vern Hill...," Anna said, failing to play off her instructions coolly. "You don't mind?" she apologized.

"No, not at all; but I don't want to discourage you," Romney said, trying to think of a way to position himself as a friend rather than a crutch. "You're a cunning girl you know," Romney continued decidedly.

Anna didn't want to answer and instead playful grabbed April's foot. Not wanting silence either, she asked Romney, "Why do you think I'm cunning? How so?"

"I mean what other girl here in Pittsburg, put in your situation, would seek out a mild gun-toting acquaintance to avoid having a date-gone-wrong find out where she lives?" Romney loosely explained as he entered the Duquesne Tunnel.

"What? I didn't even see you put that on! Did you have that on in the lobby?" Anna asked seeing the firearm attached to Romney's hip.

"No, I didn't have time."

"But when do you, I mean how do you decide whether or not to put it on? If you don't have it on, I mean, it's kind of pointless, right?" Anna rationalized, remembering Romney's prior discourse after the fundraiser.

"It's a pain and a chore no doubt, but it's routine," Romney said, returning his right hand to the steering wheel as he exited the highway. "You have to really sit down and decide for yourself, 'Where's the real threat,' and 'Can I safely carry this device to protect myself and my family.' You know there's curious children, accidental discharges, and the fact thieves try to steal house guns all the time," Romney said, feeling comfortable disclosing his views to Anna. "In reality..."

"Do you think I should get a gun?"

"If you're not scared to use it and confident in how it works; here take this."

"Oh, please don't; I was just asking," Anna objected squeamishly.

"I won't, don't worry, but there's your answer," Romney said, pressing the gas pedal harder to account for incline of the road. "The way I see it, violent crime happens in the home, at work, and sometimes in dark parking lots. Obviously, I don't carry it at home, and I don't at work either. The funny thing is, the criminals in the parking lots usually only want your money, and the first thing I'd throw at a thief is my wallet. That leaves the crazies that are just out to kill people, and perhaps some random gang related violence that can mostly be avoided by avoiding the 'dark alleys altogether,' if you know what I mean," Romney elaborated. "I'm sorry did you want the short answer?"

Anna laughed and said, "No, I want to know how your brain works and what goes on up there."

Romney laughed in reply and let a few moments pass by in silence as he turned down Anna's side street. The shadows of the two-story houses had long finished their daily journey of crossing the road, and Anna's corner house came into view.

"Monday now, you owe me remember. It's a gun free campus mind you," Anna intrepidly said.

"Is Spencer going to be there...the reason?" Romney guessed on a whim.

"Are you still going to come if I said he might be?" Anna inquired, cringing at the sound of her honesty.

"Of course, I owe you lunch?" Romney said and noticed Anna's artful guise wear off as her shoulders drooped. As a he parked the van in the shared driveway, he continued, "Though, I do have to suggest that your clear refusal will ever be more effective than my occasional presence in dealing with Spencer."

"Right."

"Goodnight, Anna; say goodnight, Pearl..."

"She's asleep," Anna half-whispered respectfully, turning to say her own farewell.

"Oh boy, early to bed means for a rough night ahead," Romney said, opening wide his eyes to shed humor on his prediction.

"And Rom, you're nothing like Spencer; thank you for rescuing me tonight."

"You're welcome, Annie."

"What? Annie?"

Romney smiled and reasoned, "Well, if you're going to get away with calling me by my childhood name, I should at least be able to call you Annie."

"Oh," Anna laughed in embarrassment. "Well, my mom called me Anna dear growing up, so have at it Rom," Anna said with a smirk and closed the door.


## Part 2 - Chapter Eighteen


"Daddy, I'm hungry," April said, curling her forehead into Romney's shoulder as Romney shook hands with an acquaintance at his church. Romney acknowledged April with a sliver of his attention as he chuckled from his focused conversation. April shifted her weight off Romney's hip, incidentally driving her knee into his abdomen. When Romney objected by letting her slip to the ground, she repeated her hungry plea.

"Okay, Pearl, what do you want to eat? We'll see you later this week, Henri; good to see you," Romney said, sinking down to face his daughter.

Henri seemed to understand, flapping his hand down at April with a silly smile before stepping toward another conversation.

"Tot-tots," April answered.

"Tot-tots? What's a...," Romney said at eye level, interrupting himself as he smiled at two passing women who seemed to have made him and his daughter a subject of their gossip.

One of the women noticed and tried to rescue her self-dignity by stating, "You treat that little one like she's all grown up."

"Go ahead and say, 'Hi,' to Ms. Melissa and Mrs. Candice, Pearl," Romney intermediated fully aware of Candice's undertones.

"She is just so cute," Melissa said in her own attempt. The wiggle of Melissa's finger in April's direction made April slip her hands around Romney's arm.

Romney offered a smile up at the ladies and let silence send the two on their way.

"Pearl, do you mean to say that you want potato-bites?" Romney asked, returning to the more pressing topic.

"Moo calls them tot-tots," April emphasized, canting her head sideways like an embarrassed teenager.

"Who's Moo?" Romney asked with a laugh.

"Moo's my friend," April explained with raised hands.

"One of your stuffed animals?" Romney suggested. "Just don't jut your knee into my gut this time, okay?"

"Okay, I won't" April lightheartedly promised and smiled as she rode in Romney's arms to the van.

Romney handed a packaged peanut bar to April as he buckled her into the van. "Should we cook your tot-tots at the mansion?"

"Can I eat this now?" April asked, ignoring her dad's question.

"Certainly," Romney consented calmly as he took and tore open the packaged bar.

The squealing of tires drew Romney's immediate attention. The crunching of metal finished the screech from a distance behind him. A few church members ran to offer help at the junction of the parking lot. Romney could hear the distant conversation of the apologetic drivers followed by simultaneous inquiries from the approaching help. Somebody anxiously laughed.

"What happened?" April asked in a cartoon voice.

"It looks like somebody didn't stop quickly enough in the parking lot," Romney indifferently explained.

"Why didn't they stop?" April asked, finally stretching her neck around to try to see the cause of the sound for herself.

"I don't know, but things will all be okay," Romney assured.

"Will they say they're sorry?" April asked, finally seeing the minor accident from her tinted window.

"Maybe," Romney answered, circumnavigating the scene on his way to the exit of the lot.

"Will they fix it?" April asked while taking her final look at the circle of people and the two cars.

"I'm sure they'll try," Romney said and steered on toward the mansion

Pleased with how quietly the van drove, Romney felt his own stir of hunger as he navigated the streets to Chapel Hills.

"Hey look, Pearl, I see police lights flashing through the trees," Romney said, leaning over slightly to determine April's level of interest. "That can't be good," Romney announced to the empty passenger seat as he rotated the wheel. The lights on top of two police cruisers silently circled on the side of the road opposite the mansion. Romney looked down the street to see if all looked normal at the Richards' house. Detecting nothing unusual, he sequentially opened the cast iron gate and the garage door. "Hey, Pearl, mommy's car. It looks to be mom's car anyway. It's in the garage; do you want to see her?" Romney said, feeling a rush of blood to his heart.

"No, I just want tot-tots please," April confessed.

"Just wait," Romney began. Then adrenaline hit him like a seizure as he saw three uniformed officers file out of the kitchen doorway toward the purring van. The officers maneuvered efficiently out of the garage, separating as they rounded the tail end of the sports car. Romney's thoughts scattered, gluing his hands to the steering wheel and his eyes to the open kitchen door. One of the officers yelled at the window in a tone of voice that would indicate he anticipated retaliation. The other two took supportive positions and all had eyes on Romney. Seeing no response from their candidate, the lead officer made visual contact with a support officer and signaled him with an inferring tilt of his head. The subtle movement attracted Romney's attention. Then the support officer moved to reposition himself behind the driver's door to try the door handle. When it proved to be locked and seeing the child through the tint, he relayed the info to his commander and genially smiled at the child.

"Mr. Daniels, we're here on a report of domestic violence. I need to see your hands while you unlock the door slowly please."

Romney returned to his wit and slowly moved his hand in compliance to the door lock, but the car lurched forward surprising everybody. The officers regained their startled footing and exchanged glances as they heard the muted apologies from inside the vehicle. Romney let the engine die with a troublesome turn of the key. He unlocked the door and unbuckled the seat belt. The aggressive lead officer stepped in behind the support officer and gave further instructions. For sake of Romney's willful cooperation, they easily placed Romney in hand cuffs, found and cleared his firearm, and secured it in a blue department labeled lockbox.

Romney only managed to say, "My daughter."

"I saw her, Mr. Daniels, she'll be with your wife for the interim until you get your release. And we'll have you out of the cuffs as soon as you're off the premises," the support officer informed him.

"Okay," Romney said, feeling a tightening of emotion in the back of his throat as he watched April apprehensively being escorted toward the open garage. He followed his daughter with his eyes and said a private prayer.

"Don't worry, you'll see her again. We get this all the time," the supportive officer comforted. Being used to void responses, he continued asking, "Should we tow the van?" Guessing his suspect's confusion, he explained, "More than likely the judge isn't going to let you back on the property, so unless your partner has a big change of heart, you're going to have to tow it anyway; unless you can get a mutual friend to move it for you."

"Sure," Romney said, trusting that the officer had courteously offered some unforeseeable insight.

"And sorry for my lead, he's the all heads in the game type," the officer said, addressing Romney more like a friend than a detainee. The supportive officer continued jovially talking as if Romney was mutually waiting at a bus stop. He told Romney the irregularity of this "DV call" and about the other "DV cases" they had recently been assigned. "I'd even let you use my phone to call your lawyer, but Charles probably would have a fit if he came out and saw it," the officer laughed at his suggestion. "How old's your daughter?"

"Two-and-a-half," Romney replied attentive to the windows of the house to see if he could see the curious little face peak through the embroidered curtains of the front room.

"You want to take a seat in the patrol car. I'll be driving you to the station and Captain Chuck probably won't be out for another twenty minutes." the officer kindly offered.

"Sure," Romney responded and took note of the perplexing venerable tone used by the officer.

"It's not all the time we make it out to this part of Pittsburg. There are really pretty homes here," the officer assessed.

"Only as pretty as the homemaker," Romney added with his defeated stride in sync with the officer's unhurried pace.

"What's that?" the supportive officer curiously inquired, looking to Romney's expression for clarification.

Romney cleared his throat and answered, "I think a home is only as beautiful as its homemaker."

"Ah-ha," the supportive officer granted, smiled, and set about intuitively digesting the comment until the lead officer returned from his private interview with his notepad in his hand.

*--- After a sleepless night in minimally furnished jail cell.*

Before Jeff said anything when he arrived at the police station's interview room, he gave Romney the 'I told you so' look.

Romney laughed, having worn out all his worry.

Jeff readily laid everything out for Romney for twenty minutes or so, and when his enlightening brief finished, he wryly said, "Get some sleep. This is the only night the city will be picking up your hotel bill."

## Part 2 - Chapter Nineteen

"Hey, I stopped by your cleaners, and they let me pick up your suit, or suits I should say," Jeff Dunnire informed Romney after he found him in the same interview room at the city jail. The gray walls and featureless furniture helped Jeff cut right to the chase. "Sandy's lawyer will contest alongside of the city's public prosecutor," Jeff briefed while motioning for Romney to sit down. "I don't think he'll get a chance to speak, as from this point the city will take charge of prosecuting," Jeff said, rambling his thoughts freely.

"Hey, am I allowed to use the phone to make some calls?" Romney asked, calling to mind the necessary contacts he had prioritized through the night.

"Of course, here use mine; we have twenty minutes though to be over in the arraignment room," Jeff informed, dipping his hand under the lid of his briefcase and removing his small device. "But two things before you get involved in your business," Jeff said, looking to the corner of the room to gather his critical points of instruction. "One, do not plead guilty...even if we later decide otherwise, okay?" Jeff queried, pausing for Romney's affirmation.

"Okay," Romney agreed.

"And two, I'm going to initially ask the judge to throw out the case based on the evidence of the photograph I took of your head, and I'll cite your testimony that you were concerned over Sandy's facial injuries that she arrived home with; you told me that you only grabbed her wrist, right?"

"Correct," Romney nodded, holding Jeff's phone firmly.

"I presume that the judge won't agree but will more likely ask the prosecutor for a statement on the request. We'll just have to see what the prosecutor says," Jeff said, quickening his rhythm out of respect for his friend's agenda.

"Okay."

"My goal is to prevent any 'no contact order' from going into effect, because if it does, you're probably not going to get to see April till our settlement or, worse case, the trial...without a visitation monitor that is. Go ahead, make your calls and get dressed, if you feel comfortable, and we'll go wait in the hallway," Jeff concluded, wiping off the tiny droplets of rain dotting his watch before pulling out a notepad to review some cursive characters he had written.

"Hey Jack, I'm not going to be into work today," Romney spoke, standing still for a moment. "No. I'm in jail, but don't worry, I should be back hard-knocking tomorrow," Romney said, finishing his track around the table to his plastic covered dress clothes. "Okay. Oh, don't worry about me, it's a formality thing. Bye now," Romney said, dropping the phone from his ear to dial a different number.

"Hey Saundra...yeah, okay...yeah, hey I'm going to promote you to executive for a day. I'm not going to be available till after lunch more than likely, kind of a last-minute thing," Romney said with a false boisterousness, passing the phone between hands as he started to change his collared shirt. "Hey, by chance do you have Anna's number...well, Anna Purse, the babysitter I told you about," Romney asked, seeing Jeff stand to his feet to loft his professional materials to the tabletop. "Well, could you apologize to her for me, I was supposed to meet her for lunch, and I'll unfortunately be detained till who-knows-when this afternoon," Romney explained, trying to maintain his happy composure.

"Oh, no tie, just the jacket; we'll do a tie at the hearings...if there are any," Jeff commented, drawing a momentary blank expression from Romney.

"Hey, thank you so much. I might be able to stop by the office before closing time; bye now," Romney said, and handed the lightweight phone back to his defense counselor. "It's so hard not to have a watch to gauge time by," Romney conceded with a repressed laugh.

"I'm sorry, you'll have that back soon enough. We have time though," Jeff reassured, taking Romney's change of clothes. "I'll take these out to my car and join you in the hallway," Jeff said, lifting all the cumbersome items over his shoulders.

Romney didn't know how to read the authoritative demeanor of the officer in charge of escorting him to his waiting place. The officer walked him along the same initial hallway that Jessica Patsy had taken, and the man-in-blue stoically held open a door at the end of the corridor. He pointed with a rigid hand, instructing him to join two others, a well-dressed citizen and a suited attorney. Each one gave him a momentary critique.

Romney tried to mind his own business by peacefully closing his eyes for the minute he waited. Jeff soon enough pushed through the door and skillfully addressed the guarding officer in a single look as he stepped over to emphasize his support for Romney. His shoulder pads bore dark dots that forewarned of an approaching downpour. "So, are you ready to confuse Judge Schwiffold?" Jeff Dunnire greeted, extending his hand to the professionally dressed civilian.

"I was surprised to see your name when I scanned the indictment summary," the prosecutor with a nearly identical name evenly responded, handling the delicacies of the professional atmosphere with confidence.

"Things running on time?" Jeff asked, recovering from his ulterior test of his counterpart's mood.

"As far as I know; two went beforehand," the prosecutor, Jeff Dunmire, answered, flattening his plain suit jacket.

"And you must be Rich M. Freckile," Jeff assumed, passing his hand over to the other present attorney.

"Representing the interests of Sandra Daniels, yes, sir," the attorney stressed.

The familiar name called Romney to attention, making him privately shudder. Romney clenched his jaw and fixed his gaze toward the blank wall to maintain his composure.

Judge Schwiffold eventually invited the quartet into the arraignment room and greeted each party separately through an interfacing video monitor. "Romney John Daniels, a domestic violence complaint has been filed by Sandra Daniels, claiming assault. Do you understand this charge and its implications?"

"Yes, ma'am," Romney answered in turn to the stern oration.

"It appears that you have selected a private lawyer already, but you should know that you are entitled to a lawyer and if for some turn of events you aren't able to afford one, the court will assign one to you; are you pleading guilty or not guilty to this domestic violence charge of assault?" the austere voice asked, leaving the question hanging for Romney to consider.

"Not guilty, ma'am," Romney confidently stated with a short clarifying glance to his defense attorney.

"I will take comments now before setting bail," Judge Schwiffold poignantly continued, driving to stay on schedule.

"If I might say briefly, Romney Daniels is a loving father and caring husband who has done no harm to his family, especially to Sandy," Jeff said, jumping to take the floor. "The domestic violence summary neglects critical details recorded from the nine-one-one response the day after this supposed incident of assault, and it also fails to accuse Romney of inflicting the recorded injuries altogether, which he assures me that Sandy had arrived home with," Jeff continued, pausing to make eye contact with the video monitor that portrayed the judge. "But as to the nine-one-one call, the first responders reported finding Romney Daniels, and I quote, '...lying face down unconscious with a significant trauma wound to the back of the cranium," Jeff rhythmically continued, redirecting his focus back to the video monitor. "The report records the testimony of the babysitter who alleges she found Romney Daniels in this state. The babysitter also found Romney's daughter locked in her play room in a dirty diaper and crying," Jeff spoke, increasing his level of frustration as he tightly gripped the substantiating report. "I would emphasize that Sandra, Romney's wife, neglected to report this life-threatening incident to police while simultaneously neglecting her daughter; willfully leaving her daughter in the presence of her alleged abuser, if in fact she still stands by her claim of assault," Jeff said, pausing longer than he did the first time. Hoping his argument stuck, he concluded, "In light of a current divorce contest between these same two individuals, I think this de minimis infraction, was encouraged by Sandra Daniels' divorce attorney, Rich M. Freckile, solely for the purpose of embarrassing my client and has no merit worth the time of this court's hearing." With his request formalized, Jeff Dunnire replaced the clenched report back into the rugged portfolio with his irritated hand.

"Thank you, Mr. Dunnire, before you respond, I'd like to ask you, Mr. Freckile, is this true?" Judge Schwiffold posed her question flatly as if anticipating an equally passionate response.

Without fluster Rich M. Freckile started, "As concerned as Mr. Dunnire is for the well-being of his client, when Sandra and I met yesterday, and I saw the injuries done to her face, I was very concerned and directly asked her, 'Did he grab you?' – he, implying her husband. – and when she said, 'Yes,' I encouraged her as any professional lawyer would, to call the law officers in to at least investigate and record the incident properly for her...and her daughter's protection." Rich M. Freckile again made his final point to the entire audience of the room, paying an extra moment of attention to analyzing Romney's flat expression.

"Did you inform your client that child neglect is a felony?" Judge Schwiffold condemned shortly.

Off his guard, Rich M. Freckile momentarily diverted his gaze to the floor before excusing, "She did not disclose the location of her daughter in my brief interview. The law officer's interview is Ms. Daniel's full testimony."

The judge sighed to express her frustration at her compounding trouble, "What do you have to say, Mr. Dunmire?"

Both Jeff's quickly glanced at each other.

"The prosecuting Dunmire," Judge Schwiffold clarified.

"With this new, before the fact, documentation detailing more of the unknowns – honestly, the recorded testimony didn't seem to accuse the husband of the pictured injuries – I'd like to have a continuance to get a chance to officially interview Mr. Daniels myself on the record and perhaps talk terms or stipulations to dismiss," Jeff Dunmire expressed humbly.

"Very well, Romney Daniels, until the time Jeff Dunmire, the prosecutor, removes said charges, you are not to have any contact with Sandra Daniels, or enter the property where she resides on Washington Street, regardless of your property rights," Judge Schwiffold proclaimed, seeming lighter in her mood. "Do you understand?" She asked, looking directly at the defendant.

"Yes, ma'am," Romney said, catching a sense of the judge's improved demeanor. He affirmed a whirlwind of other direct questions, but each new question triggered a different intuitive question, and each pair of questions amassed until he could hardly restrain himself from displaying his emotions. A few scenarios flashed in his mind's eye till a muted roar of thunder snapped his attention to the ceiling. "Yes, ma'am," Romney emotionally repeated like a scolded servant.

## Part 2 - Chapter Twenty

"Do you still have that tie somewhere in reach?" Romney asked Jeff, who had turned from fighting lawyer to friendly chauffeur.

"It's hung...I hung it on the hanger folded in the trunk," Jeff informed, pausing to check for traffic. "Come on, you're free from that choking thing. Enjoy the open air for a minute why don't you," Jeff invited.

"A minute will work out great, Lundberg is about that far up West Franklin," Romney spoke with borderline sarcasm.

"Okay, Romney, seriously back to work? I even have the rest of the day off," Jeff said, turning obediently onto West Franklin Street.

Romney's thumb hovered over his phone's keypad before selecting a square button and placing the phone to his eardrum.

"Do you want me to drop these off to your apartment...no Romney...Romney, sit back; relax for a minute," Jeff said, catching Romney assuming a business posture with his phone. "Dinner's at my house tonight, don't bring Sandy," Jeff said, smiling in attempt to lighten the irony. "And you need to see your daughter."

"How do I do that?" Romney conceded, halting long enough to show Jeff the crest of his chagrin.

"An intermediary, I'll have my wife call and negotiate a time if you don't have any trustworthy go between," Jeff brainstormed on the spot, letting his car idle out front of Lundberg as traffic passed inches from his driver side mirror.

Romney took a deep breath, unable to collect his thoughts. "You'd better remind me about tonight, because I'm all over the place; things were crystal clear this morning in my...thoughts, but the splash of reality at the arraignment has seemingly put me through the shredder."

"Two things, see your daughter, and come to dinner, but the stress I understand," Jeff said as tactfully as he could.

Romney's phone rang.

"Daughter, dinner," Jeff reminded with a laughing grin. "I'll be praying for you, brother," Jeff said, saluting his overwhelmed friend on the curbside.

"Oh, the trunk," Romney said, tapping the roof and retrieving his garments before Jeff pulled into traffic. Romney saluted his friend as he walked toward the approaching site manager. The white collared manager didn't waste time after his handshake before proudly beginning his wordy progress report.

"May I have a moment?" Romney asked the hardhat wearing foreman of Lundberg. "I was in jail this morning, and I need to figure out where my daughter is," Romney divulged with his phone out and ready to dial.

"Jail? Sure, go ahead; the added allowance has everything flowing like a locomotive around here; I could almost take the day off we're...oh, sorry," the foreman rambled.

Romney had already dialed his phone to begin his search. "Sandy," Romney said and bailed on his initial thought. "Is Pearl with you? No? Then where?" Romney asked, failing to find a gentle approach. Having located his daughter, he rallied his courage and interjected, "Sandy...," impatiently listening to the rest of his wife's lethargic excuse. "I was going to invite you to Jeff and Cheryl's for dinner, but the judge set a no contact order till the charges are dismissed."

"What charges?" the foreman interjected in a lull, but he waved his hand apologetically when Romney pulled the phone down to his shoulder.

"Sandy, do you remember the officers at the house yesterday?" Romney painfully inquired. "The police officers," Romney clarified, turning his back to the foreman.

"You didn't mean to, I know, but I really want to see April. Are you going to object to me having her for the week?" Romney transparently asked. "I'm not allowed, so I'm going to send Cheryl...Dunnire, Jeff's wife," Romney reasoned. "Put some lanolin on it...right, it's in the upstairs hallway bathroom. Okay, bye," Romney harshly concluded, returning his phone to his pocket.

"So, what's with the wife and being in jail?"

"What's that?" Romney asked, not hearing the foreman as he walked back to his clothes that were balanced on the back of a chair.

"Oh nothing, just curiosities," the foreman replied, watching Romney lay hold of the fat end of a striped dress tie.

"You said before the call, 'Smooth-goings?'" Romney probed, working the fat end of the silk cloth into a knot under his light green collar.

"Well an extra hundred grand made securing contractors a cinch, and by the way, Wellshop personnel will be by here soon to walk through the framework."

"They must have committed with an initial move like that," Romney said, reflecting some of the foreman's enthusiasm for the upcoming construction work.

"Well someone from upstairs doubled the demo floor budget, and at a perfect time too," the foreman said with a proud smile on his face and his arms crossed. "...over the weekend even. I was able to redirect enough of the upstairs steel members to nearly finish the second and first level...Wellshop's future area," the foreman spoke candidly.

"Wellshop hasn't signed anything more than an interest contract as far as I know. You say they'll be by soon?" Romney said with concern. "Can we walk through now?"

"Absolutely," the foreman said readily and led Romney through the water darkened dirt toward the fully erected tower. Other contractors in their bright vests and hard hats seemed to move with drive and purpose. One worker shouted out his greeting from an open space in some second-floor plastic sheeting meant for a large future window, and Romney waved in return.

"I don't think Bobby has gone home since he picked up his hammer seven years ago, or maybe he's been with us eight now; I don't know anymore," the foreman said, proudly leading Romney into the future foyer. The ugly framing for the triple side by side escalators promised easy access to the future second-floor tenant.

Then Bobby peaked over a safety railing and yelled, "Should be down to bring you up, boss."

"Thanks, Bobby!" the foreman yelled back as a construction elevator opened before Romney.

"Hey, Anna, I'm in an elevator," Romney said, feeling awkward in the intimate space with his cell phone. "Hey, I'm sorry for standing you up for lunch. Did Spencer ever show up?" Romney asked amidst the shrill sound of a saw screaming at a steel member from somewhere outside the opening doors. "I'll be out to look in a minute. Thanks," Romney said, letting the sound dampening doors close him into the elevator. "What's that? ...Smart girl," Romney responded, plugging his open ear to discern her abbreviated summary of the circumstances. "What's that? I'm sorry...April's with her mom at the mansion, I'm going to try to see her today. Well hey, hard to explain here, why don't you deliver your gift to her? ...Well actually, if you could bring her by my work. I hate to ask you, but it'd sure be a big favor to me." Romney said, having felt the rising elevator come to a stop. The doors opened to some chatty workers in their reflective vests and hard hats. The upper floor appeared quieter than the second floor, so Romney stepped off with the phone to his ear.

In the transaction of trading spaces, one of the construction workers grabbed a hard hat from the wall and courteously handed it to Romney while instinctively reciting, "Safety first. We all got to look out for each other now."

"Thanks," Romney replied with a smile. Though the sound of the saw had grown faint, the sound of the wind made hearing equally difficult. "Anna, are you still there?" Romney asked, looking up at the disorienting sky.

"Yes, yes, I can pick April up after three-thirty," Anna approved. "What's Sandy's number so I can call her to let her know I'm coming...Romney?" Anna queried, looking quickly at

her phone to make sure the line had not disconnected.
"Romney, what's Sandy's number so I can call her to let her
know I'm coming," she repeated to the strange noise coming
from the phone. Reluctantly giving up on her effort, she
decided to act upon her offer regardless of Romney's feedback
or further instruction. Anna let her thoughts drift slowly back to
her food, reminding herself she wanted to look busy in case
Spencer made good on his suggestion to meet her after class.
"He's a human being...embarrassed, not evil," Anna recited the
advice to herself, and her shoulders released a shudder from the
terrible memory. A few students moved into conversing range
and chatted over their drenched pasta and three-layered
sandwiches. She toyed with her napkin and watched the buzzing
campus through the cafeteria windows a bit longer. Then she
finally picked up her college books and sandwiched a pink
woven bracelet in the first one as a bookmark. After disposing
of her leftovers at the door of the cafeteria, she walked back
through the alley of booths set up for the career fair toward her
car. The first booth at the corner of the parking lot with its
three attendants had been handing out pink bracelets earlier, and
she taken one for April.

The hits radio station faithfully played an upbeat song, and
Anna hummed along as she crossed the north-south bridge to go
to Washington Street. Looking left down the street, she saw the
neighborhood gym, and gratefully clicked on her right-hand
turning signal to wait for the red light to change. After a few
minutes of winding through the suburbs, Anna pulled to the
curbside of the mansion. After unlocking the mail gate with the
memorized code, Anna followed the artisan cement work, with
its tight pattern of imitation flagstones around to the front porch
and knocked politely. She might have heard a pattering of
footsteps, but the loudness of the wind muffled her certainty.
Then the lady from the family photos carelessly opened the door
and leaned on the frame while propping the storm door open
with her forearm. She held it open enough to speak but not
politely enough to welcome Anna inside to the foyer.

"Well, if it isn't Romney's little bed buddy," Sandy said from
behind her fried head of hair.

"Hi, I'm Anna Purse, are you April's mom?" Anna said, refusing to react to Sandy's welcoming description.

"Yeah," Sandy said indifferently. "Nice car, I have one just like it."

"Yeah? ...Hey, Romney sent me to come get April, is she here?" Anna inquired as optimistically as she dared.

"Yeah," Sandy said again, walking into the house and leaving Anna to infer her actions as an invitation. "So, Rom's girlfriend has a name...," Sandy lofted her voice over her shoulder to communicate with Anna. She collapsed her limbs clumsily onto the sofa and found that Anna had followed her somewhat inside to the living room. "And don't deny it, I have pictures, I hi-had Richey," Sandy said, her vocal chords confusing her words. "I hi-heard a private investigation," Sandy proudly continued, surrendering to the fact that she was as she sounded, intoxicated.

"That's outrageous, I've never set foot in his hou...his bedroom; besides I have a boyfriend," Anna stuttered, cornering herself while flustering her defense.

"And yet, uppity-up, up, up you two went," Sandy said, seeming to find peaceful enjoyment from the implication.

"I'm sorry. I'm being honest," Anna claimed, blushing without further words of assurance.

"It's okay, missy, we all have our secrets don't we. It's just...Rom won't let me enjoy mine."

"But he loves you. He really-really loves you. He wants to help...," Anna said, shying away from clinching her courageous point.

Sandy snapped, "Does he help? No, he warns, he forbids, he denies me the only thing left in my horrifying existence that helps me enjoy life." Sandy's arm started jittering from her flippant bout of excitement, and her eyes started scanning the room meaninglessly.

"But don't you love your daughter, and this house, and...," Anna said, brusquely stopping her list when she was unable to conjure up any other heart pulling items.

"Oh, let him have his daughter...and his divorce," Sandy disputed, laying hold of a needle and managing somehow to match it with a jittering vial. She ignored her guest without remorse or further comment.

Anna imagined with disgust the rest of the ritual as she moved quickly, trembling as she anxiously called for April. April appeared armless at the top of the stairs, standing in her mother's high-heels and dragging a long train of clothing from the bedroom. "I'm all dressed up and ready to go, don't-cha like it?" April said as if rehearsed.

The childishness made Anna involuntarily give up a short laugh as she rushed up the steps. Trying to conceive a plan to prevent April from forever taking in the sight of her mother inducing her addiction, she readied April to whisk her out the front door. Yet, after her motherly actions of removing the oversized attire and of disposing the soiled diaper, the appalling thought surfaced that this may not have been a first occurrence. Her divergent line of thinking served well enough to ease her conscience, and she carried April to and through the front door.

"Bye, mom," April waved over Anna's shoulder.

"Bye, darlings," Sandy replied, satisfied with her view of the ceiling.

Anna didn't pause longer than it took to open the door and its associated storm. The storm unevenly crashed into the sturdy frame.

"You didn't close the door, princess," April contested from inside Anna's bouncing hug.

"It's okay. Your mother might want to wave goodbye," Anna deceptively rationalized.

"She doesn't ever wave goodbye to me though," April replied, as Anna paused momentarily to release the mailman's gate.

Turning to see how open she had left the door, she told herself in a whisper, "It doesn't matter."

"What doesn't matter?" April asked with curiosity.

Spontaneously repeating herself, Anna replied, "It doesn't matter, you can still wave to her."

After the scurry of buckles, she launched the car down the street but stopped abruptly at the street's end.

"Why did you stop?" April asked, looking out at the tall trees that guarded the entrance.

"I have to call your dad to tell him something," Anna said, letting her tensed nerves fumble the phone out of her handbag.

"Tell him I love mom," April said instinctively. "And I'm hungry."

"Okay...two good things to say," Anna automatically replied, focusing her attention on locating the stored number.

"Hey, Anna, perfect timing."

"Perfect is less than it seems, um," Anna quivered into the phone, unsure of how to most expediently bring up the trouble or if she could at all.

"You're calling about whether or not to get April I suppose. Sorry about...."

"No, I have April...I just grabbed; I had to get her out," Anna said, unintentionally abbreviating her speech.

"Is the house on fire?" Romney asked, naturally conveying his concern.

"No. Sandy's doing...," Anna said, censoring the rest of her disclosure.

"Now...you're sure? She's doing her illegal thing now?" Romney repeated.

"Yes, completely at peace on the couch," Anna affirmed, squeezing her eyes closed and waiting for her heart to beat.

"You're out of there? Safe?" Romney asked to be certain.

"Yes," Anna said, interpreting Romney's question to signify that she did the right thing.

"Don't worry about Sandy. I'll phone for the paramedics. Just come by work, and park in the street. It should be emptying out over the next few minutes. See you soon," Romney said, making his instructions sound inviting. "Ahhh, I'll have to find a better time to do this work thing," Romney said to himself as he transitioned to dialing the emergency number.

## Part 2 - Chapter Twenty-One

"Well, Romney, now I won't need to call to remind you about dinner," Jeff announced, comforted by the sound of his closing garage door.

"Hey, I've kind of got a situation with Sandy," Romney replied directly.

"Were you able to find someone to pick up your daughter? Because you didn't call Cheryl. I know that much," Jeff said, missing Romney's subtle vie of concern.

"Yes, Anna has her and should be arriving any moment with her," Romney answered.

"Who's this Anna?" Jeff said half-seriously, separating his portfolio from his briefcase.

"The babysitter...whom I owe massive favors and apologies to as of late," Romney rationalized, thinking more so about his predicament. He stood on the street with a bag of Butler's chick peas in the crux of his arm and his head on a swivel for Anna. "Almost like an unofficial nanny, but Sandy...I called nine-one-one on Sandy," Romney said.

"Yeah, what's up with Sandy?"

"According to Anna, she was doing her drugs with April in the house, so I called the paramedics. I would naturally tend to her myself, but...."

"Good, I'm glad you're at least thinking straight."

"But I would like someone to check on her," Romney said outrightly.

"Well, it seems that you've arranged that already. My advice...as no doubt this has happened before, and she's managed on her own, just let it play out," Jeff said and waited for Romney's reaction. Kissing the air in his wife's direction, he scooped up his son in one arm and groaned, "Oh that's enough, Justin."

Romney took the cue from the background noise to change the topic. "What's your wife cooking?" Romney asked without changing his focus on the side street.

"Not pork, though I know you won't believe me...."

"No, I believe that you believe your wife's not cooking pork, and you can be assured I'll eat your wife's pork graciously," Romney said, trying to forget what so worried him as he spoke. The sight of Anna's bright vehicle lifted his spirit, and he laughed into the phone.

"Aww come on, ye of little faith. Honey, what are you baking for dinner tonight?" Jeff questioned from across the room with the phone pulled away from his ear.

"Crust-less bacon quiche. What? I put spinach in it so it will be healthy...okay so not a lot of spinach, but I made the pigs-in-a-blanket...the ones that April liked so much last time," Romney faintly heard, focusing his attention primarily on flagging down the red car. He watched Anna successfully pulled up less than an inch away from leaving a tire mark on the curb. Putting the phone back to his ear he said, "Okay, April's here now. We should be there in about thirty minutes."

"You sure you'll eat graciously? You'll never trust me again," Jeff said apologetically.

"Don't be ridiculous; your wife cooks, and April certainly doesn't mind," Romney said as he opened the rear door to see April.

"Somebody doing some cooking?" Anna chimed in as Romney hung up the phone.

"Anna, actually can I climb up front for a minute to discuss Sandy?" Romney immediately asked as he slid the phone into his billfold pocket.

"Thank you, please!" Anna asked with obvious relief. Then she tilted her head and glanced with her eyes to inquire, "Is April okay here?"

"Anna, I've been unfairly dragging you through my obstacle course," Romney asserted without further permission, stopping to look at Anna who had diverted her gaze in respect of his tone. "You know those mud-covered obstacle courses...obstacle debacle," Romney said, feeling bad for ironically starting his apology as such. "I'm sorry and so grateful. If I have stirred up any feelings or emotions compelling or making you feel obligated on April's behalf, please know...."

"No, no, not at all," Anna interrupted, "I'm sorry, I really am; remember when I...."

"Anna."

"No, I don't want you...I mean, I want you to know...."

"Anna."

"No, Sandy said...."

"Annie! Anna dear," Romney interrupted, exhaling a smile as his chosen tactic succeeded in suppressing Anna. "You don't have anything to be sorry about, so don't apologize. You've become such a great friend that I half-wish you could befriend

my wife...," Romney said, capitalizing on his opportunity to
speak. "I mean that, I...you...just click, but seriously now, you're
way mature beyond your age, and maybe it's an intrinsic thing,
but what am I saying...," Romney said, trying to untangle his
point as Anna listened responsively. He could see her avert her
eyes to the steering wheel every time he looked in her direction.
"You're not April's mother...but please don't let my gruffness
discourage you the least bit. You've proven your capacity as
such, and I am forever grateful," Romney said and stopped after
seeing the harsh impact of his words.

"She's my babysitter!" April timely included.

Hesitant to speak, Anna's lips started flinching like a short
circuit. "Sandy told me that she had pictures of us going...up,
up, up," she admitted after a fitful breath and let Romney infer
the rest of the story.

Romney paused for a moment then slowly connected the dots,
"That all makes sense." He noticed Anna's slight reprieve.
"Sandy's messed up in the head a little and mixed up with a
smooth-talking lawyer. It is not...," Romney said and paused till
he had Anna's full attention. "...not your fault if trouble comes
to me for offering you that ride home."

"I hear what you're saying, and I'll promise not to blame
myself on one condition," Anna strategically proposed, "that you
let me keep babysitting April. Oh, why are your fingers in your
mouth again silly." April had managed to fit all her fingers into
her mouth. Then Anna continued her attempt to filibuster her
proposal into agreement by taking the duplicate pink bracelet
from her arm. "Here give me your hand," Anna instructed and
easily transferred the adult sized band onto April's tiny wrist.

April's bright eyes appreciated the jewelry with an open smile
and concluded, "It's pretty," before plugging her opposite hand
into her mouth. Then Anna nervously pursed her lips and lifted
her eyebrows with hope when her attention had no other
options.

Romney saw Anna's cheeks dimple and couldn't help but
smile, conceding to Anna's positivity with a nod. "Well, April,
pork is a waitin' to be eaten," Romney exclaimed.

"Yay!" April sang ignorantly as to what pork meant and became excited about what sounded like her favorite pointed utensil.

--- *In a booster seat forty minutes later at Jeff and Cheryl's house.*

April sat still for the time it took to consume most of the pigs in their flaky blankets.

"Look at her cheeks...just munching away," Cheryl commented with pride.

"Hey, Pearl, do you want some spinach quiche?" Romney asked blandly, foregoing the extra effort in prediction of April's answer.

"No," April said decidedly, finding space between chews to make her answer clear enough.

"Why don't we slip this out and slide this in," Romney suggested, replacing the pig with a carrot.

April didn't take to her dad's traded-in carrot. Instead she eyed Justin's plate and decided to suck on her utensil for interim entertainment.

"So, how's the progress of Lundberg coming along?" Jeff asked, careful in how he approached the luring topic of work.

"Impressively on fire," Romney returned, intending a pun. "I haven't heard about any new project starts on your end. How was the rest of your day off?" Romney asked, remembering Jeff's earlier perspective on his work choices.

"Well, you're a motivating man. I couldn't, from your lead, resist the urge to check in at work," Jeff admitted, tossing his napkin onto his plate as if he had finished at a restaurant.

Romney followed suit and turned to Cheryl to express his thanks, saying, "I'm nearly done-in with the quiche. It was good."

"Ready for a Sundae?" Cheryl politely asked, rising with hospitality to clear Romney's plate and dinnerware.

"Always ready for a new week," Romney responsively asserted, looking back at Jeff and then at his daughter.

"How about the one that comes with ice cream and syrup?" Cheryl tactfully clarified, asking her question over her shoulder as she walked to the kitchen with the collected dishes.

"Oh, oh, no thank you. I'm sorry," Romney said, leaning forward uncomfortably.

"Don't be silly; would April, or Pearl, as you call her, like one?" Cheryl said, amending her offer to the sound of the ceramic plates clanking in the sink.

"Uh...n...."

"Does it come with chocolate chips?" April asked, having found a reason to remove the fork from her mouth.

"Why yes it does, April, but ask your dad first," Cheryl said conscientiously.

April, seeing the treat within grasp, turned like a puppy to her dad and asked, "Can I have some chocolate chips?"

"Chocolate at six-thirty, Pearl, is kind of like giving coffee to an auctioneer," Romney disputed ready to deploy his tried and true fatherly tactic. "But if you eat the rest of your carrots, you may ask Mrs. Cheryl for some."

Relaying the information as if her dad had spoken to her privately, she announced, "My dad says I can if I finish eating my carrots."

"She is just so advanced for her age in her speech and understanding," Cheryl complemented over April's head to Romney. The incentive worked in April's case, and as April ate with a new furor of hunger, Cheryl slid a bowl of ice cream in front of her husband.

"We've been picking up quite a few non-profit reconstructions; people approaching us with minimal budgets for expansion or structural repair," Jeff said, explaining as he dragged his spoon up the covered mound of ice cream. "It's kind of frustrating...makes me regret ever leaving the law office," Jeff added before taking a bite. Romney waited for Jeff to continue while admiring his motivated child. "You know, small as we are, a non-profit...able project will still tie up resources for quarter of a year," Jeff said, taking another bite. "You seem to have had all the divine blessing, cause my start up...competition, hasn't ramped up at nearly the same pace as yours."

"Have you looked into having a low-cost department, like an internship staffed unit or pairing new-hires with the movers and shakers to offload their schedules somewhat?" Romney shared, knowing Jeff's compulsive tendency to find a way to accommodate everyone and every request.

"Hmm, interns...I hadn't thought of that," Jeff admitted, returning to his slumping mound of dairy.

"You set a more than fair price, I mean look at me," Romney freely compared, knowing his friend appreciated his input.

"So, interns," Jeff repeated, letting his spoon fall with appreciation into his empty dessert bowl. "Where's the best place to go looking for them?" Jeff asked, knowing his goodwill and longtime friendship would buy him a valuable nugget of advice.

"Well, I dropped by Vern Hill the other day to introduce April to the babysitter that I told you about – this is before the iron skillet incident – and you know...they have a very well-kept landscape of students. It's where I would start," Romney tipped while reaching over April's happy fingers to steal a few of her dark chips that Cheryl had gladly delivered.

"Vern Hill you say," Jeff pondered out loud.

"Yeah, the yearly fundraiser was well attended this year as well...that's where I met Anna in fact...the babysitter," Romney explained, turning again to find April's empty dish. "Isn't that right, Pearl?" Romney encouraged, removing the dish before the depleted container turned into a toy.

Still happy from her chocolate, April pledged, "Yeah, Anna let me look for a baby deer."

"My dad kills baby deer," Justin boasted on his return through the kitchen, seeing a chance to compete for attention with the younger guest.

"Justin, that's inappropriate for her age," Cheryl chided, holding the dripping dish instinctively over the sink with her rubber wash gloves.

"Sorry," Justin apologized, retreating shyly into the living room to play with his toys.

"My dad has a gun, but he doesn't shoot things with it," April informed the adults at the table. Romney took note and smiled. "Daddy, can we go outside and look for baby deer?" April pleaded, pulling at her restraints.

"No, but I'm sure Jeff would appreciate your expertise on his next hunt," Romney joked.

"Justin, run up to our room and bring April one of mom's toy dolls to play with...now please," Jeff indisputably instructed.

# Part 2 - Chapter Twenty-Two

The idea that Romney had planted had bothered him all night until finally he put it to rest by deciding he would call Vern Hill first thing in the morning. "Hi, my name is Jeff Dunnire; I'm the owner of Scales Architectural Company, and I'm wondering what the process might be to go about offering an architectural internship to Vern Hill students?" Jeff asked straight to his point. He listened to the young voice answer his question with more approval and accommodation than he expected. "Today? That's an option? Great! See you soon," Jeff replied and slammed down the receiver like he had just been invited to eat lunch with the governor of Pennsylvania. "Patrick, we're going on a field trip, and we're going to be gone all day. So, I hope you charged your cell phone," Jeff said, soliciting Patrick for his position as lead architect and for his having characteristically settled into his desk before the average morning rush.

"New property?" Patrick asked, ready for whatever awaited.

"No...new department, and I need a second head to prevent any rash decisions on my part," Jeff informed as he headed back to his office for a few personal supplies. Stopping into the supply room while still actively trying to piece together his vision, he slammed through a couple of tall metal cabinets. Realizing he would need more hands for the items he had selected, he set down the impromptu promotional materials and went in search of a box. The mail room had an appropriate container and he returned with a box as well as with a different idea. Replacing most of the special-order promotional items on the shelves, he picked up a rolled-up vinyl sign that typically would mark the entrance of a construction site and hugged it under his arm. Returning to Patrick's cubical with his briefcase and the portable sign, he found Patrick ready to depart.

"Are you sure we're not surveying a new site?" Patrick reiterated his question, walking with Jeff to the front of the office. "Because I'll change my shoes if so."

"No, we're going to see if we can find some qualified candidates at Vern Hill to hire as interns."

"Interns...good, we need a few new faces around here," Patrick said, perking up at the novelty of the trip. "Young minds, especially those immersed in the college curriculum, will be motivation for the rest of the team. Tammy would be the most recent addition, and she's been with us what, four years now?" Patrick rationalized, while holding open the administration door behind Jeff. "Mutual benefit...," Patrick continued enthusiastically.

--- *Twenty minutes later in the Welcome Office at Vern Hill.*

Jeff recognized the voice of the student behind the counter, and the student reciprocated, remembering Jeff's call. After a brief set of instructions, Jeff left the office with a detailed hand-drawn map describing the location of nearly every available career fair table.

"Contact cards with pens would have been nice."

"I almost brought the pens."

"I should go grab one of their pens," Patrick chuckled, pointing out the abundance of giveaway items set out on another table.

The vinyl sign, reading Scales Architectural Company, kept peeling off the table in the breeze, which frustrated the attempts Patrick made to productively display the hand full of general marketing brochures. After an unproductive hour, more displays began erecting along the walkway of brown tables. As soon as they did, professional looking students started arriving with questions.

"Have you guys been here all week?" A student asked, obviously looking to start a deeper conversation. He had his hair combed to one side and wore an open collared shirt. Nobody had a tie on, and the wind kept all the displays busy.

"This is our first day here. What's your name?" Patrick encouraged, deserting their defiant sign.

"Jonathan Wickfell. I'm in my sophomore year, studying architecture. What do you guys do?" Jonathan answered, noticing the problematic vinyl sign.

"We do mostly small-scale reconstruction. We've been in business for eight years now," Patrick answered, following Jonathan's distraction closely.

Jonathan let down his bag and unzipped the main compartment. "I just bought this at the athletic store; do you think it'll work in holding down your sign?" Jonathan asked in an unrelated response, offering the entirety of his new hand-tape to Patrick.

"Yeah. I think that might work, Jonathan. Would you mind giving me a hand taping it down?"

"Not at all," Jonathan said, leaving his bag where it was in the path without a second thought.

Jeff took note of the tripping hazard and interrupted his casual conversation to move the bag a couple feet to safety.

"What motivated you to pursue a career of architecture?" Jeff heard Patrick ask Jonathan from behind him.

"I love looking at something and figuring out how it ticks. I daydream sometimes of the notion that one day I'll get to see something that I imagine up here become reality," Jonathan explained, tapping his head. After successfully securing the sign, Jonathan returned the white fibrous tape to the bottom of his book bag. "Visually stunning things captivate my attention," Jonathan continued, lifting the straps of his bag over his shoulders.

"Well, Jonathan, let me get your phone number; I think we could put your imagination to work," Patrick solicited, closing the informal introduction.

"Yeah sure, in fact I have it all written down here on my resume...in my back pack," Jonathan said, lifting his book bag down off his shoulder again.

"Where are you headed off to after this?" Patrick asked as he received the hand-written piece of paper.

"Well, I was going to finish walking through the fair. I saw a few other booths that looked at least a little interesting...but then I'll be playing basketball at the gym," Jonathan explained, letting his passion escape from his cheeks.

"You have great lettering here. I would have expected a printed resume, but this is impressive."

"My teacher told me to do that," Jonathan said proudly. "He said, 'Once you have lettering to show off, show it off, they're going to ask you to letter anyway,'" Jonathan continued, turning his attention to a female student that passed behind him. Hooking his nose as if to wipe off an itch, he looked back at Patrick.

"Thank you, Jonathan, Jeff and I will be sure to look over your information here. Do you have any other questions I could answer?" Patrick asked, slipping the hand-written resume into the back of his legal sized notepad.

"Oh, a bunch, but they would likely be better saved for an interview or something more sit down-ish. Do you guys have a website?" Jonathan asked, putting his thumbs under his bookbag straps.

"Why yes, good question, in fact here, take one of these," Patrick said, reaching with one step toward the table. "This is a brochure that we distribute to prospective clients. You might find it interesting," Patrick said and turned his attention aside for a moment to another eavesdropping student. "Have fun on the basketball court, Jonathan," Patrick called back to Jonathan who had courteously stepped back and started moving away with the push of students.

Jonathan smiled and lifted his hand politely to signal that he had heard Patrick's farewell and spun to walk properly down the brick pathway.

## Part 2 - Chapter Twenty-Three

"You worked late; must be something new," Cheryl said as Jeff pushed through the front door.

"Yeah, I thought I told you," Jeff answered.

"I'm sure you did, but I still haven't mastered your dialect of telepathy," Cheryl said, leaning in for his passing kiss.

"I had to catch up after being over at Vern Hill all day," Jeff said while unloading his brief case by the office door.

"Oh, so you took Romney up on his suggestion," Cheryl said, mentally connecting the dots.

*--- The next morning after a well-deserved night of sleep.*

Walking into Scales, Jeff sat down for no longer than a minute before he took up the stack of sorted resumes. He thumbed through the top four and smiled as he walked out to the lobby for the routine morning meeting. The queer shaped lobby barely fit everyone with its three tables, twelve chairs, and standing room for roughly fifteen people. "Camille, Grace, we'll need to sit down right after this," Jeff preempted, holding up the stack of resumes. "Camelot Kitchen, Wickies House of Children, and Calvary Tabernacle all approached us over this past week with new proposals for expansion," Jeff started and paused at the reply of muttering. "All of the proposals would have been working at cost to us, and as much as I like each of these non-profits, and knowing how each serves this city faithfully, I think your efforts will be better applied elsewhere." Somebody raised an objection from behind the first line of standing employees. "I know, Howard, but taking in just one or two of these projects will tie up our staff for the greater portion of next year's peak building season," Jeff reasoned. "What I hope to accomplish with this stack of papers is...to find and hire a group of talented interns that will tackle these projects with our minimal oversight. They'll hopefully introduce us to a new generation of technologies and hopefully spur us on in our own positions to continue learning," Jeff said, surveying the appreciation of his audience. "Each intern will have a mentor to teach and oversee him or her, and though I have people in mind, this will all be voluntary," Jeff said tactfully, hoping to clearly convey the opportunity and extra responsibility all at once. "We will hire as many interns as we have mentors volunteer. How does that sound?" A few people clapped, making Jeff smile as he made eye contact with Patrick across the angular room. "Good. Patrick and I canvassed students all day yesterday and competed with probably thirty to forty other companies all hoping for the same thing, so let me know by lunch time please if you're interested in mentoring." Jeff closed and turned to Camille and Grace who sat to his right. Reducing his voice to a conversing level, Jeff handed Camille the stack of resumes with the instructions, "First thing this morning, look over these with

Grace and Patrick and call in as many of them as you think are qualified for interviews."

"Sure thing."

"Yeah."

"Set up the interviews on my calendar and Patrick's also," Jeff directed. "Draw straws amongst yourselves as to who wants to interview with us," Jeff said, smiling to signal the end of their impromptu after meeting.

Camille politely took the stack Jeff offered and started gauging the number of sheets with her thumb.

*--- After a hectic school week and a good-feeling interview at Scales.*

Jon quickly shuffled his feet, lunging forward which put his defender off balance. Jumping up for a shot he sank the basketball from a half-step inside the red painted perimeter line. The polished floor captured the squeak of his landing, and the hustle of the players flippantly tracked the ball and their opponents to the other end of the court.

"When are you going to just run around him, Jon?"

"Two is two, isn't it?" Jon defended between breaths, positioning himself an arm's length away from his opponent and square with the basket.

The opponent didn't seem to concern himself with Jon's outstretched arms. Instead he deceptively communicated nonverbally with his right-wing teammate.

Jon bladed his right foot back suggesting an open lane to his unconcerned opponent. All in a scurry, Jon engaged, creating a domino effect of movement. Jon's opponent sank to his own defensive level and, in full control, offensively pushed off Jon and mailed the ball in a skilled arch toward the basket. Timing the play, the opponent's teammate leaped into position before the ball passed the rim and hand delivered the ball to the nylon net. The smash made Jon envious, and the millisecond of lost focus allowed Jon's opponent time to pose his defensive threat. Missing the initial trajectory of the inbounding ball, Jon ended one full step shy of receiving the powerful pass. Discouraged, Jon slowed his opponent long enough for the referee's whistle to announce the game's end.

Heading to the bench, his teammate slapped him on the shoulder and said, "Don't worry, it makes it easier; this way we'll get the bye."

"Yeah, I don't know what happened there."

"Weren't you three for five?"

"What? One for three, maybe. I was ecstatic when I made that last one," Jon laughed with embarrassment, pulling his shirt away from his chest to prevent the defeating sweat from soaking into his skin.

His teammate started saying, "Drive...," but he noticed Jon's attention redirected to his vibrating cell phone and instead silently saluted farewell with two fingers.

"Hello?" Jon answered the phone while making full use of the university's gray towel. "That's great! Yes, yes, for certain!" Jon answered. "I'm sorry. What's your name again? Camille did you say?" Jon asked. His feet didn't know whether to be tired or happy as he joined a few players heading toward the general men's locker room. "I interviewed with Patrick and Jeff...and Grace. So, what's next?" Jon asked, pressing the phone to his eardrum.

## Part 2 - Chapter Twenty-Four

Jonathan sprinted from the towering gymnasium to his Monday morning Math Logic class. Luckily, Jonathan caught the door before it swung closed. Finding himself uncomfortably tailgating Professor Kovan in his brown sport jacket, he hung his head to ignore the attention he knew the entire class paid to him. While turning into his row he glanced and thought that he saw Erica smile. That smile hijacked the entirety of Professor Kovan's hypothetical thesis on statistical certainty.

As the class ended, Francisco, his table mate, won his attention by saying, "Too bad about the bye today, you're still in the tournament, aren't you?"

Jon winced and struggled to focus his attention away from the general dispersion of students on the other side of the room.

"I know it's not the fall tournament or anything, but you know...," Francisco said, trying to solicit a response from his tablemate. "Are you hungry?" Francisco continued, slowing down in response to Jon's lagging pace.

"Yeah, I know," Jon replied absent-mindedly, looking up at the wall mounted clock. "I think I'm going to sell my bike," Jon stated before making eye contact with his tablemate.

"Why?" his desk mate looked puzzled as he surrendered to Jon's new topic.

"Do you know any places to buy a cheap car?" Jon asked, further ignoring his polite acquaintance. As the students poured into the hallway, Jon searched for Erica's refreshing face.

"Have...."

"Sorry, I'll catch up with you later," Jon cut off Francisco, openly admitting his distraction to swim up the stream of students. He fell into the place he was aiming for, in front of Erica. His eyes suggested he had forgotten how beautiful she was, but his words inviting her to lunch came naturally to him.

"Sure, are you up for it, Anna?" Erica responded graciously to Jon's lunch proposal.

Jon blushed like a make-up display but gladly extended his invitation silently to Anna.

"We were heading that way anyway," Anna accepted and brushed by Jon's shoulder to suspend the door.

"Oh, much thanks," Jon appreciated as he revolved back into line with the exodus.

Anna continued holding the door for her friend and then handed off the responsibility to the next student in line.

"So, did you gals understand what Professor Kovan was saying?" Jon asked, trying to feel out his captive audience.

"I don't think it was too hard to figure," Erica honestly replied, turning to encourage Anna's agreement.

Jon peaked out in front of Erica and noted Anna's shoulders confirm Erica's assessment. "Maybe I missed it for sake of daydreaming...."

"Or dozing," Erica responsively joked, enjoying her position between Anna and the smart kid in class.

"I'm Jon by the way," Jon introduced, trying to repress the redness he felt growing on his face.

"Erica.  And this is the lovely Anna, isn't she adorable in her polka-dots?"  Erica described with a jitter.  She fanned Anna's skirt open to validate her description.

"Hi again, Anna.  Anna's the awesome person that rescued me from a torrential rainstorm last week," Jon admitted.

Erica closed her mouth with a smile and turned her eyes to the predominant foot traffic.  Making their way through the cafeteria they stood in line for a few minutes, exchanging a few awkward grins amongst the commotion.

"What do you gals want to eat?  I'll be happy to pay," Jon finally asked.

"That's kind of you, Jon, but I think all the meal vouchers are the same...yours or mine, and Anna here's rich," Erica declined.

"Yeah, just offering, what do you get usually...Erica?" Jon singled out, turning his attentive eyes away to share in Erica's perusing of the overhead menu.

"They make a good pesto panini, it's basil or parsley I think."

"The green sauce?  You like that?" Jon asked with surprise.

"It's good.  I get it all the time where I work."

"I'll have to try it...again; a pesto panini, please," Jon asserted, leaning toward the glass shield that protected the matrix of sandwich ingredients.

"What do you want on it?" the cook straightly asked almost mechanically.  His eyes seemed bothered by having to annunciate the question.

"I don't know, what should I get on it?" Jon asked, connecting with Erica's eyes for the second time since his invitation to lunch.

"Whatever you want," Erica answered, suspending her recommendation by retreating her attention to the security of her friend.

"I'll get whatever she's having on hers," Jon decided.

"She's having a salad; do you want a pesto salad?"

"No, um, whatever Anna cho...well chicken.  Chicken will be fine; just chicken that's all," Jon looked down and fiddled with the wallet stuck in his front pocket.  After being the only one to get held up at the cashier, Jonathan conscientiously grabbed utensils and napkins for everybody and walked to the edge of the seating area, eagerly searching for his female classmates.  He eventually found them involved in a giggling discussion at a private table toward the side of the cafeteria, and he assumed that he had permission to sit down in the remaining chair across from Anna. Once comfortable, he smiled and asked without remorse, "So how is the salad...and panini?"

"Good."

"Good."

The two friends unconsciously suppressed their prior liveliness to continue consuming their entrees. Jon joined them in eating, periodically smiling in lieu of attempting dialogue. Jon's phone buzzed, and he automatically brushed his hands free of crumbs to answer it, expecting it to continue its roll of delivering good news. "Matty, Matty, Matt, I'm not robbing you. I have it," Jon suppressed, stretching his arms around to the back of his head. "Matty, I have...," Jon said, trying to edge in a word. "Here with me now. I have...well, come to the cafeteria then; I'm eating," Jon said, finally succeeding in his conveyance. "I'm sorry. Would you gals defend my sandwich while I make a delivery," Jon requested, avoiding direct eye contact with Erica.

"Sure," Anna said, responding after Erica's silent smirk.

As soon as Jon left with his backpack on his shoulder Erica leaned into Anna and asked, "Do you see where this is going?"

"Kind-a obvious, right?"

"Boys get that look in their eyes, and if I give him any more allowance, he'll be stalking me where I work...never to get rid of him," Erica said, watching Anna take another slow bite of her sandwich. "I'm not ready for another one. Would you?"

"Of course, you've got to get to work anyway. I'll stay and 'guard' his food; you go...shew," Anna said, automatically forming in the back of her head the words she needed to faithfully deliver the inferred request.

"Come by Crumbles tonight, and I'll buy you dinner; you're so nice!" Erica said, abandoning the remains of her salad to ensure her escape.

"You know he seems like one of the kind and honest ones," Anna critiqued from behind her napkin.

"Uhh...you might be right, but...not worth the risk to find out," Erica explained as she hastened her farewell, and before disappearing through the glass door, she tipped her head back and authentically mouthed, "Thank you."

## Part 2 - Chapter Twenty-Five

"Oh...where's Erica gone off to?" Jon said, settling back into his seat. He performed well enough to not sound disappointed.

"She had to get off to work." Anna apologized, straightening her polka-dotted skirt from underneath the table.

Jon had taken a bite of his sandwich immediately after his question and settled into Anna's eyes. "So, tell me about you, Anna," Jon inquired after the pause before downing another piece of his panini.

"Erica just got out of a relationship that's still kind of jading her, but me...what about me?"

"Yes, what makes Anna different?" Jon said, further internalizing his disappointment.

"Oh, I love kids and history; what about you?" Anna asked, taking her turn to nibble.

"Kids, eh? I have a little angelic niece."

"Around here?"

"No, unfortunately, or I'd introduce you. It's about a ten-hour drive...south," Jon paused for a second, noting Anna's new attentiveness. "I like new things...like new concepts, opportunities, hobbies...things like that. It keeps everything interesting." The sun started beaming through the trees, striking Jon's face. He reached up and instinctively pulled down the window's visor sufficiently to shade his eyes.

"So, what was the delivery all about?" Anna asked, following his movements with interest.

"Oh, I deliver magazines from a press downtown, well not too far away, but they let me fill their orders for a little commission." Jon said, feeling the muscles in his cheeks that shy people feel when talking about themselves. "I mean it takes twenty minutes or so on my long board one way...well shorter now since I've biked, but there's a big enough market here to make the monthly trip worth it," Jon self-consciously rambled, gripping his napkin out of view in his lap.

"Are you studying business?" Anna kindly asked, sensing Jon's nervousness.

Jon reached up again to the visor and lowered it completely, shutting off their view of the serene campus landscape. "Nope, that would be logical though...architecture actually," Jon answered with a more comfortable expression. "And I just got an internship this morning! In fact, you're the first person to hear the news!" Jon continued unable to restrain his ballooning voice.

"Oh congratulations, where's the internship?"

Jon hiccupped and said, covering his mouth, "Scales..."

"Scales?"

"Arch...Scales Architecture something."

Anna chuckled, "Are you excited?"

"Really, my dad has been pressing me to get some sort of industry experience before I graduate, not that graduation is any time soon, and this is right in my field of study. Patrick Wilson and Jeff Duy-er or something were great to me during the interview, and now I just can't wait to get started."

"When do you start?" Anna asked before finishing the final corner of her panini.

"I don't know, hah," Jon convincingly admitted, smiling again with an honest shrug. "I hope somebody calls and lets me know. I just found out about it today."

"Up...my turn," Anna responded to the ring of her cell phone. "Time for my mom to...," Anna said, letting her humble emotion hover blankly for a moment as she waited for the caller identification to scroll across the screen.

"You can take it."

"No...don't need to."

"No really, I don't mind. Look at me over here. I'm not Mr. Interesting or by any means important enough to keep you from your business. You really should; you're going to make me feel bad. Okay, well, I don't feel bad now that you're looking at me like that," Jon said, unsuccessfully trying to hide his flustering admiration.

"You can look at me, I don't mind."

"Well, it's just you...cell phone, privacy and all."

"Would you walk me to my car, Jonathan Wickfell?" Anna said as calmly as she could to counteract the tension building in her neck.

"And why should I have such an honor?" Jon said almost instinctively.

"A courtesy for a friend?"

"Is that a good enough reason? Absolutely!" Jon rhetorically replied, springing to his feet. "Here, you're done, right?"

"Oh, the pickle."

"Oh, sorry; oh, Boise. I'll get you another one."

"Don't be silly, you haven't touched yours," Anna said, reaching over to his tray without hesitation.

"What a klutz," Jon confessed as he knelt to collect the fallen wedge. "Do you like brine or vinegar more?" Jon asked unconsciously.

"Brine, brine...three times more. I can't help but think of lukewarm pickles sitting on a grocer's shelf for two years."

"You do have a point," Jon agreed and stood up to his feet. "In fact, I don't think I'll ever look at another vinegar pickle the same now that you've said that," Jon confessed and consciously tried to pinpoint the source of what made Anna's answer fascinating during his trip to the trash receptacle.

Jon caught up to Anna with a double step.

"I have this suspicion...."

"Oh, hold on...," Jon interrupted, jogging a few paces back to the small table to collect his book bag.

"Phwew...I'd have to bike a good while to replace this, and then I'd have to explain how there was this girl and this brine fermented vegetable...and they wouldn't believe me and charge my account anyway," Jon rambled.

"Anna, hey," Spencer said as the couple passed through the exit door of the cafeteria.

After glancing at Anna and seeing her as blank as a white wall, Jon haphazardly enthused, "Any friend of Anna's is a friend of mine. Hi, I'm Jon."

"Spencer."

"Spencer, wonderful. Have you tried the cafeteria's pesto panini?"

"No."

"No, seriously? Anna's friend and...well, you'd better get it while you can, maybe a little thick on the tomato but worth the meal voucher."

Anna slipped her hand down Jon's forearm and into his hand.

"Well, Spencer, don't you think Anna looks lovely in her white and polka-dotted dress?"

"Certainly."

Jon looked again at Anna who had frozen in place. "Oh...kay, you ready to go, Anna?" Jon prodded.

"Yeah," Anna welcomed, breaking her trance with a short laugh. She looked one more time and victoriously read an admission of defeat on Spencer's face. "I'm glad you got to meet Jon," Anna finally spoke as she stepped away from the unwelcomed stranger. After a distance, she leaned into Jon's arm like Erica had into her that first day of summer classes, and her face came back to life. Then she noticed Jon's hand was sweating.

"So, I have this suspicion."

"Oh no, I'm not in trouble, am I? I mean we just met."

"Did we now?"

"Well, I'm mean, okay you gave me a ride back to campus, and I've seen you the past three weeks in class, and I nearly killed you at the fundraiser."

"That was you. Yup. Where's your skateboard now?" Anna asked, dropping her intended accusation of Jon liking Erica.

"Yeah, it wasn't fast enough, so I bought a bike."

"To bike uptown to the magazine press."

"Yeah, but it's still not fast enough, so I'm in process of looking for a car," Jon said, not knowing how to courteously let go of an affectionate girl's hand. "One that I can afford, maybe."

"Here."

"No, I'm not going to let you give me your car, I'm not that desperate."

"Good, it's not mine to give away anyway, but you can at least drive me to your dorm...Swanson Hall, right?"

"Ya...yeah, okay...wow," Jon stuttered, forgetting all courtesy as Anna rounded the car alone.

"You have driven a real car before," Anna assumed and let her assumption linger as a question.

"Um, I have my license...driver's license that is; this is seriously expensive looking!  I mean is."

"My mom trusts me with it," Anna said, and watched Jon climb in and get somewhat settled behind the wheel.

"Cool."

"Yeah, cool." Anna echoed with a constrained giggle.

Jon, fascinated with the luxury of everything, finally started the engine.


## Part 2 - Chapter Twenty-Six


"Saundra?" Romney called from inside of his office.  When he knew that he had Saundra's attention, he asked, "Building one, Philly, or building two, Morestown?"

"I...I don't think...."

"My whim is as good as yours.  Come on, you just compiled all three properties for the meeting," Romney said, moving to better hear Saundra's answer.

"Morestown, if you have to know my pref..."

"Why not building one?" Romney unintentionally domineered, shuffling the Morestown data sheet on top of its contestant, investigating it again in search of Saundra's reasoning.  The informal conference stopped short at the sound of tapping on the outer office door.  "George, come in," Romney beckoned as he stepped forward and recognized his guest.

"Mr. Daniels, I went to distribute the listing money for Fenndale per the in-house release from our most recent team get-together-meeting," George said, direct to the point.

"Right."

"Right, well I'm sure it's a glitch in our software, but the request consistently comes back saying 'insufficient funds.' Should I contact I.T. or did I need to wait till the next budget cycle...because I might have mistaken something, or not, from the meeting," George confessed, hoping to appear competent in his responsibilities.

"The ad budget, if I remember correctly, was something small like seven thousand."

"Twelve-five."

"That's right, Monica would have the accurate balance of the account, but last I checked, in the meeting actually, there was upwards of a hundred and thirty-eight thousand dollars or something."

"I can show you," George asserted, pulling his portable computer out from under his arm.

"We'll go ask Monica, she'll have the real time numbers; but before you go...your opinion," Romney said, spreading his arms out to separate the two data sheets.

"Philly," George said with a smile, feeling proud for the opportunity to share his opinion with his boss.

"Why?"

"There's more potential retail space, and the district is in shambles. I reviewed the Lundberg proposal and how it attracted two substantial bids before closing...."

"And right off the bat it dug into the profit margin," Romney finished.

"You and Jack see something for what it could be, and the farther the stretch the farther the competition'll keep its distance. I think anyway."

"Shambles. I'll give you that. It sure is easier to bulldoze something that doesn't look valuable."

"And that too!" George encouraged. "I'll get right in touch with Monica and shoot you a message with what's going on. Sorry to trouble you," George said, dismissing himself to go carry out his self-assigned duties.

"George keep your head up."

"Sorry, what?" George asked, turning back to Romney with curiosity.

"Your attention to detail is not troublesome; keep your head up," Romney clarified, smiling to better convey his intent.

"Right, thank you, sir," George responded and left the room with the complement affixed to his face.

"I don't know why, but didn't you tell me sometime in the past few days, that Mitchell had you re-release ground improving funds for Lundberg?" Romney asked Saundra. The distracting thought caused Romney to accidentally drop the datasheet of the Morestown property, and it immediately floated out of reach. "Well, it's a good thing I'm not superstitious."

Saundra grinned and returned promptly to her desk where she started clicking her cursor around the computer screen. Romney bent over to pick up the data sheet and walked up behind Saundra. "I'm sorry...Mitchell rang a bell for you. One hundred and thirty-eight thousand rang a bell for me," Saundra confessed the reason for her silence.

"Let me call Lundberg."

"Okay."

"They should know or have an idea of where the money off and done went to, or at least I hope so," Romney suggested, dialing the number to the hard-working foreman from his personal phone. "Hey there! I know...," Romney greeted, stepping deeper into his office. "Great update, but a big question...," Romney said, guiding the discussion into his question and the foreman's prompt answer. "Double...well right more than double; do you have that exact figure?" Romney asked and reversed his course straight out of his office into the wide aisle that split the patchwork of cubicles. "One hundred four...thirty-two; got it, thanks. I'll call you sometime tomorrow to check in," Romney said, hovering at the entrance of George's cubicle.

"It's not there," George said with worry.

"Monica?" Romney mechanically assumed.

"Yeah, I just asked...and the account was wiped...to zero; it has no money in it," George confirmed with an assuming tone.

"Odd."

"Granted it is just our imaginary line that differentiates one account from the next."

"Not to worry," Romney consoled with a sigh and kept walking down the wide aisle. "Mitchell, can I have a word with you in my office," Romney inquired, making his best attempt to avoid any nearby ears.

"I'm busy, boss," Mitchell replied.

Romney paused for a moment, awaiting Mitchell's compliance. "It'll only be a minute, but it's important."

"You already underfund my proposals and demand I comply with your tedious run-arounds. I am busy as you can see, boss, and I really want to get home to see my son's baseball game...which isn't going to happen at the latent rate I'm working," Mitchell said with anxiety and swung his office chair around to face Romney, having lost all focus.

"You do a good job and make it clearly known that you care a great deal about the success of this company," Romney said, uncomfortably addressing Mitchell's aggressive resolve. "A duplicate...well, an almost duplicate release of funds...you had Saundra release a hundred thirty-eight thousand four hundred and...," Romney said, pausing to try to recall the exact number.

"Four hundred seventeen dollars and thirty-two cents, yes, I heard you enlisting George's and Monica's services, and for those pennies, Jon now has the ability to stay ahead of target."

"Right, and I suppose you considered Fenndale in the process?" Romney proposed, resisting the urge to cross his arms and lean on the side wall of the cubicle.

"Fenndale's fully operational, the faster Lundberg launches its first tenant the faster it starts paying back in cash, and we both know this company sinks or swims around here on those double dollar signs," Mitchell mockingly said, glad to have spoken his peace. "I'm sure you've weighed the merits of all my 'verbiage,'" he continued in a disgruntled fashion, turning away to face the work cluttered office space.

"Mitchell, I know you don't mean harm in testing out your proposal before it has been approved, and your dedication is clear to all. But I can't have you disregarding company policy to prove the merits of your favorable arguments."

"You can thank me later."

"That's right, you have a ballgame to get to. What can I do to help?" Romney offered, knowing the length of dialogue had to have attracted considerable attention.

"Humph...," Mitchell exhaled, thinking of two menial tasks that could hasten his departure for the day.

Romney took the liberty of taking a piece of paper off Mitchell's notepad and scribbled a note, using the cubicle as a backboard while Mitchell continued to ignore his presence.

Replacing the pen back in his pocket and returning the noted paper to the top of the stack, he left Mitchell to his work.

"Jack, a small monetary issue has come up," Romney said, poignantly greeting his counterpart.

"You have the same administrative leeway as I do Romney, what's the issue?" Jack said, interrupting his focus to acknowledge his co-founder. "So, Philly or Morestown?" Jack proposed in the time Romney took to collect his answer.

"Philly has a larger potential in starting over from the ground up, as George pointed out, but I'm still more drawn to revitalizing the Morestown property, though we'll more than likely have numerous competitors to bid against...also, as George pointed out," Romney blankly reasoned.

"The third property is out then?" Jack assumed, reclining comfortably in his chair.

"It's under contract so it would look that way, but a more trivial matter."

"That's right. Go ahead."

"Mitchell Reed...."

"Oh, say no more; I don't like novels," Jack said, looking to relax from his hours of focus.

"Hah...yeah, though I think he has good ideas or at least intentions of good ideas," Romney defended to maintain his serious tone. "He seems to have transferred a hundred and thirty-eight thousand dollars from Fenndale to Lundberg's operating budget," Romney explained.

"So, transfer it back...."

"Well, we haven't located it all yet, or I would. It would seem thirty-four thousand dollars somehow disappeared in the process."

"Hah," Jack laughed. "That's like half of his yearly salary. Do you want to can him?"

"That would probably be easiest, but let me get the evidence together first," Romney said, objectively considering the legalities and requirements involved in firing somebody. "I hate to admit it, but Lundberg for once is ahead of schedule," Romney said and lingered pensively on his redeeming conclusion.

"Meanwhile seeing that it was done on my watch, I'll refund the money to Fenndale's account so the off-load can get up and started, hopefully before the next budget cycle," Romney said persuasively.

"Like personally refund?"

"Yeah. It's nothing to me sitting in my account and probably means happiness to everyone around here. The foreman sure appreciates the leniency over at Lundberg, and the quicker Fenndale's off our books the quicker a Philly or Morestown offer can happen," Romney said, having settled the matter in his mind already.

"Oh, don't worry about the offer. Byron said he'll fund the venture over and above his current investment," Jack assured, tossing the concern out of his mind. "If you somehow feel obligated still to reconcile this 'issue,' why not just consider it a bonus. But don't go writing a guilt check. I'd feel bad...and your bonus this year is set to be six times that anyway," Jack said, smirking as he rounded his desk to approach his friend.

"Well. Thanks," Romney said with a resolute handshake of appreciation. "I'll tell Monica to write it off and slide some funding around for the interim."

"You know how to get it done and make those big wheels turn," Jack heartened, returning to his polished desk.

# Part 2 - Chapter Twenty-Seven

"Closing-up shop time," Romney said to Saundra, walking with an optimistic beat toward the door of his office. The sun had long passed over the office complex making the open space seem gray and cold. He held his portfolio like a textbook in the same arm that held his briefcase.

"I see you've put that portfolio to good use," Saundra commented, noting the first thing that came to mind.

"Thanks to you, all my paperwork arrives crisp and clean," Romney replied, but seeing Saundra's keen objective to hustle through her remaining assignments, he refrained from elaborating his compliment. His striding to the elevator seemed to cue everybody into the time of day. Mitchell Reed especially hustled around his office finishing his checklist of items that needed to be staged and ready to go for his tomorrow's agenda. Though the elevator seemed like his destination, Romney bypassed the steel doors and pushed through the exit door into the stairwell. Romney made it to the bottom floor with a fair amount of energy left in his knees but paused for a moment to check that he had remembered his phone. When he found it, he pushed out of the stairwell into the lobby. The polished lobby bustled with a variety of employees and loiterers, all contributing to the happy noise at the end of the business day. The elevator opened in front of Romney, and sure enough Mitchell Reed hurried out with purpose in his expression. "Enjoy that ball...," Romney began, the noise and distance drowning his attempted farewell. Pressing on at his own slack pace put him ten paces behind Mitchell on the same pathway out of the office building.

"Mr. Reed," Romney heard and saw Mitchell's attention flash to a character standing next to the exit. Romney couldn't hear Mitchell's response, but the interchange allowed Romney to catch up to eavesdropping distance.

"Mr. Daniels," Romney heard from the same caller.

"Mr. Gallant," Romney replied, forgoing the handshake for sake of his shoulder bag and portfolio occupying his right hand.

"I trust that Saundra, your secretary, relayed my apology for my intrusion last week," Michael Gallant said, turning his complete attention to the Chief Operating Officer.

"She did, thank you; hey, enjoy your boy's ball game tonight!" Romney said, shifting the attention to his employee.

"Mr. Daniels, I'm sure you would be excited to know that the window of opportunity has been extended for our venture fund at F.P.O. due to an increase of interest, though the terms have slightly changed," Michael said, extending a colorful brochure. "I finally received the info packets back from the printer, please take this one," Michael promoted, holding the thick brochure steady to reinforce his offer.

"Thanks, but it's not for me today. And don't keep this one too long, he has a game to catch," Romney concluded, inching backward toward the exit.

"Yeah, I'm excited to watch his son...Chad, pitch."

"Oh, you're going too?" Romney inquired with a look of surprise, partially constraining his retreat.

"Only because Mitchell here extended an invitation," Michael humbly explained.

"Chad's your son, Mitchell?" Romney asked, correlating the pitching reference with the little he knew about his employee.

"Wattsworth," Mitchell said with a modest nod.

"I had the pleasure of meeting him briefly at a baseball fundraiser not too long ago; you're in for a real treat Michael. From what I hear, he's really good, but I'll let you two go. I have a little girl waiting for me," Romney said to his captive audience, waving his free hand briefly before catching the closing door. The street had filled with commuters. Joining them, he continued four more blocks to his apartment complex, where he took the elevator down to the parking garage and walked to his black van. A few minutes later he crossed the Mills Bridge and shot into the Duquesne Tunnel. After a minute in the dark passageway, the dinner hour of daylight returned, and he changed highways to parallel his way up Mount Lincoln to the perch where he knew his daughter would be waiting for him on Riverview Avenue. He pulled far into the conjoined driveway and hopped out ten yards from the back door. After knocking seven times, he found himself waiting and looking around the double driveway. A man, he supposed to be the neighbor, exited the neighboring house with two heavy trash bags. "Hi there," Romney greeted, and he stepped across the imaginary property line, abandoning his knocking attempts. The neighbor initially smiled but turned back inside when he saw Romney answer his mobile phone. "Anna, how goes it?" Romney inquired, peering at the unique view of the city from between the two houses. "Yeah, I'll be here. Oh, don't hurry, work is over for the day. Okay...mmm-bye," Romney spoke, and noticed the man walking out of the house with two more black bags of trash. "Need a hand?" Romney offered.

"Oh no, I need a buyer," the man countered. "My renters trashed the place again, and at my age I'm getting a little too slow to keep up with this landlord business," the man explained, taking a moment between tossing each bag into the private trash bin. He wiped the sweat from his brow, looked at the stranger, and asked, "Are you a friend of them Purses? ...Really lucky folks to have next door."

"Yes, a God send for me as well. How many more bags do you have hiding in there?" Romney asked, realizing the last black bag hadn't made it into the bin but sat atop the rest.

"Oh, about twenty. Do you want to come in and see what they did to the place? ...These disrespectful people," the man vented, pausing on the small porch.

"If you'll let me help you with ten of those bags," Romney negotiated.

"Oh, don't ruin your suit."

"Sometimes I wonder if the suit has in some way ruined me," Romney returned, stepping toward the older gentleman.

"Gab," the man introduced, extending his hand.

"Romney Daniels."

"Good to meet you, Romney. Come in...it'll make me feel better to have someone share in my disgust of human nature," Gab said, holding the door open for Romney.

"Hoe, you weren't kidding."

"Oh, the walls are nothing. Wait till you see the granite. It'll make you cry," Gab said and grabbed two more bags that he had staged by the door.

Romney followed him outside pensively.

"At this point, living on a reverend's stipend and social security, I don't even know if I have the money to make it rentable again," Gab said, holding the door once again for Romney.

"People neglect to realize the effort that goes into preserving a house and even more so into keeping a home," Romney conjectured and grabbed two more bags.

"Hold on a second, I want to show you something. Maybe you'll know what it is," Gab instructed, motioning Romney up the stairs. "Either somebody loves carving up plastic soda bottles, or...," Gab said, losing his train of thought as he battled the steps.

"Methamphetamine...perhaps?" Romney said after Gab had ushered him into one of the upstairs bedrooms.

"Metha...what? Do I need to call the police and report this?" Gab said, looking bewildered at the thought of an additional burden.

"It wouldn't hurt."

"You're not a druggie, are you?"

"Me?"

"You seemed to know what you were looking at off the bat, not that I was baiting you," Gab contested, vacating the bedroom door to return to the stairs.

"No, someone dear to me is, and I tried attending a recovery group to learn what I could do to help," Romney transparently explained.

"How do you help these kids?" Gab bluntly pondered before heading back down the first few steps.

"Well, it took a recovered-addict nineteen weeks to explain it to me," Romney said, hoping to lighten the mood. "Hey, you said you're hoping to sell; what price are you looking for?" Romney asked, following Gab slowly down the stairs to grab the awaiting bags.

"Look around. Make an offer," Gab half-jokingly replied, moving his hand from his side around to the living space behind him.

"How about sixty-five thousand?"

"Well, what do you know, that's what I bought it for twenty years ago," Gab said and exited the back door to the dumpster.

Romney followed with two bags in tow, setting one down to work his way through the door.

"Do you have the money, or will I need to pay off one of those realtors to close the deal," Gab said, pausing to assess the seriousness of his helpful stranger's offer.

"I'm pretty savvy at purchasing real estate, that's what I do for my job anyway at Hense and Daniels downtown," Romney assured.

"Is that Jacky Hense and Daniels? Brock's little boy?"

"Yes, sir."

"I met Brock once, a big brick if you asked me, but you seem much nicer," Gab said, bypassing Romney toward the rotting porch step.

"Jacky...hah, I'll have to tell him. At least Jack turned out all right. I met Brock a few times around the time we opened the business."

Gab stopped and looked back at Romney. "Prick?"

"Yeah. I could see where you get that," Romney conceded.

"Well, look where I ended up. Maybe I needed to be more of a prick to these rascals," Gab said, reflecting on his own reduced position in life.

The old man started to hobble and groaned, "Ooa, I'm getting too old for this. Sixty-five, you say?"

"In cash, as is, no need to do another ounce of labor," Romney said, looking up at the house and comparing its value to that of the neighbors'.

"Double that and you have a deal," Gab said and started patting his pockets in search for his notebook. "Now, where on earth did I put that?"

"Deal. Here's ten thousand down now, and I'll have the rest in a certified form when you deliver the clear title," Romney said, initiating his own scribbling on his check book.

"Ahh snappy, I'll get your name and number here somehow...maybe it's in my truck," Gab said, scratching his tall thin hair. Then wobbling over to the unlocked door of his truck, he cried victoriously, "Ah-hah."

"Romney, you say?"

"Daniels and my number...," Romney started but heard a car bump into the driveway.

"Ahh, here comes Miss Purse now. You know, I don't know how many times she's helped me over the years, I'd probably have a landfill's worth of garbage back here if she hadn't taken the renter's bin over every week."

"Daddy, daddy," April said, running as soon as her feet hit the ground. "Ju-inna let me drink orange juice!"

"Really?" Romney playfully responded.

"Yes."

Romney hoisted her up to his side and said, "I want you to meet someone."

"Who is it, daddy?" April innocently asked and started picking at the collar on Romney's suit jacket.

"This is Mr. Gab, and we're going to be buying his house."

"It's nice to meet you there, angel. You know, I have a granddaughter that looks just like you," Gab said joyfully.

"Nooo, that's silly," April said, scrunching her nose at the mistaken compliment.

"I'm sure he does, April. Do you want to see inside the house?" Romney asked.

"Is it for me?" April said, stunned at the incomprehensible prospect.

"Well, for you, and me, and mommy when she's allowed to come home."

"But mommy lives upstairs at the big house; where my bed-toys are," April disagreed, reaching for Anna as she approached.

"Hi, Gab," Anna greeted, happily taking April in her arms.

"Miss Purse, you're looking like sunshine," Gab said, taking liberty to gawk at Anna's youthfulness.

"Did the renters trash the place again?" Anna asked with concern, gently taking hold of April's fingers that had latched onto her braided hair.

"Not my problem."

"Oh?" Anna replied with surprise.

"The only bearable part of this place was its neighbor," Gab said, handing Romney the pen and paper. "You write your name down."

"Is tomorrow good for you?" Romney asked, finishing the scribble that Gab had started on the notepad.

"Tomorrow? The deal's for today. I know that I look as old as my truck, but my diabetic foot still is heavier than yours," Gab said, aware of his audience. "Give me thirty minutes."

"Well, take forty-five and deposit these checks before the banks close," Romney said, popping out his check book again.

"Oh, my bank's done been closed for a good long time now. You're a friend of Miss Purse's. Here, what do you think, Miss Purse, should I trust your new neighbor and his paper money?" Gab redirected.

"What...?"

Fabricating the concerns going through Anna's mind, Romney clarified, "Don't worry, we'll talk about it...the details...."

"What details? I'd two hundred percent rather you live there that those dead beat...," Anna said, censoring herself when she remembered April was in her arms. She started bouncing April to disperse her heightened animation.

"Well, let me leave you two, and I'll go get this house title...then meet you back here, so we all can get on to eating dinner," Gab said, excusing himself to his truck.

"Details...really, Rom?" Anna retorted playfully like an offended companion and slapped his arm with the back of her hand.

"What? I don't want you to think that I'm some creepy dad crowding in on you with my daughter. At least that's what I'd be thinking," Romney said, adopting his own playfully defensive tone.

"Woah, my house is messy," April observed.

"That's why I bought it, and why Mr. Gab accepted such a ridiculously low offer."

"It won't be messy for long, Pearl. We'll get it cleaned up right away," Anna said in response to the worried look on April's face.

"Hey, do you want to bring April to the baseball game tonight? I was going to stop by Vern Hill and watch a little until my mom gets off work," Anna asked and immediately sensed Romney's tension. "Gab will be back in a minute. He literally lives half-a-block away," Anna rattled, filling in the space that she desperately didn't want to become awkward.

"Under normal circumstances, I would love nothing more than to drag my family to an all-American past time, but for sake of appearances, and how greatly I value you and your mother's kindness, I'm must decline," Romney said, trading smiles with Anna.

"If Gab takes long enough, you might get to meet my best friend, Bethy," Anna said, smartly changing the topic. "Bethy Berkshire."

"Beth, you say?"

"Ba...buh...buh," April said, testing out her pronunciation. "Bubbles?"

"I met her dad that night at the fundraiser. Roger, I think."

"Roger's like the dad I never had," Anna said, hugging April with a glow on her face. "He's like a dad to me," Anna clarified when she saw a question form on Romney's eyebrows.

"I'm sure April would love an introduction."

"You too, right?" Anna queried. "You don't have to answer that, sorry."

Anna let April down to her feet, and the two adults followed her quick footsteps around to the covered front porch where they waited the few remaining minutes for Gab to return with what he thought was the transferable title. When Gab returned, Romney explained with increasing detail the actual real estate process. Once satisfied, Gab left with a solid handshake along with a time to meet Romney early the next morning.

## Part 2 - Chapter Twenty-Eight

Romney exited the newly acquired house with his phone to his ear. Not one to delay the launch of a project and already having vetted contractors at his disposal, he hung up after agreeing to a thirty percent commission with a maximum cap, having called an interior designer and a general contractor. He knew what it should look like, and this made the rest of the project a matter of minor details that specialists could manage. Across the driveway Romney saw a blond girl greeting his hesitant daughter. The girl reached out her thin arm toward April, flapping her fingers gently to say hello. Giving up on making her acquaintance, she rose to her feet.

"Romney, this is Bethy, Roger's daughter," Anna introduced.

"It's nice to meet you, Beth. Do you babysit too?"

"Uh, no, no," Anna adamantly objected. "I have the exclusive pass to babysit April."

"Ha...no, I'm actually just in town till Friday to get things ready for college in the fall," Bethy calmly said. Knowing that in some way Romney probably either knew or did business with her father, she politely offered her hand to greet Romney. "And it's Bethy."

"Bethy! You two need to be off to a baseball game, don't you? I'd a-thought it'd already started by now," Romney encouraged, simultaneously calling April with the signal of his stretched-out arm.

"Oh, you know baseball games with their eighteen innings," Anna declared, pushing April away to the arms of her dad.

"Whose car?" Anna asked Bethy, dismissing Romney to carry on his private conversation with his daughter as they eased over to the black van.

"Do we need to pay for parking?" Bethy asked.

"No, but I can drive," Anna said after making up her mind.

"Nah, hop in," Bethy decided and climbed into her boxy vehicle.

"Isn't he a little out of your age bracket? And he has a kid," Bethy accused first thing after settling into her driver's seat.

"An adorable kid mind you."

"But he's like thirty though," Bethy said, guessing.

"Well, not quite, but close enough," Anna consented. "His wife has him in a troubled spot, and you know me."

"And he's married?"

"...which is why we aren't dating."

"Flirting," Bethy said, keeping up her charge.

"This is good feedback, that's why I need you here."

"My point exactly! My dad would relax so much more if you'd move in with me as my roommate. He knows how reliable you are and probably wouldn't even charge you rent...but don't quote me on that," Bethy said, avoiding the sunbeam that filled the interior of the car.

"I tried dating once you know," Anna disclosed, knowing the explosive potential of the topic.

"No, not my Anna. And she didn't even call me before she did," Bethy said with a false air, weaving in her mild disappointment.

Anna giggled at the recollection of their bedroom promises, "I should have though."

"You know it," Bethy said, holding a serious expression for a second. "Please tell. It doesn't sound like it turned out so well."

"I was stupid...basically sums it up," Anna said, suddenly feeling gun shy at the details of how her adventure had unfolded. "But I'm hungry, are you up for Italian?"

"No girl. Ball park and corn dogs! We're going to watch some baseball, not gluten-ize our bellies."

"I'm not sure that's completely rational, but corn-diggity it is," Anna said and directed her driver to the bridge leading to campus.

"Thank you! My one chance for junk...okay, my one week for junk," Bethy said overdramatically.

"Weren't you the one that got us all dieting with eating the colors of the rainbow?"

"And you the one that signed a no dating pact," Bethy countered.

"Right, right," Anna said, retreating into her thoughts.

"You're a tough one to pitch to," Bethy rationalized, displaying her friendly teeth as she stared over the wheel.

"No, you're right. You think you're invincible until you're in the most terrifying position in your life. At least I thought I was invincible until I found myself running to Romney to save me."

"The dating pact wasn't to scare you away from dating but to get others involved in it," Bethy responsively clarified as a big sister would.

"You don't need to convince me of that anymore," Anna assured.

"Come on, it couldn't have been that bad. You're here. Aren't you?"

"I don't know."

"I do," Bethy joked but interrupted her own playfulness. "Is there something you need to be telling me, Anna," Bethy said, changing her tone.

"No, Romney helped me out of it, for now anyway. He showed back up on campus today, and didn't say much, just creepy things happened. I don't know. Maybe it was me, but I learned everyone isn't as innocent as they seem," Anna rambled, as they turned into the sizable parking lot.

"Romney or your date showed up today?"

"Spencer was his name. It was like I was in an emotional prison on our date. And by accepting his invitation, I felt somehow obligated to tag along until he was done with me," Anna said, feeling finally honest at the recounting of her confusing experience.

"Euh...well, you're my date tonight, so let's go find something that will nourish that let down heart of yours," Bethy said for lack of better tact, bouncing out of the car to play the part of a gentleman.

The two friends linked arms as they crossed the rows of parked cars, proceeding toward the gate house. The crowd cheered on the flip side of the bleachers and then calmed down to a spectating hum.

"Anna, good to see you! Who's your friend?" Jonathan Wickfell asked from a short distance behind the girls. Seeing Anna's nervous eyes swing around and peer at him, he stopped and hid his hands in his pockets.

"Ah, Jon," Anna said, recognizing him. "This is my best friend Bethy. Bethy, this was my other savior when Spencer came to campus today," Anna cheerfully introduced.

"I think the ticket window's closed, I just ran out to make a quick delivery. I have some good seats, or had some, if you'd care to join me. They should still be open," Jon offered and waited for the girls to exchange glances.

"Sure," Anna said, offering an indifferent frown.

"A pretty good turn out if you asked me," Jon commented as the three entered the park and eyed the bleachers filled almost to their capacity.

"Uh, Jon!" Anna called out, raising her voice and hand above the elevated noise from the crowd. "Concessions!" Anna yelled, pointing to her objective.

Jon smiled and retraced his steps down to follow the girls as they weaved their way up to an order window.

## Part 2 - Chapter Twenty-Nine

Anna Purse sat knees-together in her tall brown boots that rose comfortably to the top of her calves. With her eyes set on the illuminated infield she occasionally rocked her knees back and forth during the windups and pitches.

Jonathan watched Anna lean over to say something in Bethy's ear. He watched the lively interchange between the friends, and he almost commented on their conversation. But the noise of the crowd and the closeness required to effectively communicate something glued him to the steel bleacher.

Chad Wattsworth stood on the mound and sent a pitch to his catcher. While shaking his arm at the elbow his mitt instinctively rose to intercept the return throw. The familiar catcher proceeded toward the mound, and the mess of his hair flopped down as he lifted off his head gear. The mound meeting lasted no longer than ten seconds, and the catcher re-disguised himself after slapping Chad's arm with his thick glove. Chad didn't seem fazed at the interruption and still wobbled his elbow as he gripped the ball. Chad threw a strike after peering for a moment at the third baseman. The theatrical emphasis that the umpire placed in the punching motion of his fist pleased the crowd.

Finally, restlessness and the hunger bred by the presence of the girl's food caused Jon to give in to his craving. "I'll be right back," Jon said, lofting his voice to attract Anna's attention.

Bethy leaned forward to alert Anna of Jon's statement.

"Where are you going?" Bethy asked after realizing Anna hadn't heard what Jon had said.

"Your food got to me; I have to get me some!" Jon confessed with boyish crinkles on his cheeks.

"Don't be silly these are completely shareable," Bethy asserted, handing the mostly untouched food across Anna's lap.

Anna picked up on the topic and caught Jon by the shirt sleeve when he had refused the second time. The surprise of the tug returned Jon to his spot. "I bought these for everybody," she persuaded, leaning close to his ear to forgo yelling.

"Well thanks, you didn't have to," Jon yelled, without returning the enjoyable gesture. The glue on his seat felt stronger than before and stiffened his posture further.

Anna sensed his discomfort but retreated to watching the game. While trying to capture the details of Jon's expression from her periphery, her friend reacted to something on the field by excitedly grabbing her forearm. Rising to her feet with Bethy and the enthusiasm of the crowd, Anna caught sight of Chad rolling onto his side and flipping the ball to the second baseman that stood poised ready to further the uproar. Completely confused at the sequence of events, she stole a look back at Jon who still sat with their food in his lap and with fans blockading his view of the action. Anna shrugged, and Jonathan understood, shrugging back with a carefree expression on his face. She smiled at his predicament of food trays, and in return, he modestly toasted the bit of pretzel he held toward her as if to say, "Don't feel sorry for me." Anna sat back down before the crowd finished applauding and said, "Apparently Chad just did something amazing. I missed it too."

Jon swallowed and leaned close to Anna's side to explain, "He caught the hit!"

Anna pulled her hair over her ear and leaned even closer, indicating her need for clarification.

"Chad caught the fly ball. It knocked him over. I didn't see the rest," Jon said expressively.

"It knocked him down all right, and then he tossed it with his glove to the baseman!" Anna said, sensing less inhibition from Jon's posture.

"Everybody says he's the next Eric Peters...minus the fact he doesn't play short stop," Jon said, taking a break from filling his mouth with the food.

Anna reflected Jon's excitement to avoid admitting her ignorance in sports trivia.

"So, when do you start your internship?" Anna asked after a moment, but the surrounding clamor drowned out Anna's question.

"Hey, I bought a car today...sold my bike," Jon informed, in response to Anna's gaze.

"Really! How much?"

"Oh, it's a beater. You wouldn't be impressed," Jon explained with his crackling vocal cords and looked down at his dinner spread.

"That'd make a good name!" Anna said, competing at her best volume.

"Beater?"

"Well yeah! It beats junk-trunk, right?"

"Hah! Hey, do you know the catcher?" Jon asked, turning Anna's attention to the field with the tilt of his forehead.

"Terrance?"

"Terrance? What's his last name?" Jon asked. "Do you know his last name?"

"I don't know, but he's a character. Have you met him?"

"I don't know, I think so, but hey, I wasn't planning on staying too long," Jon admitted, scratching his head.

"Oh, we weren't either," Anna agreed, turning to Bethy.  "Hey, you want to go?" Anna asked.

"How many guys are on the field?"

"One, two, th...five, ten if you don't count the judges, why?" Anna responded.

"You counted ten?" Bethy inquired with surprise.

"Well nine players and a batter from the other team makes for ten, right?" Anna said, mimicking her friend's intense posture of looking out over the baseball diamond.

"Oh, I thought there were supposed to be ten fielding players.  Maybe I'm wrong," Bethy said, shrugging off her confusion.

"Maybe it's just a college thing," Anna reasoned before standing to follow Jon off the bleachers.

## Part 2 - Chapter Thirty

"I was watching my dad play softball last week," Bethy said, coasting along next to Anna.

"How is he?" Anna asked, looking at Jon as he split away from the pair.

"Good, as far as I know."

"Hey, Jon!" Anna called out before the sophomore walked into the shadow cast by the corner of the multi-purpose center.

"What?  No goodbye?" Bethy comfortably jumped in, taking her cue from how Jon whirled around with his hands buried in his pockets.

"I'll see you guys later.  I didn't want to spoil your conversation," Jon said, stopping his progress down the parallel sidewalk.

"Come on, the corn dogs were horrible, and Anna's hungry for Italian," Bethy presumptively said, glancing with energy back at Anna.  "Butler's?" Bethy suggested agreeably to Anna's bewildered face.

"Yeah sure," Anna said as optimistically as her friend.

"Butler's? I haven't heard of it," Jon admitted with interest, still frozen in his place.

"You're going to love it, and I know Anna didn't feed you enough of our leftovers," Bethy rationalized again.

Jon took a few steps back toward the girls who exchanged an obvious glance at each other. "It's really good...one of my favorites actually," Anna assured to prevent her tacit interchange from icing over the friendly atmosphere.

"Who's driving?" Bethy said, moving toward the first row of cars to set the trio in motion.

"I have to see this new ride of yours," Anna answered, finally infected by her best friend's behavior.

"No, there's no need for that. I mean I don't even have a tag for it yet," Jon said, spitting out the first excuse that entered his head.

The background noise erupted for a moment, and Anna, while making further mute conversation with Bethy, watched Jon collapse at the sound of a loud smack. Jon sprang back to his feet and again faltered, relying on his good foot for balance. His face said everything that needed to be said for a good three seconds before his voice caught up. "Oowww," Jon exhaled with pinched eyes.

Anna noticed a baseball rolling away at the pull of the parking lot's shallow grade.

Bethy constrained her nervous laughter, managing to say, "Are you okay, Jon?"

"Yeooww, my calf hurts," Jon expressed again, struggling to keep his swagger alive. Falling on a car for support, everyone jumped at the sound of the whoop made by the car's security sensor.

Bethy had no choice but to act like she caught Jon's balance as he gracelessly careened into her shoulder.

"Sorry."

"Sorry."

"Are you guys okay," Anna said, infected with the humor of the improv act.

"Yeah."

"Yeah, I'm fine," Bethy said, starting to laugh again as she grasped the entirety of the happening.

"I'm more worried about Jon," Anna said half-seriously. "He's the one that got hit by a baseball."

"Is that what it was?" Jon said, shortly wincing as he tested out his limp leg. "It felt like a bullet; there's no blood, right? Neither of you see blood, right?" Jon petitioned, twisting his leg around to assure himself of the answer.

"No, I don't think so. I saw a ball rolling toward the sewer drain over there," Anna said, still trying to rein in her giggles. "Bethy, your idea, you're driving."

--- *Twenty minutes later, entering the first-class dining establishment.*

"So, you like this place, Anna?" Jon asked as the white gloved waiter led the talkative group to their table.

"You will too, just wait," Anna promised, courteously walking at Jon's pace, which had much quickened from the parking lot.

"I'm sure I will, though the closest I've come to Italian is macaroni and cheese, I think," Jon said, showing his handsome smile to the floor before making eye contact with his company.

"What? You've had spaghetti before...and pizza," Bethy said outright.

"Well okay, if you count R&T's or the cafeteria's, but...real Italian...I can't say I've ever been to such a place like this."

"You know R&T's Pizzeria?" Bethy asked reminiscently. "R&T's is Italian, mostly."

"There's one right off campus. Well, it's a-ways off campus, but right on my pickup route."

"On Main?" Bethy asked.

"Yeah, Main, I think...wow talk about fancy...this is great," Jon said impressed at the texture of the table cloth.

The waitress skillfully rounded the table, concealing her concern over the casual dress of her youthful customers.

"You are going to have to help me," Jon admitted sheepishly, tilting the menu up and down like a mirror signaling his distress. "Because I don't speak Italian or Greek or whatever this menu's written in."

"I'll order for you; you're not allergic to anything are you," Anna asked. "Jon...."

"Not a thing, please surprise me," Jon agreed with thankful eyes and then squinted again to continue deciphering the menu.

--- *Under the warm streetlights outside after the meal.*

Still enamored by the experience and distracted by the sounds of the street, Jon didn't notice Anna tip the valet who hopped out of the car. "Who do I pay?" Jon generally asked, knowing one of the two girls would embarrass him with the answer.

"My mom took care of it, don't worry," Anna said, leaving the curbside to sit shotgun next to Bethy.

"Aww no, I know I'm broke, but your mom?"

"Well me too, broke...technically anyway, but she doesn't care; she comes here all the time, sometimes even alone," Anna said, looking over at her quiet chauffeur. The task of driving occupied Bethy, and the city sights squelched the conversation for Anna. For Jon, a burning question and how to tactfully ask it made for a silent return to campus.

"You said the second drive?" Bethy asked.

"Yeahah," Bethy's occupants replied unanimously.

"Okay, second drive," Bethy mused, grinning at her thoughts.

Jon stepped out from his back seat, but he stopped before giving up his opportunity. "Hey," Jon said, gathering the attention of both driver and passenger in the open window. "Bethy, what's the best way to ask Anna out on a date?"

"By asking," Bethy said resolutely.

"Asking who?" Jon continued, feeling the prompt need for oxygen.

"Her...my mom," Bethy and Anna piggybacked.

"Is she by chance listed in the white pages?"

"Yeah," Anna said, smiling. "But who uses the white pages any...more?"

Jon lost his breath.

"I don't know, right, who uses the white pages," Bethy rescued, shifting the car back into park.

"I'm sorry, thanks for the great night...food tonight; company...and all," Jon stuttered and stepped away from the vehicle. Jon winced for sake of his appalling fail and simultaneous reminder of his leg as he climbed the curb.

"Call her mother!" Bethy yelled out from the far side of the traffic circle as the dark gray vehicle moved toward the boulevard.

Jon couldn't see any details from inside the car due to the combination of background and the weakness of the campus's street lamps, but the benevolent guidance was psychological medicine to his ailments. Then after suppressing his ear to ear smile, he started directly for his dorm room. He needed to get enough sleep for his internship at Scales Architectural Company that started the next morning.

    --- *After departing the drop-off circle in the direction of Anna's house.*

Bethy kept the car cruising in her lane. The streets of the city felt welcoming. Anna sat silently, pressing her lips together to prevent her confusing joy from gushing out like a fool. Her cheeks flexed and lips occasionally pulsed as she replayed the details of the evening.

One look at Anna and Bethy laughed out loud, "You do! Ahhh, I see it."

"He still has to call my mom; don't get all excited."

"Anna!" Bethy energized but abandoned her comment. "Well, I'll be forewarning her soon enough."

"What do you think?"

"I like him," Bethy said already decided. "And he obviously likes you."

"Yuh think?" Anna said.

"Well, when you say it that way; I'll drop it, if you want me to," Bethy promised. The car dove into the heart of Mount Lincoln with a whoosh followed by rhythmic pulses of the tunnel's framework and eventually found its way into the shared driveway behind Anna's Victorian house.

"We'll see," Anna said, relaxing her shoulders after getting tired of the tension she had been privately entertaining.

"See what? You have me on the edge of my seat."

"What about this, 'I'll drop it, if you want me to' talk?" Anna said, trying to pull herself out of her serious mood.

"Hey, you broke the seal with your, 'We'll....'"

"Okay, okay, but I'm gonna keep the pact this time."

"Good for you...and I'm just going to go inside to let your mom know she has a responsible daughter that has this crush on a school boy."

"Wait! Can you name it something other than crush!"

Bethy slammed the car door to secure her head start. Unable to retain her glee, she reached the porch and hastened through the back door. Displaying the privileged information in her smile, she turned back and held the door for Anna to give her assurance of her joke. Anna knew Bethy well enough but poked her friend in playful retaliation anyway.

"Oh, hey girls," Julianne welcomed.

"Hi, mom," Anna proactively replied.

"Did you hear? The prosecutor dropped the charges against Romney."

"Wait...how did you find out?" Anna asked with confusion, accidentally exposing her obsession.

"How long are you in town for, Bethy?"

"A week or so," Bethy replied, leaning into the counter eager to observe the disposition of her friend.

"Mom, when did you find out? Because Romney was here when I got home, and he'd just bought the house next door from Gab," Anna reasoned.

"He did? Well, we'll finally have some decent neighbors then."

"Mom, the lawsuit," Anna reminded.

"Oh, Anna dear, I pulled in right as you and Bethy were pulling out. Romney stopped and chatted for a bit with Frank. I think I was one of the first to know actually...his lawyer called him," Julianne said, refocusing on the dishes in the sink.

"Frank?" Anna accused.

"Frank dropped me off from work and stayed for dinner," Julianne defended.

"That's what I figured. How am I supposed to trust my mom to be boy discerning when she doesn't ever set an example for me to follow?" Anna asked Bethy with betrayal before turning to escape upstairs.

"Oh, don't judge Frank; he's a nice guy. He even goes to Romney's church, I think," Julianne called as Anna rounded the stairs. Julianne gave Bethy an inquiring look to explain Anna's rash behavior.

"She has a crush," Bethy disclosed comfortably, knowing the typical contest between the two.

"Oh? Well that's not a first," Julianne smiled.

"Or a second, but this one's a good one, if I had a say. You'd be proud, her instinctive response to him was, 'Call my mom,'" Bethy said, taking a bite size cookie out of a jar kept in a corner of the counter.

"Well, that's a privilege I never thought I'd have," Julianne said, pausing at the realization. "What should I tell him?" Julianne asked as Bethy retreated to find her friend.

Bethy nodded with an approving smile, making eye contact as she rounded the banister of the staircase.

## Part 2 - Chapter Thirty-One

Jon pushed through the door of Crumbles Cafe, ringing the door chime and holding the door for the next patron. Joining the queue, he watched Erica match up two food filled plates with a hanging order tag. Appreciating how intent on her work she seemed, Jon wondered if he would have an opportunity for a brief hello or perhaps a brief acknowledgement of existence in her world. Jon could see Erica's green name tag wiggling on her chest as she handed the trays to the table servers. His turn came, and he ordered his usual corned beef and sauerkraut Rueben on a hearty wheat bagel. He waited for his food with the hope of catching a glance from Erica's brown and focused eyes. She smiled courteously at the patron much the same age behind him. Jon wondered for a foolish moment if Erica had noticed how he had held the door for that patron. The patron with his clean head of hair made Jon intensely jealous, so he vacated the premises after his food was delivered by a different smiling employee. Walking across the street he felt temporarily satisfied as he sunk into his car to eat his lunch. The clock on the dashboard didn't work, so he glanced at his watch rather often to make sure he could still be promptly early on the first day of his internship. After brushing and picking the crumbs from his lap, he stepped out of his vehicle and ensured the car was locked before turning around like a tourist to take in the top-rate architecture. "Oh, I'm sorry," Jon apologized as a pedestrian walked into him from his blind side.

"Don't sweat it, bro. Do you work here?" Spencer asked, glancing up the short flight of outdoor stairs that led toward the angled glass structure of Scales Architectural Company.

"Well, it's my first day as an intern," Jon proudly disclosed but couldn't help himself from momentarily scowling and slowly shaking his finger at the boy as he tried to place a memory with the familiar face.

"Ah, internship, I must have made it to the right place then," Spencer jovially said. "Scales Architecture Company. I'm a History major. What about you?"

"Architecture.... Have they told you anymore than they did me about what we're going to be doing here for the summer?" Jon asked as his movement toward the entrance made Spencer fall into step with him.

"Not a clue, bro," Spencer said in his college attire.

"I'm Jon, by the way," Jon introduced, stepping forward to open the glass door for his fellow intern.

"Thanks, man," Spencer appreciated and stepped inside and waited for Jon to lead him further into the lobby.

"Do you know where we go?" Jon asked candidly after looking around and not seeing any obvious cues.

"No clue, bro, but don't wait for me. I think I need to take a dump."

"Hah, okay," Jon laughed but felt unprofessional for responding as he did to the blatancy in such a clean environment.

Jon watched his new acquaintance part ways toward the bathroom, and with a glance again at his time piece, he began his search for Patrick, his designated mentor.

--- *After finding Patrick.*

Jon finished the short tour of Scales and collected some fifteen business cards from the numerous introductions. Exiting his new work area to take up Patrick's suggestion to have a look around and get familiar with the place, he again nearly collided with the strange intern. "So, cool tour, huh?"

"Yeah, you excited?" Spencer asked, distracted by some unseen objective.

"Yeah, did you hear we are going to get to...."

"Hey, do you remember where the water cooler's at?" Spencer interrupted to excuse his scanning of the room.

"Well yeah, I think I remember anyway," Jon hesitated, confident that he had seen a water fountain.

"Is this the place they have you put up?"

"Pretty-cool view, huh? I'll show you where I think the cooler's at, if you'd like," Jon offered, looking over at the profile of the intern.

"Sure. Hey, is this yours?" Spencer asked, tapping the top of Jon's silver laptop.

"Yeah, my dad bought that for me for college."

"Don't get it confused with everyone else's."

"Oh?" Jon said, pausing for an explanation.

"It looks identical to the one they just issued me, and I've seen three others that look just like it."

"Well thanks, I'll have to be mindful," Jon said, continuing out the door and down the hallway toward the water cooler.

"Here it is," Spencer said, watching Jon cruise right by the water fountain inset between the hallway's restrooms.

"Oh right, sorry...leading you on a wild goose chase here," Jon apologized, feeling ridiculous for his lack of observance.

"Don't sweat it, bro. Hey, I'm gonna keep looking around the place; see you around," Spencer said before dipping his head down to the water fountain.

Jon escaped, using the agreeable notion to rescue himself from his embarrassing plight. Upon returning to his work area, after conversing at length with Jeff Dunnire, he stopped abruptly and scratched his head. His silver laptop had disappeared from where he had left it twenty minutes earlier. Then his mentor stepped into his work area and started introducing himself more casually. He asked a few questions about Jon's hobbies and followed Jon's eyes around the room. Completely distracted, Jon gave partial answers to most of the questions and shortly smiled when his mentor extended his hand for a second time to welcome him. Too embarrassed at the thought of his predicament, he kept it hush, quietly searching until his dismissal time. When he reached his car, the recollection of the face hit him. "Anna."

*--- A few minutes later at Trist's poorly maintained apartment complex.*
"What do you mean?"

"What do you mean, 'what do you mean?' We take these to the pawn shop and sell them to pay off Wiffet," Spencer said with frustration at having to explain his illicit purpose.

"Yeah, you go ahead; I've tried that before. You'll get five hundred bucks...maybe...for all of them. Spence, I thought you smarter than the average Joe," Trist scoffed, not moving from his relaxed posture on the depreciated couch.

"These are two-thousand-dollar devices!"

"If you sell them full price at a retailer."

"Well okay, tell you what, I'll just go return them and apologize," Spencer said, disgruntled at the reality of his unproductive solution.

"You're funny, man; we need ten genies tonight...so I'm going to hit up Sandy again, you're welcome to hang here and talk with Wiffet till I get back."

"Yeah right! Wiffet? Cordial?!"

"I'm bringing Farley tonight too, because clearly you and I aren't cutting it," Trist said decidedly as he collected his t-shirt from the counter in passing Spencer.

"Yeah, you, boss…are losing it somewhere," Spencer fell to mumbling.

"You coming?" Trist asked, without acknowledging Spencer's obvious frustration.

--- *Minutes later after picking up Farley.*

"Last time I came here, the guy was stupid," Spencer testified, as the trio pulled onto Washington Street.

"He ran you off, did he?" Farley commented with an edgy voice. The red brick mansion slowly came into view.

"I got what I came for; he just gave me hell for it."

"You didn't hear then. His woman kicked him out with some court order. Now she's as ridiculous as ever. We might even get to mess around with her kid before we go. What do you say, Farley? You up for babysitting?" Trist asked sarcastically, eyeing the property.

"Babysitting?"

"Yeah, she lets her kid just roam all over, she's lucky she has a gated yard," Trist explained.

"And we're lucky that she has no idea how to change the codes," Spencer added competitively, punching in the same access code to the mail gate.

"How much is she good for?" Farley asked, impressed by the dimensions of the Victorian rotunda covering the porch furniture.

"All we need; hey, Spence you got this. I'll jump in if she puts up a fight," Trist prompted, leaning up against the brick facade out of view of the front door.

"Easy money," Farley agreed to the instruction and fell in suit against the wall behind Trist's strong figure. A few moments later, Farley saw Spencer clam up and step back from the door unexpectedly. He cast his eyes to the porch and slid his hands into his pockets.

--- *Back in time, specifically the day before in Anna's driveway.*

Romney playfully attempted to coax April into her car seat after waving goodbye to the two girls departing for the ball game. As he looked up a second time, he saw Julianne with a gentleman rolling into the driveway and felt his phone vibrate in his pocket. He instinctively answered his phone and spent the next four minutes listening to the joyful news from Jeff Dunnire about the prosecutor dropping his domestic violence charge. With one unbelieving hand on the back of his head and the other holding the phone after the call ended, he forgot about April's final shoulder restraint, and after April's polite voice jolted his heart back to life, he unbuckled and unleashed his daughter. April then ran around the conjoined driveway while he proudly conveyed the news of the dropped charge to Julianne and her male friend. Thereafter, he drove directly home with speed and tunnel vision, trying to guess what lay in store for him behind the doors of the house.

April announced, "We made it, daddy!" as Romney pulled into the driveway.

"I guess mom's out and about somewhere with the car," Romney deduced with an air of disappointment as he parked in one of the two vacant spots inside the garage. Romney placed a call to Sandy to figure out her whereabouts, and after Sandy told him a real time to expect her home, his joy returned, and he began excitedly dancing around with April in her toy room. Then he intensely set about cleaning like a hole-house vacuum, starting at the garage door and finishing in the master bedroom. Timing the completion of his work flawlessly, he finished tucking in the plush comforter with sweat on his forehead as he heard the garage bang to life. Sandy's behavior didn't fulfill his dreams, but it didn't dash his hopes either. For the first night in a long while, Romney laid in bed, delighted to be next to Sandy, who had no trouble dozing off to sleep. Content with this improved and hopeful status, he managed to fall asleep after a few minutes of pondering the duties of the next morning.

The morning rushed in naturally, and Romney rolled out of bed, as many times past, at the first stirring of his daughter. "What can I make you for breakfast, Pearl?" Romney asked, kneeling to her slumbering eye level.

April worked hard to rub the droopiness out of her remaining eye, and responded slowly, "I want chocolate-chip pancakes."

"Chocolate-chip pancakes it is then," Romney said. Romney took advantage of the short while after breakfast to cover the gaps he had missed in his rapid cleaning job the previous night. Then the day accelerated on, and Sandy came to join the happy pair just prior to lunch.

"I thought you weren't supposed to come here anymore according to the police," Sandy asserted.

"The prosecutor had the judge dismiss the ruling based on a review of the police report and lack of corroborating evidence," Romney said tactfully as if un-fazed by the insulting allegation. As he lowered April from her highchair eating-trough he heard steps at the door followed immediately by the chime of the doorbell. Wondering why the gate chime hadn't rung properly, he walked to and opened the door. Setting aside his confusion for a moment, he suspiciously watched Spencer retreat backwards a guilty step.

The next few moments were an intense blur. A blow appeared from nowhere, and he cupped his face. He felt his shirt collar whiplash his neck and then his right shoulder slam into the top pane of the storm door. Feeling his limp body pulled away from the comfort of his home, he twisted and collapsed to the brick patio step on his knees. He clamored and fought backward with enough success to regain his entrance and open the storm door. Yet, his assailants made sure he didn't hold the security handle for long, jerking him aggressively again toward the yard. Ultimately, the double chime of his front door locking assured him of his victory, and he gave up his frantic scrambling. The crack of his head on the brick walkway no longer mattered. It didn't matter whether he was being ruthlessly punched or violently kicked. His repeated groaning came out involuntarily. He gasped for breath and hugged his head, but it didn't matter. Romney indistinctly heard a siren amidst the brutal exercise and saw one assailant already fleeing. The beating didn't stop at the suggestion of police in the proximity, but it continued rhythmically in double time as if the dominance of the two remaining thugs hadn't yet been secured. Romney couldn't see any longer, and didn't care to, but finally his body faithfully told him that the assailants had surrendered and were sprinting away to maintain their freedom. He then rolled onto his back with relief and stared blankly up at the hazy sky. The aches mysteriously disappeared from his body as he recalled the victorious sound of the front door locking. However, the relief didn't last long, and pain again shrouded his face as he tried rolling further onto his broken elbow. His muscles shivered as his lungs and tears reacted to the swelling injuries. His one good eye caught a glimpse of the blood splattered around his shoulder. Then his body put his conscious mind to rest.

# Part 3 – Anna & Jonathan

# Part 3 - Chapter One

Jonathan Wickfell moved his legs faster to pick up the pace he had set for himself. He looked in the display window barely giving his legs slack to rest. "My piece of junk," Jon said to the window, comparing the rotating car showcase to his recently broken-down automobile. "I don't even know how they got you inside," Jon spoke to the shimmering car. After one more block of hustle, he arrived. The hanging name plate of the shop covered most of the small window on the front door, and all that could be seen from the street was the digital printing press, the multitude of boxes, and the stacks of supersized paper. The hanging 'Miss Doxy' sign slapped the window pane as Jon shook his tired thighs inside the shop.

"What took you so long?" Markus, the lone Doxy attendant questioned. Markus co-founded the Miss Doxy magazine and ran the associated photo-studio and the tireless printing-press with another college-graduate named Dan. Though Markus had profitably succeeded with his devilish cohort in spreading adult literature throughout the city, he usually came across disgruntled and snappy in his greetings.

"Car broke down," Jon reasoned, watching the skinny man, not much older than he was, duck down out of sight behind the heavily scuffed-up counter.

"The new one?" Markus questioned, reappearing with a red face from his abrupt maneuver.

"New...," Jon laughed. "I'd love a warranty right now, but someone lifted my laptop, and my fix-it money for my clunker has higher priorities."

"You should have kept that skate board."

"You're telling me; I should have kept that bike," Jon said as he finished stretching on the cluttered small delivery counter.

"Well, don't worry about being late, and since you came, and Noah didn't, you can have dibs on the double prints...I'll advance it, don't worry, if you're cash strapped."

"Quarter?"

"Yeah right, half. But I need the space, so I'd rather you take it now. You'll still make a killing at a half price," Markus assured and slammed two bundled stacks of magazines on the counter.

"Ahhh, torture," Jon tried to happily complain at the sound of two more thuds.

"What's that?" Markus questioned as he turned to grab the front door key from a drawer behind him.

"Can you mail the fourth...I can't carry all that much...that far; I want it, but you know...you understand, right?"

"Sure...if Noah doesn't take the opportunity before I get to it tomorrow."

"Thanks. I'm gonna die under the weight as it is," Jon said, rationalizing his request as sweat began to finally bead on his forehead.

"Sure thing, Monica finally did a special; check it out...here's an extra code," Markus said, pulling a business card out of his pocket with a six-character code pre-printed onto the back of it.

Jon didn't respond as he fit a stack into his oversized book bag and lifted the remaining two bundles by the straps. Setting one down, he pocketed the gift.

The attendant genially pulled the front door open and dismissed Jon with his three bundled paper weights as he turned back to finish his closing duties.

Thankfully the momentary decline of the sidewalk helped Jon find a rhythm to his steps. His eyebrows flared as he passed the revolving show-car, and instead of pausing to appreciate the stylish work of engineering, he muscled his way to a bench around the corner.

He slouched back angrily at the demanding exercise, and as he tried to motivate himself back to his feet, he let his tightening back muscles convince him otherwise.

He exhaled and saw a girl walking down the street that looked like Erica. The girl stopped at the cross walk in front of him, minding the traffic as she waited. The girl surveyed Jon, and Jon lost all fatigue as he recognized her.

Erica with her tall walk and small backpack started crossing the street to about where Jon sat frozen. Scrunching her eyebrows and grinning a friendly grin of coincidence, she said, "Well, hi, Jon, you look tired."

"Not the least," Jon lied, pushing his sweaty hair off his forehead with his palm. Laughing to admit his bluff, he asked, "So, where are you off to?"

"Oh, campus...just finished work. Hey, would you like a hand with one of those?"

"Oh gnaw, it's my car that broke down. You shouldn't have to shoulder any of this." Jon diverted his gaze as he felt his cheeks glowing and stomach starting to tingle.

"Well, lacking a car puts us in the same boat...," Erica said positively, stepping toward the nearest bundle. Erica hesitated for a moment, as she recognized the title of the magazine. Then trying to hide her reaction, she picked up a magazine bundle and asked, "Do you sell for Dan or Markus?"

Seeing her willingness to cradle the smallest bundle onto her belly made Jon jump into action to match her. "Markus, for the most part. I think Dan moved on, or I haven't seen him around lately. I don't know what he's up to now."

"You say Dan moved on?" Erica said, her eyes brightening for a minute.

"Yeah, I think, but I don't know," Jon replied, paying more attention to the crosswalk and traffic than her question.

After they finished crossing the busy street, he turned to Erica and somewhat succeeded in making conversation for the next twenty minutes.

"It doesn't come naturally to me, and here you're the one breaking the class's curve," Erica said, pushing Jon with her shoulder in answer to Jon's question that referenced their most recent math logic test.

"What?"

"Well, what hall are you in?" Erica asked, catching hold of Jon's eyes.

"Swanson," Jon informed and made the connection that they had arrived at his destination. "And you?" Jon asked, hoping for the miracle to continue.

"Hampton...hey, if you ever have a chance, would you ask Markus to tell Dan that I didn't appreciate what he pulled on me? He'll understand, and if Dan's really out of the business, to have him call me."

"Yeah sure; I'll see you later."

"Okay."

"Hey, Erica," Jon said, loving the sound of speaking her name. "Where you two like boyfriend-girlfriend?"

Erica stopped and looked back at Jon with a forced smile that answered Jon's prying question.

## Part 3 - Chapter Two

Jonathan, distracted by all thoughts of Erica, bypassed a few open doors of conversing classmates as he walked down the second-floor dormitory hallway. Hearing his name called out interrupted his fanciful daze.

"Hey, Jon, are those new?"

"Yeah, and half are unsealed," Jon responded, resisting all the urge to drop his baggage.

"Any loose codes?"

"One, if you get me a few full sales."

"Do I got your word on that?"

"A few as in more than one...you sure do," Jon answered, turning to finish his journey.

"You need help, man?"

"No, I got this," Jon claimed, traipsing the final steps to his room. He dropped the bundles and shuffled for his key as two girls stepped behind him and on down the hallway.

"Pay up," his roommate welcomed without breaking his focus on the computer. Jon's roommate, Nate, had a flat head of loopy black hair and a true talent for computer-coding.

Jon pulled a pair of scissors out of his desk drawer and popped the bands off a bundle of double prints. Proudly tossing a copy down on his roommate's desk, Jon said, "Here; any luck?"

"Any code?" Nate echoed. "And yeah. Do you want to see him?"

"You have a picture?" Jon emphasized with doubt.

"You own a two-thousand-dollar laptop, your web camera is taking pictures in thirty-minute intervals and transmitting them to me now whenever he's plugged in."

"I'll get you one if you get me that laptop back."

"Me? A guy who has balls to jack laptops out from under your nose is not my nemesis of choice. And no, I won't be making any recovery efforts, thank you, but I'd be happy to let you know your thief's location as of ten minutes ago, for an upgrade," Nate propositioned from his unbreakable focus.

"Or how about as a pal...," Jon said, pensively picking up and unconsciously rolling the unsealed magazine.

"Pal's good, thanks. And he's up somewhere on the corner of Brighton and North. That's probably accurate to a block or two."

"A block or two, that's like almost helpful." Jon said and trailed off calculating the probability of ever seeing his laptop again.

"That's free on me, cause we're bartering as pals now."

"Nate and Jon, rooming-pals," Jon mused, pausing until he realized his roommate still expected a wrapped upgrade. "What?" Jon objected, not realizing what had been negotiated.

"You said it. Pals." Nate said, facing Jon for the first time since he entered the dorm room.

"You're with me until we get this thing back, right?"

"Yeah, I want to see how my sniping code works out," Nate said, accepting the complimentary upgrade before spinning back to his work. "You've got to see his dumb face."

"He's slick enough to manage a broad daylight heist; I wouldn't call him dumb," Jon pointlessly defended.

"No, I mean he looks dumb, just like you and I would look staring at a screen. He's still dumb enough to plug in a stolen laptop that has a built-in camera. But, if you're defending him now, I'll let up."

"I don't know what I'm saying," Jon confessed, taking off his sweaty shirt and massaging his left elbow. "So, how are we going to get this guy?" Jon pondered out loud.

"If by 'we' you mean you and the police, I would suggest you start by...um, maybe reporting it as stolen." Nate said, making a few clicks on his screen and keyboard.

The fan blew the rumpled magazine wrapper off Dan's desk.

"I feel bad, I only lost one, Scales Architect...Company lost four, and I've already told my Scale's mentor about mine being missing," Jon said as an open-ended statement, hoping for feedback. Nate answered him with a few more clicks on his keyboard and swipes of his mouse. "I guess that's good advice. Can I copy your sniping program to help the police find the computers?" Jon asked, looking over at his out-of-touch roommate. "Thanks, I'll hold you to that," Jon dictated loudly enough to compete with the blowing fan when his roommate didn't respond.

"It's not exactly legal, so no. But it's good enough for your sake. And it's already in place. So, it will e-mail me every thirty minutes when it's able to report something," Nate said in retrospect after a long minute of gazing at his screen.

## Part 3 - Chapter Three

"Well...thanks for helping out a friend. A girl always wonders when she's left hanging," Anna said to Romney, leaning with her fair-skinned forearms on the bed rail and still toiling over Jonathan Wickfell's silence. Anna had brought up the topic of Jon not having called her mom for a week and a half when she came to visit Romney at the hospital. The one-sided conversation, due to Romney's pitiful state, had led to Jon's internship, which led to Scales Architectural Company and then to Jeff Dunnire's phone number with Romney's miniscule additions. Jeff had supplied Anna with Jonathan's contact number, and Romney had smiled to the extent of his ability when she excitedly asked him for his opinion of whether she should call.

"Four-four, he'll be right over. He's with...," A nurse spoke loudly in passing, catching Anna's attention.

Turning back and noting Romney's subtle change in mood, Anna felt pity. "Please don't stay in pain on my account," Anna petitioned, moving courteously to gather her light red jacket. Torn between her rush of joy and Romney's helpless state, she left promising, "I'll bring April by tomorrow, she seems to be doing well with...despite missing you." After leaving Romney's curtained area, she stopped and quietly peeked back around the corner. He hadn't moved and still looked up at the ceiling with his unbandaged eye. She left when she noticed him tighten his remaining eye with what looked like an attempt to force himself to sleep. She could tell his pain and made a conscious effort to keep a smile on her face as she walked out of the hospital to the parking garage. After easily navigating her car through the series of tight turns, she checked the locks on her doors as she remembered the garage would soon shoot her out into Spencer's part of town. Not after long, she pulled into her square driveway and pulled her red jacket closed as she stepped out into the breeze. She noticed the door to Romney's house looked open, and she walked over to find it missing completely. Construction material lay partially depleted in the driveway, and a fiberglass tub jutted up over the edge of a rented dumpster. Yellow siding lay bundled together with plastic wrap, and the concrete that had been removed already was replaced with what looked like a new foundation that would extend the footprint of the house out by ten feet or so. Not wanting to test if the concrete work was dry, she stepped along the makeshift planks to go take a tour of the house's renovations. Most of the remodeling work was in process but the front porches seemed untouched. She walked up to the second floor and stepped out onto the porch. She glanced over to see if her mom was outside in her usual repose. Then hearing two voices coming from the house, she exhaled and eavesdropped for a minute. She relaxed her body on the railing and looked down across the Montague River. Focusing on Romney's living complex, she began daydreaming, and without realizing it, the present world disappeared.

Anna heard a muted crack and snapped out of her daydream. A shriek, followed by yelling, came from her mother's bedroom next door. The trailing laughter provided reassurance, but the indistinct male voice reminded her of the matter at hand. Deciding her course, she put her limbs back into motion. Taking out her phone and car keys, ready for a drive, she called Bethy, knowing she was still in town, and asked if she had an extra bed to spare. Then after pulling into the gas station at the end of the street, she called and left her mom a message of her planned whereabouts as she usually did. After leaving her short message, she flipped closed her cellphone and tapped it on her

leg for a minute, clicking her tongue back and forth in her
mouth while she did.  Then she decidedly pulled the scratch
piece of paper out of her purse, that she had gotten with
Romney's help, and dialed Jonathan Wickfell's number before
her bold idea lost the upper hand of her debate.


## Part 3 - Chapter Four


   Jon's phone rang.  "Yellow," Jon said.  "Yahuh," he answered.
"Yeah, fifteen minutes, thirty-five dollars, and no checks," he
said, stretching in anticipation of making another evening
delivery.  "Well, I'll do two for fifty and you can sell the other or
make a friend really happy," he said and started sliding the
magazine bundles out of view into his personal closet.  "I have
unsealed copies, but they don't have a code...fifteen...so, you
want the full magazine?" Jon said, putting two of each product
into his smaller book bag.  "The gym would be a good spot...in
fift...yeah fifteen minutes."  Jon stepped out of his room with his
phone still to his ear and locked his roommate inside.
   "Hey Jon, any price cuts lately?" an acquaintance asked in
passing.
   "Thirty-five.  Yeah, I'll be there," Jon answered, splitting his
attention equally between the two buyers.
   "I'll take it."
   Jon understood and swung his backpack to under his arm,
unzipping the pouch to make the sale.  "Thanks, I hear Monica's
inside the special," Jon advertised.
   "Any good?"
   "I don't know, I'm too busy to watch anymore."
   "Right, he sells, but he's too busy to take his turn."
   "Whatever."
   "Hey, Boston Rob is like on a mission to get that free code
you promised him," the classmate said as he took his magazine
away with him down the second-floor hallway.
   The evening greeted him with a pleasant coolness.  Then after
a few steps, reality struck him, and he negated every part of his
delightful thirty-minute walk with Erica.  On his ten-minute walk

to the student gym he kept replaying her cold mannerisms and listening repeatedly to her cold remarks and comments from his vivid memory. Everything seemed cold behind her smile. He didn't have to wait long for his customer and began his return walk to Swanson Hall by way of the student complex and cafeteria. Seeing an open telephone book hanging from one of the three pay phones, he stopped and back-stepped to consider his hanging invitation to call Anna's mother for permission to ask her daughter out on a date. "Why not?" Jon subtly shrugged at the suggestion to himself. A few students roamed the pathways outside, and as far as he could tell, the student complex was vacant. He walked over to the hanging telephone book and let it hit the bottom of the telephone stall before flipping it open. He immediately started pulling the pages in groups back toward the beginning, and finding the P section, he found his next dilemma. "I have no idea," he decided, and closed the book with the intention of returning to his hall. Yet, the two glass doors scolded him, and his fear set his heart ablaze as he waited for his body to decide what it wanted to do. Submitting to Sean's prior advice from weeks ago, he pulled out his cellphone and dialed the first number he found under Purse. "Hi, are you Anna's dad? No? Sorry."

He hung up the phone, "Does she even have a dad?" Jon started figuring. "Ask my mom would make me think...girl name...Hello, does Anna live here? Ann...a? Oh, you're she, this is Jon from your math logic class, the one who spiked the curve," Jon said, having a hard time fitting the callers voice to his memory of Anna's. "No, you're right, I'm in college now. I have the wrong...yeah, I think so. Sorry; bye...have a good day...," Jon said, flipping his cellphone closed. Trying to ease the burning sensation on his cheeks with his fingers, he scoured the book again with what little determination he still had left in his dialing thumb. Two more message machines recorded his embarrassing introduction with his phone number. Running low on number options, he tried to make his thumb stop shaking with energy as he started dialing the next of the last three numbers. "How convenient," Jon said with aggravation at the sight of an unfamiliar number that interrupted his phone dialing. "Hello," Jon answered, expecting a 'Boston' Rob referral.

"You've got to be kidding me, I was just calling through the yellow pages...I mean white...trying to find your number. Right, trying to call your mother," Jon expressed with excitement as he pressed the phone harder to his ear. "Tonight? No way," Jon said, and tried pulling his jaw off as he critiqued his response. "Tonight's not good, um. I haven't talked to your...well, right, right; coffee at night's not a good idea either. Will I see you in class?" Jon said, willingly bumping his head down onto the open telephone book. "Of course. I hope to see you before then, Anna; hey hold...," Jon said incoherently. "Hello? You've got to be kidding me. Dude, how stupid are you? ...Ahh....ha; caller ID," Jon reprimanded himself to the silent phone, and thumbed eagerly through the menu to save Anna's number. "Hey, Anna; Anna Purse, right? Right, it's Jon. Hey, I don't know how stupid you think I am, but out of these three numbers which will get me in contact with your mom...mother?" Jon asked as if he was valiantly warding off heart failure. "None?" Jon said in surprise after citing the three numbers. "Oh, I'd better write that down, my heart's moving a million miles-per-hour. Okay, I have you on speaker phone," Jon admitted, grabbing for the pay phone's tethered pen and trying to jot down the number on an old piece of tape stuck to the payphone.

"Can you hear me okay?" Anna asked ready to recount her home phone number.

"Yeah, I can hear you; go ahead...and tonight was not a bad idea, I just...but the number...go," Jon said, lifting the phone closer to his ear to hear the string of numbers. "Okay, and I'm sorry. I'm completely bumbling tonight, can I have...yes. Perfect, and if you don't mind me asking, what's your mom...ther's name? Miss Purse, I'll be sure to...yes, of course. Well of course she's nice, look at her daughter!" Jon exclaimed, and then in the awkward silence he apologized again before saying goodbye.

# Part 3 - Chapter Five

Tired of flats and letting her high heels lay dormant in her closet, Saundra Lent impulsively selected a favorite pair. The color popped perfectly with her normal business suit, and the extra two inches refreshingly elevated her perspective as she walked out the door. Taking her time to greet her favorite colleagues on her way to her office, two compliments on her shoes made the extra strain worth it. Nevertheless, she slipped them off as soon as she sat down to start her directionless day of work.

Miss Theresa sent her an email that caught Saundra's attention with the bold characters, "DID MR. DANIELS APPROVE THIS?"

Saundra briefly replied, "Hi, Theresa, No. Sincerely, Saundra." Then clicking into her company account, she looked up the transaction number. She recognized Romney's credentials, but didn't recognize the transaction. She picked up the phone and dialed the hospital to see if she could talk to Romney directly and typed another message to Theresa while she waited on hold for the nurse to find an answer. When the line suddenly disconnected, she decided it was probably unnecessary anyway. Slipping her shoes back on, she paused for a moment to transcribe the critical information onto her notepad and went to see Jack Hense.

Jack's secretary as friendly as ever, greeted Saundra, "Oh my, where did you get those shoes? They're gorgeous!"

"Oh, I don't even remember. I thought I would give something other than flats a go today. It just felt right," Saundra replied, shyly covering her fluster. "But you're always dressed so well. You probably have a closet full of accessories I'd be jealous of."

"Are you up for lunch today?" Jack's secretary surprisingly asked.

"Ahh, I don't know, is Mr. Hense available?" Saundra said, letting a hint of her issue show.

"Yes, I think so; let me check," Kim said, instinctively picking up her phone and hitting two buttons with her little finger. "Sure, go right in. Lunch?"

"Aww, you're so sweet, honey, the answer is yes, but let me see if it'll be today or tomorrow okay...in a second," Saundra promised.

"Kay," Kim said brightly.

"Saundra, come in!" Jack said, immediately noticing the contemplative look on Saundra's face. "What's the matter? Have you heard from Romney to see how he's doing?"

"No. I tried calling the hospital this morning. But I think...well, straight to the point, if I may?"

"Yeah sure, go ahead," Jack said, relaxing in his chair to lend his full attention.

"I think someone is stealing money from the company, and I can't believe it's Romney. But it kind of would look that way in the transaction records," Saundra briefly explained, and clicked open her pen to take down instructions out of habit.

"No, Romney hasn't stolen anything; he makes the money around here," Jack said confidently, easing Saundra's tension. "But let me look it up; which transactions?" Jack typed the information into his computer that Saundra professionally conveyed to him. "Ha, that amount would tend to send up red flags. I should go see him. I need to pay him a visit anyway. Is he at UMC Hope?" Jack asked, standing up and moving his chair back into place under the wide desk.

"No, the other one north of the river."

"Allegan?"

"That's right, I don't know why it slipped my mind," Saundra confirmed, leading Jack to the door of his office.

"Meanwhile would you have Kim try to freeze that transaction. It might not do much good as that's a pre-authorized amount. And then stop by I.T.. Abdul will help you secure Romney's credentials."

"Right away, sir."

"And Saundra, don't sweat it; money comes in, and money goes out," Jack said, reaching in front of Saundra to open the door.

"You've been listening to Romney too much," Saundra said, smiling at the reference.

"I wouldn't have graduated without him," Jack said with his car keys in hand, leaving Saundra in his outer office to chat with his secretary.

"Today would be great by the way," Saundra said to the questioning eyes of the secretary.

"Yay...and you don't sweat. You're the coolest calmest person I know," Kim encouraged, having overheard the end of the conversation.

"You're so sweet, darling," Saundra said, reflecting the secretary's younger smile.

"Let's say around eleven-thirty," Jack's secretary suggested as her phone rang.

"Perfect." "Jack Hense's office, this is Kim," Saundra heard from behind her.

"Sure, I'll look up the directions and call you back, Jack," Kim said and giggled.

On her short walk back to her office, Saundra thought about Kim's newfound friendliness. "The computer's and all their fancy programs really make this place like an ice cube tray," Saundra concluded to herself as she sat down and slipped out of her glossy red shoes again.

## Part 3 - Chapter Six

"So, what's in your heart today?" Saundra bubbled as she pushed through the lobby door ahead of Kim.

"To eat?" Kim asked.

"To eat, and is your last name spelled like the family...."

"...of cats? Felidae, most people don't get that," Kim said, looking at the pricy restaurant across the street.

"That one's out of my range too," Saundra said, interpreting the look on Kim's face.

"Yeah. How about I drive us to Crumbles Café," Kim offered.

"Oh, I know that place. Mr. Daniels always meets one of his colleagues there," Saundra said, turning to follow Kim to a nearby parking garage. "It's really nice of you to suggest lunch; I really should ha..."

"Oh, it's nothing. I actually need some advice, and you're the only one in my life that seems like she has it all together enough to ask," Kim said discretely and turned into the first floor of the garage.

"Hah, together? I don't know where you'd come up with some fanciful notion like that," Saundra said as she saw the flash of Kim's headlights a few steps away. "You got a pretty good spot this morning," Saundra commented as she split away to the passenger door.

"Yeah, at least something went right today," Kim said, sliding into her coupe.

"Well, if everything else went wrong you've certainly mastered putting on concealer," Saundra said, trying to tactfully investigate Kim's claim. Saundra looked at Kim and saw the need for a different topic. "Jack must pay you more to afford a ride as fancy as this," Saundra said quickly.

"Hah, it's not mine. It's my manipulative boyfriend's."

From the time the garage attendant identified Kim's parking pass and onward, Kim looked preoccupied, and Saundra respectfully let go of the conversation till they had parked the car at Crumble's. Saundra stepped out onto the sidewalk while Kim waited for a break in traffic. Parking meters lined the sidewalk, and Saundra took her opportunity to deposit enough change in the meter before Kim could object. Kim didn't seem to notice, which made Saundra proud of her accomplishment. The tingle of the door chime seemed to trigger a flood of emotions that Saundra compassionately detected, and she ushered Kim to the most private corner of the cafe. One of the employees took notice as she cleared tables for arriving patrons.

Erica gawked a bit as the older patron hurried to say something behind her hand to the emotional girl who strikingly looked like the girl on Miss Doxy's cover. Identifying with her distress, she returned to the kitchen.

With her back to the corner, Saundra sat next to Kim. "What's wrong, my dear?"

"Everything," Kim responded.

Saundra looked kindly at Kim, hoping she would explain.

"I'm a prostitute. And I don't want to be," Kim admitted sorrowfully.

"You certainly don't have to be, my dear; you have an income of your own."

"But the car. And I signed a contract."

"You said the car was your boyfriend's?" Saundra questioned, squeezing Kim's hand, attempting to rustle her memory.

"I don't know. It seemed like a gift at the time, but he said it was in my contract."

"No real boyfriend would make you sign a contract."

"He said I needed to for his business, to give his business permission to print the pictures."

"Like a model-release?" Saundra asked, seeing Kim pull herself together in a troubled breath.

"Yeah kind of, I think he used a different term. Have you seen them?" Kim asked, pausing her forlorn expression to gather her answer.

"Seen them? The pictures?" Saundra asked to clarify. "No, I don't believe I have. Where would someone see them?"

"Miss Doxy."

"Miss...Doxy...I haven't heard, but don't mind my ignorance. You said you feel like a prostitute, which is just a horrible self-label."

"But that's what they say I have to do."

"Or what?"

"They'd make me."

"I'm sorry, dear, they can't make you, not in this country."

"They'll just do it again."

"Do what?" Saundra said boldly but saw the sore impact of her inquiry.

Kim shook her head, too ashamed to answer, and Saundra pulled her into a hug as tears started forming in her own eyes.

"What do I do?" Kim asked on Saundra's supportive shoulder.

"What we need to...to get you free of this monster."

"Here these are for you, gals," Erica said kindly, setting down two sandwiches if front of the girls.

"Oh, we haven't ordered anything," Saundra piped up.

"Oh, they're on me today," Erica smiled. "Hey, can I ask you something?" Both patrons looked up with their red eyes. Seeing her opportunity, Erica mildly sat down. Tipped from her eavesdropping, she leaned in and asked, "Are you Mon...." Erica abandoned her question to rephrase. "Do you know Dan or Markus?"

"Markus," Kim admitted, shaking her head up and down. "I'm that Monica," Kim admitted and had the courage to look up at Erica.

Erica took the information in for a moment then apologized, "I'm sorry if that's too personal. It's just, just that, I'm one of them...too," Erica managed to say politely, and left suddenly to hide herself in the cafe's kitchen.

It took a minute for Saundra to reflect on the waitress's contribution before returning her attention to Kim. "Well, it doesn't look like your alone." The young secretary, still hanging on the waitress's words, smiled and retreated from her transparency. "That was nice of her," Saundra continued, listening to her stomach and choosing one of the two complimentary sandwiches. Kim kept smiling and followed Saundra's lead. "Hey, I know Mr. Daniels and Mr. Hense have access to some powerful lawyers that could help; could I ask?" Saundra brainstormed, taking a bite of her sandwich to conceal her forwardness.

"Not Jack."

"Not Jack?" Saundra echoed, thankful that Kim didn't take offense at her offer.

"I don't want to lose my job," Kim recovered, lowering her sandwich back onto the plate.

Saundra swallowed the lump in her throat, and vocalized her suspicion, "Kim, honey, I'm not going to ask what my conscience suspects as to why not Jack, but I know two things. With your smile and positivity, you are highly employable, and if you need a hand, out of whatever, or wherever, mine's available. My hand that is." Saundra pressed Kim's slender shoulder, and Kim smiled. "I don't have one of those fancy cell phones, but my husband did set me up with one of those email addresses," Saundra said, trying to accommodate her savvier counterpart. "Here's my home number and email; you contact me anytime."

The gesture made Kim smile again, and the two coworkers continued eating their sandwiches till they were finished. "Hey, would you put this over there in that tip jar?" Saundra asked Kim, pointing with a bill she had drawn from her purse. After Kim had deposited the tip, the couple proceeded to the door together and felt the steady breeze cleaning the sidewalk on their brief walk to the car. Saundra sunk into the coupe next to Kim. "I guess somebody's going to get free parking today. I over fed the meter," Saundra whimsically observed.

"No refunds," Kim quipped back before making use of the tissue she had grabbed from her middle compartment.

"Nope, but the food was free. So, why not just think we're paying it forward," Saundra said as she watched Kim start the car and take advantage of a break in traffic.

## Part 3 - Chapter Seven

Jack Hense didn't have much to worry about and enjoyed the sound of the wind flapping through the windows. With thoughts of life in the front of his mind, he drove to the hospital, forgetting the best route that his executive assistant had prescribed.

"Hello, officer," Jack greeted plainly, courteously placing his hands on the steering wheel.

"Hello, sir, may I see your license and registration please," the officer said before stepping to the rear of the car to watch the driver collect the requested documents.

Jack didn't rush or dawdle but collected and held the two items passively on the steering wheel.

The officer responded to the gesture and returned to the window. "Thank you, Mr. Hense," the officer said before walking away to his idling patrol car.

Jack closed his eyes to return to his stretch of ideas for the new property. Something about the history of Morestown lured his mind into creative mode.

"Mr. Hense, did you realize that you were speeding in a construction zone?" the officer said, interrupting Jack's creative spell.

"Ooh, double whammy, no sorry, sir. I did not; I must have missed the reduction. I'm normally good at catching those."

"I see. Well, I won't keep you any longer. Here is your ticket, license, and registration. Have a good day." the officer said without much emotion.

"You too, officer," Jack said and turned on his flashers, upon realizing he had forgotten. Pulling out his cellphone, he called his accountant, "Hey...good and you? Yeah, that's right. You have time to make it? Well great, I'll see you there. Sure, who you got for me? You have good taste, put her next to me at dinner. Hey, before I forget, I just got this ticket...no not pawning one today, but I need to pay one today. Yeah, strange right! I think I'll have it framed to memorialize it. I'll have Kim fax it over when I'm back in the office."

"Sir, you need to move on now," the officer commanded with his mega-phone.

"Oh sorry, don't want another one. Yes, I'll see you there," Jack said, hanging up the phone to convince the officer he had heard his instruction. After arriving at a nearly empty parking deck, he rolled up his windows and proceeded into the hospital intent on finding Romney. The receptionist seemed busy, so he waited and folded a ten-dollar bill into a swan. He greeted her cold face with a smile when she finally seemed to have a moment.

"Let me check," she replied to his inquiry, warming up in return to his kind expression.

"You get a lot of echo in here. It probably gets pretty loud when things get busy."

"Things get dramatic on the other side of the building. Here it's usually pretty quiet unless they decide to set up free lunch," the secretary commented while mechanically punching the keyboard to find the patient Jack had requested.

Jack elusively set the swan on the lobby counter in front of the receptionist as she read Romney's whereabouts from her computer monitor. Jack relished the fact that she didn't notice the gift until he had disappeared down the cathedral shaped hallway. The nurses in their ugly patterned scrubs were all particularly attractive to Jack, and he almost tried to stop one to ask for directions.

"Who are you looking for, young man," an elderly woman asked from behind him.

"Romney Daniels, and whom do I have pleasure of speaking with, young lady," Jack responded more gladly than ever.

"Oh darn, I lost that title fifty years ago. I'm Suzy. Romney, did you say? Daniels?"

"Very good, yes, and any help would be wonderful!"

"Down the hall and to the left I think," Suzy said roughly, trying to clear her throat.

"You look like you're out for an afternoon stroll, would you be so kind as to walk me there? I've already lost my way twice."

"Sure, sure. You're going to have to do it slowly though," Suzy declared with a warning tone.

"It wouldn't be an afternoon stroll otherwise, would it now?"

"No, it wouldn't. I used to take a walk every day. We had a nice park path down the street...seeing the kids playing and screaming on the playground. Oh, it was nice," Suzy reminisced at her own pace.

"I don't have a purpose to go sit at a park, though I did build one recently," Jack said, shooting the breeze.

"Oh, a builder! I'm sure you included all the popular knick-knacks that the kids love," Suzy said, pushing her metal walker one step at a time.

"We sure did, and the play-equipment company even had this new rope gym pyramid that we threw up in one of the corners, where kids can climb ten feet up this rope webbing," Jack said, proudly smiling as he curled his fingers into the shape of the pyramid.

"We? Aye?"

"Well, I'm taking the credit, but my business partner Romney designed the entire grounds. I just signed the order form," Jack admitted, swinging his shoulders away from Suzy.

"Don't waste your money there," Suzy said, following Jacks eyes.

"Pardon me?" Jack said, returning his gaze to see what Suzy referenced.

"I see your eyes to know enough.  But the gal sitting behind the desk would be worth your time."

Jack silently looked with closed lips and interested eyes toward the gal Suzy spoke of thirty feet ahead at the corner of the hallway.

"You're going to grow old and ugly like me one day you know," Suzy said to fill the silence.

"Why would you trust a wandering eye with a nugget of gold?" Jack asked before recognizing April's pigtails bouncing inside of a room.  "Oh, I think this is it."

"I guess so.  Well, Jacky, I love you, honey, will you be home for dinner?" Suzy asked with heartfelt sincerity.

"I'm afraid Suzy you might have me mixed up with a different Jacky," Jack apologized, giving Suzy his full attention one last time.

"Sorry, dear, you're not my Jacky," Suzy agreed readily and continued stepping toward the corner of the hallway.  "Have you met my Jacky?" Jack heard clearly from behind him as he stepped into Romney's hospital room.  "You two would make a good pair," Jack heard again and grinned to the floor, stealing a look at the nearby conversant.  "Well, it looks like he's been good company to my Miss Suzy.  Are you done with your rounds, Miss Suzy?" Jack heard the kind conversant respond.  Then Jack stepped out of earshot and into Romney's hospital room with his typically warm, "Well, hello."  He saw Romney stir in his bed.  "Oh, is he sleeping?" Jack asked, hushing his question to the youthful red-headed girl that was monitoring April.

"No, I don't think so."

"No," Romney gargled, trying to address the familiar voice. "No, I'm not, but I'm completely bored of lying in this position, Anna could you raise...."

"Sure thing!" Anna said, rising to her feet.

"Jack, thanks for coming," Romney said as hardily as he could. "This is Anna, a great friend who's been taking care of April while Sandy's been busy."

"Hi," Anna said, putting her hand on April's inquisitive head as she rounded the corner of the bed to comply with Romney's request.

"Hi, I'm Jack Hense, this guy's boss," Jack greeted Anna and heard Romney laughed with pain.

"That's funny, Jack," Romney managed to say with his one eye slightly cracked open.

"Laughter's good medicine."

Romney tried speaking more, but his voice had left him. He recovered his attempt by whispering to Anna, "Ask April if she remembers Uncle Jack...family friend."

"Hey, little Pearl, do you remember Uncle Jack?" Anna vocalized to the pig-tailed girl who was playfully twisting on the bed rail as if at a ballet lesson. April responded with a laughing snort that showed her top row of happy teeth. "Well, April's getting a bit restless, and I have to get her back to Sandy soon," Anna explained to Jack to dismiss herself. "April, say goodbye to your daddy, and give him a kiss. I think he liked that a lot last time."

Anna watched the daughter's endearment and then said goodbye to Jack as she guided April out into the hallway.

Jack turned back to Romney and said, "You've got yourself one super-nanny. Oh, don't use any more energy on me, Rom. I just came by to see how you were doing. They sure make it a hassle to get across town these days. If the traffic doesn't slow you down enough, the cops do. I got my first ticket...ever...in Pittsburg that is...," Jack said and interrupted himself when he heard Romney clearing his throat.

"You don't drive like you used to," Romney said thinly with enjoyment.

"You've given me enough stress with the successes and woes of Hense and Daniels. Just give me a car that removes the bumps from the road, and I'll be happy," Jack said, moving over to sit in the corner where Anna had been sitting when Romney relaxed his head.

"Hey, I don't mean to bring my work to you here, but Saundra, not your wife...but Saundra came in today like you did earlier this month and told me about missing funds. I think we've found the hole and plugged it, but you said it might have something to do with Mitchell Reed. The transfers looked the same from my glance this morning. Have you...did you have time to look into Mitchell's case before these bullies knocked you senseless?" Jack said with his typical carefreeness.

"No."

"I didn't think so, but hey, I'll take care of things on the mothership. Morestown looks promising. You don't have any second thoughts on Philly, do you?" Jack asked suggestively, setting his elbows on the chair arms and forming a pyramid with his fingers.

"Always, liked the Philly property better, but it doesn't make sense. Make sure...," Romney started but lost his voice again.

Jack waited patiently for Romney to recuperate.

"Make sure you have proof. Legal...," Romney managed and finished his statement with flat lips.

"For Mitchell? Right, I'll send the minds to work...before I can the guy that is. Hey, did he have any good ideas in his manifesto?" Jack asked, remembering his prior curiosity.

"He did."

"Well, I just might have to get my hands on a copy to see for myself. But regardless, I need you to get better, and I think you've earned the time off. If you're okay with it, I'm going to move Theresa into your position while you're out healing."

"Good call," Romney responded softly.

"She's...what's that?" Jack asked.

"Six months," Romney said again, taking a hard breath.

"Six months. Well, if that's what the doctors said, then Romney Daniels can do it in three, rest assured," Jack said jovially, taking the subtle cues in Romney's mannerisms to rise to his feet in preparation to leave.

"Great friend," Romney said as a goodbye with a turn of his head toward Jack.

"That goes two ways, but you have lots of work to do friend, and when you get that arm of yours out of that cast, you'd better be giving me a call on that cellphone. Bye-now!" Jack said and left Romney to rest. Taking a right turn out of the room, he headed for the highlighted nurse's station. The same kind nurse sat busily attending her eyes to something flat on the desk. "Hello," Jack said plainly.

"Hi," the gal said professionally.

"You're going to think I'm creepy and that I do this all the time, but I honestly don't...ever really. I'd like to have lunch with you...sometime, my name's Jack Hense, I'm Romney's friend."

"Not Suzy's boy?"

"Suzy sure seemed interested in her match-making, didn't she? But she had the highest regards of you," Jack said and straightened up quickly when the counter wobbled from his weight.

"I'll think about it," the nurse said coyly. She started turning the plastic pen around in her hands after a distracted moment.

"Well good, I don't expect you to tell me your name, Nancy," Jack said, reading her name from her tag. "...but if the thinking turns into a yes, ask my buddy Romney to let you in on all my little secrets and my phone number; he's known me since early college."

"He comes with references rather than a pickup line and a bottle of beer."

"Up, that's one thing I don't partake in. ...Tried it yes, toasts okay, but...you're not a drinker, are you?" Jack asked, comically wincing his cheek.

"No, it's just the boring stereotype," Nancy responded, as a screen below the desk grabbed her attention.

"Now, I'm serious. Ask Rom; I kind of want to see what he'll say," Jack said, pushing himself back from the wobbly counter with hope.

# Part 3 - Chapter Eight

The sounds in the hallway had become routine, and Romney looked hopelessly punished between sleeplessness and fatigue.

"How are we doing this afternoon, Mr. Daniels?" Nancy greeted cheerfully, moving around the foot of the bed to a tray with some medical instruments.

"I'm glad you act like we're in this together," Romney said in return, trying his ugly lips at a greeting.

"Of course! When you walk out of here with your life back in suit, I'll be just as happy as you'll be," Nancy said, pausing her task to address Romney's stiff face.

"That's the goal."

"Sure is!" Nancy said, preparing a dose of medicine for the IV. "So, tell me about Jack Hense."

"Jack's a good friend; do you know him?" Romney inquired, tracing the lines on the ceiling to Nancy's face with his eyes.

"No," Nancy laughed nervously.

Romney wiggled two of his fingers to the extent he could.

"So, he's a good guy you say?" Nancy prompted, hoping to spur more information out of her patient.

"Best," Romney replied, rolling his head as far to the side as he could. Seeing that Nancy was busy at her task, Romney rolled his eyes back to watching the ceiling. "My left foot feels like it's burning."

"That's what the green button is for, Mr. Daniels," Nancy instructed calmly without interrupting her charge.

"It doesn't hurt; it just feels like it's boiling," Romney explained without irritation.

"The doctor might come in before he leaves for the day, but I'll take note of it," Nancy said, already jotting down what she had promised. She walked around the end of the bed toward the door, but a surge of boldness stopped her. "Would it be worth my while to accept a lunch invitation from Jack...Hense?" she asked, turning back to take in Romney's answer.

"If he asked you?" Romney semi-queried, moving his chin a little toward Nancy's gaze. "Yeah, that would be good," Romney said, forming a questionable smile as he saw the betraying expression on her face.

"I find it strange," Nancy commented and lost her thought from an internal distraction.

"Me too."

"You too? Why would he tell me to ask you for his number?" Nancy asked, dropping her bedside manner for a moment.

"Strange that he asked at all," Romney said, hearing clearly Nancy's predicament.

"Okay, please explain," Nancy pushed but scolded herself when she saw Romney exhale. "I'm sorry, you look tired; I don't need to bother you so," Nancy followed up, snapping out of her curious mood.

"Ha, no bother," Romney said, inhaling to gather the strength to reply. "He probably wanted my opinion of you."

Nancy watched, mulling over Romney's meaning.

"He's...a fairly guarded guy. Lots of people like...the rep...reputation, but not many...like Jack," Romney said, embarrassed at his own slow babble.

"So, would Jack be...lunch be worth my while?" Nancy rephrased.

"Do you want his number?" Romney said, relaxing his eyelids.

"I don't know," Nancy exclaimed after a thoughtful moment. "You don't seem to be too vying to give it to me."

"I almost slipped, sorry."

"What?" Nancy laughed at Romney's confusing confession.

"I don't think anybody has Jack's number, except maybe his grandmother."

"But you do," Nancy tactfully accused, exposing the error in his statement.

"Yeah, like I...said," Romney said, inhaling deeply. "Jack's guard...places a load of trust in a few...people."

"Ha, like an introvert," Nancy laughed at the notion. "Well, I'll think about it."

"Okay."

"Thanks, I'll see you tomorrow...early," Nancy said with her typical cheeriness.

"Wait!" Romney gasped, making Nancy jump. "Catch that nurse!"

"What?"

"That nurse that just passed!" Romney said stilted up on his shoulder as if his life depended on it.

"Oh sure, but relax; don't hurt yourself, Mr. Daniels," Nancy said, moving with alarm back to the bedside to help Romney recline. Then hurrying away, she pursued the nurse without asking why.

Returning age-long moments later, Romney, on his back, was poised eager with his question.

"Yes, sir, may I help you?" the unfamiliar nurse questioned with worry.

"Sandra Daniels. I swear I heard you say as you passed," Romney quivered.

"Yes, sir, do you know her?"

"Is she here?"

"Yes, sir."

"What for?"

"Well, what's your relation to Sandra Daniels?" the nurse asked, acting like she might be in trouble if she answered inappropriately.

"My wife," Romney said in a whisper with the effort he had remaining.

The nurse looked at Nancy, who returned a neutral expression. "Well, she was admitted about two hours ago."

"What for?" Romney queried to egg on the nurse's answer.

"A drug overdose; I'm sorry."

"Alive, dead?"

"She's very alive, sir. When she woke, she put up such...she struck...well, we had to restrain her for safety's sake."

"Would you...would you tell her...that I'm here?" Romney said, concluding his interest with a look of pain.

"I certainly will, sir."

"Thank you...and, Nancy?" Romney said, claiming his last moment of opportunity.

"Yes, Mr. Daniels?"

"I need you to make a phone call please."

"I...I could do that," Nancy said, unconsciously asking her coworker with her eyes for permission.

"Could you call Hense and Daniels, and ask for Saundra, my executive assistant?"

"Sure."

"The number's in the phone book. Explain about Sandra Daniels...they'll all understand."

"Hense and Daniels...let's see…and your wife's name Sandra."

"Also, my executive assistant is...."

"Saundra, right."

"Thank you," Romney said, desperately pinching the slack green button for a relieving dose of morphine.

Romney closed his unwrapped eye, hating his helpless condition. After mentally toiling for a minute, he fell asleep.

# Part 3 - Chapter Nine

Nancy walked to the corner booth quickly. Rounding the corner and swinging through the half door, she grabbed a pen from a cup and slid a square pad of paper to within writing distance. She scanned the books and folders next to the nurse station and then the short book shelf behind her for a phone book. She kept reciting the company name to herself. Without success, she picked up the phone and dialed down to the receptionist's desk to expand her search.

"Hi Julie, this is Nancy. I have a favor to ask...sure, I can wait," Nancy said, looking down the corridor and seeing Suzy approaching again. She thoughtfully smiled before diverting her attention back to the square notepaper with her agenda of names. "Yes, one of my patients has requested I contact Hense and Daniels with some pertinent information, and we don't seem to have any phone book up here at this station. Could you? Thanks," Nancy continued and looked down at her slightly crooked name tag. "Yes, I'm supposed to have punched out already, but you found it? Yes, and ready. Yes, Romney Daniels is one of the patients on my round today. The guy that came to see him? Tall, a little stocky, round face, sandy hair? Yes, he introduced himself as Jack Hense, I think. He seemed nice; Mm..hmm. Thanks for looking up the number, Julie," Nancy said, hanging up the phone with purpose. Picking the phone right back up again, she punched in the scribbled number. Listening to the phone jingle under her chin, she continued fiddling with the pen between her thumbs.

"Hello, you've reached the corporate office of Hense and Daniels. This is Kim; how may I help you?" Kim greeted happily, her eye drawn to the office door.

"Hey, Kim," Jack greeted from the entry frame but hushed as he noticed the phone to her ear.

"Mmhmm, you're looking for Saundra Lent. I'll transfer you right over. She should be at her desk. Well, there's two of us here to take calls, Saundra's on the other side of the building.

Well, there's a few divisions. Here at the office...forty-five people or so, but depending on if you count the contractors, about two to four hundred at any given time. Sure, I'll patch you right over. Well, I work mostly as a secretary for Jack Hense. What's his role?" Kim looked up at Jack who had taken a seat to wait his turn. "He's the owner, or more so one of the owners here at Hense and Daniels; oh, my pleasure," Kim said and punched a few buttons on the number pad before hanging up the phone.

"Have you taken lunch already?" Jack asked, standing up after the phone call.

"Yes, Saundra and I went to Crumbles Cafe for a minute."

"Crumbles?! I love that place."

"Yeah, one of the servers gave us food for free which kind of surprised us," Kim said overly cheerful.

"Ha, who said there's no such thing as a free lunch? They didn't make you fill out a survey or sign up for any gimmick, did they?"

"No," Kim laughed.

"Well, could you fax this to my accountant? Them hard-workin' policemen were out doing their job today and caught me speeding."

"Oh no," Kim reacted, straightening her expression instead of chuckling at his feigned drawl.

"Well...I'm gonna count it as my three-hundred-and-sixty-four-dollar contribution to the city's road re-construction project," Jack said half-seriously in his own voice again and passed the carbon copy to Kim with a crumbling grin. Jack turned to go close himself in his office, but swung back and added, "I almost forgot; check Mitchell Reed's calendar and set me up with an appointment ASAP...or why don't you give him a ring and ask him what the first logical break in his schedule might be to have a chat."

"Sure, right away," Kim said, not letting her forearm think longer than a moment before starting on the task.

"Good," Jack said and finished the four steps into his den.

"Hi, Mitchell," Kim greeted while scrolling down Mitchell's calendar that was displayed on her computer screen.

"Hi, Kim," Mitchell sanguinely responded.

"You're a busy guy I see."

"Work, work, working if I'm gonna get this kid through school," Mitchell said proudly.

"Well, Jack just asked me to set up a meeting for you and him at your first convenience," Kim explained, covering her mouth to avoid letting extra air into the phone.

"Okay, about what?"

"You know what? He didn't say, but I'll be sure to ask and add it to the calendar event I'm creating," Kim assured, placing her hand back on the computer mouse to move it to the corner of the screen. "What time might you be available to meet?"

"Ahh, man...how about ooh; I have... aye. Never? Or how about now; your pick."

Kim laughed at Mitchell's inflection.

"I live with a ten second agenda at any given time; so, surprise me. Say it's mandatory, and I'll be there."

"Okay," Kim said, laughing again at the unconditioned reply. "I'll call you back if it's soon. If it's not, you'll be watching your calendar, right?"

"Yes, ma'am. Thanks, Kim," Mitchell said politely, hanging up the phone and glancing at his watch. "Hmm," he said to himself and picked the telephone back up. After holding it in deliberation for a moment, he set it back down. Then after rustling his courage, he picked the phone up again and called his son.

"Hey, I saw your last game, Chad," Mitchell said, taking a brown paper bag out of the bottom office drawer. "Chad? If you're busy I can call back after work," Mitchell responded to the ambient talking he overheard in the background. He listened intently for a reply as he removed a dry looking sandwich from his lunchbox.

"Yo-hey, dad, sorry. What's up?" Chad responded hesitantly as he retreated out of the lunchroom clamor to commit his attention to his dad. "Thanks, we still lost. Coach does that when he thinks my arm is getting tired or when he thinks it's a strategic advantage for the opponents line up. Oh, I don't...I don't worry that is. The next one is two weeks on Thursday. Did you want a ticket too? Mom will be there," Chad forewarned, slipping his hand into his pocket as he paced along the few patterned lines on the floor. "Yeah, mom wanted to come to this one though. Okay, maybe it would be easier next time...the next-next time." Chad conceded, and turning around, he caught his roommate leaving the cafeteria. "Well, I got to go, dad. Be well," Chad said, jogging to the door. "Yo-hey, Sean, wait a sec!" Chad yelled at Sean and Veronica, who stopped and turned to see Chad hanging out the cafeteria door. After Sean nodded, Chad ran back to the cafeteria to grab his bookbag. Rejoining his friends, he sarcastically miffed, "You guys just leaving me hanging?"

"No, we didn't know how long you'd be with your dad and all."

"Yeah, yeah, right, you know I'm just kidding. He was at the game last Thursday, I think," Chad said in stride with Sean.

"Really, he should've told you and maybe you would have thrown a few more strikes," Sean said sarcastically. When Chad responded with nothing more than the same bemused smile, he continued, "Hey, let me say goodbye to Veronica, and I'll catch up; whoa look at Terrance with that girl, that girl from the party...you know her."

"Anna Purse," Chad Wattsworth said, having paused to take in the pleasant sight.

"What kind of last name is Purse?" Veronica audibly critiqued.

"I don't know; she lives with her mom," Chad offered.

"Yeah, you would know," Sean cracked, glancing at Chad.

"Know what," Veronica asked after Chad had started lingering behind to greet Terrance and Anna.

"Mrs. Purse...is hot," Sean said and turned red in the face.

"Mrs. Purse? Is what?" Veronica offensively asked.

"Mrs. Purse is hot," Sean said committing to his statement with a giant grin.

"You think, Mrs. Purse...."

"I don't. Chad does," Sean said, excusing his statement as he wrapped his arm around Veronica on their trip to the parking lot.

"Hello, Terrance...Anna," Chad expressed, making eye contact with each. "Are you guys off to class?" Chad assumed by their obvious direction.

"Yeah, man, but hey it looks like you spilled mayo or something on your shirt, and that's a nice one too," Terrance said and flipped Chad's nose with his finger as Chad looked down to where Terrance was pointing.

"And you put up with this guy?" Chad joked back to even the score.

"Oh, believe me," Anna said, rolling her eyes.

"So, this guy pitches to me, right? He pitches to me again…and again, the same three pitches and then he must go light headed, double vision, or something, because then suddenly Mr. Gunner throws one straight into the umpire. The ball gets stuck in the poor man's mask, like an inch away from his right eye," Terrance said, putting two fingers up to demonstrate. "The runner's rounding third base to come home because the umpire's like falling all over himself, and I'm looking at him thinking, 'Do I help him, do I push him over onto the plate, or what,'" Terrance said, animating his words to his two humored classmates.

"This wasn't me pitching by the way," Chad clarified, seeing Anna's beautiful teeth.

"No, no; this is from my better high school days," Terrance agreed, grabbing the door for Anna.

Anna walked through to the classrooms and recognized Jonathan Wickfell leaning against a wall. "Hi, Jon," Anna chimed, but didn't speak fast or loudly enough to catch his attention among the exiting crowd.

The commotion interrupted Chad's connection to Anna, and he waved a lonely farewell to dive into his classroom.

Anna tapped Terrance and said, "I'll see you inside." Then walking over next to Jonathan, she bumped into him purposefully to gain his attention from his upright study posture.

"Oh, hi, Anna. Sorry…last minute cramming; you know how that goes. How goes it?" Jonathan asked, almost returning his eyes to the text he held in his hands.

"As it goes you still haven't called my mother."

"What? Yeah, about that, I uh, yeah." Jon said, attempting to clear his head. "I didn't forget, I promise, but the number I have sure doesn't call your mother. It dials someone named Dasha Markova, and she's very nice, mind you, but she doesn't have a daughter...and her son's name is Jason, Jason Markova." Jon looked at Anna's smile and pen scratching on his forearm.

"No excuses now," Anna warned, stepping away to her classroom with enough energy to make her hair bounce. "Good luck on the quiz."

"Thanks," Jonathan replied, taking out his phone and discovering his entry error as he cross-referenced the blue ink on his forearm. "The professor's probably going to think I'm cheating," Jon surmised to himself as he collected his bookbag to walk into his classroom.

## Part 3 - Chapter Ten

Anna ignored the first unknown number that scrolled across her cellphone, but when Romney's work number popped up, she thought it urgent enough to dismiss herself from the class. She missed the call, but as soon as she exited the room into the hallway her phone buzzed with a voicemail. A man re-introduced himself as Jeff, the lawyer, shared his brief concern over April's whereabouts, and left his number twice at the end of his message. Before the message had finished, Anna's phone buzzed again, and she curiously looked at it.

The second voicemail was not from Romney as she had thought, but from a lady who introduced herself as Saundra Lent, and she shared a similar concern about April's whereabouts, stating that she had passed along her phone number to Romney's lawyer, Jeff Dunnire. Anna recorded the second number below the first on the back of her left hand and returned to class for fear of being missed.

The lecture finished shortly after she returned, and she stayed seated, punching the first number into her cellphone.

Having noticed Anna's departure, Terrance asked, "Hey, is everything okay?" before Anna put the phone to her ear.

With tense nerves, Anna looked up at Terrance with a disguising smile.

Reading Anna's concerned face, he continued, "I'll leave you alone, sorry."

"No, sorry. It's just a phone call I need to make; I'll see you next week?" Anna recovered.

"Yeah, yeah," Terrance said and stepped away.

"Hi, is this Jeff Dunnire? Yes, this is Anna Purse," Anna answered, turning halfway to stow her pens. "She's with my mother...our home on Riverview Avenue; can I ask why?" Anna said defensively. "Oh," Anna said and almost nervously laughed at hearing the irony of husband and wife being admitted to the same hospital. "Your home number? Cheryl? Right, my mother will be good taking care of her until then, tonight," Anna said, loosening up as she began to grasp the nature of the issue. "We live up on Riverview Avenue. You'll stop by afterward, you say? Okay," Anna echoed the plan and gave Jeff her house number.

After hanging up she finally tidied her pens and quickly grabbed her notebook to vacate the room for the next class.

"Have you called my mother yet?" Anna said to the tune of her own humor as she recognized Jonathan waiting for her.

"No, but now I have the brain space to form a coherent sentence with that quiz off my shoulders," Jonathan said, glancing at Anna's hand wrapped around her notebook.

Anna caught the direction of his gaze.

"How do you know, Jeff?" Jon inquired weirdly.

"Jeff?"

"Yeah, Jeff Dunnire?" Jon clarified, and immediately realized he needed to explain. "His phone number is on your thumb, and name is on your notebook there."

"Oh, he called me during class strangely about...," Anna said, stopping to gather the best words to explain the entire ordeal.

"You gonna be interning too?"

"Interning? No; oh, like the career fair? No," Anna said, finally allowing her nerves the freedom to laugh.

"Oh, Jeff's my boss at Scales Architect Co, and you're wearing his number's why I ask," Jon over-explained.

"Oh," Anna said, chuckling a bit more at the coincidence. "He's going to be watching the girl I've been babysitting."

"Cool," Jon said as they started walking slowly for the exit.

Jon looked down at Anna's hand again.

Anna again saw his look and released her hand from her book.

Jon felt the tip of Anna's finger sweep by his. Then, confirming Anna's open disposition, he slid his fingers between hers.

Walking hand in hand together to Anna's car, Jon's hand ached when Anna released it to open her door.

"I'll see you...then?" Jon asked, starving for Anna's attention through her window.

"We'll see," Anna responded to her steering wheel before showing him her confident lips.

"Phone call, mother, yeah. Cool...," Jonathan promised, rolling back on his heels as Anna pulled away.

"...lest...best...ever!" Jonathan celebrated privately, nearly leaping into the air.

With all the confidence in the world he marched to the curb and dug out his cellphone to dial the number that was transfixed to his forearm, but as soon as the cellphone was open to dial, his thumb stiffened in terror. His shivering legs carried him to the bus bench. Incapacitated in the face of his task, he ran his fingers through his hair and felt utterly foolish. Then, using the little power left in both thumbs and referencing each number from his arm for correctness, he let his throbbing thumb press the call button.

"Hello, hi...my name is Jonathan Wickfell, I'm calling for Anna...Anna's mother, Mrs. Purse. Uh, well, with your permission I would like to take Anna out on a date for dinner. ...She asked me to call, and I wanted to call and ask...," Jonathan said and listened to Julianne's careful response. "Well, I have no place in mind specifically...she asked me to ask you before...," Jon stuttered, unable decide what to admit as he answered and as Julianne's continued asking her questions. "I don't know. What does she like?" Jon jumped up in disbelief of his words and spun around, feeling even more foolish. "Okay, is she available tonight or tomorrow? ...Today? ...Yes. ...Okay. ...I'll be picking her up. ...Well, I bought it; I own it. I own the car. ...Just dinner. Does she have a favorite place? ...That's right, we went there with a friend of hers, Bethy," Jonathan said, finally growing a little more comfortable with the questioner. The conversation ended shortly, and Jon sat down with fatigue like a fifty-pound sack of flour hitting the bus bench.

# Part 3 - Chapter Eleven

"Ma'am, ma'am, please return...," the officer stated while physically restraining the uncooperative patient.

"There's nothing wrong with me let me go," Sandy protested, pushing back against the blue uniformed officer.

"That's not my call, ma'am. After the doctor clears you, you'll be going in for processing regardless," the officer informed, finally moving back to position himself as a barricade to the hallway.

"Well, where is he? Let's get on with...with this," Sandy provoked, feeling her elbows tremble as she broke into a fit of helpless emotion.

The officer tended to his duty, having been forewarned by the prior guard.

A short while later a nurse entered on her round. Finding Sandy facing the ceiling, she paid acute attention to Sandy's movements while she did her routine. When she finished, the nurse said, "Thank you, Sandy, we'll have you back on your feet in no time."

"When is the doctor coming?" Sandy asked plainly.

"She's coming around, but I think she has a late surgery scheduled for today, so she might be a bit longer this time," the nurse replied, already halfway to the door. "You're not the first anxious patient we've had. I'd think that just about every patient can't wait to hear the doctor's words," the nurse continued encouragingly, but the thought of her patient's circumstances removed the positive expression from her cheeks. When Sandy didn't respond, the nurse tried to apologize by saying, "You're lucky your body responded so well to the naloxone antagonist and especially lucky that the doctor instantly saw the discrepancy on the paramedic's paperwork."

"Thank you," Sandy said pleasantly, the corner of her fluffy pillow hiding her mouth. "Do you know I have a little daughter?"

"Yes, yes, I think I've even saw her here earlier today," the nurse said, mostly hearing her question as she referenced her next assignment.

"Romney does that...takes her everywhere, and he's always concerned about me getting enough quality time with her," Sandy said and giggled as if trying to contain her joy. "Was I sleeping?"

"No, your older daughter or your caregiver brought her to visit her dad," the nurse said, refocusing her attention on her patient chart.

Sandy's smile slipped off her face for a moment as her memory slowly sharpened. "Can I see him?" Sandy asked.

"Who?" the nurse asked, pausing her agenda again.

"My husband," Sandy clarified.

"I don't see why not," the nurse answered, checking her answer with her watch. "I'll ask the officer if he'll take you, and if he can't, I'll help you up there in a few minutes," the nurse said, empathizing with Sandy's long expression.

Sandy stared at the ceiling drifting in and out of consciousness for twenty minutes until the nurse stepped back into her room and said, "He's awake. Do you still want to see him?"

"Yes," Sandy said, moving slowly to a standing position as if unsure that her ankles still functioned properly.

"Here we go, would you like a chair?" the nurse asked suggestively.

"Sure; well, no. I'm okay."

"Okay?"

"Yes," Sandy reassured, stretching the high-tech bracelet attached above her ankle bone.

"It won't be on much longer, I think, at your impressive rate of recovery," the nurse commented at Sandy's indicative ankle movement.

"Everybody's so nice here," Sandy said after they had started toward the elevator. She looked around at the furnishings of the hospital and smiled with a shrug when the nurse caught her inquisitive eyes.

"Good, good, that's good to hear," the nurse said as she continued, walking at Sandy's pace down the hallway.

When they had walked around the corner station and into Romney's room, the nurse said, "I'll help getting you back downstairs to your room when you're ready."

"Thank you," Sandy said again and turned, waiting at the frame of the door.

"There she is," Romney said meagerly, leaving his head to relax on his pillow.

Something about Romney's endearing tone in its truth uncovered Sandy's guise. "Yeah," Sandy said and picked up a pair of steel scissors laid out on Romney's nurse's tray.

Romney closed his eyes to memorize the pleasant expression Sandy had on her face, but he already knew it was fake.

"What's this?" Sandy inquired pulling on the tubing at his bedside.

"Five-hundred-dollars-worth of Morphine," Romney resigned and heard three clicks of what sounded like his pain reliever button. "I'm glad...glad I could help San...," Romney finished.

"Enjoy your sleep...husband," Sandy said contemptuously and walked to the other side of the bed to sit in the guest chair.

With a good view of the corner station and her optimistic nurse, she went to work on her bracelet. The plastic came off easily, and she could feel the buzz of energy through the steel scissors as she crimped and sawed at the safety wire. Seeing that she almost had earned her freedom, she walked into the bathroom and filled the sink with water. With a small final clip, she let the technology fall to its watery death. The chirp was immediately hushed, and she carefully walked back to her seat to watch. Nobody outside seemed concerned with her action, so she stepped to the doorframe to check for her nurse. She found her nearby and preoccupied with a computer screen. Looking from where she came and seeing nothing but a clear shot to the open elevator, she walked to it and patiently let the elevator doors close behind her. Three floors below turned out to be a waiting room for parents and children, so she stepped off the elevator, approached the receptionist's desk, and asked to use the phone. The nurse receptionist gladly assisted her in dialing the number she knew so well. After making her short arrangement, she went to the bathroom and locked herself inside to wait for the arranged time. The longer she waited, the more remorseful she felt, but the momentum of her plan trapped her. She listened anxiously to the chatter outside for more than ten minutes and let the excitement of her chosen adventure have control of her heartbeat. A cry that sounded like it came from a newborn caused lump of compassion to form in her throat. The lump grew so intense that it drew her out of the bathroom stall and back into the waiting room, but when she saw the baby and the fierce attention that the mother paid to the child, her compassion dissipated. Her craving reminded her that her ride would be waiting. Not wanting to risk having Spencer aggravated, she marched to the elevator, descended to the lobby, and strolled through the foyer. The foyer was tended by a few people in flowery scrubs. At the end of the welcoming space, she saw a black coupe approach. A rush of success put a smile on her face, and she moved through the exit. Ignorant of the nurse that took a double take, Sandy enjoyed her stroke of lucky genius. Once in the car, Spencer didn't need to take instructions but hastened his departure from the paramedic's circle.

# Part 3 - Chapter Twelve

The car sped through the streets away from the hospital. Trist's place wasn't too far away, and in his usual manner, Spencer didn't make much conversation with his customer. When he finally looked at Sandy, he stated plainly, "You look like you need a fix." When Sandy didn't respond right away, he continued, "Heck, I need a fix." His customer silently continued chewing on her knuckle with a carefree smile. "You up for one?" Spencer asked, turning into Trist's apartment complex.

"Since yesterday," Sandy queerly responded.

"Here. I have some words for Trist, and I'll be back."

Spencer got out of the car and walked up the gray flight of stairs. After rapping on the door, he looked out and surveyed the parking lot. When Trist didn't answer, he rhythmically bounced down the stairs and jumped back into the car. "So, why were you at the hospital?" Spencer asked, assuming an obvious answer.

"Cause I had to be." Sandy said with her head against the plastic sidewall.

"And when did you get a conscience about your hubby?" Spencer huffed, checking the streets as he handled a tiny vial. "This stuff doesn't do much."

"It's kind of weak," Sandy agreed. "And why'd you have to beat the bad out of Romney anyway?" Sandy said drably, rolling her cranium across the headrest to see her companion.

"I don't know," Spencer said, falling silent and tapping the vial from finger to finger. "You know I need to stop this dabble, or else I'm gonna be full swing by Friday."

"You mean like last year?"

"No, I've got me under control," Spencer said, putting the vial back in his pocket to prove his point to himself.

"We all got this under control. Stopping tomorrow, are we?" Sandy asked with calm sarcasm and let the silence overwhelm the confined space.

Spencer's eyes glazed over completely, feeling the tug between guilt and the itch in his pocket. "So, why were you in the hospital?" Spencer snapped.

"I got arrested," Sandy smirked.

"Naaah...you'd get taken to jail if that was the case. Why were you at the hospital?" Spencer repeated, further feeling the ping of reality from Sandy's convincing answer.

"They just dragged me in as if I was dead already," Sandy explained with an indifferent frown, swiping her hand across her lap, demonstrating the manner of how her limp legs might have looked at the time.

"Shhh...Sandy! And you called me?"

"I couldn't as well have called Romney now, could I? Cause you kind of laid him out for a while," Sandy said with a tinge of contempt, pulling at the latch in a feeble attempt to get up and out of the car.

"That's just great," Spencer muttered half-aloud.

"Great like bacon; your car door is broke."

"Just get out and...and leave," Spencer said, still trying to bury the matter on his face. Leaning over he popped open the door with the handle that Sandy had let snap back in place three times. He pulled out of the parking spot and took one last look at Sandy who had already collapsed and sprawled out contently on the girth of grass below Trist's second floor apartment. Spencer drove all the way to the parking lot of the police station with the bi-polar idea of turning himself over to the police. He shut off the engine with a rash turn of the key. The silence convicted him, and his wrist started shivering. The heat of the sunlight warmed the dashboard quickly, making a strange odor. There was a church next door with an advertisement on its sign that said, "AA, NA, GA - All Welcome." "Right...you need more than God right now," Spencer relented as his opposition changed from one thing to the next. He entertained the new idea long enough to exit his car and walk up to the front door of the small church. The metallic handle, having had hours to absorb the heat of the sun, hurt his hand when he grabbed it. While shaking the pain from his hand away, the door swung open from the dark interior, and an apologetic voice flew out. "Sorry, please, don't mind the handle; you almost need an oven mitt to manage it. But come on, lad, come on in!" a gray-haired gentleman welcomed. After watching the deliberation for a moment on the lad's face, he continued, "I'm Gab, we have water and A/C inside."

"Your AA/NA meeting?"

"What's that, son?" Gab queried, tilting his weak ear more toward the sunlight.

"Your sign says...."

"Oh, oh," Gab said, jumping to an understanding. "Wednesday, evening; It's always on a Wednesday."

"Right," Spencer said, turning away.

"And don't park at the Police Station! Six-thirty to seven! Don't be late!" Gab said with increasing volume. Then he let go of the door after watching the boy trespass the tree line.

Spencer turned around with an intrigued smile but couldn't see anything through the tinted glass door.

# Part 3 - Chapter Thirteen

"Shoot, what's the rampage about?" Nate asked as soon as he stepped into the dorm room.

"A date–date, and I've got to go like yesterday!" Jon said, wrenching on his final accessories.

"Well, at least the room smells good for once."

"Good, good. Bye," Jon said, shooting out the door. Feeling the shower water drying off his sideburns, he bolted down the hallway.

"What's with Jonny?" a classmate asked mockingly.

"A date–date, like with the toilet apparently," Nate said shortly toward the door of his room.

"Ahhh...a date–date, got it."

"Hey, close the door, would you?" Nate instructed before the classmate stepped out of sight.

Jon splashed down the circular stairwell with a crazy blend of nerves and joy. Twenty minutes later he rounded the corner of Anna's house for the second time and glanced at the windows wondering if twenty-three minutes was too early to knock at the door. He rolled up his windows to let the air conditioning pound out as much cool air as possible. He looked in the mirror and saw his hair still hadn't dried. On his third trip around the block he slapped his knee in disgust, disappointed that he had come without flowers or any other girly fancies. A gas station on the corner caught his eye, and gauging that he had twenty more minutes till his proposed time, he decided to pull in and see if they might have a convenient gift. The sticker covered window invited him in with a jingling chime. A few customers were perusing the shelves, and two were in a sort of make shift line where the cashier worked his machine. Jon turned down the first aisle, trying to figure out the method of organization. His eyes scanned for chocolate that would be fitting for a first date. Pretzels and bags of chips covered another full aisle. He had all but ignored the surrounding refrigerators full of beverages when he noticed a pickle in a bag. "Huh...," Jonathan said to himself. Picking up the pickle after opening the cooler's door, he felt the coldness start to condense on the plastic wrapper. Running his strange idea through his head to see if it passed inspection, he looked around with an infectious smile on his face. The cashier's line had disappeared, and Jon slid a debit card onto the counter next to the pickle-in-a-bag.

"Do you have cash?" the clerk inquired, causing a look of confusion to cross Jon's face.

"Cash, yeah...but no, not for this," Jon replied, reading the clerk's unconcerned expression.

"There's a minimum five-dollar purchase on all cards...it's posted...there...and there...and here, and when you came in, on the door."

"Right, right," Jon said, happy to oblige as he saw a chocolate rose on the end cap display two steps away. "Here," Jon said, replacing his card next to the two convenience items.

"That comes to four fifty...want anything else?"

"Good deal, hmm...add a donut there; that should do it, right?"

"Yeah, just don't wait too long to eat it...six dollars and forty-nine cents," the clerk stated passively.

"Noted, thanks," Jon said, accepting the advice and taking his items. Putting the donut instinctively in his mouth, he pushed through the door and immediately gagged. He turned toward the sticker covered glass to hide, and his violent cough began flushing his face and neck a crimson color. A single glance inside told him that the clerk found his predicament funny as he helped the next customer with a smirk. He stepped back to his car regardless of his desire to spit out the dry donut. With the car door wide open, he took a second bite, illogically trying to find some way to appreciate the unpalatable grittiness. His mouth resisted an early attempt to swallow, and as he chewed, the thought of ingesting the dry mass only grew more repulsive. Finally, convinced of its disgust, he climbed back out of the car and marched to the trash can and spit out the donut. Noticing again in detail the rust that ran along the bottom of the side panels of his resurrected car, he returned to the driver's seat and turned over the engine to fight the rising temperature of the cabin. After five minutes of watching thin trails of smoke rise over the hatch of his car, he pulled out of the lot and started creeping up the residential hill toward Anna's house. The top of the city came into view with the last few yards of his short drive. Pulling in and parking next to a white utility truck and trailer, he got out and walked around the house in search of the front door. Seeing the panoramic scene of the cityscape, and still with ten minutes left till his proposed calling time, he decided to look both ways and crossed the street to the view appreciating walkway that paralleled the string of houses. A mild breeze kept the sweat from forming on his forehead while a slow-moving train kept him entertained. He gazed until a person grabbed his attention from his periphery.

"A great view?"

"Anna! Yeah, but the great view is you. You ready to go? I didn't want to knock too early in case...well...are you hungry?"

"Yes," Anna responded with a cheery smile.

"I was thinking Butler's Station downtown, or your...."

"My favorite," Anna said, and placed both hands on the strap of her small purse. "You're driving?"

"I'm driving," Jon said proudly. "Hey, your mom, is she home?"

"Yeah, she's there...see in the window, with April," Anna said, pointing to the first floor of the house.

"April; your sister?" Jon asked, looking at the window without any luck at seeing the characters veiled by the shadowy porch.

"Oh no, I babysit her, and my mother takes over when I'm at school, or I guess for times like this," Anna said, waiting for Jon to start leading her back across the street. He eventually took the clue and led her at an arms distance across the street and around the side of her house. "So, this is the new purchase," Anna said with her typical hard to discern tone.

"New to me; nothing like yours of course," Jon said ambiguously, leading Anna further around to her side door.

"One step better than mine actually, because I don't technically have one yet. My mother said you own this. That's nice."

"Well, you're the one to give all the car ownership advice; I should have solicited your help," Jon said, trying to read how comfortable Anna was as she climbed into the hot car. Jon stepped up to close the door but stopped when he felt the wave of heat hit his face. "Oh sorry, the A/C works. I promise. I'll leave your door open till I get it started," Jon announced as he hustled around the back end. The engine turned over easily and started blasting a stream of air at the two passengers. After a few seconds the stream turned cold, and Anna and Jon closed their doors simultaneously.

## Part 3 - Chapter Fourteen

"It's weird how the city sits in a flat bowl surrounded by these crazy inclines," Jon said, paying careful attention to the cars parked on the side of the narrow sloping road.

"And Vern Hill sits in the center of it all."

"Down the road from the ginormous hospital, Hope is it?"

"I think so, I've never been higher than the third floor," Anna said, glancing outside at a neighbor as the car rolled down to the stop light.

"Is that a good thing? Hey, I got you this...and this," Jon said after careening his head around to check for traffic.

Anna accepted the two gifts and looked them over with confusion. "Eh...okay, I understand the chocolate, but explain the pickle," Anna said, rolling the squishy bag around in her hands.

"You like pickles, right?"

"Well, refrigerated ones."

"Yeah, that one came from a refrigerator, granted it's not as cold as it once was. Oh man, I'm sorry, I so promise there is no innuendo going on with the pickle," Jon reasoned and slowed the car to get through another bottle neck in the road.

"Oh?"

"Oh, what?" Jon asked, following Anna's laughing eyes outside the car.

"Oh, there's J.J.'s."

"A good place to eat?" Jon tried asking.

"Mediocre. Do you know how to get to Butler's?" Anna questioned bluntly.

"It's not this way? Well, I'm out of luck to turn around; this is steep."

"Don't worry. We'll just cross at Concourse Square."

"That's a plan," Jon said, appreciating Anna's graceful solution. "Have you ever been there?"

"Nope, should we go sometime?"

"If you're not bored of me by tonight," Anna said, responding to the tenseness in Jon's voice.

Jon laughed and resisted all temptation to look over at Anna's face to see if it reflected what he was thinking. The road curved to a stop.

"Left here, then straight," Anna instructed.

"Got it," Jon replied happily.

"All through high school I would come with my best friend down this way, and we'd end up at Shymark Stadium, watching the Stellar Hans play," Anna said, trying to find a comfortable topic.

"The Stellar Hans?"

"The soccer team, they have football and other tournaments, but...."

"There's another train! Wow, I saw two while I was waiting for you and now another; good thing we don't have to cross the tracks."

"Trains, boats, barges, planes, Pittsburg has it all."

"And look...going both ways now; don't they ever keep you up at night?" Jon asked like a wide-eyed-kid at an amusement park.

"Nah, they don't ever blow their whistle, and even if they did, it's nothing like living next to a subway in New York," Anna said, watching the brown and black train cars for a moment while they waited at a stop light.

"You've lived in New York?" Jon said, intrigued with the notion.

"Me? No, but I stayed there for a week once," Anna admitted, looking back at Jon's profile. After studying him for a moment, her smile flared, and she threw her eyes out the window before Jon could notice.

Jon felt a hand touch his, and his fingers went into cardiac arrest.

"Unless you don't want to," Anna stipulated.

"No, I want to. I'm sorry," Jon said, fighting down the pace of his heart.

"They are playing next Saturday night," Anna said as a surveying invitation.

"The varsity?"

"Oh, no. Not at school, the Stellar Hans at Shymark Park."

"That sounds fun. Go alone? Or is this a group thing?" Jon asked, feeling a bit more comfortable with Anna.

"Us alone might be exciting," Anna responded accordingly, feeling the texture of Jon's palm.

Jon looked over at the bridge that had taken him to Anna's mountain. "Ha, two ways!" Jon exclaimed, turning his eyes to reference the bridge. He met Anna's eyes a longer second time. "Double-decker bridge!" Jon explained and pointed with his head when his heart stopped hammering his lungs.

"Right!" Anna echoed, catching sight of the familiar Daniel Mills bridge.

Jon moved his thumb along Anna's finger, sparking another mutual glance. Jon single handedly crossed the bridge and drove to within sight of Butler's Station. "So, what's so special about Butler's Station," Jon asked with extra formality. "I mean other than the great food and service...and perfectly white table cloths?"

"Oh...let's see, the great food and perfectly white table cloths," Anna said, pausing to watch Jon's lips. "My mother taught me to like it," Anna clarified, conscious of her sarcastic voice. "Oh, pull right up. They'll park it."

"But there's a free garage right around the corner."

"Ooh, free; let's do free."

"Free agrees we me," Jon said, executing his plan. Anna and Jon found their way back around the corner of an office skyscraper still hand-in-hand. "I actually just got my car back from The Boys Garage," Jon said, looking back in the direction of the parking garage.

"Expensive?" Anna asked, looking at Jon with every opportunity.

"Surprise! I'm not good with cars, but when the steering wheel shakes every time you turn right, you get this uneasy feeling that something's gonna break...like the front wheel is going to come flying off halfway through an intersection or something," Jon animated with his free hand. "Here we go," Jon continued, pulling Anna into a clearing of traffic to cross the street. They happily ran to the entrance of the restaurant where a hostess warmly welcomed the couple and led them to a general booth behind a full dinner party. Taking their seats across from each other, they opened their menus after the brief introduction and promise from their waiter that he would be right back.

"Okay help! I'm mean, I got this," Jon said, breathing in his correction.

"You got this," Anna encouraged, hiding her mocking smile. "Tomatoes and pasta, don't mind all the fancy titles."

"Yes, chick peas right away, please," Anna said decidedly after the waiter's second brief introduction.

"What's an Italian drink? Italian ice? Is that an Italian drink?" Jon asked the waiter.

"That'd be more ice and fair-food," Anna answered in his place. "They drink wine a lot, I think."

"I'm not quite there yet," Jon admitted, tucking his nose back into the menu.

"We have soft drinks, tea, and milk."

"And water? Water would be wonderful," Jon said, making confirming eye contact with Anna.

"Me too," Anna said.

"Great! I'll be right back with those," the waiter again promised while tucking his ticket book into the stretched-out pocket of his apron.

Anna watched Jon turn his eyes back to the menu. "Really, it's just pasta and tomatoes," Anna said with increasing pleasure.

"Forgive my nubile behavior; I'm buying by the way. And remember, you have to show me your favorite dessert!" Jon insisted.

"Okay," Anna agreed, before hearing a crystal-clear mention of Romney Daniels name from the dinner party table.

"Yeah, I just visited him today."

"Is it true about his wife?" a lady spoke.

"You know...Romney's had a bad run of luck lately, but he takes it eyes-open, face on. I couldn't ask for a better partner in crime," the speaker said, touching his comment with an upstroke of optimism.

"I think I'll have this 'Bucatini Pomodoro.' It looks a lot like spaghetti," Jon commented, before looking up to find Anna's redirected attention. When Anna's eyes apologized for their distraction, Jon continued, "I know, tomatoes and pasta."

"Their salads are good too!" Anna said convincingly.

"Salad?" Jon said with surprise. "Good?"

"I heard he's seeing some eighteen-year old while his wife is out of service," the comfortably postured lady suggested.

When the lady quickly leaned back to survey the effect of her comment, Anna saw Romney's business partner that she had met earlier in the day.

"Romney? Why...that'd be mud made of sand and water. You'd have a hard time making that stick," the partner defended, laughing to show his opinion of the matter.

Anna searched her brain for his name.

"You okay?" Jon asked after two or three private glances between Anna's eyes and the table next door.

"Sorry, I met that guy today at the hospital. I just can't remember his name; I mean it's right there...Hense!"

"Hense! There you go...what a name."

Anna blushed as she thought Mr. Hense might have caught wind of his name from their table.

"Which salad?" Jon asked, seeing the waiter approaching from the royal red strip of carpet running down the aisle of chairs.

"Spinach with pecan and the house dressing is best," Anna said.

"Is that what you're getting? May I order for you?" Jon asked and saw Anna's intelligent and approving smile as the waiter squared himself up to table. The waiter rocked side to side and scribbled Jon's two orders on his ticket book, which gave Jon a moment to study the pattern of freckles on Anna's nose. "What color is your hair? It's your natural color, right?" Jon asked curiously.

"There's red in there somewhere, sometimes more than other times."

"Do you like your freckles...," Jon asked as if out of the blue, "...because...."

"Do you?" Anna rebounded seriously.

"Is it appropriate to say they're perfect," Jon said, disclosing his weak nerves.

"Jack! Jack! Sit down. Come on, finish dinner. We're all just friends here. She doesn't have an agenda," an overbearing voice complained and momentarily cleared the room of private conversations. Jack's response was unintelligible. The lady seated next to Jack, looked sheepishly flustered for a moment before recovering herself. Jack quietly took the arm of a passing waiter. Anna only heard in part, "Make sure Tonya has a free cab home, leave her with my apologies." The waiter responded, respectfully addressing Jack as "Mr. Hense."

"Oh, hello, Ms. Purse...great choice of restaurant," Jack greeted to Anna and inclusively toward Jon. Then with a timely tilt of his head, he departed down the road of carpet that led outside.

## Part 3 - Chapter Fifteen

For a minute, it was difficult to respect the privacy of the dinner party table, but without saying anything, Jon made Anna laugh as if they were devoted to their own conversation. Then the restaurant crept back to its normal hum for the rest of their meal. "How much do these entrées run. I didn't see any prices," Jon asked at the end of their fun conversation.

"You didn't get the priciest meal, and meals with drinks definitely run up the tab, but thirty to forty-dollars," Anna said, recalling that Jon had promised to buy her food.

"The salad too? Was good, wasn't it?" Jon asked, looking at the empty plates.

"We can go Dutch if you'd like."

"No, no, I'm fine, and what kind of poor date would I be if I left you with half the bill?" Jon reassured. "Here let me take that up," Jon said, taking the bill from the waiter and rising to his feet.

Anna let him get two steps away before realizing his purpose. She slowly reassembled the dishes on the table to make it easier for the busboy to do his job while she waited. Then after patiently looking around without any sight of Jon, she rose and took the few steps to the back of the restaurant to use the restroom.

"Oh, I thought you had disappeared," Jon said when she returned.

"On the contrary, I thought you did. You took a while," Anna said, folding her hair around her ear before accepting Jon's bold hand.

"It took a long time to run my card for some reason."

"Or more like you were waiting to talk to a manager for something," Anna kidded, releasing Jon's hold to get through a congested space.

"And I did. He was very much dressed in a cook's outfit, really quite befitting for an Italian joint."

"You met the chef, a cook, or the manager?" Anna asked untimely, as Jon was distracted with the valet and the door. "...And I'm sure you told him his spaghetti was immaculate!" Anna said, pecking back at Jon's fingers in front of the restaurant.

"Well, spaghetti did come up, but he was more the one that mentioned it," Jon said.

"It was fun. We should come back," Anna said, resisting Jon's attempt to disconnect.

"I'll definitely be coming back, definitely," Jon emphasized with a misleading smile and another appreciating look at Anna as they walked. Jon stopped and twirled her around in a surprisingly skilled move.

"You know, Anna, I had a great time tonight. Are you ready to head home?"

"Sure, unless you had something else planned, Mr. Dancing Man," Anna said, having enjoyed the surprise turn.

"Next week, eh?" Jon surveyed, stepping back up to Anna's side.

"Uh yeah! Soccer game!"

"Soccer or baseball?" Jon asked to clarify.

"Me or next week?" Anna asked.

"Which sport do you prefer?"

"Baseball, hands down," Anna confided, checking Jon's face as he spotted traffic at the corner.

"Well, then the Vern Hill Varsity is where it's at! For baseball lovers anyway," Jon said. As they came to the parking gate, Jon privately thanked the cashier's window for being vacant. "Should we take the double decker bridge or the shortcut?" Jon asked, maneuvering the car out of the garage and onto the street.

"It depends on how long you want to keep me," Anna responded, adjusting the blast of cool air back to a more appeasing flow.

"My parents are coming, by the way, on the train for some reason. Do you want to meet them?" Jon asked, quirkily raising his eyebrows.

"Wouldn't it be faster to drive, and then they'd have an option to go wherever?" Anna commented, silently contending the fact that Jon had changed the topic.

"Yeah. I'm not too sure if they're all level-in-the-head, but they surely reminded me that their act of paying my tuition is their deposit for my goodwill cab service."

"Hah, when are they coming?" Anna said, seeing Jon's earlier nerves returning.

"Next week...Saturday," Jon answered, realizing, his date was looking for more details.

"Okay."

"I guess I want to clarify something...about this," Jon said, seeing a general connection with Anna being willing to meet his parents. "You do want to meet them, right?"

"Yes." Anna said, predicting the topic.

"Is this like? I mean are we...."

"Boyfriend-girlfriend?"

"Type thing," Jon finished with relief.

Anna smiled, but immediately tucked away her prior certainty and said, "I had a good time with you."

"Oh no, just good? I'm not a killjoy, I promise. I didn't want to presume you wanted to keep going. I'll take you for ice...or a walk in the park, or a stroll through...."

"Only if it's Italian Ice."

"You want to?" Jon interrupted, getting nervous about the entanglement of what was almost a straightforward jubilee.

"Not tonight. I think you're right; the more rain checks I have to cash in, the more I'm going to get to see you, so...."

"Tomorrow?" Jon suggested with youthful blush painted on his forehead.

"I can't wait," Anna said, finally communicating her sentiment as Jon wound the car through the inclining streets.

"Just no titles yet," Jon stated after a minute of difficult driving.

"Unless you feel the need for something different, 'friend' is still a meaningful title, isn't it?"

"Boy, girl, or just friend; that works, no need to clutter something of value with formalities," Jon said, dancing around with his extraneous thoughts.

"Just don't overthink it," Anna said, giggling away her concern as she opened her door to egress from the car to her driveway.

"Oh, and," Jon said, rushing out to meet her at the front corner of his idling car. "May I walk you to your door," Jon continued as if he had planned and waited all night to ask permission.

"Why yes, you may usher me along my voyage," Anna said, raising her arm to accommodate his request before taking her final three steps to the garage porch. Leaving Jon with her dizzying smile, Anna stepped inside to the cheer of a little girl. "And I've been meaning to say there's a gas station right down the street!" Anna mention before disappearing inside to the further heralding of the two-year-old.

"Ah yes, I remember," Jon said, forcing a thankful smile at the reminder. He climbed into his car and immediately traded the air-conditioning for the windows. He considered the solid gas light illuminated on his dashboard until a car turned for Anna's driveway and almost blocked him in the square of pavement. Unable to clearly see the driver, Jon eventually took the hint and backed out into the road. When he came to a stop, his engine stalled and came to a quick hush. The patient car responsively took Jon's predicament as a courtesy and finished his turn into the driveway. Then Jon looked twice and winced at seeing his boss step out of the vehicle. After laying his head on his hands to somehow gather his ego, he shamefully looked up and smiled with his eyes closed as he heard his boss's footsteps approaching.

"Fancy seeing you here!" Jeff Dunnire said cheerfully, guessing at the cause of Jon's quiet car. "You know these electric cars are pretty cutting edge, you've got yourself a nice one."

"Yeah, my battery's a bit low on petroleum-ion," Jon said, playing along.

"You know there's a gas station at the bottom of the hill? I have a couple of minutes, if you're up for a boxcar run," Jeff offered, glancing down the street to assess its decline.

"That would be wonderful," Jon agreed and looked up at his boss. "But I have no money," Jon admitted, hoping his boss would laugh at his candidness. "I don't know what I was thinking or what I'm doing...taking a girl like this to Butler's and expecting it to cost me the price of a ballpark hot-dog. I guess I wanted to reciprocate, or not bring her down. I don't know. I have no money."

"You don't know, or you do know that you have no money?" Jeff asked humorously to cut off Jon's rabbit trail.

"No, that...that. That I do know," Jon emphasized. "No computer. No car. ...And guess where I get to work off my unpaid check...starting next...next, I can't even remember."

"At Butler's Station?" Jeff guessed.

"That's the one. I mean, what would you do, if you kind of liked somebody and finally had the guts to ask her out? And she, for real, said, 'Yes!' ...But she's like her and just spends money...just has money," Jon rabbit-trailed again away from his question, stopping for a long enough moment to suggest he might want a reply.

Jeff waited for a moment longer before accepting the challenge to offer advice. "If she said yes to you because she thought you'd dazzle and dine her with your finances...well, that wouldn't put her in a very good light, would it?" Jeff commented.

"No."

"You have a lot less to be dilly over if you stick to reality...I mean this is the girl, if I'm guessing, right, that babysits for free because she loves it."

"Yeah," Jon said, picturing himself rolling uncontrollably down the hill in front of him.

"Hey, you lost your computer, and you don't have any gas. Tonight, you won't have to worry about either...as long as you don't have a hundred-gallon tank hidden somewhere in the trunk," Jeff decidedly encouraged. Your brakes are obviously still working, right?" Jeff queried.

"I hope so."

"Let me hop in. We'll roll to the bottom. I'll push you into the station – if I can – and buy you a tank of gas, if you'll drive me back up to the top. Deal?" Jeff negotiated and waited for permission to act.

"Yeah, I still have no money."

"That'd be true, but you'll at least have a tank of gas, which at the very least will get you to your new job...and your internship for a week," Jeff reasoned as he hopped into the passenger seat and nodded to denote that he was ready for the coaster ride to begin. "Oh, and I found out today that our business insurance is covering the theft of the laptops; we should have new computers up and running by opening time on Monday," Jeff said, watching Jon struggle with the wheel as he slowly directed his car to the center of the street. "I made sure yours is mobile, so you'll at least be able to use it at school until you get your personal claim back."

"Thanks, I know who stole the computers by the way," Jon admitted.

"You do?"

"Well, what he looks like and relatively where he's keeping the computers...or at least mine," Jon explained as he let gravity freely pull the car to the bottom of the hill.

"Well, you'll have to explain it all in a minute, let me get out and push," Jeff said as the car coasted as far as gravity allowed. "Well, you might need to get out too and push from the door; though, I'd hate to see you soil your nice clothes," Jeff advised after an unsuccessful attempt.

"Oh, the least of my worries."

# Part 3 - Chapter Sixteen

"Didn't go so well?" Nate asked after Jon entered the dorm room.

"What?" Jon asked, glancing briefly at Dan's computer screen before trying to avert his eyes.

"You're back like at nine!"

"With a full tank of gas."

"Yeah, with...a full tank of gas...ready to go somewhere?" Nate asked curiously, twirling his chair back to his computer.

"You're always staring at that thing!" Jon exclaimed as he grabbed his book bag and swung it over to the closet.

"Well, you sell what I look at.  Hey, I think your guy tried to offload your computer.  Have you gone to the police yet?"

"I thought I told you that I did."

"Nope.  You've said a bunch of strange stuff.  But in my opinion, he wasn't successful, because he popped up over here, and I, out of curiosity, cross-referenced it to see if it was some sort of pawn shop or something.  And it was."

"And?" Jon said, pulling out the stack of magazines.

"An hour-and-a-half later the thief turned your O.S. back on in the same location it was before."

"Interesting," Jon said, slightly preoccupied with the straps of his backpack.

"I told my boss about your program tonight."

"Oh yeah, you looked awfully slick to have left for a date with your boss," Nate said, losing interest in the conversation.

"Right," Jon replied, taking the hint from his roommate. Having finished restocking his backpack he continued, "Well, I'm out."

"The sun's going down, you sure you're going to get her home before her bedtime?"

"Yeah-yeah...what you're saying is, 'I got one and you don't!'"

"Ohh, and he comes back biting!" Nate said and leaned back, excited to have sparked more interchange, but Jon was already heading through the door.  Jon walked through the campus to where he had just parked his car.  His phone kept buzzing with new messages.  "Yeesh, I'm coming already," Jon said to his flashing phone. Hopping into his car, he started the engine and sped out of the lot. Ten minutes later, he pulled back into the same parking garage he had utilized with Anna on their date. "This could have been done more efficiently," he remarked to the empty teller window. Retracing the steps, he kept his eyes on the illuminated windows of Butler's Station. Stepping into an office building lobby that was across the street from Butler's, he put his thumbs in his pockets and turned his eyes up to the high ceilings. "Hi," Jon called as he recognized the face of the man stepping off the elevator.

"I hate to trouble you so late."

"Trouble? No worry, this is what I do. It comes with the job."

"Thirty-five? Wait, wait, what's this?" Jack Hense asked as if he were being gypped.

"I don't understand," Jon said, aborting his motion of pocketing the cash.

"This...this is my...this is wrong; I can't take this?"

"Why not?" Jon managed shyly, holding back sudden jitters.

"No, she's centerfold, right? The code in the back? The girl on the front?"

"Usually," Jon said, noting the internal struggle on his customer's forehead.

"No...no, keep the money. Take your magazine. You're feeding an addict," Jack said with guilt while shaking his head in disgust of himself. "Man, I'm sorry; I thought I was someone better."

"You sure...you don't want your money back?" Jon proposed, but the proposition seemed to dismiss his customer back to the elevator.

Jon held the door for a man in casual business dress as he exited the lobby.

"Thanks."

"No problem," Jon responded and proceeded on his way.

Mitchell Reed walked over to the elevator to scan his badge against the wall. The door opened, revealing Jack as he leaned against the back wall.

"Oh hi, Mitchell!" Jack said, recomposing his countenance for his dress-down employee. "What? No fancy tie?"

"Oh, I'm sorry, no," Mitchell replied after glancing down at his plain collared shirt.

"No, no, no what brings you here this late?" Jack inquired, rubbing the flat part of his forehead one last time.

"Really?"

"Really, you're not up to no good, are you?" Jack asked in a lighthearted fashion, while recalling the uncomfortable topic set to be discussed Monday morning.

"No, my computer gave up the ghost," Mitchell said, stopping as if silently confessing his motive.

"Ahh, I see...well you know how to get a job done!" Jack responded.

"I actually had no intention of working, but I was going...."

"Sure, the network's all yours, whatever you need. But hey, on another note, we got a few unauthorized transactions to an F.P.O. Company recently through Romney Daniel's credentials. The money transfers corresponded with some of your job site funding requests and all. I won't bore you with the details," Jack said, glancing toward the light he had left on in his office. "Does F.P.O. ring a bell?"

"Yes, kind of," Mitchell replied after a second of shifting his eyes around the top of his eyelids. "I talked with a financial advisor who works for Financial Principle Organization, and he referred to his company as F.P.O."

"About a week or two weeks ago?"

"Yeah, about that, and more recently...how much were the transfers? You said there were a couple?" Mitchell said, finding the connection outlandish at best.

"Thirty-eight something, and a hundred and forty-one thousand I think."

"Strange...," Mitchell admitted, recognizing the two generalized numbers. "He had gotten me all excited about this investment opportunity, where I pay in a minimum of a hundred and eighty thousand and in ten years' time, if left untouched, I'd have double that, but...strange...."

"Well, don't waste too much time thinking about it, we secured all the login credentials in question. I'll have you look at the account records on Monday morning to see if we can get any more hints as to where...where the money ended up. But it's not the end of the world," Jack said with obvious distraction.

"Yea...yeah. I'll call my guy. His name is Michael Gallant, and yeah I even have his business card in my office."

"Monday, don't trouble yourself this weekend."

"What else does a single guy have to do?" Mitchell said, trying to echo Jacks nonchalant attitude.

"Oh, get out to that ballgame tomorrow. Your son's still pitching, right?"

"Wouldn't miss it. I can buy you a ticket, if you want one?" Mitchell offered.

"Not this time, but thank you," Jack said, moving towards his office.

"Huh...," Mitchell sighed to himself. Then after spending the next three hours on the internet scouting out deals on computers, he found a listing that read, "Perfect laptop for college, dirt cheap." After contacting the seller via his work e-mail and finally deciding on a time and place to meet, he shut down his station and left the office without interrupting Jack.

## Part 3 - Chapter Seventeen

"Hey, this is Mitchell. Yeah, I'm here. Oh, you're not coming?" Mitchell said into his telephone after having waited at the designated meeting spot for ten minutes. "Well, thanks for the heads up," Mitchell continued, unsure of whether he was okay with the change of plans. "Your place? I guess that's fine; how far away? Oh, that's not far," Mitchell said as he listened to the seller's directions. He relaxed back into his bucket seat before reaching for the key to crank his car's engine. Then pulling back into traffic, he drove by way of the memorized instructions down the street and turned at a stoplight. The morning was empty. After passing a wall of pine trees, the gray complex came into view. He pulled in and took another look at his watch. Trying to ignore a muted argument coming from one of the apartments, he watched his rearview mirror. The seller had promised to show up shortly, and Mitchell had already assumed that he'd probably be left waiting again from the way that the private computer seller had apologized. Mitchell laid his hand on his front pocket, feeling his short stack of twenties. Relocating the bills to his back pocket, he reflected on his weakness as a haggler and how he had come ready to pay the full asking price for the laptop. After a few more minutes a black coupe sped through the entrance and pulled up right next to Mitchell's car. Mitchell flashed a friendly smile, and the individual, though looking stressed and in a hurry, looked back amiably enough.

"Hi, sorry, I've been running all over the place this morning. I've got the computer upstairs," the seller dressed in a worn printed t-shirt said.

"No problem, I'm Mitchell," Mitchell said awkwardly, unsure if the seller's rushed vocabulary was an invitation or not. After a moment's hesitation, he chose to follow the seller up the staircase.

"Oh yeah, come on up," the seller said after realizing Mitchell was following him. "You said it was Mitchell?"

"Yes, sir."

"I'm glad somebody finally is interested in taking his thing off my hands, I've been trying to sell it for forever, but it seems nobody's interested in old stuff that works just fine anymore," Spencer said, courteously turning around to face Mitchell as he neared the top step.

"Well, my old thing went down the tubes two days ago, and I finally gave up trying to fix it last night. So, I went into work...found this...you, and well," Mitchell stammered as he watched the seller dig out a key for the lock. The opening door interrupted the passionate dialogue coming from inside. The aggressive voice changed to a warm welcome until Mitchell stepped into the doorway.

"What's this freak doing here?" Trist asked gravely, following the stranger's curious eyes as they began to wander around the room.

Mitchell caught sight of blood on a girl's forehead and shame cast eyes, trying to avoid attention.

"He's here for the computer," Spencer let on, as he moved decidedly toward the back room.

"Well, welcome, to our tech paradise," Trist sarcastically grumbled at the stranger.

"Thanks," Mitchell responded. He tried to mind his own business, but his eyes fell back to the girl and then to a gun laying on the kitchen counter.

Trist was bothered by Mitchell's interruption, and the intention of getting back to his suspended argument crossed his face twice. Then he too noticed the firearm, and he took four steps to pick it up, maintaining his annoyed scowl. "You're here for a computer," Trist commanded. "Why don't you wait outside."

"What's to fear?" Mitchell fumbled, feeling a violent upstroke in his heartbeat.

"Your here for a computer, fool, why don't you wait yourself outside," Trist repeated, having shoved the handgun into a deep pocket.

Mitchell didn't like his conscience at that moment, but he couldn't resist it. "Can I talk to your girl...can I talk to you for a minute?" Mitchell asked, shifting his attention mid-sentence to the fifteen-year-old-looking girl.

The girl shook her swelled up head as Trist witlessly answered, "You can't afford a conversation with her, stranger."

"I believe she has a right...," Mitchell started, facing the intimidating figure.

Trist grabbed Mitchell with two hands by the collar and forced his body up to the kitchen island. "She has it right. You have it wrong and had better leave!"

Mitchell looked straight into the convincing face of the aggressor. "You know you can leave too, right?" Mitchell spoke indirectly, hoping to encourage a response from the girl.

"Get out," Trist ordered, releasing Mitchell with inertia toward the door. "And where do you think you're going?" Trist said, exchanging Mitchell's hold for the girl's shoulders, and whipping the girl back to the couch.

Mitchell tried moving himself to her defense at the sound of her shriek, but Trist again intercepted him with a strong forearm and sent him sailing back toward the door. The girl bolted for the opening, and the aggressor brandished his impulsive judgement. Mitchell pushed himself back with his panicking hands and feet toward the fatigued doorframe. He heard a deafening crack and saw the girl collapse to the floor. Caught between his freedom and his conscience, his body impulsively decided he was committed, and he rolled up onto his left hand and tried to encourage the struggling girl from the floor. But her weight and the extra shout of thunder hampered his assistance. Mitchell struggled further as his aggressor walked up to him to a point where he couldn't miss. Some sharp words were said that Mitchell couldn't understand, and then another deafening pang ended his movement. The thin looking boy darted into view behind the ruthless man as the feeling in Mitchell's chest slowly acknowledged the gunshot.

"What? Have you lost it?" Spencer screamed with panic, a table having stopped his approach. His partner didn't answer but displayed combined frustration and acceptance of the casual losses. "You don't go shooting my customers!" Spencer illogically scolded, looking back toward the room where he had gone looking for his merchandise.

"Your customer?"

"He didn't have anything to do with you!" Spencer cried, developing his frustration further.

"Your customer...," Trist repeated, stooping to lift the body of the motionless man by the belt and shoving his hand into the bulging back pocket. "Your customer's...paid you," Trist heaved, dropping the man and slapping the three hundred dollars onto Spencer's chest.

Spencer caught the money as he watched Trist turn back to his victims. The weight of the two bodies didn't seem to concern Trist as he dragged them out the door and lifted them down the stairs. Spencer couldn't control the guilt pooling in his lungs like a plugged bathtub. He turned back to the interior room once and then took advantage of his own opportunity to leave without having to reengage Trist.

## Part 3 - Chapter Eighteen

Mitchell woke up when the weight of the girl had landed on top of him. He felt a perpetual sting in his left shoulder and his jaw felt repulsively hot. The girl lay on top of him, not moving, and he couldn't focus well enough to determine if she was breathing or not. The sunlight didn't last long, and a crash closed in the darkness. He knew that his head rested on something soft and that something sharp jabbed into his side. His right arm felt like it could move, so he tried it but found no strength in it. He feared making a sound at the recollection of the beastly man, yet everything crinkled around him at the slightest movement. His senses returned in a rush to inform him that everything pungently smelled. Then the hair of the lifeless girl started tickling his face, and the throbbing pain started to amplify in his shoulder. He thought of his telephone in his pocket and how to speed dial his son. He was scared with confined panic until he heard the voice of his son through the speaker. "Chad," Mitchell whispered hoarsely with a stretch of his remaining energy.

"Dad? Hey dad, practice is about to start. I can't hear you," Chad said, putting the phone to his ear as he tried to finish tying his last shoe in a hurry. He looked back at Coach Paddernick to judge how much time he had to talk. With no time at all, he heard the hush fall over the locker room and Coach's voice begin. "Dad, I don't know about a dumpster. I've got to go; call me later," Chad tried to conclude, to prevent further tardiness.

"Chad! Who's on the phone?" Coach Paddernick asked, redirecting the entire attention of the group toward Chad's locker.

"My dad; sorry, sir. I'm ready now," Chad promised, abandoning the laces on his shoe to devote his full attention to the group.

"Go outside and call him, please. Join us when you're done," Coach Paddernick instructed, silently inferring the post-practice consequence associated with Chad's tardiness and interruption.

"Yes, sir," Chad said compliantly, hopping toward the exit to avoid tripping on his shoelace. Once outside he did as he was told and held down the number eight on his keypad to speed dial his dad.

"Hey, dad, you just got me kicked out of practice...," Chad said with suggestive undertones. "What? Dad, that doesn't make sense! You are, or why are you telling me about throwing out trash?" Chad tried to listen more carefully to the hushed voice over the sound of the competing whisper of wind. "You know that means a lot to me, but I have to go, maybe I'll see you at the game tomorrow," Chad said before hearing his dad clearly cough and groan. "Dad, are you okay? Dad! What? Tell me, tell...you have my attention. What happened?" Chad asked, starting to accept the seriousness of the phone call. He listened with all his capacities as his teammates started to pour out of the complex toward the baseball diamond. Chad listened without acknowledging the passing herd and felt the full weight of his dad's farewell message. "Dad, dad, I mean...I'll come, I mean right now. I'll call the police, where are you?" Chad said frantically. Chad listened as carefully as he could and repeated what he heard in a broken format unaware that his coaches were standing behind him.

Chad hung up the phone and shivered with confusion. He didn't breathe until Coach Paddernick asked him about the state of his call. Unable to restrain himself or communicate meaningful statements he fell back against the wall to keep himself from collapsing.

"Do you know where?" Coach insightfully asked.

"North of here in some dumpster."

"Do you know how far?"

"Yeah," Chad said, still snagged by his emotion. "North of the west bridge, first light, one mile...gray apartments."

"Jamerson, tell the team we're going...now!"

"Okay!" the clipboard-toting assistant chimed without objection.

"Hand me your phone!" Coach Paddernick ordered and started marching off toward the center of the half-filled parking lot.

The strict direction of the coach magnetized Chad's shoulders and pulled him along until he was almost clipping the coach's heels. The coach's introduction was stern to the police dispatcher, and with a mid-sentence inquiring-gaze at Chad, he relayed the information he had skillfully understood. When Chad had latched himself inside the coach's V10 truck, he looked up to see the entire varsity team moving toward the parking lot with purpose. Coach Paddernick didn't pause or let on that he noticed, but he throttled out of the parking lot at three times the posted speed limit.

## Part 3 - Chapter Nineteen

The girl, with her scattered hair, hadn't moved, and it had been many minutes now since Mitchell had awakened to his nightmare. Her body still lay motionless and heavily on parts of his left side. What were seconds after his phone call had felt like minutes of worry. He forced his bones stiff when he reflected on how strategically stupid his phone call was to his son, but the resurgence of light didn't come as he kept anticipating and waiting. He heard nothing, but he couldn't be sure. Gaining courage, he tried engaging his pinned down arm, but it stayed frozen underneath what he assumed was most of the girl's weight. When he moved from his arm to testing his legs, something in the dumpster reverberated. He lost his courage for a long minute while he fatiguingly listened for a response. He relaxed, letting out a sigh of relief, and then he refocused his work of uncovering himself. He felt around with his free arm for something to leverage after his body refused to coil. The plastic bags crinkled as he pushed them about without success, and he continued his search until he grazed something sharp. He couldn't tell if he had opened another wound on the back of his hand or not, but he started feeling about more carefully. After spending many more careful seconds of searching, he happened to lay his hand on the girl's wrist. The girl's deathly presence reminded him of the pain rising and falling in his chest. After the resultant minute of sorrow had ended, he scolded his arm back to work. Suddenly a crack of light appeared above, and Mitchell saw the blinding sun followed by an eclipse of something large. That something was a heavy bag of trash that perfectly landed on his head. Thinking of nothing more than self-preservation, he frightfully flailed like a drowning victim.

The young teen-aged boy that had hurled the trash bag into the dumpster froze at the strange sound, fully alert to the possibility of danger. He smartly decided to leave his curiosity alone, but when he turned to leave, an enormous white truck sped into the apartment lot. The darting monster-of-a-truck screeched to a halt, having swerved with intention toward the dumpster. A tall baseball-ready athlete exited the vehicle before the vehicle had settled back onto its rear wheels. As the athlete sprinted to the dumpster and lifted the lid, the boy, whizzed around to see four other vehicles dashing recklessly into the small apartment complex. The boy lifted his eyes up to the second floor of the complex and saw the notorious man observing from his window. When the boy turned back to the dumpster, the athlete was already squatting on the ledge, carefully spotting out a place to land. The boy turned again to see more athletes gravitating with uncertainty toward a loud man with a cellphone that had emerged from the monstrous truck. Sirens started winding up in the distance. The boy glanced back to the second story window with growing panic; it was vacant. The man with the cellphone started barking orders in every direction, and each ball player that bore a large VH emblem rushed obediently to his task. Two more cars rushed into the parking lot but were directed right out of the way into a corner. The four prior cars all began moving simultaneously with brisk intent to cram orderly into the same corner. Four or five tall guys rushed by the boy with complete focus on assisting the first athlete that had already dove into the dumpster. Then as another athlete approached him by saying, "Hi there," he saw his alarmed mother.

The parking lot was now mostly organized as the sirens reached their peak. The boy clung to his mother as he moved away, watching the rest of the confusion. The man in charge intercepted the two police officers that moved ambitiously to engage the organized crowd. The boy heard an athlete yell, "Two, there's two!" This announcement seemed to set the police officers off in a different direction, and an ambulance arrived seconds later. The mother was ushering her boy away

when the first stretcher flew toward the dumpster. The boy
looked up at his mom and back as a white bag of trash flew out
of the bin. The mother kept forcing the boy's cheek away from
the working men, but she stopped her mothering once a police
officer interrupted their escape. The boy saw a small body
emerge and saw the rolling wheels of a gurney flop down to
receive a girl. The team hastily transported her over to the
flashing parade of vehicles. The process immediately repeated,
except that the second moving bed seemed more important than
the first.

The police officer prompted the boy through some leading
questions and started searching around the complex. A trail of
evidence was easily discovered, and the police officers started
assembling their taskforce. The baseball team of cars obediently
left in a slow procession as a new mashup of squad cars
crammed into the lot. Then a special team was selected and
dispatched up to the brink of Trist's apartment. They poised in
a filtered line until the officer in charge shouted an order to enter
the unit. The boy stood by with the other antsy tenants,
watching it all unfold.


# Part 3 - Chapter Twenty


Hungry, Trist Palanco walked into a nearby gas station and
looked at the cashier. Knowing that he wasn't going to be
paying for his shopping experience, he slipped what he really
wanted into his back pocket. Then he picked up a bag of chips
and opened them as he walked toward the front of the store.
He put the first handful into his mouth, and instead of
approaching the register, he continued toward the exit. As the
cashier started to protest, Trist played dumb and approached the
counter.

"Why are you trying to steal from my store, huh?" the angry
cashier scolded. "That's what the register here is for, at the
front; there's no way you couldn't see me, guy!"

"Dude, cool it. My head's not here today, and don't go all up
and showing me flack; I don't have to pay for these! Heck, man,

I don't even want these anymore; that's not the way people treat people," Trist intentionally escalated and threw the open bag onto the counter.

"Awe come on, man, what's that for?" the cashier said with aggravation as he looked at the mess that had spilled from the counter to the floor. "Just leave," the cashier concluded, mostly ignoring his customer.

"My pleasure," Trist said spitefully and walked out of the store. A few steps later, he dug his hand into his deep pocket, and out came his cellphone along with a sealed bag of drugs that flopped onto the ground. Trist stopped to pick up the bag and switched out the bag for the item he had just swindled from the convenience store. "Hey, Spence, I'm taking your bed tonight...what?" Trist said hatefully into the cellphone when he realized his listener had hung up on the other end. He called back.

Spencer listened for a few moments longer the second time as Trist berated him. Anticipating Trist's demand for money in lieu of a threat, he hung up the phone and proceeded to continue driving through the streets. He finally pulled into his parking space at his own apartment and instinctively shut off the car. Opening the car's door to expel the growing heat, he let his thoughts blackout his surroundings. After a minute, his eyes came to focus on the dashboard and how the dash looked like it was covered in dust. The dash may have been dusty at one point, but now the dust and the dash were one and the same, part of the car. "What now?" he challenged himself. He looked out at his apartment and then down at where the time would have been displayed on the dash. He hobbled out of his seat after a few seconds and walked lethargically up to his front door. He grabbed his hair with his fist and let it go with a puff of undirected emotion. When the door to his apartment swung open behind him, he spun around defensively with surprise.

"Sorry to surprise you, big-boy."

"Baby-sis! Why? Surprise me already," Spencer said honestly.

"You really should lock your door when you leave," Katie said matter-of-factly. Katie didn't have the same coveted hair and face of her brother, but she did have a radiant smile that her brother loved to see.

"Yeah," Spencer said as the distraction of parking lot traffic caused him to uncharacteristically ignore his sister's playfulness.

"Well, hey, let's get lunch!" Katie said as she bounced out of the doorway, pulling the door closed behind her.

"Let's get lunch," Spencer echoed half-heartedly. "This is probably best," Spencer said in response to his intuitive conversation.

"What? What's best?" Katie queried with interest.

"Do you have your license?" Spencer asked.

"Yeah, I'll grab it from the car."

"Did you leave anything inside?"

"No, why? Do your roommates steal stuff?" Katie asked.

"Yeah," Spencer said, almost laughing.

"Well, you've got disrespectful roommates."

"No kidding," Spencer agreed and watched his sister gather her things.

"Where we goin'?" Katie chimed as she slammed her car door shut and used the key-fob to lock it.

"Is dad at home?"

"We're not going there. Kay is in an uproar over his not eating sugar again. He refused to eat her pancakes because they were doused with maple syrup," Katie said, letting herself into the passenger side of Spencer's car.

"You know what? How about you drive," Spencer decided after settling into his seat.

"Really?"

"Yeah, I'm not up for it," Spencer said, as he stepped out and looked around the complex again.

After swapping cars and swapping places, Katie took off toward downtown.

"So, how's this girl you told me about?"

"Girl? Oh, Anna. You'd love her," Spencer said, feeling a bit better in the presence of his sister.

"Yeah?"

"Well yeah, but yeah...," Spencer exhaled, returning to his thoughts.

"No? Not the one?" Katie asked, taking a glance over at Spencer and tracking his forward gaze.

"No, not the one. It didn't ever really get off the ground."

"Well, she wasn't good enough for you then."

"No, Katie, that's not true," Spencer said somewhat humored but was unable to explain.

Seeing the deadness of the topic, Katie moved on and asked, "So, you still going to show me around campus?"

"We'll see," Spencer said to avoid promising her something. "But they do have an awesome tour; you're a big girl now. It's pretty easy."

"Wait, wait, wait! What's going on with Crumbles? Why aren't they open?"

"I don't know," Spencer said glad for the new distraction. He read the sign in the window, "Closed. Thanks for your patronage over the years. New owners coming soon!"

"Well, I hope the new owners are as good as the old ones," Katie lamented.

With a sprout of courage, Spencer changed the topic and asked, "Hey, sis,' I hate to drop out on you, but would you drop me off there...right past the police station?"

"What? Are you going to confession?"

"I was thinking about it," Spencer tried joking. "The church. Right there, and I'm hoping, if the minister is in, to see him."

"Will it be long?" Katie asked, sobering her tone.

"Yeah, but you don't want to stay for this, and it's a near walk home," Spencer rationalized, but could see his sister didn't believe him. "Could you relay a message to dad for me?" Spencer asked.

"You mean after mom's done with her earthquake?"

"Preferably, just tell him I'm sorry for everything I did to cause him to give up on me," Spencer said, searching his brain for answers to the anticipated follow up questions.

Katie blinked at Spencer a few times and then shook her head when she finally comprehended Spencer's words. "Whoa that's deep, do you think he'll let you back in the gate this time?" Katie prodded tactfully, after Spencer didn't continue his confession.

"No. At least I wouldn't, if I were him, but maybe he'll come out." Spencer's sister could tell the tender nature of the issue and kindly agreed to do as he had asked. "Hey, Katie, be sure to lock your doors at night; bad guys yesterday are still bad guys. Kay, kid?"

"From baby to kid now, huh," Katie said lightheartedly, trying to break through Spencer's serious tone as she watched her brother rise out of the vehicle. "Should I wait?"

"No, he's here; see the cars?"

"You sure?"

"Yeah, he'll get me where I need to go next. Thanks, Katie," Spencer said and departed for the church's door. "Oh, Katie, whatever you do, don't go back to my place again. It's not safe." When Katie scrunched her face in disbelief, Spencer explained, "I'm mixed up in some pretty bad stuff, and I'm pretty sure my roommates won't like me after today."

## Part 3 - Chapter Twenty-One

Spencer opened the door to the church and walked inside. The secretary was busy on the phone, listening with an occasional, "Mmhmm" and "Uh-huh," but otherwise it was quiet enough to eavesdrop on the minister's office. The crack of the door let out a rather mixed testimony. He couldn't tell how old the man was that was speaking, but he could hear Gab's occasional encouragement. "Pornography...it's embarrassing. I feel alone; I can't talk about it...or get rid of it, I mean," the man confessed. Spencer rolled back on his foot, but his motion crossed into Gab's line of sight and caused Gab to come out of the office.

"Spencer, right?" Gab said, emerging to shake Spencer's hand.

"Yes, sir. Do you have a moment to talk; I'm mean you're busy with someone else, and I didn't call or anything. I'll come back," Spencer said flippantly.

"No, no. Conversations take time, and as you see this place is not your Friday night hangout. So, please wait a few minutes. I'm sorry. Elena's chatting with the phone again; take a seat. I'll be right around," Gab said lightheartedly, before hobbling back to his prior guest.

Spencer watched him close the door entirely and understood much less of the conversation. Elena finally hung up the phone and smiled her comfortable smile at Spencer. "So, what brings you in today?" she asked.

"I'm in trouble, and I need some advice," Spencer admitted, feeling somehow that he could shed his secrets in this place. But he still turned his gaze to the highly-trafficked carpet.

"Well then, you're in luck since we're running a special on great advice. You caught Gab at a good time," Elena said with a smile, looking for some feedback.

Spencer caught her humor and smiled politely. "Do you know how long he'll be?"

"Hours, so you'd better take a bag of pretzels and get some water to wait it out," Elena continued, pointing out the refreshments on a cart in the corner.

"Hours?"

"Oh no, honey, he'll be out in five minutes, he's not long-winded; but these are my favorite pretzels to buy from the grocery store. Have you heard of them?" Elena said and welcomed Spencer more properly by serving him a bag of the pretzels.

"No."

"No? Well, you're in for something else then!" Elena continued, taking the pretzels back out of Spencer's two hands to open them. "They sometimes...are a bit...ahhh...tricky. Here you go."

"Thanks," Spencer said politely and watched Elena walk over to the water cooler to fill up a cup for him. Then Elena disappeared into the shadows of the church as he ate patiently. Gab's finishing seemed to coincide with his finding the bottom of his pretzel bag, and he looked on as Gab escorted the middle-aged man out to the parking lot with some humorous chit-chat.

"So, Spencer, it's not Wednesday, what can I do for a troubled-looking youth, such as yourself?" Gab asked after ensuring the privacy of the foyer.

"I need some advice," Spencer said, humbled by the prospect.

"Good. Advice is free all week long, and if you're determined enough to burn your hand on that door handle twice now, you must really want it," Gab said, showing him a welcoming arm towards his office.

"Thanks," Spencer said, walking toward the invitation with his trash items.

"I'll take those," Gab said.

"Thanks," Spencer repeated, relinquishing the items to Gab. Slipping his hands out of sight, he entered the stuffed office. Scanning the wall of books, he waited beside the one welcoming chair.

Gab picked up on his distraction and took the opportunity to open the topic of his choice. "So, is it possible to pay penance for the wake of damage that drugs have done in your life, Spencer?" Gab asked after taking a seat.

"Penance?"

"Righting your wrongs through money, apology, community service, and so on," Gab defined apologetically for using an unfamiliar term.

"I don't know, but I'm on the cusp of finding out," Spencer admitted, shedding a flash of light on his intention.

"Explain," Gab commanded with interest, happy that his opening assumption hadn't put Spencer on the defensive.

"Well, I came in today to tell you that I probably won't make Wednesday's meeting," Spencer started and then stopped reluctantly.

"I'm sorry to hear that...."

"But I wanted some sort of support to go through with this," Spencer continued with renewed grit before hesitating again.

When Spencer didn't continue, Gab pre-diagnosed, "Spencer, it sounds silly to ask in a church, but are you thinking of killing yourself?"

"Hm? No, I'm not that...not that," Spencer said.

"Good, I'm glad you have a little perspective. What's this you're trying to do and go through with then?" Gab asked more specifically.

"Well, you called me out on it, I do drugs and sell drugs. I guess it's kind of obvious."

"You're not the first person who's come, trying to kick that addiction. I've had some of those troubles in my lifetime," Gab said to give cause to his earlier statement.

"Addiction," Spencer involuntarily repeated while his mind continued. "I've watched my – I don't even know what to call him – boss, if you'd like, abuse girls, beat and beat down poor people, and...."

"Have you been a participant in these crimes?" Gab said, hoping to expose Spencer's ownership.

"Y...yes, more than that sometimes. Now I realize I'm done, and I'm done...done. And I can't...I tried...but can't get...through," Spencer unsuccessfully admitted, clenching his jaw and pointing at the window that perfectly framed the police station next door.

Gab listened patiently, and when his turn came to prod the confession, he asked, "So, what's going to happen after you walk through that 'door?'"

Spencer stared as Gab's fingers made quotation marks, and he honestly raised his shoulders, admitting, "I don't know, I just know I'm, that I, I don't have any other doors but yours and that one to walk through." Spencer looked lost, and when Gab didn't help carry the conversation, Spencer asked, "Do you? Do you know?"

Gab twisted around to make sure the police station was in fact visible through the window behind him and took a shallow breath. Then committing to his thought, he leaned forward and said, "Adventure."

Spencer laughed a short disbelieving laugh.

"Come on," Gab invited, rising to his feet. "What story doesn't have some unpredictable leap of faith woven into its storyline?" Gab encouraged.

"But I'm free now," Spencer said, objecting feebly.

"Free? Really? Okay," Gab said and paused for a few seconds to change his approach. He looked as if he didn't know what to make of Spencer's expression and started to return to his seat. "You know, I don't know if I have an answer for you today, Spencer," Gab said, lowering his brows with concern. "But...for a moment there I was excited to keep flipping the pages to see what was about to happen in your story."

"My life isn't some story though, it's not some made up novel where heroes die and magically come back to life. I'm done for, or I'm dead, if I...I'm done if...."

"There it is. You. You. You're good," Gab said, pointing at Spencer. "That-there emotion is real; I can feel the conflict. You have me back rooting for you, Spencer."

"Aren't you some pastor and supposed to be talking about salvation in Jesus or...I guess you did talk about this penance thing already," Spencer said, backpedaling.

Gab smiled without interrupting for a few pleasant moments. "I'm gonna grab some water and pretzels; you want some more?"

"No thanks."

Gab left and came back with the snacks. "So, let's clear things up. I'm glad you've been open with me this far," Gab said.

"I...," Spencer said, letting his legs bring him to his feet. "The thing is, you get to walk out. I don't, won't get to...maybe."

"True, but if we're thinking about the same thing here, then you're thinking of doing the right thing...manning up and taking ownership. That's the stuff fathers are proud of. Plus, I'm not in the business of selling forgiveness, and once you've had a run in with trying to buy forgiveness, you'll be in a much better place to value this free-gift of forgiveness from this Jesus person you just mentioned," Gab said, rising to Spencer's level. "You ready?"

## Part 3 - Chapter Twenty-Two

"Hey Elena, Spencer and I are heading over to the station. But before we go, Spencer could we take a moment?"

Spencer stopped in front of Elena's desk when Gab paused. Seeing Gab close his eyes, he respectfully followed suit, but opened them again to glance at the two somber individuals already praying.

"You'll open doors, protect, you'll guide. Convict us and expose us that we might have courage to humble ourselves, that we might seek that rocky adventure you designed, that we might turn from our wicked ways, so that you'll hear us, forgive us, and heal us, and especially this Spencer here as he's standing at his 'cusp ready to find out.' Amen."

Spencer looked up as he was familiar enough with the foreign closing phrase.

Gab reached over and encouragingly slapped his hand on Spencer's shoulder. "So, has your heart skipped a beat yet?"

"Yeah, I guess you could say that," Spencer replied, taking the hint to start heading to the door.

"No car today?"

"No need for a car today; you weren't able to talk me out of doing this."

"Talk you out of it?" Gab questioned as they started to cross the small parking lot.

"This is crazy!" Spencer animated, losing awareness of his advisor's train of thought.

"Crazy! Good, how far would you like me to take you?" Gab asked, following Spencer to the edge of the pavement. "I'm savoring my steps these days."

"What am I going to say?" Spencer asked, having fallen silent for a few more eager seconds.

"I'd ask for a lawyer, if I were you, but if you're confident from here, I'll leave you to your adventure, Spencer," Gab said, saying farewell with a turn of his shoulders.

"A lawyer. This is stupid," Spencer replied, stepping through the small path that joined the parking lots of the two buildings. After another twenty paces, he made it to the station doors.

"Hi, there. How may I help you?" a secretary greeted Spencer from behind her protected window.

"I'm here to confess to a crime, or a couple of them."

"Okay, one second...fill this out describing the crimes you've witnessed, and you'll be contacted by an officer as time permits," the secretary informed while sliding a clipboard through a slot in her protective window.

"Okay, this is new for me...and how do I report crimes where I'm the criminal?" Spencer asked, after identifying the purpose of the form from the title.

"You? Well that's not the right form if you're not reporting a crime." The secretary said, taking the triplicate form back. "Do you need to talk to somebody?"

"Yes, ma'am, if there's somebody to talk to," Spencer said, pounding the counter lightly.

"One second, and what's your name?" the secretary asked as she pushed away from the counter on her rolling stool.

"Spencer Dorkan."

"Okay, Mr. Dorkan; I'll be right back in a second," the secretary promised.

Spencer felt a shiver run through his shoulders as he stepped back into the lonely lobby. Spencer had hardly paced the room twice before a disturbing click from the security door beckoned his attention.

"Mr. Dorkan, Spencer, right?"

"Right."

"How's your dad?" the officer asked, inviting Spencer through the security gate and back towards his office.

"He's fine; we haven't been on the best terms lately," Spencer said honestly.

"Well, I'm Marty Petrone, if you don't remember," Marty said, stopping to introduce himself with a handshake a few steps away from his office door.

"Yeah, you used to work at my high school."

"...Did, and still do occasionally. You know, I just talked with your dad last week, and you came up. And, you know...," Marty said and laughed. "I never thought you would give me the pleasure of a conversation. What's going on, Spencer? Pull the door closed behind you," Marty instructed, settling back in his chair.

Spencer smiled as his courage swelled. "You treat me with the respect that my dad deserves. I c...."

"Heritage is a blessing; your dad said you were out trying things on your own these days. How's that going for you?" Officer Petrone guided.

"Not good, my dad doesn't know I'm here. I just talked with the pastor next door, Gab, I think," Spencer said and hurried to continue, "I'm in trouble, and I'm really here to confess."

"Well, I'm all ears, and hopefully I'll be able to help," Marty said, putting his hands behind his head.

"Well, I stole some laptops recently from the business across from Crumbles Cafe," Spencer admitted.

"Are you going to return them?" Marty asked.

"Is that an option?" Spencer asked with surprise.

"I'm sure whoever's laptop you stole would love their laptop back."

"It's not that simple."

"It usually isn't, but go ahead," Marty invited, glancing over at the wall.

Spencer glanced in the same direction and saw a wall clock. "I'm sorry to take your time, and I don't know how to go about this, but I've been dealing drugs for the past year, doing drugs off and on, and that's why my dad and I aren't on speaking terms right now. With that, I've seen my, uh, my contact abuse girls and put them on the streets as prostitutes," Spencer admitted, folding his arms uncomfortably as he rashly confessed like a can of dry beans being poured into a justice scale. "I don't know how I rationalized this for so long, but I know I've been an accessory to crimes and have hurt...people. There's got to be some law I've broken that would put me in jail."

"Oh, there is, but keep going," Marty invited again.

"It culminated today when my guy, in his drunken stupor, shot another guy that I was trying to sell a laptop to...right after shooting a girl he was prepping to put on the street...and I'm supposed to just go along with this?" Spencer rhetorically asked, pausing only long enough to allow him to catch a breath. "I don't want a part of that anymore, whatever it costs me...which brings me here," Spencer said.

"If it would make you feel better, I could walk you down a hallway and lock you up in our station jail for a few hours," Marty said, genially hinting at his view of Spencer's problems. "But here's what I'll do instead. I'm going to remember our conversation, have you fill out a report-a-crime form, and make a few phone calls. You don't look like you're going to resist arrest, if that be the case. So, why don't you wait in the lobby for a few minutes, and I'll come out and let you know if the district attorney's office has use for your testimony."

"Okay," Spencer agreed and rose to his feet. Marty Petrone escorted him out through the security door that led to the lobby and dismissed him for the time being. To Spencer, the air in the lobby felt lighter. He walked to the tall lobby windows and gazed at the church for a few minutes. Then he sat on one of the dense plastic chairs and took to tapping his heal nervously.

Ten minutes ticked by, and he stood to meander around the waiting area again. After a citizen entered, discoursed with the secretary, and took a seat across the room, he detected some marching and liveliness occurring beyond the security door. Two arguing characters proceeded toward him, trailed by three uniformed officers. The officers were obviously charged with detaining Spencer and flew to their easy task.

"The criminal should be...."

"You don't have any wit in the situation."

"I'm completely aware of the situation."

"You're throwing away this wide-open opportunity...."

"I'm throwing a criminal where a criminal belongs."

"Well, that goes without saying. Justice will have its course, but you're missing the big picture," Marty Petrone pointed.

"Please enlighten me," a well-dressed man in a gray sport-jacket said.

"Here's a kid, whose dad will buy him out of jail anyway, but who's, right now, wanting exoneration from his guilt. Use him," Marty Petrone spoke emphatically, disclosing his ploy to everybody.

"Let's move this to private quarters and see if he's even willing to entertain your version of exoneration," the man in the gray suit said, scowling at having to negotiate.

"Gentlemen, I'll escort Spencer to the briefing room, if I may," Marty said, revealing his frustration in the orders he gave to his attentive audience.

"Spencer, meet your public servant, Jeff Dunmire," Marty said after the parties separated.

"Nice guy," Spencer said, echoing what he thought was sarcasm from his old-school officer.

"At lunch or a dinner party for certain, but that's not his job here," Marty clarified. "You're gonna want a lawyer before you talk to him, but would you do me a favor?"

"Will it clear my name?" Spencer asked.

"Now you're thinking smart, Spencer," Marty said as they navigated the patchwork of desks that separated the lobby from the briefing corridor. "You've seen how your actions, and those of your friends, have hurt people and are still hurting people, right?"

"Yeah, I'll help or whatever," Spencer said, detecting Officer Petrone's inference.

"Good, but use your head," Marty said and dropped his voice to a friendly whisper, "Negotiate...through a lawyer nonetheless; Jeff hates me anyway as you can tell," Marty said and joined up with another police officer before he opened the door to a briefing room. Spencer looked up and down the hallway without any sight of the equally frustrated public official before he stepped into the briefing room with a different guarding officer. The officer invited Spencer to sit down and make himself comfortable. Then after a few minutes with nothing but a few glances, the officer finally asked, "So, what'd ya do?"

"Nothing I'm proud of," Spencer replied.

"Well, at least you came forward about it; that's noble," the officer commented. "But people don't come turn themselves in over stealing candy from a convenience store; so, what's so large that you're trying to get off your chest?" the officer asked straightly.

"Would this be a good time to ask for a lawyer?" Spencer responded nervously, remembering Marty's recent short bit of advice. An angry voice resurfaced from somewhere behind a wall, and Spencer heard a single pound on some out-of-sight desk.

"Maybe you're right. Do you have one?" the officer asked.

"Kind of, if you let me use my phone," Spencer responded.

"Sure, it'll save me from having to walk you down the hallway," the officer said loosely.


## Part 3 - Chapter Twenty-Three


"You're up and about now!" Anna Purse remarked as she entered Romney's hospital room behind April.

"Yeah, this is a new excursion for me; excuse me for a bit," Romney said as he was being assisted heavily by two nurses into a wheel chair.

Once Romney was in the chair, Nancy looked at Anna and said, "You're more than welcome to wait around here, or...well, you know the waiting room has heaps of toys; you've been here enough."

"Thank you, Nancy. Hey, April do you want to go read a book with me in the waiting room?" Anna asked, turning her attention to the toddler who was already trying to intervene with her dad's transfer.

"No, I'm going to walk with Daddy!" April said, proudly climbing off the wheel of the wheel-chair to claim her spot beside it. April and Nancy exchanged glances of mutual approval. "Where are we walking today; hah-ha-ha, I was being silly. You're not walking," April self-critiqued with an adorable laugh.

"To the restroom, Pearl."

"Can I hold your hand, Daddy?"

"If you can keep up, Pearl," Romney invited, watching his daughter dance and skip while grasping his stationary hand. Anna followed behind courteously.

"You do a good deed," Nancy said back to Anna with a smile of encouragement, indicating her involvement with April. Anna smiled back politely, aware that they were only a few steps back from Romney and his daughter.

Not far down the hallway, Anna held April back and picked her up to her waist. As Romney was assisted into the restroom by the two nurses, his daughter wiggled back to the ground and gleefully called up to Anna, "Let's go to the store."

"To buy what?" Anna giggled and scrunched her nose.

"Sunshine."

"Sunshine?" Anna echoed, grabbing hold of April's hand.

"And new socks, and coaties."

"Coaties?" Anna asked. "Do you mean jackets?"

"Yeah, jackets," April responded, wiggling her arm enough to get Anna to release her hand. She ran up to the bathroom door and yelled out, "Knock, knock," in unison with her fist.

Anna heard an entertaining voice from inside say, "Who's there?" and April responded, "No, I'm actually knocking."

Anna beckoned April away from the door with an embarrassed voice, saying, "Hey, April, knock, knock. Now you say, 'Who's there?'" After April responded as directed, Anna prompted, "Woo," and looked at April's perplexed face, trying her best to keep her smile from flooding into laughter. "Then you say, 'Woo who?' Like this, 'Woo whoo,'" Anna repeated with energy. Anna laughed at her attempt to communicate the juvenile humor to April, and as she rose to her feet an older man dressed in a suit jacket approached the pair.

"I'm sorry to bother you, miss. But I'm looking to visit a Mr. Daniels, and this looks like his little girl," the gentleman said, looking down mostly at April.

"Sure, I'm Anna. I'm waiting for him as well. He should be back over this way in a few minutes," Anna said, taking April by the hand and moving toward Romney's hospital room.

"I'm Sir Byron Dorkan, an old friend of Romney's, and my wife should be in trail shortly," Sir Byron said, pulling his suit jacket together. At the doorway of Romney's hospital room Sir Byron stopped and observed the length of hallway from the corner to the elevator. April ran over to the seat she had claimed earlier and returned to looking out the window.

A few minutes later Romney returned behind Byron's compassionate wife, Kloe, who introduced Romney's arrival by saying, "Look who I've found."

"Yes, I conquered the bathroom yet again," Romney returned in good humor as Anna went and sat quietly by April at the window.

"We were sorry to hear about the attack and would have come sooner," Kloe said thoughtfully, walking over and leaning on Byron's shoulder.

"But everybody comes in those first few days when you're feeling your worst, but now's when you need the cheer," Sir Byron added, putting arm around his queenly wife. "It looks like you've got a good team keeping you in check.

"Yes, sir, they're taping me up all over the place," Romney replied during his slow maneuver back into the hospital bed.

"Well...," Sir Byron started, but was interrupted by a floor pager and a brief hustle of employees in the hallway. "Well, you know Theresa's been sitting in for you and doing a great job. So, you'd better be getting better fast, or you might not have a position to come back to," Sir Byron said jovially.

Romney smiled widely enough to put the billionaire at ease and said, "How are those two kids of yours?"

"They...," Sir Byron said, but was interrupted by Kloe who whispered into his ear. "What about Spencer?" he asked with a scowl on his face.

Kloe spoke up to the volume that Sir Byron had chosen, "He called me from jail, saying he would like to talk to you and your lawyer. My apologies, I could have saved our family troubles till...."

"Did he say which jail or what for?" Byron asked completely distracted by the information.

"A bunch of bad choices, and yes; he said police station number two."

"At least he knows why he's in there, and he best know I'm not in the bail bonds business."

"He didn't ask for that, honey; just you and our family lawyer," Kloe said, trusting her son's words.

"That'll cost more than bail," Sir Byron said, remembering Romney and the other occupants. "Well, Romney, looks like you'll be served dinner before us tonight; what do you think Kloe, does R&T's Pizzeria deliver to the penitentiary?" Sir Byron asked, indicating to everybody that his departure was imminent.

"Kloe, thanks for stopping by, and, Sir Byron, don't give Theresa too many more ideas," Romney asserted so the two could leave gracefully.

Sitting quietly for a few minutes from the time the Dorkan's departed, Anna occasionally shepherded April away from danger. "Do I pay you enough?" Romney asked Anna out of the silence.

"Not nearly...," Anna replied, instantly blushing for not finishing her thought. "...Enough compliments."

Romney husked out a laugh and said, "You about had me cracking a joke about your stubbornness in accepting money."

"Stubbornness! Why I...," Anna said, returning Romney's misshapen smile.

"Stubbness," April echoed.

"I have a question, seeing that the awkward is inevitable," Anna stated, connecting with Romney as he rolled his head toward her on his pillow.

"Sure," Romney invited.

"Have you heard of Miss Dixy? It's a magazine, I think," Anna explained and looked away at April who had conveniently picked up one of her dolls and started to play.

"I've heard of something similar, are you thinking of Miss Doxy maybe?"

"Yes; Doxy, right," Anna said, and when she realized Romney was asking for more of a lead by his silence she continued, "I've caught a glimpse of it around campus, and did I tell you that I'm meeting Jon's parents tomorrow?"

"Oh really, are you excited?" Romney asked, watching Anna's changing expression.

"I've never done...it's kind of scary in how it's foundational, making it official, I don't know," Anna said, bending her fingers stiffly.

"You sound nervous," Romney teased, expecting Anna's genteel smile.

"Nervous...maybe," Anna said and diverted her eyes to the corner of the room. "I feel like...like I know what it means to 'meet the parents,' and I've thought about asking you to meet him first."

"And why not your mom?"

"There's something validating about...what? Why not my mom?" Anna stopped. "She will, I mean she has for all real purposes already...I just kind of want your approval," Anna confessed, finding it difficult to look at Romney.

"Well, you know where to find me...for a little while longer anyway," Romney said, finally catching Anna's floating eyes.

"What is Miss Doxy?" Anna asked, returning to her prior thought.

"What do you already know about Miss Doxy?" Romney asked.

"I know it's not for sale at the school bookstore, but I don't know much more," Anna lied, having seen the magazine and its contents clearly from one she had taken from Jon's backpack.

"To me it's pornographic, and it very well may be full blown by now."

"Really?" Anna said with uncommitted astonishment at the prospect. "How do you know...I mean, say," Anna said with almost a hurt look on her face.

"It's been around for a while and...," Romney started. "And I supported them with my, with my viewership for a good while. Call it a vice that I had to battle for many a day."

"And what about now?"

"Wow, you cut right to the heart of it."

"I'm sorry, forgive me to answer...to ask, I'm sorry," Anna said, scattering her eyes amongst her thoughts again.

"That's why I had to stop."

"Why...what?" Anna asked, desperate to understand in the moment.

"If you could see yourself, that's why," Romney said, but saw confusion from his comment. "Do you know the story of Job, the Bible one?"

"Of course, it's classic...we, we studied it senior…as a senior I studied it for English," Anna explained, balancing her focus between Romney and his daughter.

"So, you know that Job underwent terrible strife and suffering."

"Yes," Anna said, looking back at Romney.

"In the middle of one of his discourses, in the pit of his suffering, he mentions out of nowhere something like, 'I made a covenant with my eyes; how then could I gaze upon a virgin?' Out of nowhere.... It's a struggle I believe every man faces for sake of the chemistry in our body. I'm just one that decided, like Job did, to make a covenant with my eyes not to entertain myself with...well, it," Romney said, straining to keep his voice clear.

Anna listened, letting her thoughts collect on her face.

"Hey, I don't want to concern you too much, but if it's an important issue to you, you don't have to compromise your expectations," Romney said, trying to be sensitive.

"I don't know if I exactly follow you, but did you, have you?" Anna asked quietly.

"Stopped? With Miss Doxy? Yes; but is a drug addict ever 'cured' in this life of his drug of choice?" Romney reasoned with pause.

"Right."

"Or are addicts all alike and ever recovering...with the commitment to the fight against their...."

"Desire?"

"Yes," Romney said, rolling his head back to the ceiling to digest his own words.

"I haven't told him I took one of his magazines; the last time we were together," Anna confessed.

"This is Jon we're talking about?" Romney asked to clarify Anna's statement.

"Yes, sir."

Romney smiled with amusement and rolled his head back to the white ceiling. "You called me, 'sir.' And you stole a magazine from your boyfriend."

"What? It's not that serious of a crime." Anna said, as Romney's smile pulled her out of her deep thoughts.

"You know...," Romney said, chuckling contagiously.

"No, I don't...I don't know why he would be selling these magazines. He had three, and he's vaguely alluded to 'selling magazines' from a press downtown, like it's normal." Anna said instinctively, gradually releasing her frustration.

Romney stopped chuckling. "He's distributing them, Miss Doxy? Wow," Romney commented after Anna flashed the direness of her distress again with her eyes. "I do know that, if you and he are going to work out, you'll have the boldness to ask and that he'll be honest enough to respond...honestly," Romney said, checking Anna's attention twice. "I'll gladly meet this Jon if he really cares about my Anna," Romney said, finishing his inference with a turn of his attention to April.

"It's about dinner time, isn't it?" Anna asked rhetorically, watching April dance her doll on Romney's arm cast to avoid responding.

"I want to eat with daddy," April said, sealing her request with her own burst of delight.

"I guess we could go down to the cafeteria and bring back your daddy's dinner for him. Do you think he'd like that? Why don't you ask him what he wants," Anna suggested convincingly. "I have to drop her off at the Richard's after 6:00pm for her sleepover with Alex," Anna reminded Romney, forcing her own bit of excitement for April's sake.

"Oh, right, the Richard's were feeding her tonight," Romney reiterated.

Anna smiled and watched April playfully take her father's dinner order with her nose folded in the menu.

## Part 3 - Chapter Twenty-Four

"Mr. Jonny-no-pay, sir, follow me," Chef Marco instructed without any pause. "Normally I would've let my manager deal with you, and normally I would have expected you to not show up a'tall."

"Well, I pay my debts, sir, and I really am sorry; thank...."

"Okay, now you wash dishes like Toretto there," Chef Marco interrupted and started to leave in response to a pressing call from the kitchen.

"Turret who?" Jon inquired.

"Toretto. Doesn't he look like the guy from the furious race movie, guy? Now don't bother Chef Cannavacciuolo. Dishes don't ask questions, they just cry 'clean me, clean me,' and no unclean dishes leave your fingers, you understand, guy, Jonny?" Chef Marco grimaced and then smiled with characteristic passion before scurrying away to his next task.

"Toretto?" Jon asked and waited, having been left alone to introduce himself. When the uninterested man scrubbing away behind the sink didn't respond, he looked around and grabbed the same obvious tools, girded himself with a big rubber apron, and started mimicking the indifferent heavyweight at the second wash basin. The dishes came, and after referencing the heavyweight's precedent method, he picked up the easy routine. After thirty minutes, it started to become natural, and Jon sank into his thoughts as dishes moved through his hands and into the dryer. Every ten minutes or so a stack would come out and a new stack would go in the unit. The first time the dish dryer finished was the only time Toretto said anything. Jon figured out the rest and started enjoying the race of receiving the dishes. Facing a wall in the back corner of the kitchen, Jon worked diligently under the fluorescent lights. The only irritation after a short while was that his shoes and socks soaked through from the water puddled at his feet.

Losing track of the time, Jon lost himself in the monotony of the exercise when he heard over his shoulder, "Now, where is that octopus? And why are you still washing dishes?"

Jon paused and set a dish onto the waiting stack. He used his forearm to wipe his face that felt spattered and smeared with food. With no way of knowing for sure whether he was presentable, he turned to address the unique voice of the chef.

"I thought I told you to do...same as Toretto?" Chef Marco chided.

"Yes, sir."

"If Toretto left an hour ago, then why are you still armed in rubber?" Chef Marco inquired sternly.

"I, I got carried away with the dishes that somehow kept coming. I didn't even notice...."

"You have a job where I pay you for octopus' duty; dollar per arm, you consider it and come back tomorrow to work if you say, 'Yes,'" Chef Marco instructed. "Toretto hates da' job; he never says anything, or yes, sir, or no, sir; you take his job."

"Um...that doesn't sound cool," Jon said, worrying that he had just gotten his reserved wash mate fired.

"If it's no good to you, you don't come in, and then I call Toretto and beg him, 'Come back.'"

"So, you won't fire him?" Jon asked, standing poised in his heavy attire.

"Toretto? No, he quits every week. He only comes back when he needs da' money again," Chef Marco said with his big smile.

Jon finally noticed the hush on the restaurant floor. "I'd better hurry, would you like me to finish these up?"

"I offer you da' job didn't I, hurry, hurry! You treat my dishes like my mother's china," Chef Marco said with gusto.

"Yes, sir," Jon said, slamming the power washer back on full blast. A moment later, Jon glanced to his side to see Chef Cannavacciuolo arming himself with Toretto's wet suit and starting to lift dishes from the stack into and out of his delinquent wash mate's basin.

# Part 3 - Chapter Twenty-Five

Rolling out of bed with a few minutes to spare, Jonathan Wickfell started his morning routine. Ignoring the presence of his sleeping roommate, he made his way around the painted cinderblock room to gather his personal tagalongs. Deliberating off and on between moments of distraction and grogginess, he opened a map on his computer to determine the best route to the train station and had just about picked up his car keys when his phone buzzed. He flipped open his phone and started to read as he pushed through the hallway door with his elbow. "It hasn't changed since the last time you asked," Jon spoke critically to the stale hallway. Using his thumb, he typed out his dry response, "The usual $35...all tips appreciated." He finished the stretch of hallway and felt his phone buzz again. "Why do you want thirty copies, Zach?" Jon asked the empty stairwell as he hopped down the stairs. He thumbed out his reply, "Why so many, bro?" He pushed out of the dormitory and paused to read Zach's third message. Before he finished punching out his reply it dawned on him that something must have happened to drive up the price of Miss Doxy, or so he reasoned fancifully. Jon then deliberated on how much to ask Zach to pay, but before he landed on a certain figure, Zach convinced him with his fourth buzz. Jon smiled and nearly broke out in laughter. "You're crazy, dude. $3000 is insane for thirty copies...even if you want them in the next thirty minutes," Jon said and looked around to find the campus mostly empty and the shaded areas still dew covered. Before Jon made it back up to his dorm to collect the absurd order, his phone buzzed again with the same question from a different contact. "$110," Jon replied. In his dorm, Jon counted out the remaining magazines. Leaving only a handful of units in his closet, he headed out in a hurry without forgetting the time or that he still had to pick up his parents at the train station.

Surprisingly, the large dollar transaction went faster than Jon had expected, and he found himself zooming through the streets of Pittsburg to Anna's side of the river to claim his parents. He came to the southern shore and followed the expressway around to the flat bridge spanning the Montague River. Not familiar with the layout of the train station, Jon toured the block once, hoping for a non-metered place to park. Spotting his parents on the second lap, he pulled mostly out of traffic and considered tapping the horn. Instead of honking, he opened his door and peeked his head up over the roof of the car. Only a moment had passed before he heard the obnoxious objection from an inconvenienced driver. The still air helped draw the attention of his parents and the rest of the mingling passengers.

"Hey, son!" Brian Wickfell welcomed, ignoring the minuscule traffic backup. Brian moseyed along next to his wife, Cassidy, who was skinny and well put together in comparison.

Jon apologetically waved with a smile at the few cars that were idly waiting. He hurried around behind the car and sped hugged his mom before tossing the luggage into the trunk. "What's this?" Jon asked, nodding at the dense box his dad had retrieved and handed to him.

"I have my suspicions, but it's heavy and addressed to you," Brian answered without stopping his route to the passenger side of the car.

"Oh, I know!" Jon said and almost forgot to hide his excitement.

"Well?" Brian asked before the trunk slammed shut.

Jon quickly hid his springy smile and acted like the trunk and traffic were at the front of his mind as he hurried himself back to the driver's seat of his old boxy car.

"So, are you hungry?"

"Brian, he probably has long had breakfast on campus already," Cassidy Wickfell preemptively chided, hinting at a prior conversation.

Jon put the car into motion and said, "Actually, the cafeteria doesn't open until lunch; it's a Saturday."

"Still your father has been talking about Pittsburg food since last week."

"I'm human, honey, and I need to eat," Brian said, looking to Jon for support.

"Are you buying?" Jon responded jokingly, glancing at his dad before accelerating the car onto a cross street.

"Of course, it's our getaway vacation, your mom's and mine."

"But we just had breakfast on the train, and even then, you seemed so worried that you were going to miss something."

"And you don't think I know that I just had thirty dainty calories? I'm hungry again," Brian said, humoring himself.

"Okay," Cassidy said and looked in retreat over her rings out the window. "What river is this?" Cassidy asked, after the silence started to annoy her.

"We call it the Montegreen."

"Oh right."

"But it's actually called the Montague," Jon corrected after his glance in his mirror told him that his mom had believed his answer.

"Oh, Montague."

"How about this – and, dad, this will make you happy – I need to stop by a bookstore in town and it's by a cafe that I've eaten at a few times. It's actually right across from my internship."

"Really? We'd like to see that," Cassidy said with vivacity.

"Honey, I think Jon's trying to say we could all grab lunch at this cafe he's eaten at a few times; am I right?" Brian said, shifting the focus back to Jon to cut off any dissidence.

"It is the best cold-turkey-and-brie sandwich in town...if they're serving lunch that is; you know it is still kind of early," Jon said, squinting his eyes at the dashboard to see the dim clock.

"So, this is the new hot rod on campus. You know, I can fix that dash backlight before I go, if you can get me to an auto parts store," Brian offered, tapping the dim display

"Great! Yeah, I haven't had time to take it apart."

"Maybe you didn't hear me, I'm offering to do it for you," Brian said and laughed at the lull of silence he caused.

"That would be great, dad. Strangely, I have class this afternoon, well two classes and a lab actually. So, I can leave you guys the keys," Jon said, turning onto the street where he had first met Anna in the downpour. "You can get parts for the dash's backlight then, and if it doesn't take you long, you guys might try out this place downtown called Butler's Station," Jon said enticingly.

"That sounds fancy. Is it good?" Cassidy questioned.

"It's real Italian; kind of pricey, but, mention my name and Chef Cannavacciuolo, I call him Chef Marco for short, might give you a discount. I don't know for sure," Jon said, looking side to side for a break in traffic.

"You're not wasting all your money on this girl at fancy restaurants, are you?"

"Yes, when do we get to meet her?" Cassidy chimed in with interest.

"Anna? Well, she deserves first class meals, if you ask me."

"Son, girls take advantage of your wallet when you let them, and starting a relationship based on...."

"Dad, no. She's not like that. I mean she's first class to me, and can probably afford it too, but she's never asked for anything...yet," Jon defended passionately.

"Well, there you go. 'Yet.'"

"Wait till you meet her, dad. You're gonna be impressed," Jon said, standing his ground.

"Brian, don't judge the girl unfairly."

"I'm not judging her. I'm just saying a tidbit of wisdom, not directly about...Anna, but about girls in general," Brian said to concede his unwelcomed point.

"I hope we don't have this conversation in front of Anna," Cassidy groaned.

"Oh, bummer look at that," Jon said with disappointment.

"What's that?" Brian asked, following his son's eyes.

"It's closed."

"What, the restaurant?" Brian clarified with an absurd tone.

"Crumbles Cafe, it says it's closed in the window and looks pretty torn apart inside; that's a bummer."

"Do they mean 'closed-down' or 'closed for breakfast,' I wonder?" Brian added critically.

"Is this where your internship is at?" Cassidy said, glossing over the disappointment that flowed from the front of the car.

"Uh yeah, it's Scales' headquarters," Jon said, pulling the car to a stop. "I'd use the garage, but I don't know if I could get in on a Saturday," Jon said, pausing for a moment to observe the building with his mom.

"I'll only be a few seconds in the bookstore," Jon said, pulling his lightly loaded back pack up from behind the center console.

As Jon walked to the arranged delivery spot, his parents watched him stop and reference his phone twice.

## Part 3 - Chapter Twenty-Six

"Hey guys, thanks for waiting," Jon said, sliding into the driver's seat seconds after his delivery.  "Anna's on campus now; do you want to meet her?"

"Why, certainly I do. What do you say, dear?" Cassidy jumped in, showing her approval after sightseeing her son's place of internship from the car window.

"Yeah, I'm up for whatever," Brian said in favor of the general mood.  He watched the multi-story structure bearing the insignia of Scales Architectural Company swing around and pass him on his side.  Turning to his son, he noticed his son's foot heavier on the gas pedal than it had been on the trip over to the bookstore. With both traffic and conversation light, Jon parked and jumped out of his ride with enthusiasm.  Cassidy could tell her son was nervous and enjoyed the few moments diagnosing his smile. "Well, where is she?" Brian asked half-seriously while straightening his belt.

"I'd let you try and guess, but that's her dancing around with the kid."

"Kid?" Cassidy worried.

"Must be a pretty girl," Brian chuckled unable to see any detail amongst the canopy of trees.

"Brian, please."

"She is, dad," Jon said passively, starting across the parking lot toward the grassy area.  "And she helps a friend with babysitting, mom.  It's not hers; the kid isn't hers that is," Jon explained, letting his parents catch up to him.

"That's generous of her."

"She looks to be good with kids, from what I can tell," Brian said, offering his hand to Cassidy.

"Hey, Anna!" Jon yelled, catching her attention.  He watched Anna turn and saw April continue in the twirling game till she ended up collapsing in playful giggles. Anna let Jon arrive before she offered a polite greeting.

"Play with me, play with me," April begged, ignoring the strangers' formal exchanges.

"In a few minutes, Pearl; let me meet Jon's parents, kay?"

"No, make them play too; it's funny," April said, restarting her game of spinning while using Anna's hand as a pinion.

Anna dropped down to April's level and conservatively said, "How about I introduce you as Princess April." When April's face didn't surrender its look of disappointment, Anna added with a giggle, "and I as the queen." Picking up the slow-to-agree child, she turned back to Jon's parents and followed through with her appeasing suggestion. "Hello, this is Princess April, and I am Queen Anna of 'Babysitter.'" April laughed, causing both parents to smile warmly.

Jon saw his parent's reaction and then felt his phone vibrate. Instinctively opening it to read the message, he gushed out, "More? Really?" Seeing that he had interrupted the warm moment, he apologized and shook his phone to explain. "Hey, you guys keep talking. I'm going to grab something from the car, so you guys can use it while I'm in class."

Anna let April down to the ground and took both of her hands to keep her entertained as she listened to Cassidy talk about their train ride over to Pittsburg. When Cassidy ended her story with a question of where Anna and Jon had met, Anna answered, "Math Logic class; he was almost late."

"Oh, I'm not surprised."

Jon stumbled back carrying the heavy box he had put in the trunk. Anna noticed the branding on the box that Jon clutched and acknowledged him by stating the obvious, "Miss Doxy?"

"Yeah, late delivery, and I need to walk this back to my dorm before class," Jon answered as normally as he could, and then he addressed his dad as he dangled his car keys underneath the weighty box of magazines. "Here you go, and I'm sorry, I got to run, if this is going to happen."

"You don't want to be 'just about late,'" Cassidy said, causing Anna and Brian to laugh.

In good humor Jon smiled and started walking backwards down the brick path. "By the way, are you free after my classes to come hear me play and sing at open mic?"

"You play?" Anna asked, surprising Jon with her look.

"I was thinking about it."

"Well, that'll be something to see; did you know he was playing...and singing too? Open mic?" Anna asked cross-referencing the glances between Jon and his parents.

"No, but Jon was always playing his guitar in his room all through high school. Only occasionally would he share one of his original songs with us," Cassidy said, loving Anna more every minute.

"Has Jon given you both a tour of the campus?"

"We've been on the campus tour, but we'd love to get to know you over lunch," Cassidy invited, guessing at the meaning of Anna's question.

"Sure, if April can tag along. I'm not the strange one that has class on Saturday like Jon does," Anna said, leading everyone slowly toward the cafeteria.

"What are you studying, Anna?" Brian asked from a comfortable distance.

"History," Anna said ready to elaborate.

"And where did you two meet?" Brian asked.

Anna paused for a moment, thinking she had already answered that question, and graciously replied anyway, "Math Logic class, but we actually literally ran into each other a couple of days before that; he's a good friend and smart too."

"What's your favorite part of history...I mean as a whole?" Cassidy asked to return to Anna's short answer.

"The painters, I'd say."

"Have you ever studied the Sistine Chapel?"

"Oh...yes, definitely worth seeing."

"See, Brian," Cassidy said, referencing another earlier debate.

"Have you ever been to Italy?" Anna asked.

"Italy is my favorite and my mommy's too," April said, gathering all three sets of surprised eyes for a moment. Anna facilitated Jon's parents through the cafeteria line, spending most of her time catering to April and trying to interest her in some form of healthy sustenance. After sitting down to eat, Brian

Wickfell asked Anna's permission to say a prayer over the food. Anna consented and did her best to make April follow the appropriate posture.

As soon as Brian finished, Cassidy spoke, "Anna, I am so impressed; I can clearly see why April's parents trust you so much."

"Thank you."

"Yes, I pictured you much differently, but you carry yourself very well," Brian added to the compliment.

Hesitating before taking a bite of her sandwich, Anna smiled and said, "Okay, so I want to hear the two sides of the story of how both of you met." A moment happened between Brian and Cassidy where they silently exchanged a look that somehow decided who was going to tell what and which part first. Lunch didn't last much longer than the telling of their story, and Anna left the pair where they had met.

Then convincing April that it would be exciting to go watch the baseball team practice, they walked over to see the team's activities happening on the field. After spending a few lazy hours there, she received a text from Jon saying, "So, did my parents behave themselves?" Anna typed back slowly, "A lovely couple. When is show time?"

Jon quickly answered and figured out where Anna and April were spending their pleasant afternoon. Meeting in the middle of campus thirty minutes later, Anna found Jon lugging two musical suitcases with a patchwork of cords.

"What is he carrying?" April asked.

"Can I help you?" Anna offered before answering April.

"Oh no, only if you'd clap and cheer after my performance," Jon said, pushing on with his load toward the parking lot. "And you know, I just realized that I don't have a car to get there."

"Well, it's a good thing you invited me along then, huh?" Anna asserted, and slipped her hand into her purse to remove her car keys.

"Sweet, arriving in style! Is your mom working tonight?"

"You guessed it, she's done at eleven, but I'm supposed to drop Pearl off at Alex's house, her other babysitter, before seven. So, dinner at the open-mic place, then we'll have to split," Anna said, walking blithely across the parking lot to her car.

"Dinner? Yes, and you're gonna be impressed with this place's food." Jon said, jumping onboard with the suggestion and taking the cue of the popped trunk to stow his musical gear.

"Will you drive?"

"At your command," Jon said, allowing Anna plenty of time to buckle April into the car seat.

Anna could tell a difference in Jon as he would jitter a bit when he'd talk, as if having to gulp milk before he spoke. "Nervous?"

"Ahh, that's what that feeling is! Every time you get near me...nervous," Jon said, noticing Anna enjoy his reply.

"So, are you?" April clarified with a cute form of aggravation.

"A little bit, but a little 'nervous' is a good thing I'm told. Especially when performing for someone who knows great music like you."

"I'm not a music critic by any means," Anna said with openness.

"No, but your mom is the real deal, and I'm not quite up to par with her, I'm sure," Jon said, trying to lower Anna's musical expectation.

"Baa, you'll convince everyone that you're a great," Anna said half-seriously.

"Ahh, my phone keeps buzzing."

"Yeah? I'll check it for you," Anna said, looking down at Jon's lap to guess where the phone was hiding. "Do you want me to check it for you, Jon?"

"Nah, I'm good. We're almost there."

"Kay," Anna said and looked back at April who was staring out the window. "How many songs do you have planned?"

"Two...two for you."

"For me?" Anna said, acting honored at the prospect of having two songs dedicated to her.

"Yeah, I was writing a song when I met you and then one came to me just this past week," Jon said somewhat sheepishly, peering into the pub's alleyway parking lot to see if there were any gaps left for them.

"Wrote? So, these are personalized songs."

"Well inspired, I don't say your name or anything."

"Good, I wouldn't want to blush in front of April," Anna said almost blushing.

"This place is hopping for a Saturday afternoon."

"Look, the burger man!" April screamed with delight.

"Pearl, that was a bit loud," Anna said, unbuckling herself before she saw Jon searching for the trunk release button. "Under the door handle."

"Oh thanks," Jon said, finding the button and leaning into the door to open it.

Anna calmly unstrapped April while trying to be available to Jon who was fidgeting with his musical parcels. "Got it all?"

"Yeah, thanks. You just worry about April."

Anna couldn't keep up with Jon who made it to the door of the pub with his gear ahead of them. A few paces back, Anna started picking up the message of the middle-aged gal leaning out the door.

"I'd recommend calling ahead next time if you're looking to get on early."

"When's the earliest, do you think?" Jon asked.

"Nine? Maybe?" the gal said, and seeing Jon internalize the time, she smiled and tucked her head back inside the bustling pub.

Jon exhaled a mix of disappointment and relief.

"What's she saying?" Anna asked as soon as she had caught up to the side door of the pub.

"The roster's full, but she has her evening slots open, but I don't think you'd want to wait that long; and April...," Jon said, remembering their tagalong when he saw her standing patiently, holding Anna's hand.

"Well, they've got good food at least, right? Do you still want to go in?" Anna asked, studying Jon's uncertain expression.

"I don't know," Jon said, looking inside the yellow windows where he could see cheery faces already relaxing around most of the front row tables. "Noaah, let's...."

"Hold on," Anna instructed, stepping in front of Jon to catch the open door. "Watch April."

A couple of customers stepped through the breach in the door, circled up to each other, then looked down at Jon's equipment and courteously started moving away. One asked shyly from behind a cigarette butt, "So, you playin'?"

"Not tonight, all the slots are full till late," Jon answered and pulled his buzzing phone out of his pocket. "Hey, Dan, what's up? They found them? Well, right, I'm assuming all the laptops are together, but you're saying they found them, or they, or it...the computer," Jon said, running his fingers through his hair. When he didn't see April where she had been standing, he spun around with an exploring look on his face. Only seeing the two guys who were both contently smoking, he stepped in the pub's side door with the phone pressed to his ear. When he didn't see Anna after a scoping of the room, he stepped back out because he could hear better and thought it less consequential if April had disappeared inside rather than outside. "Dan, are you telling me the police have my laptop, or are you just telling me that it's been moved...maybe and yes; okay, I understand. Hey look, I got to go, I lost something a little more important," Jon said, taking a few steps out into the tight parking lot.

"Jon," Anna called from the door.

"No, not another laptop, a girl; we'll talk soon," Jon finished and looked concerned while trotting back toward Anna.

"Hey."

"Hey, good news," Anna started but assumed Jon's concerned expression.

"Oh good, she followed you inside," Jon interpreted with relief.

"Where's April?" Anna asked confused.

"I took my eyes off her for a second; she could have only followed you inside," Jon explained.

"Well, come on then!"

"You go in, I'll guard the stuff by the door," Jon said, starting back along his perimeter search route. The sun had been blazing until a small cloud cast its shadow on the street. Jon scratched his head more nervously now than on his drive to the pub and started running through the parking lot, checking between every car.

Two minutes later, Anna came out with the same gal that Jon had talked with about the roster. The gal wore the same worried expression as Anna and continued a string of questions detailing

April's age, clothes, where, and when the child went missing. The gal, Alicia, who owned and managed the pub, already had the pub house phone in her hand and began dialing some number.

"Shoot," Anna fretted, curling her hair up and over her ear nervously. Jon apologized to everyone at the same time and felt his stomach twist into a horrid knot. "Where, April, where?" Anna asked, ignoring Jon's blanket statement. Her feet kept moving, as did Jon's and the pub manager's. Alicia aggressively interviewed the two smokers, who answered with sympathetic shrugs and guessing directions. Then she demanded their help in watching the door and ran to catch up with Anna and Jon who had taken up a post at the street corner and were peering every which way.

Then before the worried manager had a chance to reunite with the search party, everyone heard a loud 'whoop' from kiddy corner of the street. A large man hollered, "Hey! Hey!" and stuck his hand high in the air. The man's apparel suggested he had been working with grease as a cook for more than his fair share of the day. "Hey, you guys looking for a little girl?" Anna didn't have the volume to respond but immediately set out through the intersection. Jon, concerning himself more with the traffic, faithfully bolted along at Anna's heels. The pair watched the cook tuck himself inside the small burger establishment, letting a heavy screen door smack the frame behind him. Anna saw the only patron inside, happily chewing before an entire combo of fries and a kid-sized burger. Reassuring herself that April was safe, she scuffled up to the table and slipped into the booth beside her little friend.

"You want a burger too? The burger man cooked me a burger...and fresh fries!" April said enthusiastically.

"Ooh," Anna said, looking up at Jon and the manager.

"Hey, Jon."

"Yeah, I'm so sorry."

"As I was saying earlier, good news; Alicia got you in, if you wanted to go on first," Anna explained proudly.

"Really? I don't know with all the commotion."

"No, no, go get set up. I'll walk over with April in a minute after she's done with her 'fresh fries,'" Anna insisted.

As Jon and the manager exited the burger shack, April concluded, "That boy's not so good at looking for me." The cook didn't hide the fact that he overheard the candid comment and let out a hardy laugh. "I sneaked away, and I didn't even make him count," April continued proudly as if she had planned and executed the entire ordeal.

"Not a good thing when you didn't ask me first, Pearl; how did you make her food so fast?" Anna said, directing her question to the cook who had returned to his cooking spot.

"The food's always ready, ma'am. Would you like a plate yourself?"

"Please," Anna said.

"I saw that little thing prancing up to the door so politely," the cook said as he prepared an identical plate of food for Anna. "I seem to remember someone like her, and she seemed to remember me."

"The burger man," April said happily.

"I'm the burger man!" the cook accepted proudly. "She came in and sat down and ordered herself; a bold little one, I'd say, but you might want to buy her a monkey leash, if you'd be lettin' her wander across roads and things like that," the cook commented tactfully as he laid the fast plate of food down and returned to minding his own cooking business.

Ten minutes later Anna and April returned to the pub where Alicia greeted April as warmly as a middle-aged grandmother. Jon was already playing his first song as Anna and April were ushered to a seat by an arcade machine. Anna didn't understand most of the words Jon sang and focused more on cuddling with April on her lap. A handful of minutes later Jon put his guitar away and promptly seated himself before the start of the actual first act. Neither Jon nor Anna wanted food, so they set out conveniently after the second opening-act finished. The hush of the parking lot lowered the tension of the pair, and as the sun started to set in the sky, they all climbed back into Anna's car.

"You driving?" Jon asked after stowing his musical gear in the trunk.

"Yes, if you don't mind."

"No, not a bit," Jon replied and felt their friendship turn awkward as he buckled himself into the passenger seat. He waited patiently for Anna to get April situated, breathing in a few times to start a conversation that didn't feel appropriate in the moment. Then Anna started to drive back to campus silently. Jon occasionally looked over at her serious profile, and once they were halfway to campus, he finally mustered courage to say, "Hey, look, I'm really sorry about losing track of April."

Anna kept driving and after a moment of reflection said, "Okay." Anna saw Swanson Hall approaching after more minutes of silence and took her last opportunity to pour out her thoughts. "What is Miss Doxy?"

Jon took his own moment of reflection. "It's a magazine...I sell for a job."

At the spark of his honesty, Anna carefully questioned, "If it's just a job, can you quit?"

"I could, I guess."

"If I asked you to quit, would you...be able to?" Anna asked, letting her voice trail off as the car coasted to its stopping point.

"You know, Anna, it sounds like you're hinting at...making me out to be some bad person with a hidden life, like a lot of the guys I know, but that's not me. It's a job and one I'm known for. I can make a lot more money answering my phone and delivering Miss...than washing dishes or giving my time away at Scales," Jon explained as positively as he could with a tinge of both logic and shame.

"I see," Anna responded passively. "So, if you could quit this lucrative job, and I asked you to abandon Miss Doxy...would you?" Anna asked in summary.

When Jon looked up, he was trapped by Anna's fearless eyes, and for a moment their gazes locked. Jon finally concluded with protest, "I don't know."

"Okay," Anna graciously replied, letting Jon get out of the car and gather his musical items from the trunk. As Jon started walking away from the vehicle, Anna rolled down her window and called loudly enough to gather Jon's attention, "Jon, I'm sorry, but it's me or Miss Doxy, you got to choose." When Jon had nodded and turned around, Anna started driving away.

"He must love Miss Dossy an awfully lot," April said, cranking her head around to keep her eyes on Jon as the car accelerated around the circle.

Over the next two days, Anna tried placing three calls to Jon's phone. Each message she left him felt progressively worse, and when he averted his eyes to avoid acknowledging her in class, Anna knew it wasn't because she wasn't trying.

## Part 3 - Chapter Twenty-Seven

In two weeks, roughly four weeks total, Romney had made impressive progress, so the doctor staff released him ahead of their original plan.

"Quick! Or we're gonna miss it!" Anna called to April who seemed reluctant to leave Alex's house, where she had been playing for nearly four hours. Anna was wet with sweat, and her loose-fitting work clothes had taken a toll from the delinquent chores of the mansion on Washington Street. "I just got the call; you'll get to see the ambulance, if you're fast enough," Anna said, trying to incentivize the two-and-a-half-year-old. "Come on, Pearl!" Anna said again.

"Is my daddy coming home?"

"Yes, today...right now! And thank you for watching her last minute and all, Mrs. Richards," Anna said to Romney's pleasant and helpful neighbor while looking up at from her fitful task of putting on April's shoes.

"I still can't understand your obligation in the manner of Mr. Daniels, but you have a good, good heart, Anna, and have helped that dear man so much," Felicity Richards complimented as she walked behind Anna and April to the door.

Anna had left the driveway gate open so that the ambulance could pull up to the house. She had planned to be out front to welcome Romney home, but Anna could only walk so fast for April's sake and was delayed further when April started kicking rocks, explaining, "My daddy lets me do this."

"Okay, Pearl. Oh, look it's coming," Anna said, pointing at the approaching ambulance. April suddenly wanted to be held, and Anna consented to speed April along to the house. "Don't worry. We'll be there with perfect timing, because people always get out of the ambulance from the back," Anna encouraged, responding to her private thoughts as April bounced along on her hips.

"The ambylence is a truck!" April commented, clinging to Anna's neck as an anchor. April and Anna finally got to a spot close enough to watch Romney hobble away from the platform.

"My, my, there's a welcoming party at the end of the long parade!" Romney said from between his crutches.

"Remember not too hard," Anna said to the departing daughter who had started charging along to embrace her dad.

"It's okay, Anna. All this was over the top, and the only reason I have these is because I paid for them," Romney excused, referring to the crutches under his arms. Catching Anna looking at him introspectively, he admitted, "All this makes me look intensely crippled, doesn't it."

"Well, seeing that you said it," Anna said, laughing from where she stood emerged in her thoughts.

"Come inside, I'll make you lunch – with what food, I don't know – but I have a few ideas and some good news to tell you before Jeff comes at two," Romney invited, changing his direction toward the house before giving Anna a chance to decline. Anna heartily smiled and stepped further out of the path of the departing ambulance. The ambulance team carefully finished pulling out of the driveway and left the trio with the fading rumble of their engine. "Here, hold these," Romney said, grinning widely as he lowered the set of crutches down to April. "And make sure I don't fall."

"Daddy, they're too big," April naturally protested, struggling to obey her father's facetious instruction.

"You're ridiculous, Rom!" Anna defended, letting on that she wouldn't play along as she stepped up to lend her shoulder. When she had gotten close enough, she felt Romney's heavy hand fall on her for support, but also felt his other hand pull her other shoulder around to face him. Anna challenged his stern expression.

"Anna," Romney said, pumping his lower lip.

Anna couldn't help but let go of her confounded expression.

"You are a great friend, and I have some great news!"

Anna contrived a smile, thinking of her own news that she had been mulling on privately for more than two weeks.

"They found Sandy, and get this, they incarcerated her on not just one, but numerous criminal accounts, and just in the nick of time too for the preliminary hearing!" Romney said in a rejoicing manner.

Anna laughed outright, "And how is this news good?"

"No drugs, no stress, and I can ask to see her at my leisure. What more could a good God give?" Romney celebrated, releasing Anna for the support of his black van.

Anna shook her head and proceeded to start helping April who hadn't let up on tugging the aluminum crutches.

"Whoa, Anna celebrate with me!" Romney said, noting Anna's mood fall.

"You know Rom...Romney, I'm almost jealous, I am jealous. I'm jealous of Sandy because...because why can't I have her...her blessing? This daughter? Boyfrie...husband whatever," Anna said, then shot Romney a painful look.

"Anna, Anna," Romney said softly.

"No!"

"Anna, three things and then...well, I'm stunned. Maybe lunch isn't the best...idea for now," Romney said, changing his voice to command Anna's attention. "One, you don't know who Sandy was, and I do. Two, you are truly amazing, and I have never trusted myself with anyone for my own sake, but that's how far above reproach you are. And, and three, I said there'd be three things... Anna, that desire you just shared is a good desire, and it's not, and has never been, out of your reach," Romney said before he stopped flinching. Anna looked down in distress, and Romney stood silently, analyzing Anna's comment until he concluded what must be going on behind her eyes. "And if I could squash that jerk-of-a-guy, Jon, right now, I would...in fact, April, give me one of those crutches," Romney said intensely.

Still hugging herself, Anna stepped into Romney's chest.

"I want a hug too!" April denounced in objection.

"So, I've changed my mind," Romney said after letting April hug his and Anna's leg.

"How so?" Anna said, standing on her own again.

"I am going to make you lunch, and you're going to tell me if I'm right to be upset with Jon," Romney declared.

"Okay," Anna said, appreciating Romney as a friend more than ever.

Romney let Anna get the door for him as he climbed after April into the smell of roasted turkey. With complete surprise Romney remarked, "What's all this I smell?"

"Oh...lunch is ready, sorry to wreck your generosity," Anna apologized glumly, moving more slowly than she had imagined toward the kitchen to reveal her preparations.

"Wow!" Romney exclaimed. "Okay give me both those crutches; I think I know what this Jon boy looks like; I'll be right back...wow, you know how to impress. Thank you," Romney said, choking up for a few seconds again as he finally allowed all of Anna's blessings to settle on his shoulders.

"Well, it's ready, whether you're hungry or not," Anna directed, picking up steam as she moved two final food items to the preset table.

Halfway through the meal, the doorbell rang, and Romney glanced at his watch. "That must be Jeff already. Where does time go when you're in good company?" Romney let Anna get up as a hostess would to answer the door. "Jeff," Romney shouted from deep in the house, "Come get some turkey!" Knowing things would be slow going, Jeff had wisely arrived early to make sure they would arrive in plenty of time for the courtroom appointment. Jeff respectfully joined the trio for the rest of their short lunch, talking lively until it was time to start heading toward the courthouse. When Romney had instructed Jeff on how to get April out of the house and to the car, he moseyed that way himself. "You sure you don't want to take the van?" Romney asked again.

"No, Cheryl went through all the trouble of digging the car seat out of storage and tying it down," Jeff declared as he walked carefully between the father daughter pair.

When they were halfway down the driveway, Anna saw Jeff turn around and mention something to Romney about her, at which Romney stopped and turned around to somewhat include her in his response, saying, "She hasn't lost my trust yet, and April hasn't had as much quality attention as she's had with her...ever." He then proceeded on after waving another thank you to Anna. "In fact, I should look into putting her name on my checking account."

"Right, I'm starting to think your doctor has a wee bit over prescribed you." Jeff said as he buckled April into the back seat.

The trip to the courthouse was cheerful, then serious, then happy again as their moods shifted between their friendly chatter and the nearing proceedings. Then they slowly tackled the courthouse stairs after Romney insisted, "There's a straight line between the curb and security, and I'm not going to wait here and be blown over by the wind while you go scurrying about looking for a wheel chair. Besides, Sandy is somewhere in there waiting." So, for the extra couple of minutes, while Romney balanced and worked his newfound legs, April danced around at the top of the incline. Once inside, the polished floors glistened, openly inviting hope into the room. Romney felt himself sweating, and while he reached for a tissue in his pocket, a familiar stranger split from a group of suited individuals across the lobby and walked straight up to him.

"Mr. Daniels, sir, may I speak with you?"

Jeff saw a few nervous muscles pulse in Romney's face at the proposition.

Spencer sensed the same hesitation and took a fair step backward to give Romney space to answer. When he didn't grant or deny permission, Spencer dauntlessly took his chance, saying, "I've done you and your family harm, sir, and since the courts won't charge me for what I've confessed, I need to know how I can make things right; how I can repay you for the damages I've caused?"

"Apologize," Romney Daniels stated abruptly.

"Sir, Mr. Daniels, I'm sorry," Spencer promptly said, expecting more tangible consequences to follow. "I'm sorry for...."

"I forgive you, Spencer," Romney interrupted and renewed his original direction and pace.

"But, Mr. Daniels, I want to make things right. What can I do?" Spencer objected, almost reaching out to prevent himself from losing Romney's attention.

"I don't say, 'I forgive you' lightly, Spencer," Romney replied without stopping.

"But what of justice or fairness, I feel like a horrible street rat...at least let me pay you back for the lunch you bought me!" Spencer insisted, moving around Romney. But he felt the protective hand of Romney's attorney impede his progress for sake of his abrupt movement.

"Some things can't be repaired by human hands, Spencer, but if you would like to satisfy your conscience as to what...," Romney said, interrupting his increasing tone. "As to what I mean when I say, 'I forgive you,' and what this forgiveness cost me, follow...me, us."

"Yes, sir," Spencer conceded. The party that he had separated from looked on critically as he proceeded gradually through the lobby. Spencer realized that he did not belong to the 'us' but instead had been instructed to follow. Not knowing what lay ahead, he obeyed and eventually sat down spaces away from Romney's party outside the courtroom where he had freshly been exonerated from his professed crimes. After a short time of waiting, his dad found him, and after exchanging nearby greetings with Romney, he privately chided him, "What are you doing, son? Do I need to pay and to thank my lawyers too?"

"Hey dad, I am thankful, but this is one of the people...many people I've wronged," Spencer admitted and hung his head under his dad's stern face. When his dad again showed his grievous dissatisfaction, he obediently rose and fell in suit behind his father to again offer his sincere gratitude to the lawyers whom had helped clear him of his charges. Then as soon as the Dorkan family lawyers finished their familial chatting and divided up to the lobby exits, Spencer bolted back up the stairs. As he topped the steps, he saw Sandy walking compliantly between two guards to the courtroom. Humiliated, he followed at a courteous distance and saw the polished pews of the small courtroom. Romney's daughter had begun to entertain herself by following the vacant rows back and forth. The girl stopped when she saw her mom and ran to hug her.

About the time Sandy started walking with April to the front of the room, the judge entered, and Spencer occupied the first available seat. The judge started his welcome before his robe had deflated on his chair, saying, "I'm sorry that things are overlapping today. I trust all parties are here and ready for sake of the schedule."

As Sandy entered the gates behind April, she turned to follow her daughter to where Romney was standing next to his representation. When the guards restrained her, she tugged with her arms, nearly yelling, "Let me sit next to my husband." Everybody including Romney looked startled.

When the guards released her at her request, the judge after a short moment broke the bewildered silence, questioning, "This is new. Mrs. Daniels, as this is a divorce case, are you not the one who filed for this divorce proceeding?" The judge in his position of power held up his hand to silence Sandy's attorney from interrupting Sandy's answer.

Sandy paused for a moment, and then after digesting what she had verbally said, whether by choice or by accident, her face changed to match her words. Then privately to Romney she said, "And I've been drug free for almost five days now."

Tucking away his suspicion as to Sandy's motives, Romney didn't care. Taking his wife in his arms and disregarding all civility, he lifted her off the floor despite her bonds.

## Part 3 - Chapter Twenty-Eight

Anna looked around at the refreshed house that she had spent the prior month on and off cleaning. After working another hour on the counters and dishes from the welcome home lunch, she finally had the place clean enough to her liking. Her sigh of contentment felt good to her inside, but as she gathered her things to depart, she caught a look of her well-worked clothing in the hallway mirror. "Nothing to be desired," she instinctively commented to her reflection, lifting the plain shoulders of her loose-fitting shirt. "I could have picked something better," she concluded judgmentally and then shouldered her bag of supplies to leave. After fitting the mop from corner to corner into her car, she pensively drove home. The thirty-minute trip turned into forty-five minutes due to an emergency vehicle on the side of the road, and she spent the extra time deliberating whether to call Jon again and what she would say.  When she finally arrived home, she juggled the two handfuls of cleaning items up to the back door and stopped for a moment to appreciate the progress made on the neighbor's remodeling.  Once inside, she could hear her mom from the master suite working through another episode of her morning sickness.

"Are you okay, mom?" Anna shouted and cocked her ear in anticipation of a muted reply.

"Don't ever get pregnant, Anna dear," Julianne replied from somewhere out of the room.

Anna didn't see the need for such a dramatic statement and instead thought about what her own pregnancy would be like until the Jon's unsettling glance crept back into her mind. Picking up the scattered dishes from Julianne's disorganized lunch to shew away further self-critique, she set about boiling a simple dinner, much simpler and blander – by Julianne's ongoing request – than her welcome home lunch for Romney.  Opening the refrigerator, she noticed another jar of pickles snugly shoved into the door.  Fitly smiling, she removed the older jar and again garnished Julianne's plate of mashed potatoes with four brine-soaked spears.

*--- Another beautiful morning shortly thereafter.*

Jonathan Wickfell's alarm scolded him again for the second time to get out of bed, and finally his roommate knocked his alarm off his nightstand with an autographed baseball.

"Strike," Jonathan moaned without being much encouraged.

"Get up Jon-man, Doxy's out today," Nate said, swinging back around to his computer with the energy of a full night's sleep.

"Doxy?  Man, I'm supposed to be at the station to talk to Officer Petrone and claim my computer," Jon said indifferently.

"Didn't you get a new one from your internship company?" Nate said, snapping his fingers rhythmically.

"Yes, kind of, but I had files on it...mine, that I need to remove, and Jeff said that they might even give me the whole thing back, cause the insurance company really doesn't care," Jon said, finally removing the covers from his legs as he sat up on the edge of his bed.

"Bummer," Nate said, trying to conjure an inquiry from Jon. When Jon didn't bite, Nate continued, "People are starting to ask me when the new magazine's coming to Swanson, and if I can put in a good word for you to hold them a copy."

Jon only half-heard what Nate said as he slid into motion, leaving his sheet and pillow wrinkled and disorganized. Jon slowly started slamming about and eventually made it out of the dorm room.

--- *An hour later at the bustling police station.*

"Good morning," the receptionist greeted.

"Good morning, I'm here to speak with Officer Petrone about my computer," Jonathan replied, harnessing all his energy to make his stated purpose believable.

"I se...."

"I'm kind of late," Jon admitted, scratching at his ball cap.

"I see, I'll give him a call. Please take a seat," the receptionist instructed responsively.

Jon sat down and started answering the string of unanswered texts about Miss Doxy. Between every text, Jon tried putting his phone down and ignoring the periodic buzzing, but he would no sooner convince himself that he was going to quit the business than he would rationalize another two sales. As he started recording his fifth new contact, Officer Petrone came out from behind the buzzing door. Jonathan aborted sending his most recent text message, which was an excuse, "I'm picking them up shortly."

"Jonathan, thank you for waiting. I have the computer back this way," Officer Petrone invited, propping open the door with his back.

Jon thought about speaking, but instead refrained and shoved the phone back into his pocket as he scuffled to shake Officer Petrone's extended hand.

"Your roommate – Nate, is it? – has quite a program to have tracked down your computer. What does he call it again?" Officer Petrone asked, keeping up the pace through the network of desks.

"He calls it a sniping program."

"Well, he really has one of our investigators quite excited over it. I think he might really have something there," Officer Petrone said conversationally. As Officer Petrone pointed at an entryway, he admitted, "In all reality this is quite fortunate for you to get your device back like this. If it hadn't been recovered in conjunction with a different investigation that involved a shooting, it probably would still be out there somewhere wiped clean in some pawn shop."

"Really? Even though we had its exact location and all?"

"In a perfect world, we would have the resources to track every thief...and have a deadbolt lock with finger print scanner on every door," Officer Petrone mused and paused while he signed a sheet handed to him through a window. "But the truth is, you're much better off purchasing a consumer insurance policy like home or renter's insurance to safeguard your items."

"So, I'm lucky."

"Lucky and alive, who could be more grateful?"

"Thank you, sir," Jon said, receiving his fortune. "And didn't you want to speak to me about something?"

"Oh, your police report, I'm going to close it out, that is, if you're happy with our findings," Officer Petrone said, with a shallow grin.

"Of course, sir."

"And tell your roommate to copyright that code before he loses his chance to make a million bucks," Officer Petrone said, walking ahead of Jonathan back toward the entrance.

Jon chuckled briefly but straightened his smile when Officer Petrone bent his eyebrows back at him.

"I'm serious, you might be in college, but if he waits even a week, his code might be public domain, and he'll have copiers like my coworker here before long," Officer Petrone reasoned, dropping the issue to focus on the coming exit.

"Thank you, sir...and for the advice," Jon mumbled, thinking he had lost the officer's attention.

"You got it, sir. And don't let me catch you behind the wheel drinking. Good day," Officer Petrone said zestfully, surprising Jon with his response before he let the security door slam closed.

Jon pulled out his cellular phone and started typing responses to the continued inflow of text messages. Then as the phone continued buzzing, he moseyed his way back to where he had originally been waiting for Officer Petrone. When the receptionist gave him a look from behind the security glass, he asked, "Is it okay if I sit here for a bit?"

"As you wish," the receptionist replied, easing the curiosity in her face.

"All these messages."

"Is having that mobile phone worth it? I had thoughts about getting one," the receptionist spoke loudly enough.

"I hate it, cause once you have it, for some reason, you can't get away from it," Jon explained and returned to the middle of typing a reply message. Yet when he saw an attractive look from the receptionist, he lowered his phone and continued, "I mean, there's no more fussing with coins for the payphone or remembering telephone numbers or...and it...."

"Yes," the receptionist encouraged, giving Jon as much attention as she could from her awkward angle.

"But it...you lose out on the real action, the human interaction," Jon said, connecting with the receptionist's eyes a moment longer than he intended.

"Yes, you make a good point," the receptionist said, without losing her composure.

Coming apart, Jon blushed and tried hiding his eyes in his phone for a moment. Then when he looked up and saw the eyes of the receptionist still fixated on him, he smiled sheepishly and left the lobby. One of the messages he had received on his phone was from Markus at Miss Doxy. "Stacks of Miss Doxy here, calling your name; come by noon and I'll drop you an extra bundle." Jon had messaged back, "Okay, on my way." That response was twenty minutes ago, and noontime was imminent. As he exited the lobby toward his car, he received another message from Markus: "Bring your car, I had to make Dan mail your last bundle." Then a few seconds later: "I took the liberty of doubling your order. I'll explain when you get here before NOON!" Irritated, Jon made two more sales, again to new customers, before putting his frustrated foot on the gas pedal. When his phone vibrated again after he had pulled out of his parking spot, he tossed it aside with annoyance and surrendered his attention to the radio. The radio host announced a tune he had liked so well because of Anna, and anticipating its obnoxiousness, he slammed the radio dial off again. Lowering the windows, he let the flapping wind distract him as he used the remaining strength of his car to guide him toward the small magazine distribution office downtown. When he arrived at Miss Doxy, the street was bustling with its pre-lunch crowd. He parked and sat there with a convicted conscience for a minute. "It's me or Miss...you don't care...or Miss Doxy...really?" Jon mumbled to himself until he popped his door open to silence his gibberish. The door to Miss Doxy looked the same as it had the month prior, and he pushed through it to find Markus again in a white shirt worked through with sweat. The disgruntled looking owner stopped when Jon came through the door and tried putting a smile on for show.

"Your pickup time was eight a.m., dude, do you have a problem keepin' track of it? You have your car back, right?" Markus initiated, moving toward the back room.

"No...and...."

"No? Really, you're going to lug all eight reams?"

"No, my car's working again; I finally got the money to fix it," Jon explained.

"Good," Markus said as he slammed two solid blocks of magazines on the small front counter. "Six more's a-comin'," Markus said without slowing down.

"Say, what happened to the price of Miss Doxy last month?"

"Last month?" Markus grunted, as he swung two more bricks onto the counter. "We had to pull all the second printings and didn't have time to revise the issue for the usual third and fourth printings," Markus explained, pausing for a moment to start his answer.

"Did the printer go down or something?" Jon asked, wondering how he had earned his small fortune. "Who's this?" Jon suddenly asked, fixated on the lewd cover of the magazine.

"No, the printer didn't go down; one of the models falsified her age when we interviewed her, and her family lawyer swore to sue the devil out of us," Markus answered, only hearing Jon's first question. The fifth ream nearly pushed one of the first two off the counter, and Jon caught the falling bundle in the cradle of his arms.

"That's...is it?" Jon said with astonishment, looking up at Markus with a face flushing with heat.

"Oh, Dan got his old girlfriend to finally go nude on the front cover. The guy's a demon, but the girl...man, I even bought an issue! And I own the place!" Markus remarked, misjudging Jon's remark as he walked over to the remaining bundle of magazines.

"No! Noo!" Jon exclaimed, throwing the block of paper to the ground with a deep thud. "Nooo!" Jon yelled wildly, scolding the lifeless picture that stared back at him with attractive eyes.

"What the...," Markus said, not having reached the remaining bundles.

"No!" Jon yelled, turning his fury on his pseudo boss, and kicked the horrific delivery. Jon kicked it again up against the counter. "Why?"

Markus, in return, walked up to Jon and grabbed his shirt and pushed him back off balance. "Get out, lunatic!"

"No, I'm sorry, I'm sorry; I'll take them, I mean I paid for them already, right?" Jon responded, dramatically changing his tone as he sat himself up on one arm from his punishing fall. His thoughts were as ludicrous as Markus accused. He impulsively swore to himself that he would take and hide all the magazines, and then burn them, and then tear each one into hateful shreds. Though his brain was not yet cured, the shove to the floor had fixed his face enough to convince Markus that he would be glad to take all three-hundred and twenty copies to his car on the double. Markus skeptically backed off and watched Jon clownishly move in and out of the front door to his trunk. The last time Jon heard the dangle of Miss Doxy's front door bell, he glanced shamefully up the street and paused in reignited fright at a striking image of Anna Purse a mere stone's throw away. He chased himself out of his momentary trance and threw the last bundle haphazardly into his trunk. Then he scrambled for the cover of his car. After checking his mirrors multiple times and seeing no one familiar he laid his head on the steering wheel and felt cold with sweat. Two taps on his side window scared him straight. With wide eyes he saw Anna's unmistakably made up face and heard her half-hearted voice. His own heart sank, and his embarrassment made it impossible to stay looking at Anna. Jon's confusion settled barely enough to hear Anna muffle through the glass, "Please, Jon, let me in, and explain this to me." His neck refused to accept any more weight, and he hung his head. Without acknowledging Anna's third light knock on the window, he turned over the engine and pulled the car into gear.

Anna watched Jon drive away and felt her heart bleeding as she stepped backward all the way to Miss Doxy's front window. Anna sunk down, using the business's tall panes of glass for support when her knees shook like they were the pillars Samson himself was pushing against.

From inside of Miss Doxy, Anna's bump on the window caught Markus's attention, and after watching the red-headed girl slide further down the window, he thought it noble enough to check on her. He stuck his head out the door, causing the dangling bell to interrupt Anna's focus.

"You okay, Miss?" Markus asked with his most sincere tone.

Anna looked up at the man looming out the door and caught sight of the Miss Doxy sign sticking out overhead. "You don't work for that horrible Miss Doxy too, do you?" Anna objected, carelessly flinging her opinionated tone.

"Now whoa, I'm not a moralist, and you can check, I've paid my taxes every month on time. If this was illegal, okay, let the government shut me down. But people love buying Miss Doxy, so don't be hating me for obliging them," Markus said defensively, moving his back foot to the sidewalk to legitimize his height.

Anna didn't respond for a moment and didn't worry about raising a defense. Anna did though screw up her face at the intense sunlight bending through the front door of Miss Doxy as Markus started to retreat from his position. Tracking his movement, Anna spoke at the final moment, "Do you know Jon? Jonathan Wickfell?"

Interested that the girl had responded, Markus replied, "Yes, I'd say I do, depending on who's asking."

Anna couldn't get out another cohesive thought and let Markus disappear with his self-validation. She took a moment longer, plaguing herself with second and third guesses of whether it was right for her to have posed herself as a Miss Doxy buyer to catch Jon red-handed, or if she should have let him alone with his dignity, or if she should have approached him in some less definitive way. A thump from behind her encouraged her to her feet, and Anna saw Markus's backside and then the shocking cover of what he had dropped alongside the window. She then, with a hesitating step, hurried back to her car and disappeared into the lunch hour flow of traffic.

## Part 3 - Chapter Twenty-Nine

"Hey, Cheryl! I'm out!" Jeff Dunnire shouted upstairs to the hallway.

"Okay," he thought he heard in response.

"Hey, dad?"

"Yes, bud?" Jeff asked his son.

"What do pigs eat from the grocery store?"

"Uhh, I don't know, Justin, what do pigs eat?" Jeff said, mindfully wrestling between his commute to work and the call for attention from his son.

"Grosseries, dad, they eat grosseries!" Justin replied, laughing at his own joke in his pajamas.

"Hah, that's a good one, Justin. Keep your mom happy, okay? And come here and give me another hug."

"Okay, but I love you more, dad," Justin said after releasing his dad's neck.

"No, I don't think so, I love you more," Jeff said, hugging Justin again harder.

"No, I love you more; I won!" Justin said, giggling as he scrambled out of reach of his dad's arms.

"Bye, Justin!"

"Bye, dad!" Justin returned, watching his dad close himself out of the house.

"Now, where to recruit?" Jeff said to the rearview mirror as he backed out of the driveway. The recent uptick in profitable business had his board of directors pressing him to expand his leadership team. Naturally, Jeff had wanted to promote his current employees, such as Patrick or Camille, but the board already had disqualified each of his suggestions. After seeing a helicopter clap overhead, he started to dream up the ideal solution to fill his vacancy at Scales Architectural Company. Forty minutes later he set down his phone and stood up to greet

Jack Hense from across the cafe table. "Thanks for meeting me on such short notice, Jack," Jeff said, cordially offering him his hand.

"Well. I'm nervous, and not for your sake. I'm uber early for my first real date in a while...a long while," Jack admitted, sitting down and surveying the view. "You're not going to be more than a few, are you?"

"That depends on how long it takes to convince you to let me hire Romney away from you," Jeff said confidently.

"Romney? Daniels? We'd have to change the name," Jack said, obviously distracted and planning for his next event. Jeff's eyes soared with hope. "But...and you know Rom – probably better than I do now – Romney's a big fish to catch, and he's loyal."

"Well, let's trade fishing advice then," Jeff suggested, catching Jack's attention for a moment.

Jack chuckled and looked at the table, having given himself away. "Let me guess, you want to know what I think it would take to get Romney to leave his own company to work for you," Jack guessed, recovering well from his break in character.

"I know Jack Hense doesn't date frivolously, so my advice is to be a friend. And if you befriend this gal, and she is servable...serve her till she smiles...every day," Jeff said, leaning back in his chair to signal he had done his part.

Jack again looked half-interested and tilted his chin back as if still considering the trade. Then he picked his phone up and dialed a number. "Hey Romney...yeah, yeah; I'm sitting across the table from Jeff Dunnire. Yeah, Jeff Dunnire; he wants to hire you, and I want to buy your part of the company...all of it. You're ridiculous, okay, then twenty-percent. Well, think about it. I was thinking about demoting you to Theresa's spot anyway, you've been slackin' all this time lately," Jack negotiated and then laughed. "Yeah sure, for real Jeff is workin' hard behind your back. You'd better give him a call and set things right. Yes, sir, Nancy will be here in a bit. I'll call you later about it, and think about your price for twenty."

Jeff stood up with more hope than ever in his success, and the waitress came running over. Jeff started briefly explaining the situation to the waitress. Then Jack interrupted by calling out to a lady that had entered the cafe. Jeff glanced at Jack and then in the direction of his holler. Supposing it to be the gal in question, he turned and picked up his coffee cup and replaced it with an inverted cup from the next table. Disappearing toward the cash register and letting the waitress take over the task of making the couple comfortable, he paid his bill and paid the couple one last glance before he left the cafe for his office.

## Part 3 - Chapter Thirty

"I want to look pretty for mom!" April said adamantly.

"I'm not saying you can't, Pearl," Romney said with his arms stuffed in the closet. "In fact, I think that's a good idea!"

April sunk to the ground to pout. Breakfast had turned into a disaster after Romney poured the last bit of April's prized cereal into his own bowl. He hobbled around as skillfully as he could manage to get dressed for their first visitation with Sandy.

"How about this? It's a pink one," Romney encouraged.

"Mom likes pink," April said, budging from her fussiness.

"Oh, maybe we shouldn't choose pink then; we don't want mom liking your dress more than your pretty face."

"But I want the pink one!" April said, latching onto her new disappointment.

"Oh, this one?" Romney toyed.

"No, that's not a pink one," April said with a child's scolding tone.

"Oh, my bad, the pink one," Romney continued and carried on for a few more minutes till April was dressed in her perfectly pink outfit. The drive was short enough, and Romney occasionally looked back at April to see her still gazing curiously out the window. The longest part of their crosstown trip seemed to be over the numerous speed bumps that led up to the penitentiary. Halfway down the long and straight entrance, April started giggling at the lurch of the van.

"You think the speed bumps are bumpy, don't you?" Romney accused, losing his disgust for road bumps for sake of his daughter's attractive attitude. Then Romney slowly moved with his daughter into the visitation center. The guards didn't at all match the rigid and cold mood set by the numerous gates and check points. When the dog came to sniff April, she latched onto the dog's collar to pat it on the head. The smallness of the girl didn't faze the tough dog, but the dog eventually barreled back when it wanted to be finished with the inspection. April tried for a shy minute to get her dad to stay with her so that she could play more with the K9 officer's pet, but Romney reminded her that it was about time to see mom.

When April stepped into the visitation center, her eyes lit up. Sandy sat there waiting amongst a few other families and stood insecurely to her feet. Then April hit her with a charging hug. Romney's proud look caused Sandy to break into her old smile, and she lowered her hand down to April's silky head of hair that was pinned against her leg. Romney stepped up and gave his wife a hug of his own. "You should have seen how much love April tried to give the guard dog a few rooms back," Romney said.

"You look so adorable!" Sandy said, dropping down to April's height.

"She picked it herself." Romney commented.

"Yeah, cause you like pink so much," April claimed proudly.

"I do, I do," Sandy said and then moved back to sit more comfortably on one of the low picnic tables. "Join me, would you, handsome?"

"Certainly, beautiful."

"You've always made suits look good," Sandy said, still savoring the touch of her daughter.

"What's all this complimenting," Romney said, half-skeptical of Sandy's new outlook. Sandy simply smiled, and Romney followed the curves of her face around to find her eyes subtly admitting an apology.

Sandy averted her gaze to April while touching her eye with her knuckle and explained, "You'll see, hopefully."

"The food good?" Romney asked, though more curious of Sandy's vagueness.

"Best food I've nourished myself with for a year. Maybe I'll plump up," Sandy claimed, puffing out her cheeks and nestling April's resultant giggles.

"Let me, mom.  Let me!" April reminded, asking to poke her mother's air-filled cheeks.

"Let me try," Romney said playfully, reaching up with his right hand.

"Do mine, dad," April begged, puffing out her own cheeks.

Romney complied with her request and simultaneously felt Sandy drop her head to rest on his shoulder.  "How can I apologize, Rom?" Sandy asked privately.

Romney interrupted his game with April and encircled Sandy with his other arm.  After a moment's thought, he suggested, "You know a wise woman once told me, 'I'll forgive you when you don't do it again,'"

Sandy laughed when she identified her own words in Romney's answer.  "You know, Rom, I didn't ask you to forgive me just now."

"You didn't?"

"No, I want to know how to apologize for something like this," Sandy said, avoiding Romney's eyes again by looking at her daughter.  "But seeing that you brought it up, will you?  Forgive me?" Sandy said, ready for anything to hit her ears.

"Every time you walk through the front door you're forgiven," Romney said with a smile on his face.  "So, long as it's our front door, and by the way...," Romney clarified.

"April's hair is so long; look at it."

"By the way," Romney repeated, "I bought us a new home on the top of Mount Lincoln."

"Oh really, please don't say it's yellow," Sandy said playfully.

"What? You stopped liking yellow?"  Sandy's wet eyes laughed at Romney's reaction.

"It's yellow, mom!" April spilled with laughter.

"I know," Sandy said, rubbing the side of April's arm.  "You know that whole hiring the private detective thing I have to apologize for also," Sandy continued, directing her disclosure at Romney.

"None needed, but I do need to know something," Romney answered.

"Oh, hold on, April, daddy has a question for me," Sandy said, hushing April's new call for attention and her tug toward the nearby pile of toys.

"What's your opinion of Anna Purse?" Romney asked.

"Did you have sex with her?" Sandy asked.

"No."

"Did she 'sleep' over in my absence?"

"No."

"She behaves like a marriage-breaker," Sandy said clearly.

"Hah," Romney said, thinking of the validity of Sandy's perception. "I...," Romney started and fell quiet as he watched April start to play with another child in the visitation room.

After a toilsome minute, Sandy asked, "Why didn't you?" Sandy looked provokingly at Romney, then turned down her chin for a second. She waited for a long second for Romney to speak, but she spoke instead to quiet her doubtful thoughts. "I was kind of hoping we were even somehow." She saw Romney curl his lips up to repress the tinge of emotion that lined the edges of his eyes. "I understand if you hate me; you have every right...."

"I hate what you did, Sandy, but never you," Romney corrected. "I can't wait to show you what the crew has done to the yellow house. It'll be a good house for us, unless you want it a different color," Romney diverted.

"Are you kidding?" Sandy said, grabbing her husband's hair with both of her hands, looking for permission to kiss him.

Romney and Sandy diagnosed each other's looks after they shared a light kiss for the first time in over a year. Then Romney noticed other families starting to filter out of the visitation room, and he looked for direction from the visitation monitor before admitting the time to Sandy. He stood and reached for Sandy's hand. Taking it in his and calling for April, he said to Sandy, "Jeff Dunnire called and offered me a job doing what I'm doing now for less money at his company. Maybe we can talk it over when you call next time."

"Only if it's a phone date," Sandy propositioned, gathering April in for a long hug. "Till next time; keep your dad company for me, Pearl, will you?" Sandy asked. "And kiss him every night for me too."

"Do you like jail, mom?"

"No, it's a horrible place, bunny," Sandy said, scrunching her beautiful nose.

"Then you should come home with us," April said innocently.

"No, Pearl, prison is a good place for me right now, and when the prison doctor says that I'm better, I'll come home to you; so, keep your room clean and be good for dad," Sandy said, tearing up as she spoke. "Cause when I come, I'm gonna have presents." Sandy said, forcing her cheerfulness.

"Do you hear that, dad?"

"You bet-cha."

"When mom gets better, she's gonna have presents for me," April said, dancing over to Romney's other hand.

## Part 3 - Chapter Thirty-One

Terrance didn't stay in one place in the cafeteria very long as he spread the news. Three other teammates along with Terrance agreed to surprise Chad with having the school turn out at the hospital to cheer him past the news that his dad wasn't recovering well. This group of four were last out of the locker room and briefly planned the idea over their three-minute walk back to the cafeteria. Each agreed to put in five dollars with the intention of making their idea come to life. Rob, the first baseman, assigned the duties on a good whim. Sean collected the petty cash and headed to the bookstore to buy some cheerful things at Rob's bidding. James agreed to call the hospital to arrange for a crowd of people and avoid being a nuisance. Then Rob took it upon himself to somehow organize transportation for students that couldn't drive. Terrance naturally took to the task of spreading news of the idea and finding people to come. After ten minutes of aggressively approaching every seated group in the cafeteria, Terrance got a call from the accountant of the group saying that he needed at least two hundred more dollars 'to make this epic!' Terrance had no problem including a donation pitch to the cause of cheering up his friend. Fifteen minutes later he texted back to everybody, "We have $635 dollars now, any ideas?" Rob, the spontaneous leader, didn't sit on the information long, but sent word along to the transportation organizer of the college to check if he could rent a bus for the day. Terrance had also told Rob that a hundred people had tentatively agreed to show up, especially if they could find a lift. Terrance kept telling the students what was happening, where to go, and when they had planned to meet. "You're an attractive girl. Do you have plans for this afternoon?" Terrance extemporaneously asked a gal that had smooth blond hair.

"No, I'm not interested. Thanks," Bethy responded confidently, instinctively sending her attention away from the strange bold boy.

"Well, that's too bad, do you know Chad Wattsworth from the baseball team?" Terrance asked rhetorically, unwavering. "You see, his dad was attacked and was sent to the hospital last week, or a few weeks ago really, and he got word a few days back that his dad's not recovering well and might die. The news has really been affecting his game and school work like you'd expect it would," Terrance said effectively, easily keeping up his pitch for the girl's participation. He continued, "A couple of his friends, me included, wanted to try to cheer him up a bit and thought that we'd extend that opportunity to everybody. If you don't have time to go see him at the hospital today, maybe you could donate a couple dollars instead, or if you have a vehicle maybe you could drive a couple people."

"Oh, I don't have one. I'll be an incoming freshman this fall semester," Bethy interrupted a bit presumptively.

"Oh-hah, and they don't let freshmen drive, I see," Terrance said, connecting the presumptive dots after translating Bethy's objecting finger and hand movement.

"But my friend Anna has a car, and she could probably take me and three other people. What time is the rally?"

"Oh, it's not a race, just a little cheering up episode of...well, maybe we should call it a rally. That's a happy sounding thing, right? But it's at two-ish," Terrance said, not one for party planning. He laughed along with Bethy's magnetic giggle. "There's gonna be a bus, if your friend Anna can't make it happen," Terrance added.

"Oh, a bus rally! Does this Chad person know you're doing this for him?" Bethy asked, now interested in the details.

"Well, I hadn't thought of that. I hope Rob is – he's the cheerleader – I hope Rob's given him a call," Terrance said, looking again at Bethy's sparkle.

"I hope so. It sounds like it's gonna be fun...or at least full of cheer," Bethy said, briefly glancing around the cafeteria while letting Terrance go away to catch another couple walking down the lane. A few seconds later she caught his fast wink back at her. After she had looked away in search of Anna, she heard Terrance return to her spot with a general apology.

Terrance leaned over the table and personally said, "I'm sorry, I've been so rude. I'm Terrance, people call me 'T.' for terrific, and I didn't get your name," Terrance introduced and saw hesitation in Bethy's blue gray eyes. Terrance instinctively picked up, "Okay, don't tell me. Let me guess...Bianca, Jessica...Maria?" looking for clues in her reactions.

"You were close the first time; it's Bethy."

"Bethy, don't forget to invite your friend, Anna. That's not Anna Purse by chance, is it?"

"It is! I'll tell her."

"Good!" Terrance said, bounding away to the couple he had caught moments prior to his belated introduction.

Bethy sat calmly for a few more minutes, her ears entertaining her thoughts as she listened to Terrance floating boisterously to other groups in the cafeteria. In the midst a happy thought that prided itself on her lips, Bethy saw Jonathan Wickfell. Thinking they might have a similar agenda of meeting Anna, she tried calling out his name. When he didn't seem to respond, she gave up, not wanting to draw too much attention to herself. Jon transferred through the cafeteria a minute before Anna entered. Anna recognized Bethy with an eager hand and walked up to her. "I just saw Jonathan. You can probably catch him if you hurry," Bethy informed, matching the energy of her friend as Anna lowered her books.

"Ah, I'll let him go," Anna said uneagerly. Bethy put on an investigative left eye until Anna noticed. "Oh yeah, I don't think Jon and I are going together anymore," Anna explained, laughing away the mute critique. Anna felt guilty, so she continued, "Jon's a great guy, but I think we're on different pages. That's okay, right? I mean, what do you think?"

"Yeah, yeah, don't let me fret you any," Bethy said. "You know him more than I did, for sure," Bethy said, giggling as briefly as Anna did out of sensitivity.

"Yeah...," Anna agreed with a sigh. "He's a good guy, don't read me wrong!" Anna expressed again. "He's the one who walked me to the car when Spencer came and tried intercepting me on campus. You remember?"

"Yeah, you told me." Bethy said.

"He had no clue but played along perfectly."

"That's too bad, he was dating a great girl," Bethy said, trying to feel out Anna's true sentiment.

"Nah," Anna discounted with an appreciative smile.

"Of course, you're the one with the crush on this businessman...and his daughter," Bethy playfully punched when she sensed Anna shutting down.

"Romney?" Anna replied instinctively. "Okay, you got me. But he said it best."

"What? You actually talked to him about it?"

"He's smarter than you think, but he helped me see what it was and what I was infatuated with; he's very much taken," Anna said, looking down at her dancing fingernails.

"So, Jon didn't measure up then." Bethy concluded for Anna.

"How could he?" Anna said, feeling better that she hadn't thrown Jon under the bus.

"How did he take the news?" Bethy said curiously.

"Well, it...it kind of was an unspoken thing. You'd think he...or I'd be more emotional about it," Anna said, scrunching her eyebrows while looking again for validation in her best friend's face.

"Hey, change of topic, do you know a Terrance or a Chad? Chad Wadsworth, I think," Bethy said, keeping her mood positive.

"Wattsworth is the pitcher for the Varsity baseball team, and T. is the catcher."

"Tease the catcher?" Bethy questioned teasingly.

"Yeah, Terrance. Well, actually it's T. I might of misspoke, but he is quite teasing sometimes," Anna explained.

"Well, Terrance approached me about a rally at the hospital for Chad's dad, I believe at two today. You want to go?" Bethy proposed.

"Sure, what happened to Chad's dad?" Anna asked as honestly and curiously as an investigative reporter would ask.

--- *Meanwhile in a sketchier part of Pittsburg.*

With a fresh conscience and good intentions to shun his dishonest drug-dealing days, Spencer successfully made his way to a bus shelter on the outskirts of town after he had sold his car to a nervous lady buyer who had contacted him by phone that morning about his online classified. She had paid on the spot in cash and only afterward had she queerly inquired as to his intentions for selling the car and his plans for the money, which he honestly divulged to her rather immaturely. Presently, a tall man dressed in thick jeans at a bus stop noticed Spencer's shivers and tapped his breast pocket in search of a cigarette. "Hay man, you need a fix?" he asked, offering his open pack to Spencer as a far cry solution for the boy's obvious discomfort. Spencer declined after a contemplative moment, but seconds later he swept his own pocket, looking for the comfort of a small package that wasn't there. Then he tightened his fist on his small duffle bag. As his long bus ride dragged on toward one in the afternoon, the gray mess of the sky finally sprouted sunshine. He watched a few intriguing characters on the side of the road while thinking back to the strange part of town where he had turned his car into cash. The whole private sale of his car seemed off, yet regardless of the lingering uneasy feeling, he had pleasantly gotten the asking price of what he thought his car to be worth. His plan of heading to the hospital with the good intention of compensating the courageous man who had stood up against, and got shot by, his old friend, Trist, replayed in his eyes as the world blurred by in the scuffed-up bus window. He had Mitchell Reed's name from the e-mail interchange and had a good lead as to his whereabouts from a call he had placed to the nearby hospital. As the hospital complex came into view, his temples started pulsing again. Then he got up from his seat to disembark and noticed a mean-looking car prowling by the bus. Hunching down to watch it for a blurry second, he discounted the likelihood of it being his, though it certainly was of the same

make, model, and color. Spencer tracked the progress of the
look-a-like car for a few more seconds as he proceeded to step
off the bus toward the hospital. Tucking a hand into his pocket,
he tightened his grip on the small duffle bag until the familiar
sound of his old growling engine caused him to turn around.
The suspicious car screeched into position while Spencer took a
few more disinterested steps.

In a cold second, the window was down, and Trist yelled from
inside, "Hey, look what I found!" Trist's friend, unfamiliar to
Spencer, got out of the passenger side of his old car and started a
slow pursuit. Trist roared the engine and let it hush before he
yelled again, "So...who gave you the go ahead to start ignoring
my calls? Wiffet isn't happy with you by the way."

Spencer looked ahead at the half mile run to the hospital and
thought hard about dashing to the proximity of safety, but when
he glanced behind him, the pursuer, who by far exceeded him
physically, was already within a tackling stride.

"What's the point, Triston?" Spencer complained, giving up on
the idea of making the long sprint. Before he heard Trist's
answer, his body stopped working from a sharp knock on his
shoulder blade.

The strong youth easily caught Spencer and pulled him to the
car in his brief state of paralysis.

In a delayed response, Trist proudly explained, "I'm here to
collect the proceeds from the sale of your car...the car itself
being my reward for bringing you in to have a talk with Wiffet."

Spencer's shoulder and neck ached horribly from the prongs
of the stun-gun, and as he rubbed what he could reach he said,
"You're ridiculous...and out of money again."

"At least that thing didn't zap your brain clean," Trist said in
his twisted manner. "Though the stupid in the twerp still made
him think he could disappear," Trist said, addressing his
counterpart. "And this is Farley's cousin by the way, not that
you care anymore about your homeboys."

"And how's he treating you, Farley's cousin? You getting a cut
of the car?" Spencer asked, starting to get annoyed at his
predicament that was taking him farther away from his planned
course.

Farley's cousin exchanged a glance with Trist, then said, "Give it to me," referencing the bag strapped over Spencer's good shoulder. Spencer didn't resist, relinquishing the small purse.

"Count it," Trist ordered, as he drove intently toward somewhere.

"You know, Spence, I'm kinda disappointed. We had a good thing going," Trist admitted at a stop light.

"You lost me when you started hurting people," Spencer said, secretively handling his phone before shoving it deeply into his pocket.

"It's all meant to hurt people; but forgive me if I started hurting your conscience," Trist said unapologetically.

"Twenty-eight...thousand," Farley informed dryly.

"Where's the last hundred bucks?" Trist flashed back to Spencer.

"I ate lunch with a homeless man and bought him a new shopping cart," Spencer said dispassionately.

"You would have been smarter to have kept the car," Farley's look-a-like reasoned.

"Shut up, and keep him in the car," Trist ordered as he parked in front of a brick storefront. A sign with the prominent letters F.P.O. jutted out over the unblemished glass door. Trist walked confidently into the pristine one-story building. Two well-dressed guards intercepted Trist when he started walking directly toward Wiffet's office, and a short scuffle proved Trist the superior fighter. The senseless match interrupted the meeting taking place in the transparent office, and the other business looking guests appeared a bit more concerned than Wiffet did when they turned around from their cushioned seats. The groomed businessman excused himself and solicited the assistance of his secretary to comfort the concerned guests.

Trist nearly punched the bag of cash into Wiffet's stomach, saying, "There you go."

Having approved the details of the private deal, Wiffet simply handed the bag off to a guard and instructed the guard as Trist had done already, "Count it." Then addressing Trist, he simply said, "Mr. Palanco, we'll settle this out back, but you currently have upset my customers. Please excuse me."

The two suited guards led Trist out the side of the lobby and down a hallway to the back of the brick building. Acting professionally courteous until the door pounded closed, the two guards had no problem pacifying Trist when they had the upper hand of surprise. When the two men relieved the towering guest of his handgun, Trist noticed they had put on black gloves. Trist didn't lose his pride and stood up to his intimidating height as Wiffet appeared from the same door a few seconds later. Then three more similarly dressed men appeared around the corner, following a less than compliant Spencer.

"Mr. Palanco, you'd make a great bodyguard, and I'd be inclined to offer you a job...," Wiffet said, trailing off as he put on his own set of gloves, but continued, "...That is if you didn't owe me ridiculous amounts of money." He took Trist's handgun that was handed to him and inspected both sides of the barrel as Spencer approached. "But...this is a good sign...this is a sign of good faith." Then without warning, he raised the barrel at Spencer and fired a round. The bullet sounded nothing like a bullet but more like a closing dumpster lid. "I do say," Wiffet continued with aghast, "Your sights are terribly out of alignment."

Spencer collapsed helplessly unconscious under his own weight.

Wiffet inspected the open side of the barrel once more then took extra aim at Spencer's still body and pulled the trigger again. "You'd better get that fixed, or you're going to end up accidentally shooting someone," Wiffet recommended as he handed the weapon back to a member of his security team. Two suited guards already were lifting Spencer by the hands and feet, readying to swing him into the nearby alley dumpster. Wiffet finally removed his gloves, and definitively said, "You're one hundred dollars short, Mr. Palanco, but that's not impossible to have here by closing time, right? After all, you were able to pull off your creative little ploy. Well...almost." Wiffet turned his attention to the guard holding Trist's gun and asked facetiously, "We close at five-thirty today. Don't we?" After the guard nodded and Wiffet disappeared, the guards ensured Trist left by way of the alley.

Spencer stared up at the sky from the open-air dumpster, wondering if his dad had received his short distress message, "Help," from the short drive over. And if he did, Spencer wondered what he would make of the message. His thoughts drifted to Romney and how he looked on the ground after he and his crew had laid him out on his lawn. Then they fell to Mitchell Reed and how he must have felt trying to survive his similar fate. But in his final seconds, he smiled at the thought of his redemptive motive and hidden accomplishment, however failed it might look to everyone else, as the blue sky turned gray.

## Part 3 - Chapter Thirty-Two

"Hi, may I help you boys?" the receptionist asked the two athletes who approached her counter in the back of the hospital lobby.

"We're here to see a Mrs. Hannah Wenzel?" Rob questioned, looking for clarification at James.

James smiled at his taller teammate to tell him he spoke correctly.

"Oh, you're those boys; I'll dial her right away," the receptionist said with experienced fingers.

"Thanks," Rob said with energy, listening to the reverberation of his gratitude in the grand lobby. He tapped his foot and listened to the small slap of the sound against the walls. "This could get quite loud; what are your ideas?" Rob observed, looking for input from his teammate.

"I think, get a line of people starting as far back as needed on that long drive up to the hospital," James suggested.

"Yeah, that's good. Let's try to make sure his closer friends are inside here but not past the elevators."

"The people outside need the biggest signs."

"And the most energy...and they'll need to know somehow which car to start going crazy over," Rob added.

"Flashers, like at a funeral! Funeral's a bad example, but I'll tell Sean to turn his flashers on as soon as he enters the drive," James volunteered.

"You know that phenomenon when the crowd starts chasing the car and ends up collapsing in on it as it arrives?" Rob asked.

"Yeah?"

"That's the image I'm picturing," Rob described.

"I think, put me in charge outside and you organize the inside crowd, so we can 'boost' him to the elevator where he'll disappear, and then I'll dismiss the crowd back to the buses and cars," James suggested.

"Perfect...."

"That sounds good, gentlemen," a solid voice said from behind them. "I'll admit, I was worried a bit about upholding the decorum of the hospital when one of you told me the number of students that you had planning to come. Hi, I'm Hannah, and this is James and his team, in charge of security."

Rob and James had spun around as Hannah interjected her introduction into their brainstorming. "I'm Rob and this is James too, except he guards third base. Terrance and Sean will be arriving with Chad Wattsworth at two-thirty or so."

"This is a first for us here at the hospital, and believe it or not, I just spoke with President Allen Vye from Vern Hill. He was telling me how you represent the college well on the ball diamond, and he trusts that you'll do the same here."

"Well, I can't take all the credit, the four of us...."

"He's also planning on attending," Hannah remembered.

"Oh boy."

"I just got expelled," James said with a theatrical face.

Hannah finished settling the agenda of the boys and gave a few private directions to the security officer before dismissing herself. Rob called Sean on his phone after Hannah stepped away from the huddle and communicated the new plan. Then Rob listened to the supplies Sean had gathered and purchased. As soon as Rob hung up, he said, "We have two buses coming, and Pitts Limousine Service is donating both. We just need to tip the drivers." Rob had started looking at his mobile phone, reading as he spoke. Then he added, "And R&T's Pizzeria is providing pizza at cost if we pay for delivery."

"Will it be enough to feed everybody?" James said half-bewildered. "...And what if not as many students show up as anticipated?  Then there's passing it out and the clean up!" James fretted almost seamlessly.

"Good points!" Rob admitted.  "Hannah!" Rob shouted, catching the gray-suited manager before she disappeared into an elevator.  Rob took a couple of quick steps in her direction.  "We have pizza coming, and a lot of it, like one hundred boxes worth."

"Don't worry a bit, I got this one; just have whoever is delivering the pizza drop it off at the far end of the lobby, and I'll send down our expert kitchen staff to take care of the rest."

"There might be lot's left over," Rob stated with concern.

"Employees love that kind of thing," Hannah assured.

"Great!"

"Great," Hannah said, smiling grandly as she gravitated back toward the elevator.  "And thank you for caring about your friend and his dad so much."

--- *Less than two hours later in Anna's sporty ride.*

"So, this Chad person asked you to the formal thing?" Bethy queried, looking over at Anna who looked very uncomfortable handling the steering wheel.

"Well, yeah, but the fundraiser is really my mom's thing, and she likes going with somebody," Anna explained.  "It's awkward for her, so I offered to go when I knew she was hoping."

"Hoping for what?" Bethy said, feeling a bubble of excitement.

"A date; wouldn't you?" Anna asked but continued, "She's never had anybody."

"What?  Anna come on!  Your mom?  You've told me yourself, how many unpleasant men you've found in your house...ever since I've known you!" Bethy said, drawing her defense from conversations of years past.

"No, not like she's never been 'with' somebody, I mean she's pregnant now; but nobody has ever...nobody has committed...men just use her because she's available.  And I can't blame them, it's not like she plays hard to get."

Bethy paused her interest for a few moments, then said optimistically, "So, you're going to be a big sister; imagine, I always wanted to have a baby sister."

"Yeah, I remember that, like for a whole year in middle school!" Anna said, laughing with her rosy cheeks.

Anna didn't take long to find a spot to park on the parking deck, and soon Anna and Bethy we're following the convenient signs to the hospital lobby where they ran into James for a moment who pointed them toward the front door. Both girls could smell the pizza and watched for a moment as three R&T's Pizzeria employees where carrying in stacks of boxes in from the far side of the lobby. They found their way among a few other students up to a different table stacked with blank poster boards and open boxes of thick permanent markers.

"Take one and walk out to the entry way. Write something encouraging to Chad," someone directed. "Thanks for coming. Keep the pen, come back for pizza after Chad arrives," the same person announced.

"I guess the pizza is for us," Bethy said with surprise.

"I guess so," Anna agreed, taking a fat pen.

"Get a different color, Anna; I took purple," Bethy suggested, having passed through the line first.

"Sure," Anna responded, tossing the similar color away in exchange for a blue one.

"What should I write?" Bethy asked as the girls fell in line behind of a few other early arriving students.

"I don't know...was about to ask you the same thing," Anna said weakly. After they walked a few paces out and found a spot to hang out their signs into the drive, Bethy scribbled some big letters on her sign and showed Anna. "That's good; should I write the same thing?" Anna complimented.

"Noo," Bethy said, bumping into Anna's shoulder. "You got to be original."

"I'm not coming up with anything that sounds right," Anna said, waving the open marker around at the blank poster.

"Okay...I know you're preoccupied with something that you're not telling me, probably Jonathan Wickfell, but...."

"Yes," Anna interrupted. "Would you tell him I don't have any hard feelings, and that it's not anything...not anything...that it's not...," Anna stumbled.

"Meant to be? You should write him a letter," Bethy suggested.

Anna considered Bethy's idea for a moment, then said, "No, I just need to pull up my bootstraps and tell him."

"You'd sleep better and feel better; but I still don't get it...it being why you stopped liking him," Bethy said, giving back into her curiosity.

"Why should it be all about this mutual liking; it started off – I mean our relationship – started off well...maybe with a bit of that, but...," Anna said, losing her train of thought as her sign caught a burst of wind.

"You've been a little busy lately," Bethy stated. "Whoa buses, and those are like charter ones."

Anna didn't look, but instead she scribbled a bold message on her flimsy poster board.

"This makes more sense, why they sent us out here. Look," Bethy said, pointing.

Both girls watched and moved briefly with the flow of students to a new spot down the curving driveway, listening to the student in charge loudly repeat the same instructions as he made trips around the poster supply table. "So, we're looking for a car with flashers," Anna remarked in response to the distinct instructions given over the general noise of the crowd.

"With these many eyes looking for the same thing, I doubt we'll miss it, and look, they even have the security officials. I guess they know how college students behave," Bethy said, enjoying herself.

After a few false alarms of different cars over the course of thirty minutes, the crowd finally discovered Terrance, Sean, and Chad. Chad looked pleased while Terrance climbed out and started engaging the crowd. Terrance saw an inspirational poster and yelled out the words while signaling everyone to chant. James, who had already started curling around the back of the slow pacing car with a few other students, caught on immediately, echoing Terrance, "We love Chad!"

"I can't hear you!" Terrance shouted, cupping his ears.

"We love Chad!" everyone continued. The speed of the chant picked up until most students gave up yelling and resorted to cheering as the three ballplayers rolled up to the hospital lobby. The sound of the crowd was deafening for a moment as Chad exited the vehicle with a disbelieving smile and entered the hospital. When the noise died down to a general humming,

James and Rob shouted the next instructions, which rang with effect through the student body like a surfer's wave.

"Pizza's inside, he said," someone nearby relayed.

"Alright; I hope the insiders leave a slice for me," his neighbor responded.

"I think I'll just go wait on the bus."

"Really?"

"Yeah, it's too early for dinner."

"Kay, suit yourself."

Anna and Bethy overheard the interchange, and when Bethy looked over at Anna, Anna spoke up, "I'm going to pass on the pizza."

"You're not going to hate me if I partake...if I stay? I'll take the bus back."

"No please...please don't let me stop you," Anna said.

"Anna, you go; I'll take the bus home," Bethy said, pulling close to Anna's ear when she had realized the guy heading toward the bus was Jonathan. She observed Anna, wondering how long she had known that Jonathan was nearby. A few moments later she saw Anna intentionally bump into Jon like a friend and saw Jon turn with shy surprise. Completely intrigued, Bethy stepped out of line to observe the interchange. After an indistinguishable dialogue, she saw an awkward moment happen between the two and both looked timidly to the ground. Then Jon said something that made Anna laugh, and the two looked at each other with a pause. Anna reached out and barely touched Jon's shoulder again like a friend leaving a dinner party. Both students looked over at Bethy briefly, and after a small wave to her friend, Anna departed for the parking garage. Bethy stepped back in line for the pizza and grabbed a whole box of pizza at one of the hospital worker's bidding. Then she walked around the table of leftover pizza boxes, knowing exactly where she wanted to sit to eat. Proceeding directly to the first bus, she stepped up the stairs and scanned the few students onboard. Not seeing Jonathan, she stepped off after a polite apology to the driver and walked to the second bus. After greeting the next bus driver, she saw Jon's head pop up over one of the captain's chairs. With a few more steps, she plunked down into the chair

next to Jon and said, "So what's going on with you and Anna?
You want some pizza?"

"That's a big box of pizza."

"Yeah and they have like fifty more inside. I'm not even a
college student yet, but you know this is pretty snazzy."

"Snazzy, that'd be a pretty good way to describe your friend,
Anna," Jon said, elusively tucking away his phone.

"Here; sorry, they were out of plates, but they had these dinky
napkins...so, I grabbed a stack," Bethy explained, turning the
pizza box toward Jon.

Jon considered the offer twice, then reached for a slice. When
Jon saw Bethy waiting for him to start explaining himself, he
said, "Anna...wow, you have an awesome friend."

"Then what happened?" Bethy accused after a lull, when Jon
didn't elaborate.

"I'm new at this whole dating thing, and we agreed that we
both were so busy with school and stuff that...yeah," Jon said.

"I normally don't think of break ups going down this way, they
need a little more heartbreak and drama," Bethy admitted
between bites of pizza.

"Anna?!" Jon said, nearly choking on his food. "Dramatic?"
Jon negated, shaking his head over his wad of napkins. After
successfully swallowing, he continued, "You know when you sit
down with somebody for a conversation and you run out of
words, and you can tell they want to leave, and in fact you want
to leave too, but neither of you want to be rude?"

"Okay, did you guys run out of things to say?"

"Basically," Jon agreed, tilting his head before he started on the
wide end of his pizza.

"Cause see, I don't believe that," Bethy blurted out
convincingly.

"What?" Jon said as playfully as Bethy did.

"Anna's way too pretty, and you're way too interesting to just
mutually fall apart," Bethy said decidedly. "Besides, you act like
you're in mourning."

"Okay, I see why Anna and you click; you're like a nutcracker,"
Jon said, covering his mouth with his folded slice of pizza as
Bethy smiled proudly. "You don't stop until you get nut cases
like me to open up," Jon said to explain his insult.

"Is this seat taken by the way?" Bethy asked, randomly.

"I'm afraid so, Beth."

"Bethy. You better not call me Beth again, and I can move whenever whoever comes back."

"Bethy, nobody's coming back."

"Good," Bethy said. "Then I'll stay awhile; Anna left me here anyway."

"Yeah right. Anna would only leave you if she had to rush somebody to the hospital, and we're at the hospital."

"That's what I don't get! She's more loyal than anyone I know...so, what's going on behind all this mutual parting facade?" Bethy said, doubling down on her investigation.

"You're good."

"And you're not telling me everything or anything."

"Well, what do you want to know?" Jon said, smiling with tension.

Bethy gave Jon her flirtatious inquisitive look.

--- *Minutes prior, after Anna and Jon's parting.*

Anna privately ventured back into the hospital and up the elevators. Getting off at the familiar floor, she hoped to find a familiar face to ask about Chad's whereabouts. Walking to the corner nurse's station, she found Nancy eating her lunch. "Hey, Nancy," Anna said with her envious smile.

"Anna! What are you doing here? I've missed seeing you these past weeks."

"I'm here for Chad Wattsworth this time," Anna eagerly explained.

"He's one floor up, I believe," Nancy said.

"How's Jack?" Anna said, with a teasing expression.

"I know, it's so embarrassing," Nancy said, hiding her face with her hands. "I don't ever date. But Jack has been spoiling me."

"I'm just teasing, Romney mentioned something over dinner."

"You...and Romney?" Nancy inquired with surprise.

"Oh gosh. Everybody probably thinks that," Anna answered, turning red. "He's helped me out in more ways than one, and I was fortunate to find a way to repay him by watching his daughter."

"You're too sweet, but I won't hold you back from your destination. Thanks for stopping by!"

"Oh, no problem," Anna said, taking her cue to step toward the elevator. After ascending one floor, the elevator opened, and she saw the small huddle of teammates in the hallway. A bit intimidated, she turned around, but she was too late to step back onto the elevator and pressed the down arrow instead. Then she heard one of the teammates inform Chad as she waited. "Anna!" Anna heard her name as the elevator opened. Swinging around, she saw Chad standing outside the hospital room in front of his friends, looking her way. Seeing all their eyes fixed on her, she called upon her smile and asked her heart to speed up. Walking shyly to meet Chad as he too stepped toward her, she asked, "So, how's he doing?"

"He's doing well," Chad replied at the awkward meeting spot halfway between the room and the elevator.

Anna then finished the remaining distance and gave Chad a hug. "And how are you doing?" Anna asked, feeling the further weight of everyone's attention.

"Good. This is all too much for me. I can't thank everybody enough. Thanks for coming! Really!" Chad expressed. "I think I saw your sign driving in," Chad continued, nervously saying the first thing that came to mind.

"One of the many out there, I'm sure."

"No, but I saw you," Chad said and glanced back when there was a sound of some commotion at door of his dad's hospital room.

"Well, I won't keep you, I just wanted to see...to see how you were doing."

"Yes, thank you. I'd ask you to stay, but he's going off to surgery soon...but...," Chad said, turning around again to look at Anna. "Thank you. Hey, I'd like to talk...to talk with you about...about sometime talking about the fundraiser. I'm sorry...," Chad said, retreating after he heard his name urgently called out from behind him.

"Sure," Anna replied and saw Chad stop for a moment to acknowledge her. Reading the obvious look on his face, she offered him her consoling smile before he stepped off toward his dad, who was being wheeled away on a hospital bed.

# Part 3 - Chapter Thirty-Three

Bethy shoved the devoured pizza's box with its few remaining pizza crusts down to the floor of the bus when Jon had started to explain his upcoming assignment at Scales Architectural Company.

"Willies?" Bethy inquired. Bethy had her shimmering straight hair draped over her shoulder, and the confidence from her natural beauty sparkled. Blond and hardly in need of makeup, she was a magnet for the eyes of each male student that periodically boarded the bus.

"Wickies...great charity actually; Patrick introduced me to the family that runs the orphanage," Jon replied.

"Have you got to meet any of the kids?"

"Once, but only a few were awake. My job was to map out the house and design the extension."

"You got to design it?" Bethy clarified with her interest. "I mean where do you even start?"

"You start by looking at what you've got and then sit down to ascertain what the occupants envision. But more so, because it isn't a heavily funded project, I've had to whittle down the grand vision to something practical that will meet their needs," Jon said, catching a few of Bethy's straight looks.

"Wow, do you get to build any of it?"

"Patrick said he might let me manage the project a bit, so I'd be that guy in the white construction hat with the big design scroll mapping out...."

"Hah," Bethy responded.

"What? It's serious business." Jonathan said, grinning from underneath his sideways ball cap.

"Here we go," Bethy commented at the releasing of the bus's parking brake. Jon pulled out his phone after it buzzed a few times, looked at it, then tucked it away. "You're a busy boy," Bethy said as she watched.

"Yeah, I need to retire from something," Jon responded, pushing back in his chair to stretch.

"Like what was that about?" Bethy asked.

"About one of my jobs; it can wait," Jon said, trying to look amiable. "Actually, I'll need to head to the bank because of it."

"You said, 'jobs,' as in more than one, which I assume you're counting your internship," Bethy said, sending her attention across Jon's face and out the bus window.

"Well that's one, the...I picked up a pretty good paying job on the weekends at Butler's Station too," Jon listed.

"Where we all went!"

"We did, we did; and I didn't realize how expensive it was," Jon said, squirming a little into his arm rest. "Well actually it's because...," Jon started then shied away from his addition.

"Yeah?" Bethy prompted to prove she was still interested.

"Well, I guess you can tell Anna," Jon said, looking into Bethy's uniquely colored eyes.

"Like no secrets? Thanks for not trying to tear best friends apart," Bethy said, acting like she lost interest in the rest of Jon's story.

"Actually, I took Anna there, but I couldn't afford the bill, so I had to work it off that weekend."

"And you got hired?"

"Yeah, apparently, you don't need a college degree to wash dishes."

"You need to do some banking...the one on campus?" Bethy reminded with amusement at the implications of Jonathan's disclosure.

"No, but it's not too far. Do you want to tag along?" Jon said, then backpedaled on his invitation. "You by no means have to."

"I'd rather hang with you than by myself, waiting for my dad on campus."

"Bah, you wouldn't be alone very long, if I had to place a bet on it," Jon said, attempting a compliment.

"So?" Bethy said, watching other talkative students rising to exit the bus.

"So? Walk or drive?" Jon said impartially.

"Walk definitely. We just ate a pizza!"

"Okay. It's...it'll be about a mile; shall we?" Jon invited, following Bethy off the bus. Bethy started down the smooth path at the edge of the large parking lot that led off campus.

"You know we might have to book it, 'cause I think the bank closes soon," Jon said, looking at the vehicles littering the parking lot.

"How soon?"

Jon slipped out his phone to look at the external time display. "Thirty...thirty-three minutes," Jon declared with stressed lips.

"A mile? We got this," Bethy said, frolicking down the sidewalk ahead of Jon. Jon smiled and hopped into a limp jog. Bethy came back to Jon and grabbed his wrist, pulling him playfully up to her trotting speed. Both jogged youthfully and came to a stop at the crosswalk to the main road, but neither looked like they wanted to admit that the quantity of pizza they had consumed might be affecting them. Both held in their pride until they looked at each other and laughed. "Okay, we'll walk...like descent human-beings across this...this busy street here," Bethy said, acting the part of an expert in charge. They laughed again, until the crossing light turned white. "Which bank again?" Bethy asked as they started between the parted traffic.

"Trusted Union; do you know it? Three more blocks, right, then three more blocks."

"Thirty minutes, bah," Bethy scoffed again playfully. "Do you race?"

Jon looked at Bethy with surprise at her question and asked, "Race?"

"Do you race?" Bethy said, hiding something within her expression.

"No, you might get a jogging mosey at best out of me," Jon said, forgetting about his destination as he tried decoding Bethy's face.

"Well that's too bad...because loser buys dinner."

"Wait! What?" Jon objected as Bethy took off running toward the end of the first block. Jon heard Bethy coltishly yell something out to the breeze. Without understanding her message, he started into his own overtaking pace until the first stoplight put both runners back at the same advantage.

"I so get to start first," Bethy said with her hands on her knees, supporting her shoulders.

"Nuau-a, not with dinner on the line," Jon contested, ready to race after he felt his heart catch up to the increased demand that he had placed on his calf muscles.

"No, you were so five seconds back."

Jon looked at Bethy's convincing eyes and said, "Well okay, only if we agree to walk across the street...no more of this skirting death dodging cars stuff."

"Okay, mom," Bethy said grumpily as if disappointed.

"Hey, I don't want to see you hurt," Jon said authentically, glancing at the cross lights in anticipation of the restart.

"Me hurt? You don't know who you're dealing with here," Bethy espoused, straightening her back.

"What; are you some secret track star that's trying to snooker me?" Jon asked skeptically. When Bethy didn't answer and instead inventively grinned, Jon continued, "Oh boy, I'd better up my game."

"Oh, you're taking this seriously now?" Bethy accused, trying to disrupt Jon's more focused stance.

When Bethy took off at the recommencing signal, Jon shouted, "Liar!" and quickly scanned the street for moving cars. Jon hesitated for a moment but knew a five second lead would leave him more than thirty yards behind the racing girl.

The next light fortunately caught Bethy and gave Jon enough time to catch up before the crosswalk changed. The timing worked in Jon's favor and Jon sportively yelled, "See you there," as he passed Bethy's stationary starting position.

"Hey, you little cheater!" Bethy objected, leaping into action.

Jon turned around and ran a few hobbling strides backwards but gave up immediately as Bethy intensively closed the short gap he had created. Impressed with Bethy's speed and flapping ponytail, Jon called out jestingly, "Well...I'm gonna call you lightening!" Only then, as Bethy pulled into the lead, did Jon notice that she had on sneakers, and active outdoorsy type clothing. He started smiling as he trailed and struggled to keep Bethy from launching ahead. Bethy reached the front door of the bank first, turning with pride to Jon who had conceded from his position a few yards behind the winner.

"You owe me dinner, and soon," Bethy touted.

"Ha...how about double or nothing; I'll race you back," Jon said, huffing a bit as he tried to upright himself to approach Bethy with dignity.

"I don't know, you look beat already."

"I'll hand you that, you take my breath away," Jon said, trying to match Bethy's wit.

"Oh, do I?" Bethy asked suggestively, playing up the boldness of Jon's double entendre.

Jon stepped up and opened the door before he realized that Bethy might have been waiting for him.

"Oh boy, looks like we made closing time rush," Bethy announced.

"Glad you made it," a well-dressed manager said after they entered the interior set of doors. The atmosphere of the bank was lax as a few people waited. Both Jon and Bethy noticed a few people pull on the locked doors and resort to the automated banking machine outside.

Jon filled out a bank slip and signed a few of his checks, and after they had stood in line for a few minutes, Bethy said, "You're lucky...and still owe me dinner."

"Why so? The lucky part," Jon asked, distracted by a beefy customer that seemed to be having difficulty with the automated machine outside.

"They obviously don't close when you thought they did."

"Oh right," Jon said instinctively. "Oh right!" he repeated when the fact had sunk far enough into his distraction.

"We actually got here ten minutes after they were supposed to close, according the times posted there," Bethy said, pointing to the outside window.

"You can read backwards," Jon absently commented to Bethy's blank face.

"I don't think smashing the ATM will make money appear," Bethy independently observed as Jon was called up to the teller window.

"Can I do tens, twenties, fives, and ones, but mostly fives and tens," Jon queried to the smiling teller who also was distracted by the large man who had flippantly transferred his frustration with the ATM to his yanking on the locked doors. One exiting customer allowed the heated man through the first set of doors.

The few remaining occupants of the bank seemed to be nervously waiting for the bank manager to return and deal with the unusual fury. The teller nimbly finished with Jon's transaction and started clearing her station. When the barred customer noticed this, he started expressing his rage in Bethy and Jon's direction. The teller continued her hurry to the backroom as Jon began tucking away his withdrawal into the offered tight-fitting envelope.

Fortunately, the teller reappeared from the back hallway with the manager, and the manager briefly addressed Jon and Bethy. "Could you wait for a moment?" the manager asked while proceeding to the bank doors. "May I help you, sir, the bank lobby is closed," the manager politely inquired after letting himself through the first set of doors.

"Aw no, you have customers standing right there."

"Our automated teller system can...."

"Is broken garbage, and I need my money," the man provoked.

"Okay come with me, and let's see," the manager invited the intimidating customer back outside.

"No, I'm not falling for that; you're going to help me inside."

"You'll be doing us both a favor, because I need to know if the machine is actually broken, and you'll be serviced faster if I can get it working for you, because it appears to be working now," the manager said, pointing to a customer walking away with money in hand. The man reluctantly complied and followed the manager outside.

The jittery teller approached Bethy and Jon with two leftover cookies on napkins. "Would either of you care for these," she said, referencing the cookies.

Accepting both the courtesies, Jon said to Bethy, "Here you go, dinner is served."

Bethy couldn't keep her disapproving face straight while looking at Jon's facetious smile, and Jon couldn't keep his eyes from Bethy's model face.

When both heard a thump against the outside glass, Bethy objected, "Nuh-uh," and courageously rushed to the doors. Jon saw the customer shove the manager into the glass a second time and stood momentarily in disbelief as Bethy made it through the first set of doors. Jon reactively spun into action as he saw the continued physical rage of the furious customer. Bethy didn't seem to notice that the assailant was much larger, but she charged anyway, intent on interceding for the balled-up bank manager. Jon intended the same for Bethy, objectively predicting the outcome of the mismatch. Luckily, Jon caught Bethy who had exchanged her approach for some aggressive words. Jon wrapped Bethy in his well-meaning arms and saw a wrathful hand coming at him as he swiveled Bethy out of the way. Jon felt the painful tug of his hair and released Bethy to fall to the ground. A second after he had let go of Bethy, he felt his trajectory reverse, and the angry fist sent him to topple on top of Bethy.

The abusive man bent down and jawed through his teeth, "Don't mess with someone else's business." Then without pausing, the man removed Jon's envelope from his back pocket and walked off immediately.

"So, what in the world?" Jon reacted, rolling off Bethy's back.

"I do declare there, Master Jonathan that you seem to be falling head over heels on my behalf," Bethy quipped, as her adrenaline rush came abruptly to an end.

"Funny girl," Jon said, holding his head where the man had grabbed him.

"Are you two okay?" the manager asked with much concern, after recovering enough from his own state of shock.

"...Will be, after I treat this girl to dinner," Jon said naturally.

"Dinner? Yes!" Bethy announced with a victorious fist.

Almost laughing, the manager smiled and continued, "The man just took off with your bank envelope, sir, please come back inside, if you're able." Sirens were heard a few blocks away as the threesome moved slowly through the locked bank doors. Once inside the lobby, the manager announced his reaction to the nervous teller.

"You'll be wearing that one for a week," the teller replied with relief, shivering at the sight of the manager's split eyebrow and swelling eye cavity. The bank manager then proceeded to the back room to see if he could find something to address his forehead.

"You okay?" Jon asked, touching Bethy's shoulder. "You just marched right out there and were about to engage some six-and-a-half-foot dude that had arms the size of my thighs," Jon continued after Bethy didn't respond.

"I'm hungry," Bethy said with more confidence than Jon had expected. Then the police pulled up and sprang out of their cars defensively as if a robbery was still in progress. The manager rushed to meet them with a string of satisfying words, and the teller surprisingly walked up to Jon, handing him an identically stuffed envelope along with a sincere apology. Jon and Bethy felt trapped as the lead officer talked back and forth with his dispatcher on his deafening hand-held radio for long minutes, obviously prioritizing them last to interview.

"Can we leave?" Jon asked the manager on the side as the officers filtered in and out of the bank.

"Could I ask you both a few questions before you do?" the officer stoically replied instead, overhearing Jonathan's shy request.

"I'll go check and see if the security footage from the back is ready," the manager said independently, already moving away from the whirling confusion toward the back offices.

The few questions seemed comprehensive enough and were answered in spurts of awkward laughter on the couple's part. Then the couple left and ate simple food at one of the few restaurants they found on their walk home. From there, they walked back to campus and continued talking in the cafeteria without either one feeling a second of the two hours that passed.

Jon asked Bethy, "Why don't you have a purse? I've been meaning to ask."

Bethy said, "I'll get it tomorrow from Anna; I forgot that I'd left it in her car." Then they continued their rounds of laughter and teased each other as they waited for Bethy's delayed father to come by the school. Roger Berkshire eventually showed up with a simple apology to his daughter. Declining the apology, Bethy tried introducing Jonathan Wickfell.

"It's nice to meet you, young man," Roger said briefly, before informing his daughter of his packed agenda with a single look. "Thank you for accompanying my daughter tonight, Mr. Wickham," Roger said flatly before he departed.

Jon tried to correct his name but surrendered when Bethy interceded and apologized with a flash of both her blue-gray eyes and knee-weakening smile.

Bubbling with energy, Bethy retold the story without so much as a single interruption from her dad all the way to their hotel. Roger seemed remotely interested at the end of her account, but he seemed more interested in Bethy's earlier encounters and opinions of the indoctrination tour. Eventually they glided contently up an elevator and said goodnight to each other as Roger waited outside his hotel room for Bethy to close her door. After Roger heard the noise of Bethy's interior latches, he snuck into his own suite to join his sleeping wife.

# Part 3 - Chapter Thirty-Four

Earlier in the day with plenty of time before dinner, in their gated mansion that lacked nothing a billionaire would desire, Sir Byron and Kloe Dorkan had invited Jack Hence and Jack's new hospital friend, Nancy, over for an evening meal. Of course, news of Jack Hence dating was news indeed, and Jack, having been a highly sought after and wealthy bachelor, had few people he confided in more than Kloe Dorkan, who was the wife of their prime investor, the proud Sir Byron Dorkan. Jack privately wanted her opinion of his girlfriend, Nancy, which Kloe of course had already determined within five minutes of them arriving.

"Your phone's vibrating, Byron," Kloe called from the kitchen.

"Let it vibrate," Sir Byron replied without concern. "You guys just started dating?" Sir Byron continued.

"Is that what we're calling it?" Jack Hense replied to Nancy's happy face.

"I guess so," Nancy said. "Can we say that after only spending a handful of afternoons together?"

"Nancy, what do you do?" Sir Byron asked like an interruptive parrot.

"I'm a floor nurse...."

"Byron, your phone's vibrating," Kloe called again.

"Well answer it, if you will," Sir Byron called, twisting his shoulders around to look at the kitchen.

"I think it's a letter message from Spencer."

"Oh, what trouble has the drug-lord gotten himself into now. What does his message say? Bring it here." Byron responded, holding out his hand to wait for Kloe to deliver his phone. "Help. Now that's super descriptive," Sir Byron commented after reading the text at arm's length with strained eyes.

"When has Spencer ever sent you a letter message like that?" Kloe asked, taking a seat in the open chair next to Nancy.

"Last time he asked for help it cost me twenty-five thousand dollars to bail him out of his guilt trip."

"You were proud of him for that though," Kloe reminded, making Byron grumble with admonition.

"Give him a call, Byron," Jack invited.

"Nah, he can wait. I'll help him after our conversation. We need to discuss Romney."

*--- Two gunshots and a bank tussle later, Trist fled with frustration.*

"Awful people," Trist steamed, after climbing into Spencer's old car and launching back to Wiffet's hideout. He pulled the petty cash out of the patron's envelope to count it at the next stop light. As tough and cold-hearted as he typically was, the memory of Spencer falling to the ground welled up Triston's face like a painful ankle might infuriate a runner. As soon as he found a red light, he tore his mind away from the thorn-ridden memory and picked up the cash to count. Then halfway through his counting, a whoop of a police siren caught his attention. Putting down the cash, the light turned green, and he started through the intersection. He relaxed as the siren waned away from him and continued the few more blocks to park in front of the brick and mortar F.P.O. building. Trist finished counting the two-hundred and fifty dollars there and pulled out enough twenties to pay his immediate debt. Climbing out of his friend's car, he strutted like a proud man into the open office and dictated to the two guards that had overpowered him earlier, "I'm here for Wiffet."

"Why don't you take a seat?" the guard mockingly offered.

"Keep dreamin'. This ain't a holiday joint," Trist refused.

Wiffet finally appeared and looked up from a document he was reading. He looked disturbed for a moment as he looked passed Trist and then offered, "What can I do for you, sir?"

"Don't act like you don't know me. You get your money, and I don't shoot up the place," Trist said, pulling out the one hundred dollars to slap down on an open counter. Suddenly alerted by the sound of screeching tires, Trist turned to find his getaway vehicle blocked in by squad cars. Officers strategically surrounded the car, and after they surveyed the area, they noticed a suspicious figure bolting to a side hallway inside the building. Instantly forming a plan, the lead officer directed his counterparts around to the side of the unit. They proceeded cautiously and maneuvered progressively around the second corner of the building in pursuit. The air was fowl with smell, and one of the officers pointed out some dried blood splattered on the ground, the place where Spencer had been shot mere hours earlier. The officers moved silently and communicated their guesses as to their next move with their hands. After clearing the concealed sides of a few boxes that were stacked against the wall of the dead-end, the lead officer suggested, "Let's go question the guys inside." They all began to retreat to the street front, when one of the officers threw up his hand. The search party froze. One by one they all agreed that they heard some muffled vibration coming from the large open-top commercial dumpster, and they all obediently took shelter at strategic positions. Then the lead officer started blindly negotiating, "We're blocking the alley. Come out of the dumpster. We're here to take you in for questioning." With no response after multiple attempts, the negotiator sent the trailing officer back to the squad car for a smoke grenade and orders to call the situation into their dispatcher. When the officer returned with the grenade, the lead took it and said loudly, "Casey, you have a good arm. Get ready to put this right in the center of the dumpster, and don't miss. Sir, for our safety and for your own safety please identify yourself and climb slowly out of the dumpster." After another final warning, the lead officer said, "Throw it." Casey complied and put the armed smoke can right in the center of the dumpster. Initially there was scurrying around the dumpster, then after twenty seconds as smoke started

slowly rising, the suspect started coughing for air.   After a
minute with the lead officer growing impatient, the group heard
Trist give up, between choking gasps.

"Okay," Trist surrendered.  "Okay."

"Climb out slowly and lay down facedown with your arms
out," the lead officer barked.

"Okay, okay, what's the big deal anyway?" Trist objected.

"What are you running from?" the lead officer questioned.
"Pat him down and read him his rights.  He matches the
description from the bank assault."

The lead officer walked over to the back of the unit and
touched a strange chip in the wall.  "Casey, call back to dispatch
and see if you can get a forensics team out this way before
nightfall.  That looks like a bullet scar and this looks suspicious,"
the officer diagnosed.  "I'm going to climb into the dumpster in
a few minutes to see what kind of evidence the suspect tried to
bury."

"Sir, the manager of this place said that they are closing now.
He just locked up the front door," a respectful officer said after
hustling to relay the timely information to his superior.

"See if he will come and make a statement."

"He made a short one already, he said...."

"Bring him back here, if he'll come."

"Yes, sir," the respectful officer said and hustled away.

Wiffet came, following the respectful officer a half-minute
later.  "Sir, I'm Officer Marty Petrone.  Do you know this man?"
Marty investigated, pointing to Trist.

"Not personally, but he's a customer, officer," Wiffet
responded.  "I'm Michael Gallant, by the way, please let me
know if there's anything I can do to help.  As far as I know he
was coming to finish repaying the cash advance I had loaned
him.  He hasn't done anything wrong by me as far as I'm aware."

"Well, you might be lucky, because a guy matching his
description just assaulted a bank manager not more than ten
minutes from here and not more than a half-an-hour ago," Marty
said, pulling out his note pad and writing something down.

"It's not the best part of town, but the security team I employ
does a great job mitigating the obvious threats."

"Do you have any security footage of this alley here I could have access to?" Marty said after finishing a scribble.

Wiffet smiled as if embarrassed and explained, "Money's tight, but that was the most recent recommendation. And as you might imagine, this is a prime spot after hours for all sorts of things I'd rather not think about."

"Seems so. Do you mind if we have a team canvass the place? I need to get in that dumpster, unfortunately, in a minute to see if I can find anything our suspect didn't want us to see."

"That doesn't sound fun."

"Hey, Mr. Gallant," Marty heralded as he saw the manager turning to dismiss himself. "Could you send me the transactions for the loan you spoke of earlier for your customer? ...Something that would identify him here."

"You know, Mr. Petrone, I slipped already in disclosing the information about the transaction. Something we advertise to our customers...to build trust, but if you come back with a warrant, I won't give you any trouble," Wiffet promised.

"That's all. Thank you for your cooperation," Marty said, turning back to the dumpster. Putting on a full gas mask and some leather gloves that a teammate had brought him, he climbed up over the edge of the open-air dumpster. "Well, our day just got dirtier," Marty admitted, standing up and lifting his mask off for a second. "Call for a stretcher, we have a body in the dumpster. I'll need another someone to volunteer to get up in here to lift the body out. Don't argue too long please," Marty said, sliding down again onto the floor of trash. Marty squatted carefully next to the body, trying to forget the stench of the surrounding trash and the irritation of the gas that had slipped inside his mask. When he heard the same vibration noise of a phone in the boy's pocket amplifying itself against a scrap of aluminum, he said, "Why thank you little guy." Then he stuck his hand into the boy's pocket to retrieve the device.

--- *After dialing the last number used on the discovered cellphone.*

"Hello, who is this?" Sir Byron Dorkan greeted fifteen minutes after he had initially returned his son's call. "Officer Marty Petrone, well, good evening. I take it my son is somewhere nearby. Well, I suppose he'd be calling me in a minute for the 'help' he was requesting earlier. Let me guess, station number 2.

JOSIAH HUTCHISON

Oh, you wouldn't be assuming anything. He's gotten himself into things too bad to speak of in the past. ...Yes, sir. ...Yes, sir. ...That'd be an accurate description." Byron said, and then he listened to Officer Petrone as he briefly described the lifeless state of his son. "I'm sorry. Thank you, officer," Byron said, holding off all emotion. Concluding the phone call, he sank down into the couch. Kloe happily came into the sitting room but stopped when she read the blankness on her husband's face. After one look at Kloe, Byron's jaw started trembling terribly, but he managed to say, "W…we need to go the station, dear."

--- *Before the end of the final summer semester.*

Anna Jane Purse had two note books full of class notes sitting in the passenger seat of her car, and each note book corresponded to a final class exam scheduled for that morning and afternoon. Though she had had ample time to study for the tests and had already finished her other summer course exams, she still planned to arrive to Vern Hill early and gloss over the notes. Leaving the worries of Julianne and her pregnancy at home, she sped across the bridge with the car windows open. The galloping noise of the beams reminded her again of Daniel Mills, which reminded her of Romney Daniels, and which reminded her of his precious Pearl. Once into the city, she past the horrid home site of Miss Doxy, which she had not been aware of before Jonathan. Yet after Jonathan, she soon started noticing the vulgar covers constantly around campus. In her final conversation with Jonathan she had told him directly, "I hope you have the will power to quit." She didn't really understand his blank stare or what had come over Bethy when she called the next day to tell her about Jon and the bank incident. But that was already two weeks in the past. She pulled into the large parking lot and found a spot facing the baseball field. Seeing players on the diamond, she decided to grab her notebooks and take to the bleachers for a few minutes of studying. Choosing a spot a few rows up the vacant rows, she took a seat. Then she looked over and saw a few older onlookers observing from behind the home plate and another in the bleachers near the away team's dugout. She easily picked out Chad Wattsworth and then Terrance. After spectating for a few minutes, she dropped her head down into her first notebook and let the comprehensive notes resurface all the key points of her second summer semester's history class. After forty minutes or so, she had finished her final review and looked up to relax for a minute. There weren't as many players on the field as she had expected. She only counted eight, including the batter and coaches. The coach was shouting something foreign to the players, and Chad responded by lifting his hand and showing the ball to the fielders. Then pitching it with little effort, the players went through some rehearsed motions of some play. When the coach seemed satisfied, he dismissed the few members standing on the field, and everybody started walking down the sidewalk back to the towering gym. Anna caught Chad Wattsworth's eye, and he lingered for a minute around the exit. A few of the ball players looked up at Anna then back at Chad, grinning to each other as they filtered their way through the exit in the fence. When Chad waved Terrance on, Anna's heart started beating more intensely. Then Chad stepped up the bleachers rhythmically and sat down next to Anna without asking for permission.

"So, you gonna ace these exams like you did the last ones?" Chad said, expressing the thought he had contrived.

"It should be easy enough," Anna admitted. "You? Do you have any left?"

"We'll see how I did on this one," Chad said unenthusiastically.

"Like as in baseball?" Anna questioned.

"True. I was contacted by a scout. You might have seen him standing by the coach."

"Really?"

"He said that I might have a second-string offer waiting for me in the majors," Chad said. "The offer's even before graduation."

"Before the fall?" Anna asked.

"No, before I graduate as a senior." Chad explained.

"You wouldn't be finishing then," Anna clarified.

"Right, that's the downer. Hey, I caught Jon in the lunch room the yesterday – your Jon – and we got to talking about you," Chad said, redirecting the conversation.

"I didn't know you two hung out."

"We don't, but we live in the same dorm, different floors, but still...are you okay?" Chad said, expressing what concern he felt he could muster.

"Yeah. What's he saying?"

"We didn't talk much...he just looked depressed, and I had heard you two were together. So, I sat down and asked. He confirmed it and then said you two weren't anymore, that it was something he did...stupidly," Chad said, trying to abbreviate the hour-long conversation.

"That's nice, Chad." Anna said, her voice faltering.

"I don't mean to intrude."

"Have you thought about Julianne since you saw her last?" Anna asked weakly and looked harder than ever at the star pitcher to see his reaction.

Chad couldn't keep his head up. "Yes, a thousand times over." Chad said with embarrassment.

"Do you know she's keeping the baby?" Anna said, ready to analyze Chad's reaction.

"Baby? Anna, I did not have sex with...your...," Chad defended himself when he read the presumption on Anna's face.

"Okay, good. Though I wouldn't have blamed you if you had," Anna said honestly.

"You're looking at a guy that has no idea what he's doing. And I mean, I was interested all semester in you, and call me dumb and stupid, but I wanted to meet your mother to ask her...to ask her about you," Chad spoke with a defeated hand waving in front of his face. "And that debacle of her inviting me over made me second guess what I wanted...and she's pregnant, and you've been thinking all this time that I'm crummier than I even thought I was myself," Chad said, feeling his nerves come loose. "Oh, boy. I'm sorry. I'm really sorry. None of that's directed at you, but you're sitting here. Wow, what's it been two and a half months now? Pregnant, wow, I didn't see that one coming."

"Yup, very pregnant," Anna said, laughing to relieve some of the tension she had created. When Chad looked out at the green ballfield with concern, she joined him. But when she glanced at him next, she noticed his face had relaxed. Anna glanced two more times at Chad's expression and continued to feel a little more relaxed herself.

"I still want to...get to know you, but I can't imagine how you'd feel with everybody knowing or thinking they know some twisted version of why I wasn't on the bus ride home. But, you Anna, I never thanked you. There I was in the middle of embarrassing you and your family, and you didn't even blink. And even more so now, all I was thinking of is what people thought about me." Chad laughed at himself again and concluded, "Selfish." He turned to Anna and explained, "I'm talking about me being selfish. I still want to get to know you." The weight from the Anna's silence pulled on Chad's neck and lingered so long that he turned back to the field for reprieve. "Would you let me; I should ask your...or should I ask?" Chad said tautly, his jaw jittering from its bounce of courage.

"Yes."

"Yes, to what?" Chad asked.

"You should ask."

"So, can I pick you up on Friday?"

"No."

"How about Thursday then?"

"No."

"No?"

"No, not until you kiss me first."

"Umm," Chad said, reddening severely. "Kiss you first? That usually comes later, right?"

"Usually. But this isn't a usual kiss."

"What do you mean?" Chad asked tensely.

"Kiss me in front of everybody...first, and you'll know how I felt."

Chad looked with concern at Anna's cheek. "To be honest, I don't know if you're teasing me, but I'm going to take you up on that."

"Good. And if you do...we'll see," Anna said with piercing eyes that burned from holding back her tear ducts.

"Okay," Chad agreed. "Well, I know one thing. You're going to ace your final exams, providing you haven't aced them already," Chad continued, referencing the tightly clutched notebooks on Anna's lap. "How is your mother?" Chad asked.

"Like I said, very pregnant," Anna said, feeling her grip onto her notebooks starting to tingle.

"What should...can I do?" Chad asked, laughing a bit from his uneasiness.

"Don't make me compete with her. And don't just disappear," Anna said with a gulp and stood up to start towards her first class. "By the way, what was this whole slow-motion thing you guys were doing on the field today?" Anna said to bury Chad's chance to respond to her rigid plea.

"What? Oh, Coach Paddernick calls it our 'habits' or 'habit plays.'" Chad replied, noting Anna's relaxed expression as she started stepping down the bleachers.

"And don't make me wait too long," Anna said further before walking out of earshot.

Chad sat stupefied for the time it took Anna to walk out of sight, and then he snapped back to reality and bolted to the locker room to catch up with the team. "Anna Purse," Chad overheard clearly in the background as he reached his locker. Chad turned around to see who might be talking about the person he was thinking about. Seeing only smiles and targeted attention, he turned back to his own preoccupation. When he heard Anna's name again, he intentionally spoke clearly to his scrunched-up duffle bag, "If you've got any good intel on Anna, hit me with it."

"Are you planning on digging through her purse too?" James said, triggering a round of laughs.

"Digging through her purse? I'm not following."

"I wouldn't try to, bro," Sean advised, ready to head off to his student lifting room job.

"No, it's all good," Chad said over another round of laughter. "Enlighten me, please."

"Man, I'm just making fun, that's all," James said, rosy in the cheeks as he leaned back to grab his own things. "But I have to know. Did you really hook up with Anna's mom? I can't live with rumors anymore!"

"You really need to ask...to figure that out?" Chad asked bluntly.

"Uh yeah, I'd hate to live another day on hearsay."

"Anna's really cool, and if hooking up is what you mean by 'digging through her purse,' I'm glad that I could be the brunt of your joking for a minute."

"Well, don't jump to conclusions, my friend. That's exactly what we've been talking about! Please tell me you got a picture!"

"That's right, you and your pictures," Chad said, shaking his head.

*--- Not more than five hours later.*

Anna eagerly rushed through the garage door back home. "Mom!" Anna said, canvassing the kitchen and living room in one glance. "Mom!"

"Yes, Anna dear?" Julianne answered faintly from her bedroom.

"Mom, you have to promise me!"

"Promise you what, Anna dear?" Julianne asked, rolling off her bed from her evening nap.

"Are you carrying Chad's baby?" Anna asked, simultaneously feeling how awkward the question sounded.

"No darling. I thought I told you quite clearly, that boy was stiff as a straight-jacket," Julianne explained and started to yawn. "Have you really been worrying about that this whole time? How'd your exams go?"

"The exams were exams. Then whose baby is it?" Anna anxiously reiterated.

"Frank's, I think."

"You think? Or know," Anna said, begging for clarification.

"Oh, don't be like that, Anna dear."

"I really need to know," Anna expressed, unable to disguise the tension in her hands.

"I know they have those DNA paternity tests, but that would ruin his marriage for sure, or at least I would think it would. Don't make me do that," Julianne said sloppily, wiping off her last bit of late afternoon sleepiness.

"What's this don't mess around with married men thing then?" Anna prodded, finally believing her mom's answer.

"And don't be like me. Why is my baby's paternal half so important to you all of a sudden...again? It's been like two and a half months," Julianne said more pensively, walking out of the room ahead of Anna.

"Cause apparently everybody believes that you hooked up with Chad."

"Is this about Chad?" Julianne said, suspecting the real issue.

"Mostly."

"Is it him or you that's...."

"Both, but one of us is very apprehensive," Anna admitted.

"I can see that."

## Part 3 - Chapter Thirty-Five

Chad looked up at his ceiling for hours. Late into the night and deep into the morning, Anna papier-mâchéd his thoughts. He repeatedly analyzed the meaning of the word 'kiss' and what Anna might expect 'in front of everybody' to be. For all he tried, he couldn't find a position under his covers where his mind would allow his body to go to sleep. The sharpness of one of Anna's expressions on the bleachers kept bothering him. With a fatiguing mind, he finally decided that, before heading to the locker room for the next day's doubleheader, he would race to Anna's garage doorstep and ask her to come to one of the games. The moment after his thoughts were decided, his thoughts turned into a dream, and he awoke from the all-too-real feeling of Anna slapping him in the face. The cool blueness of the morning was more agreeable to him than his dream, so instead of rolling over for another rhythm of sleep, he figured he would throw on some clothes and go down to the cafeteria to see if he could grab some unusually early breakfast. After dressing quietly, he left his room and eagerly hopped down the stairs toward the exit. In taking the left turn toward the cafeteria, he almost missed the gray figure sitting on the curbside facing the traffic circle.

"There's only one guy on campus I know that lives with his long board," Chad greeted when he had stalled long enough to identify the student. "You waitin' for somebody, man?"

"No, just couldn't sleep," Jonathan replied without much movement and looked at the long board he had just purchased again from the store.

"Me neither. Must be the weather."

"Hah, I wish I could make that my excuse," Jonathan said pessimistically, spinning the wheel on his comforting long board.

"You want to grab some breakfast at the cafeteria?" Chad offered benevolently.

"Are they open?"

"Probably not, but that just seems like...."

"Have you ever been rejected by a girl?" Jonathan asked with preoccupation.

"Funny you ask, no, but today might be a first."

"All I did was write her an e-mail," Jonathan said, conceding his train of thought.

"Are you talking about Anna Purse? I thought you told me you two actually broke...."

"No, I screwed up with her," Jonathan corrected and fell quiet.

"And you're already onto another girl?" Chad observed suggestively. "You wrote her a letter?"

"An e-mail, it's faster. You get to fall on you face faster too." Jonathan said, trying to acknowledge his glumness.

"Says the skateboarder."

"Hah," Jonathan chuckled involuntarily and realized he probably appeared rather absurd to the campus star. "What about you not sleeping?" Jonathan asked, realizing Chad wasn't as much of a stranger as he would like to have listening to his confession.

"Girls have that effect it seems. Anna. Anna Purse kept me up all night."

"Really? I don't see her as an all-night talker."

"No. I need to make something up to her. Something I embarrassed her with. Now it's my turn for embarrassment."

"It's not about Romney Daniels, is it? She was always talking about him."

"I don't think I know a Romney. I hope he's not competition," Chad said, showing his worry for a second.

"Competition?" Jonathan reacted, over-emphasizing the question. "You and Anna then?" Jonathan recovered.

"I don't know, but you and everybody else I'm sure will be talking about it by the end of today. You sure you don't want breakfast?" Chad asked again, as he rose from the curbside and stretched his back.

"No, I'm good. They open at 6:30, I'm pretty sure," Jonathan reasoned, wanting his loneliness more than a plate of questionable protein.

"Ahk, well, I'll be first in line," Chad said confidently, also glad to have his own privacy back.

*--- A peaceful walk to the center of the cafeteria later.*

Chad sat alone, toying with a napkin until the gate to the kitchen rose with invitation. Ready to eat after the night of stress, he went and grabbed a tray. Halfway through his eating his breakfast, someone set a piece of paper down in front of him. Looking up quickly, having been lost in thought, Jonathan's flat look met his. "You want some breakfast now, I take it," Chad said, inferring an invitation for Jonathan to join him.

"Yeah, hey, I printed this off," Jonathan said, too preoccupied to observe any social norms. "It's from that girl, Bethy, Anna's friend. Best friend it seems," Jonathan trailed off. "I don't know why I'm asking you to read it. But maybe you can tell me what you think...I should think. Well, for the time being," Jonathan asked roundaboutly with fleeting eye contact.

"Sure thing, on two conditions. First, you go get some food, and second you then tell me about Anna." Chad saw Jonathan shake his head with a look of obedience, so Chad read the personal letter while Jonathan took a turn around the cafeteria to gather and pay for his breakfast.

"And," Jonathan said after setting down his food tray.

"So, you've got bad timing," Chad said, as he finished a mouthful. "I don't know that any respectable guy wouldn't want to be this 'Marshall' boy in your letter from Bethy...bold enough to ask her dad, and lucky enough to win the dad's favor...and to the tune of a daughter that seems to trust her dad enough to entrust him with the job of filtering and directing her life love...love life...and waiting for him to approve of the guy before she dates him, if that's how it real happened. I can't completely tell by the letter," Chad spoke convincingly, but he realized Jonathan was tearing up as he spilled his feedback. "I'm sorry, man. It looks like you missed out on a ruby, but you never know, this Marshall guy that this special girl mentions in your letter might fall through." Jonathan looked too emotional to respond and started putting food in his mouth. Knowing he had an agenda of his own, Chad said, "Look, I've got to run, but keep your head up. You'll be in Marshall's shoes one day soon, if you want to be."

"Thanks," Jonathan replied. "Anna's great, you two will be good for each other."

"Thanks, I appreciate that," Chad replied sincerely and walked off with his tray to the trash can. Chad didn't know what to do until a decent time arrived, so he went and sat on the pitching mound for an hour. When he couldn't wait any longer, he launched into motion back toward the cafeteria phones. After calling the familiar taxi company, he rode his way to Anna's doorstep alongside the first blazes of sunlight. Deciding the front door would be less awkward than the strange backside of Anna's corner house, he boldly rang the doorbell and backed up a step. Shoving his hands in his pockets, he turned around and tried his best not to look in the windows. Then feeling uncomfortable, he removed his sweating hands from his pockets. Eventually, Anna answered the door with tired eyes. Chad saw her try to smile away her early morning look and returned her pleasantry, explaining, "I promise I'm not here to ask you out on a date, it's just an invitation to a baseball game. We have a doubleheader today." Chad gasped, having forgotten to breath since Anna had opened the door.

As if it were an additional item to add to a to-do list, while holding back a yawn, Anna said, "Okay." Without further courtesy, she closed the door. After a good twenty seconds of staring at the back of the ritzy partition, she opened it again and stepped outside with confusion pulling down her eyebrows. Chad had disappeared, and, shaking her head, she almost wrote the entire ordeal off as a dream. But Chad peaked his head back around the corner, refuting her doubts.

"How'd you know I would ace my tests?" Anna asked, finally sparked with a draught of adrenaline.

"Well, you've aced every single one I've seen you take, so I'd say you have a pretty good track record," Chad said, waiting for a more positive invitation to approach.

"Oh," Anna responded shortly, as if hearing a satisfactory answer. "And why are you here?" Anna asked, wrapping her arms around her night garments.

"To invite you to a game, a baseball game."

"What time?"

"Any time after two, but sometime at least before eight-thirty."

"You're not picking me up?"

"It's not a date. It's an invitation from a friend that likes you," Chad said and found his shoes instantly ten pounds heavier. Anna's lips curled up into a small smile before she slid happily back inside more like Chad had expected. Chad left the second time with a similar but larger grand expression on his face.

--- *Four timeless hours later.*

"The game's at two, right?" Sean asked Chad as he watched his roommate lift his locker room bag over his shoulder.

"Right, I need to talk to coach," Chad said, shoving his small ring of keys into his pocket.

"You don't think you'll have plenty of time during dress-up?"

"He's always busy then."

"Not so busy that you can't talk to him. What's it about?" Sean asked, debating the topic in attempt to get Chad to talk.

"Anna Purse."

"Anna Purse? The girl Terrance took breakdancing?" Sean questioned, choosing the less circulated event to expose his surprise.

"Did he really? I can never tell if people are fabricating things," Chad said, progressing toward his agenda outside their dorm room door.

"Are you trying to get her a ticket, 'cause you know you can have mine."

"No, but thank you, I need to do something strange, or special...especially strange for her between tonight's games," Chad sporadically explained.

"You're not hiding roses anywhere, are you?"

"Is that normal?"

"Dude, if you're going to ask her out, do it somewhere private. Not that you're asking for advice, but you don't want to make a reputation for yourself, more than you already have," Sean said cynically, turning back to his own business.

"I have my hopes, but I feel like this is more of an apology to her than it is for me to try to be her prince charming," Chad said, rebuking himself with a frown.

"You don't have the right hair color for prince charming, but I'd find some roses whether it be an apology or whatever. Roses are normal," Sean said to answer Chad's forgotten question.

Chad hopped out of the door, down the stairs, and onto the brick walkway with the same intensity he had had that morning. However, the nearer to the gym complex he came, the more he felt like his muscles defiantly turned against him. Regardless of his hesitations, he arrived at the locker room and entered it alone. The lights turned on at his presence, and he walked to his aisle to begin dressing. All the while he kept rehearsing his plan semi-audibly, talking himself into and out of the whole venture repeatedly. Finally, the coaches arrived and stopped when they came across Chad sitting dressed and ready to go in front of his locker.

"This can't be good," Coach Paddernick said, seeing Chad in uniform. "You're not quitting, are you?"

"No, sir. But there's this girl," Chad started and remembered to breath. He paused longer than he meant to when his coach reacted. "And I want her to feel special, so I was hoping to ask permission to speak to her between the games, she's coming to one of the games."

"Well, you know my stance, Chad. I don't care how good you are, or how much extra work you've put into the team. You need to be focused for sake of your teammates."

"Yes, sir. I hope you'll understand, it's something...."

"I'm not going to give you permission," Coach Paddernick interrupted, "You're not going to get permission to do what I know you're going to do anyway." Coach Paddernick said with a sigh of disappointment, finishing the conversation by continuing to his office. "I don't like distractions!"

"I understand, sir," Chad said with a brewing grin.

Chad incrementally felt less odd as his teammates trickled into the locker room, bringing with them the more familiar noise and chatter. The time moved forward slowly enough to count each locker slam open and closed, but fast enough to where Chad found himself walking onto the game field with Terrance beside him. Before they parted ways, Chad said, "Anna's coming today to watch, I think."

"It's a trap! I'm walking away, you see me? I'm walking away," Terrance said as he split towards the home plate. "No really, don't mess with me," Terrance emphasized, pointing at Chad.

After a few warm up throws, the game began, and Chad started pounding in his pitches. The first inning was over without the ball contacting a bat.

"You must have been serious, is she here yet?" Terrance asked as they approached the dugout.

"I haven't looked yet, but she seemed to indicate she'd be here, last I knew," Chad said as he funneled into the lineup.

"You gonna let anybody else play today, Chad?" James encouraged in team spirit, sitting down between the catcher and pitcher.

"Chad's girlfriend is coming," Terrance said, forking the topic of the moment.

"Oh, the pressure's on!"

"Or is she not your girlfriend yet?" Terrance said, intentionally enjoying his abuse.

"Not yet," Chad admitted, shaking his head.

The top of the second inning finished in much the same fashion as the first. "Is she here yet?" James asked, knowing his answer by the distracted eyes of his teammate. "You know it would be more impressive to your non-girlfriend-soon-to-be, if we actually had points on the board when she arrived."

"You think that would impress her?" Chad said, acting naïve. With a smirk, he got ready to jump up the three stairs on deck. Looking as much as he could embarrass himself to look in light of all the attention, he split his focus from his bat to the crowd until he stepped up to the batter's box. He smacked the second pitch into the side of the mound, splitting the second baseman and short stop. Arriving easily at first base, Chad fought his focus again back onto the game at hand and stole second base. After the fourth inning, Chad remained the only one attentive to the fact that Anna had not yet arrived. After the ninth, the coach pensively celebrated the shut-out score and their nine-run lead, still with no sign of Anna.

Reading the facts on Chad's face as he scanned the crowd, Terrance said, "So, you warmed up yet?"

"Are you asking for more fast balls?" Chad countered, trying to hide his anxiety.

"I will say, you feel a few m.p.h.'s slow. What are you going to be throwing when Anna arrives?" Terrance said, assessing the agitated state of his friend.

"Hopefully something over the plate," Chad said, hearing Terrance's friendly optimism.

"It's 'cause you don't have a rose, didn't I tell you to get a rose," Sean said, slapping his friend from behind.

The second game started without intermission, and the away team came out fighting. "Chad, come on, focus! She's in the crowd, now pitch," Coach Paddernick said pressingly, as he watched his star pitcher divide his attention between his throws. The coach's shout directed Chad's prompt compliance. Chad still hadn't seen Anna. And having missed his opportune window to make things up to her during the intermission, he started pitching off his disappointment. Terrance responsively called a time out after catching his fourth walloping strikes and approached the mound. "Um...I was just kidding about pitching slow, and I have many more exciting ways for you to damage your arm."

"Sure."

Terrance stared at his distracted friend and adjusted his tone. "I don't care how fast your lightning is, you still have a wimpy changeup...that's slow enough for me to score on. You don't want to be throwing changeups for the last seven innings, do you?"

"Sure," Chad said, keeping his ear tilted toward his friend.

--- *At the same moment that Chad's next pitch hit Terrance's glove.*

"Hey, Erica! Are you going to the game tonight?" Anna queried, taking off her fifth outfit, and piling it to the side of her large closet as another possibility. "Where are you working? Crumbles closed. Yeah, it's been a long time hasn't it. Sorry, I've been a stranger," Anna said as she looked over another outfit. "Look, Chad Wattsworth asked me to the baseball game tonight, and I don't want to go alone...and I don't know what to wear, so I was hoping...," Anna confessed, fitting a ball cap on her head and then removing it just as quickly. "Six? I'll pick you up!" Anna stressed, pushing her hair up over her head. "Oh, I'll bring them all, if you'll decide for me!" Anna looked again at her closet with apprehension one last time before grabbing all her ideas along with three other pairs of everything and slumped it all into an available laundry basket.

"Did the washer break?" Julianne asked from her reading chair at Anna's passing.

"No," Anna said dryly.

"Are you moving out?" Julianne asked with interest.

"No," Anna said without changing her course toward the garage door.

"Are there moths...."

"Chad invited me to his baseball game this afternoon, and I'm going. But I've never been so nervous in my life, and I can't for the life of me figure out what to wear, so Erica...so Erica, my friend, is going to help me," Anna said fitfully, while pausing at the corner of the kitchen counter.

"Exciting! I'm almost jealous."

"And I left you out of it, so you wouldn't ruin it a second time," Anna mustered with half the boldness she had practiced and turned to press toward the garage.

"Anna Jane," Julianne objected, standing immediately up from her repose. "Anna dear, don't leave me with hate. Hate my mistakes, but they're only mistakes, I'm sorry. Chad deserves you more than I deserve you," Julianne said and started crumbling with remorse from the abrupt sincerity of hurt that Anna had poignantly fired. Anna's glance at Julianne was filled with coldness and distrust. "Anna," Julianne said with sorrow spontaneously filling her eyes. "I'll...I'll be here. I'll be cheering for you, and I'm giving you a hug in my heart if that means anything."

Anna listened with the side of her head and started toward the kitchen door after Julianne had finished her choppy rebuttal. But she stopped for a toilsome moment, holding up her pile of clothes. Then taking a strong breath, she continued and made her way through the garage to the car. With her clothing settled into the back seat, she defiantly turned over the engine before she hit a conscious road block. Trying to push past the heat growing in her head, she shifted the car into reverse, but her foot wouldn't come off the permissive brake. After a minute of tense idleness, she shut the car off and walked uncomfortably back inside to the living room where Julianne was once again hiding behind the book she had been reading.

"I don't want you to ruin things," Anna admitted again more shamefully.

Julianne tried to smile, but she couldn't hold up her frail cheeks. "You're right, I probably shouldn't be there. I'll probably interfere to your usual disliking. But...I'll be here, waiting for your news," Julianne said hopefully. "Go to your friend, she sounds like a good one to keep," Julianne encouraged as she rose to receive the hug she had wanted.

--- *Minutes later, after driving to where Erica was.*

"What a way to get me running around like a mad woman and shewing customers away," Erica said, hustling to gather Anna from her waiting spot at Erica's new place of employment.

"You didn't shew anybody away," Anna said, rising to follow her to the exit. "Do you think they'll care if we use their bathroom?"

"You need a bathroom?" Erica inquired, pausing her momentum.

"To change, I have my clothes in the car."

"I'm sorry, Anna. You're too cute! And I mean it. I would die to have your wardrobe," Erica said, grinning. "But as much as I'd like to dress your envious body to my heart's content, baseball games don't last forever."

"Chad said there were two, back to back."

"That means, we have about half a game left to catch," Erica said, wrapping an ushering arm around Anna's shoulders.

When Anna didn't pick up on the right level of intensity, Erika asked, "Maybe, I should drive."

"Okay," Anna said, but as Erika put the car into gear, Anna started rethinking her allowance. Anna grabbed the seat belt as the car peeled around the fancy brick lot and out the exit. "I didn't know my car could squeal," Anna bumbled as she finally succeeded in clicking her seatbelt closed.

"Have you seen rush hour traffic in Pittsburg before? At least we'll be going into the city," Erika remarked, finding it difficult to contain her delight amidst her hurry. "You don't know this, but before you called, Veronica called me about you."

"About me?"

"Yeah, apparently, Chad talked to Sean, Veronica's boyfriend, and Sean mentioned it to Veronica."

"Oh boy," Anna said, melting her eyes with her palms.

"She called me right before you did. So, when you called, it confirmed everything! Now all I have to do is get you past all this traffic."

"Na uh, don't even think about it," Anna said, seeing Erika eye an empty lane across the double yellow line.

"What? Okay, okay," Erica said with a huff, using her hand to hold up her chin. She sat staring at the red light hanging over the string of cars that blocked the left turning lane and started tapping the steering wheel. "So, do you like him?" Erica asked, returning to her excitement.

"I do. I asked him to kiss me."

"Kiss? Chad? That's kind of forward."

"Got to love it when my mouth speaks before my brain thinks."

"Meh. That's not as bad when it's someone like Chad who wouldn't know how to unhook...a girl's shoe."

Uneasy with Erica's honest yet crude comparison, Anna self-consciously replied, "You must know something worse to put it that way."

"Yeah," Erica said, squirming in her seat. "That's right, I haven't told you about Dan."

"No, it was too fresh, last time I weaseled into your business."

"Have you seen the cover of Miss Doxy? Speaking of the whole campus knowing someone's business," Erica said, showing her buried frustration of the topic.

"Hah, that's why I broke up with Jonathan Wickfell."

"That's right he sells for Markus," Erica said, connecting the dots. Then seeing general interest on Anna's face as the cars started moving, she explained, "Dan and Markus, both run Miss Doxy, Dan and I were dating, then we weren't, and then we were when he asked me to help him out. Big mouth-small mind here volunteered, and now I'm the face that every pervert on campus gets to masturbate on...sorry, it's still fresh."

"No, no, you're honest. You should have told me though. Shame on you," Anna said, winning a short laugh from her friend.

"So. I know Chad, from knowing Veronica and Sean, and Chad's not like the horror-bot that I got suckered into helping."

"I understand why you might take a break."

"Girl, that's what I tell myself two seconds before I trip over the same bump in the road," Erica resonated and looked at the dashboard clock. "Wow, so you're going to miss the game at this speed, you'd better start hoping they're tied going into the ninth!"

"Oh no," Anna said sarcastically without much emphasis.

"No, no, no! Chad's not at all like Dan, believe me!"

"Uh-huh...okay," Anna said in a funny voice.

"You don't believe me."

"I dated Spencer, once. That wasn't very encouraging."

"Spencer?" Erica said with outrage. "Didn't I tell you not to date him?"

"You said to be careful."

"Code word for...don't date him," Erica said as she turned down another street lined with cars.

"Then I dated Jonathan for a month, and that turned out swell," Anna said sarcastically again.

"Swell, listen to you," Erica echoed.

"Well...good, but it was like I asked him to remove his right eye when Miss Doxy came out."

"Money and girls, there you have it...the crushes of all men," Erica said. "Up, now we're moving."

"So, there's Butlers, let me treat you to dinner," Anna asked strategically.

"Not on your life, but I'll give you credit for trying. I wouldn't miss Chad kissing you for the world series!"

Anna watched her favorite restaurant go by at a walking pace.

"Do you really think he'll do it? I mean what type of conversation ends up with kiss me at your next baseball game?" Erica said after a lull, trying to piece all the gossip together.

"He crushed me the last time...when he had invited me to the fundraiser."

"Did you go with him?" Erica asked, sensing the disgruntlement in Anna's dodging answer.

"No, I went with my mother," Anna answered, looking at Erica's healthy glow.

"So?" Erica said, inching the car forward.

"So, he went home with my mother."

"What?" Erica gasped in disbelief.

"Nothing happened, and he apologized.  And my mom admits she has a problem," Anna explained.

"Well, if you're hungry, that restaurant you mentioned, is it good?" Erica said, cranking the wheel over with the intent of making an immediate U-turn.

"So, I told him to kiss me, so I could slap him.  He just doesn't know the slap part yet."

"Nah, I don't think you could bring yourself to deliver that type of retribution.  You'd crumble."

"Well, the world does play out differently than it happens in my mind most of the time," Anna admitted, trying to hide how happy she was to have been figured out by her friend.

"You're bluffing, you brought clothes...like all your clothes," Erica accused.

"Right, what do you wear to commit an act of vengeance?" Anna said, breaking out her smile again.

Not completely convinced, Erica turned the car around into the empty lane and toured into the parking garage adjacent to Butler's Station.


## Part 3 - Chapter Thirty-Six


The second game lasted shorter than the first, and no one dared address Chad who refrained from the miniscule hoopla after the away team's finishing pitch.  Chad's friend and catcher diverted from the group heading off the field and slapped Chad on the shoulder with his glove.  "You know I think you looked stupid, even if it was a long string of bad calls, right?" Terrance said in his excusable manner.  Terrance carried on when Chad shook his head and frowned at the ground.

"Get to the locker room.  I'm not impressed," Coach Paddernick said forewarningly to Chad when he came within earshot.  Chad perked up with fear and glanced up at the scoreboard defensively.  The scoreboard confirmed that they had shut out the team in the same manner as the first game, but Chad knew coach's reason and obediently followed his direction.  Once closed inside the locker room, the coach forcefully called everybody together, and a hush fell over the team.  Coach Paddernick paced back and forth as a few teammates shot questioning glances to each other.  "Did everybody play their best?" Coach Paddernick petitioned.  "I don't care if we beat them by a hundred runs, did everybody play their best?" The coach clarified, scanning the room.  "Sean!  Were you there one-hundred percent?"

"Yes, sir."

"Rob!  Were you?" Coach Paddernick asked without hesitating.

"Yes, sir," Rob answered, and the team started whispering their objections to the coach's antic.

"Chad?  Did you have yourself pulled together out there?" Coach Paddernick fired passively.  When Chad, diverted his gaze to the floor, Coach Paddernick ordered, "Chad, stand up!  That's not an option, stand up."  Coach Paddernick stared at Chad.  "Terrance, please inform the team of what you told Chad on your fourth trip to the mound?"

"Sir, Chad was freaking awesome, and I tried telling him to be less awesome so that he could survive the game.  But he just kept on being awesome till we won."

"James, what do you think about Chad's freakish performance?"

"He seemed out of character and was kind of scary to watch at the end, sir."

"Thank you, at least there's one honest person in the room," Coach Paddernick said, taking another walk back to the front of the circle.  "Composure!  How do you think your composure affects one another?  Who's looking forward to celebrating tonight after Chad's scary display?  Who's looking forward to practice tomorrow?  There is no team, if you're here playing only

for yourself.  There is no team, if you won't listen to your
teammates."

"Coach," Chad interjected.

"Chad, I'm not saying you're a bad athlete, but don't forget
you represent everybody standing around you.  Listen to your
teammates; you're freaking, scary good.  But from what I saw...."

"Coach, team, I'm sorry, I have no excuses," Chad said with
embarrassment written all over his face like unsightly pimples.

"That's a little more team-like.  Somebody put your hand on
Chad's shoulder and remind him where his team's at."  The
hands started patting Chad's shoulders and back as the coach
dismissed himself to his office and the players started revolving
to their lockers.

"Hey, I'll see you back at the room later," Sean said to Chad,
before rushing to the exit.

"Sure thing," Chad responded as he had fallen behind the
normal changing rhythm.

Chad finished changing last and lifted his bag of soiled clothes
over his shoulder.  He intentionally walked by the coach's office
on his way to the exit and said, "Coach, I wanted to say sorry
again."

"You'll have better composure next time, no doubt."

"Yes, sir," Chad responded and made his way out to the
evening light.  The heat of the day had already fallen, and the
scattered clouds looked like they had obtained terms of peace
with the wind.  He walked at his own pace back to Swanson Hall
and climbed the stairs to his floor.  He locked himself into his
room and found himself alone after he flicked on the overhead
light.  Tossing his athletic bag at the foot of his bed, he sunk into
his desk chair and turned on his computer.  He stared at the start
up screen while toying with the scroll ball of the mouse.  Ten
unproductive minutes went by before he opened an application
to check his e-mail.  He listened as a couple of students chatted
their way down the hall, and when another set of footsteps
stopped outside his door, he swung around ready to hear the key
of his returning roommate in the lock.  Instead a rhythm of
knocking brought him to his feet.  When he looked out the peep
hole, he saw Anna holding her elbow.  Chad opened the door
wide enough for Anna to see the setup of the small room.  Then

Chad closed himself into the hallway two feet away from Anna's toes.

"So, I missed your game, well your games," Anna admitted and bit the corner of her bottom lip.

"I'm glad you did, they didn't go so well," Chad said, telling the rest of the story with how his eyes fell to his feet. "My roommate told me to buy you a rose."

"A rose would have been nice," Anna kindly acknowledged and held in her breath.

"Would you like to find a place to talk?"

"Yes," Anna said, exposing her heart.

"Let me grab my key," Chad said. Completely confused and equally rushed, he closed himself behind his door for the moment it took to retrieve his key and his walking shoes.

Anna reran her fingers through her normally stingy hair and looked down the length of the hallway.

"Shall we?" Chad invited after locking himself out of his dorm room, already knowing where he wanted to adventure with Anna.

"How is your Dad?" Anna asked as they walked out into the cool of the evening.

"He made it through the first of a few surgeries, but it was the most difficult one," Chad said, pulling his shoulders together. "Thanks for asking."

The couple walked along the brick path that led toward the baseball diamond. Both had multiple topics to discuss and apologies to make, and consequently their conversation lingered in the slight breeze that swept the grassy areas of campus. "You know, Anna, you taught me something about myself," Chad commented, flapping his elbows out before digging his hands deeper into his pockets. Chad took Anna's pleasant expression as a cue to continue and said, "When you claimed that I would know how you felt, post-fundraiser, on the bleachers yesterday, it was like scales fell from my eyes. Up until then I was interested in getting to know you because you're pretty, smart, considerate, kind, and the whole ten-yards."

"Isn't the phrase, 'the whole nine yards?'"

"Well, I figured it pertained to football, and why stop at saying nine?" Chad admitted, loosing track of his point for a moment.

"What I've read is cloth back in the mid-1800s was usually sold in increments of nine yards, then became a common military phrase during World War 2 when aircraft machine-gun belts were nine yards long, and hence the phrase, 'Give 'em the whole nine yards, Mac.'"

"You're only proving my point," Chad expressed, fighting to prevent his mouth from reflecting Anna's pleasure. "...But you brought the other side of the word 'relationship' into focus. A girlfriend like you is something I wanted, but really that's as selfish as saying...as saying, or as the guys who scope out girls and give cat-calls. I don't know if that makes sense."

"It does."

"Good, I'm starting to shake, I apologize. So, I don't know how to conclude this...this, I don't know what you'd call it."

"Realization."

"Yeah, realization. So, when I say I want to get to know you over breakfast tomorrow morning, I'm not saying it because there's something I want from you, but more because there's something I want to bring to you...to put myself on the breakfast table, so to speak," Chad said, wiping his hand across his eye like he had regrettably smeared embarrassment on his forehead.

Anna Jane Purse at that moment started rehearsing what her name would sound like as a Wattsworth, and she slipped her arm around Chad's elbow. Her touch silenced Chad's soliloquy for the remainder of their walk to the baseball diamond where they officially selected their spot on the bleachers a few rows up. It happened to be the same spot where Anna originally had seated herself during Chad's baseball scrimmage at the end of the spring semester. They exchanged apologies and explanations, both laughing at their acknowledged absurdities and faults, and they talked and talked until they finished their five-hour conversation next to Anna's car at nearly two in the morning. Chad walked back to his dormitory alone, shivering both from the chill of the night and from his jubilance over the date he had planned with Anna the next morning, a breakfast date where he undoubtedly would lay on a table for the sake of his slip-of-the-tongue words and for the sake of Anna's captive enjoyment.

*--- After the year-long task of securing Sandy's release from prison.*

Bins were piled everywhere, and countless moving boxes were piled on top of out of place and disassembled furniture everywhere else. The Daniel's mansion on Washington Street had a For Sale sign in the yard, and over the course of a few weeks Sandy Daniels had found it harder and harder not to express her joy in their choice to move to the renovated Riverview house. Only a few unpacked items remained, hiding mostly in untraveled corners of the mansion. Romney rushed in with the sound of splashing keys after work at his new job as the C.O.O. of Scales Architectural Company and clapped his briefcase on the kitchen counter. April had heard his arrival and came down to meet him. "Where's your mom?" Romney asked, picking April up in a hug and then setting her down again.

"She's upstairs making me mad," April replied.

"Why on earth is she trying to do that?" Romney asked, moving in that direction.

"She's throwing all my dolls into the recyco-ing bin," April whined, looking for a doll rescuer.

"Naah, I doubt that, Pearl, she bought those for you; I'm usually the one that throws your toys away. But even then, you'd have to have made her pretty mad."

"I didn't. I promise," April pledged.

"Let's go see."

"Hey, dad?" April asked from her stationary position in the kitchen.

"What's that?" Romney replied, pausing long enough to turn around.

"Might I have some chocolate chunks in the pantry?"

"Hmm, would you stop at just one?" Romney approved.

"I kinda think I want two, or maybe three. Is three okay, dad?" April negotiated.

"Umma, no. I think two would be enough don't you think?" Romney said, wincing one eye in April's direction that made her run happily off toward the pantry.

Romney leaped up the stairs and found his wife's golden smile in the master bedroom, wrapping up porcelain crockery in his fat sweaters.

"Look who's home!" Sandy said, continuing her work on her lap after pausing long enough for a kiss.

"I'm going to change. And April's quite concerned about her dolls; are you donating them?" Romney asked as he continued for the master bathroom.

"No, I'm not donating them. I read an article about moving and it had all these space saving ideas, like using tubs for toys, and clothing for packing material."

"Those movers will be here in the morning, and dinner's at Jeff and Cheryl's tonight," Romney reminded as he moved out of sight.

"That's right, I should shower," Sandy said, standing up and briefly stretching out her healthy legs. "I can use the guest one," Sandy added when Romney poked his head out of the master bathroom.

"You sure?" Romney checked while sliding his tie out of his collar.

"Yeah; you're certainly dustier than me," Sandy assured graciously, walking into the closet to grab the evening dress that she had set aside earlier in the afternoon. "April, we'll be upstairs, and once again we aren't donating your toys. We're just moving them to the yellow house," Sandy shouted from the staircase balcony.

"Kay," Sandy faintly heard.

Sandy walked into the guest bathroom and bent down to grab a towel from under the cabinet. She heard a click-clack sound after she had taken the towel and didn't think anything of it until the cabinet door wouldn't close properly. When she opened the door to figure out why, she saw the obstructing needle and a vial. Recognizing her old paraphernalia, she let go of the cabinet door and watched it bounce back onto the jammed plastic. Rising to her full height, she paused for a minute. The minute could have been an hour, but Sandy stood frozen, staring down into the dark crack. Her body finally shivered, and she argued with herself, "I can't; no, Sandy, you can't." She shook her head and disrobed after starting the shower. After a good five minutes of shivering debate, she climbed in and tried thinking about something else. By the end of her shower, her neck, her shoulders, her stomach, and her forehead all physically ached with craving. Pounding her head, she took the soft towel and stepped out of the shower to dry off the water. The crack in the cabinet door hadn't changed, and she stared at it again, continuing her struggle. She heard little footsteps in the hallway, then silence. She opened the cabinet door again, but she retreated and pounded her head three more times in defiance. Hearing heavier footsteps heading for the staircase, she pulled every string of willpower she had left in her bones and called out, "Rom!" The footsteps stopped abruptly and promptly opened the door.

# Afterward

An Interview with Jonathan Wickfell - May 31st, 2006

J.H. - "Hi, Jonathan, please take a seat."

Jonathan - "You must live in hotels."

J.H. - "Pretty much goes with the job."

Jonathan - "I didn't know authors travel that much."

J.H. - "No, actually the author thing is quite new...as are my interviewing skills.

Jonathan - "That's cool, man, no pressure; last time I talked your ear off. Where were we? Boston?"

J.H. - "Yeah.... I just have a few questions in the back of my head, and I'm sorry if they don't flow together neatly. I'm just trying to tie together a few remaining loose ends of the story."

Jonathan - "No worries, man; fire away."

J.H. - "Hopefully I'll be able to plug up some holes, so if somebody decides to actually read it, it'll make sense. But first off, you got through reading the rough draft, all hundred and forty-five-thousand some odd words. What do you think of it?"

Jonathan - "Hah! After I finished telling you my story, like three years ago, you had asked me if you could craft it into a novel."

J.H. - "Right."

Jonathan - "You wanted to use my name and make a kind of biography of 'Jonathan Wickfell' so to speak."

J.H. - "Right."

Jonathan - "Well, where in world did you come up with all those names and places? And why did Anna Purse get her name in the title and not me? I'm just joking, but I must say that I had a hard time figuring out who was who, and who I was supposed to be. You're calling me Dean Fischer, if I'm not mistaken. Right?"

J.H. - "Yeah. I asked you that some years ago, and you seemed so hesitant about using real names."

Jonathan - "No, no, I know why you did it, but when I read it, I was like...like a little disappointed. Here I was reading about me, but it didn't seem real. 'Cause you used all those...those other...."

J.H. - "Pseudonyms."

Jonathan - "Pseudonyms! That's it."

J.H. - "Well, okay. Would you like me to take Dean Fischer out and use your real name?"

Jonathan - "Yeah...yeah. I think I'd like that, even if it was only for my benefit...when I read it."

J.H. - "Do you think you'll ever read it again? I mean you've already read it this once."

Jonathan - "Uh, yeah. Like every year. I'm going to give it to my future kids to read, my neighbors, the clerk at the supermarket...no, but really. It would mean more, I think at least to me, to see my name printed on the pages...even if it's not on the front cover."

J.H. - "Okay, but I'm curious about the rest of the novel; I mean you obviously know the bit I made up."

Jonathan - "A bit? I'm kind of glad you did, I was worried at first when you said you wanted to write a novel...that it would just be this big long sob story.

J.H. - "Right, well, what I really want to know is about Bethy? You know who I'm talking about when I say Bethy, right? I want to hang out on Bethy for a minute, because that's where you left me off back in Boston, and I didn't want to go off the deep end creatively, plugging that hole. What ever happened to you guys?"

Jonathan - "I know. I kind of figured that's the whole reason you wanted to meet up. So, I brought this for you to read, and feel free to use it, just...just remember to change her name and all."

J.H. - "Of course; would you mind me skimming it now?"

Jonathan - "Go right ahead, I'm going to take a phone call while you do, if that's okay? And it's not to sell a magazine."

J.H. - "Yeah, yeah."

--- *Referencing the newly printed sheet of paper.*

Dear Jon,

I had a great time with you last week, and I got your lovely letter. I'm sorry that I didn't take the time to handwrite this. I should have for the sake of your kind words. E-mail just feels a little cold to me. Please don't take it as meaning I don't care, but I thought you should know this sooner rather than later. When I got home to Little Rock with my dad and mom, I had already told them all about our experience and that you seemed like a quality guy. Well, that next Sunday they introduced me to a fine gentleman at church. This was novel to me, because it's something that's never happened before now. Anyway, I didn't think anything of it until afterward at lunch when my dad told me that this gentleman, whose name is Marshall, had approached him a month before to express his interest in me. My dad then asked me to consider letting Marshall pursue me, like date me, and I'm not even officially in college yet! When I told him thereafter about you and your letter, he told me that he wasn't settled in his spirit about it and left it at that. I trust my dad. My mom and I are planning to have Marshall and his family over for dinner come middle of the week, and I'm nervously excited! I asked my dad about corresponding with you like we are now, and he said that he trusts my judgment. So please write, and I'll see you this fall at school!

Sincerely,

Bethy

*--- Jonathan had returned and sat patiently as J.H. finished.*

J.H. - "I honestly had imagined this going a whole different direction, but at least I won't have to write a sequel!"

Jonathan - "I know, right?"

J.H. - "Sorry, that's my joke for the day. What did you do after you read the letter?"

Jonathan - "Ha. I walked alone and ended up at my elementary school park. I sat on this great log playground structure and just sat till I finally felt sorry for me feeling sorry for myself."

J.H. - "And the past three years...anything?"

Jonathan - "Nope, I kind of fell out of that group pretty quickly. I stayed busy though; my internship turned into a job before I graduated. Anna's friend...Romney? He, became my new boss shortly afterward, strangely enough."

J.H. - "What about the whole Miss Doxy distributorship?"

Jonathan - "That was a deeper issue than I thought.  I quit, but I was like a walking hypocrite for a while.  I still am to an extent."

J.H. - "Would you care to explain?"

Jonathan - "Care to?  No.  But for posterity sake, and it'd probably be good to get off my chest, akhem, okay.  I struggle, and I don't fully get it.  How you get caught up in something that's not seemingly bad at first, but at some point, you realize that it is.  Then when you decide you want to change, the allurement doesn't just disappear like you'd think it would. Instead, you're left fighting your desires tooth and nail.  I hate how pornography controls me, and it's like this struggle where my body cries out for it from the inside.

J.H. - "Did your roommate ever succeed with his tracking program?"

Jonathan - "Nah, he was a porn addict, I mean like 'almost dropped out of school' porn addict.  For real, when I stopped doing Miss Doxy, it was like I'd betrayed him."

J.H. - "You said you've been fighting tooth and nail this pornography struggle.  Have you figured it out any, or learned how to tame it?"

Jonathan - "Yeah!  There's this blue and green pill they sell at the vitamin store down the road called, 'Don't Start.'"

J.H. - "Hah...right!"

Jonathan - "Josiah, to be honest with you, the only thing I've learned is that I broke something, and if I broke it, I need to make things right.  Pornography isn't who I am, it's what I've done.  I mean there was a time when I didn't know porn existed, and I was fine with that.  I just need to get back to being the real me somehow."

J.H. - "That's good.  I need to hear that myself.  Did I tell you that I'm recording you?  I apologize."

Jonathan - "I kind of figured as such with the whole voice recorder thing on the table."

J.H. - "You should have seen me the last time.  When I got back to my hotel room, my whole arm was sore by the time I had finished writing down everything I remembered."

Jonathan - "Yeah.  And look, you remembered just about everything.  I like it.  Hey man, that was my acquaintance.  He's a bit early, sorry."

J.H. - "Any last thoughts?"

Jonathan - "You gonna give me a cut if you make a movie deal?"

J.H. - "Are you volunteering to act?  ...For posterity sake?"

# ABOUT THE AUTHOR

Josiah Hutchison was born in Michigan and attended High School in Portage where he began his pursuit in writing lyrical poetry. For the birth of his son in 2011 he self-published, 'The Story of a Cloud,' a children's bedtime story of a cloud racing the sun to the top of the sky. Then after many conversations with friends concerning the epidemic topics of the day, he set out to write the fictional story of Anna Purse. The storyline was inspired by countless Ravi Zacharias podcasts, by Leo Tolstoy's famous 'Anna Karenina,' and by a unique four-hour long conversation with a stranger Josiah met on a YMCA basketball court. Upon finishing the manuscript, Josiah set it aside in 2016 to cool it off and meanwhile completed work on two other topical pieces. Then in 2018 he returned to the initial script, then titled, 'FoAP,' and after heavily reworking its parts, the novel eventually took the black and white title, 'The Monstrosity or Anna Purse.'

54501668R00271

Made in the USA
Columbia, SC
02 April 2019